The will was short and to the point. Even Patrick understood it.

Oaklands was to be sold. He was glad of that. At least, he would not have to live *there*. Lawyer Atkins was appointed his legal guardian, but Patrick was to live with an uncle or aunt until he was twenty-one when a sum of money so enormous that it had no meaning for Patrick was to be his. He was to choose for himself the relative with whom he preferred to live. Having made his choice, there could be no change, unless the chosen one died. But in order that he might know what he was doing, he was first to live with each uncle and aunt for three months. When he had done this he was to make his permanent choice.

Patrick desperately wrapped his legs around the chair rungs again. Aunt Lilian might look her eyes out, he thought, but he had to do something to steady his body.

He didn't want to live with any of them. If he could only go to Glen St. Mary now, and live at Ingleside! The very thought seemed like heaven. But, alas, the Ingleside people were not related to him, except so distantly it didn't count. *If only Patrick had some other relative, a kind and loving one, to choose. . . .*

The Road to Yesterday

L. M. MONTGOMERY

Published by
Dell Laurel-Leaf
an imprint of
Random House Children's Books
a division of Random House, Inc.
New York

Visit us on the Web! www.randomhouse.com/teens

Educators and librarians, for a variety of teaching tools, visit us at
www.randomhouse.com/teachers

ISBN: 0-553-56068-9

Reprinted by arrangement with McGraw-Hill Ryerson Limited

RL: 6.0

Printed in the United States of America

First Dell Laurel-Leaf Edition February 2003

20 19 18 17 16 15 14 13 12

OPM

Contents

Canadian Twilight

A filmy western sky of smoky red
    Blossoming into stars above a sea
Of soft mysterious dim silver spread
    Beyond the long gray dunes' serenity,
Where the salt grasses and sea poppies press
Together in a wild sweet loneliness.

Seven slim poplars on the windy hill
    Talk some lost language of an elder day,
Taught by the green folk that inhabit still
    The daisied field and secret friendly way,
Forever keeping in their solitudes
The magic ritual of our northern woods.

The darkness woos us like a perfumed flower
    To reedy meadow pool and wise old trees,
To beds of spices in a garden bower
    And the spruce valley's dear austerities,
I know their lure of dusk but evermore
I turn to the enchantment of the shore.

The idle ships dream-like at anchor ride
    Beside the piers where wavelets lap and croon,
One ghostly sail slips outward with the tide
    That swells to meet the pale imperial moon.
Oh fading ship, between the dark and light
I send my heart and hope with you tonight.

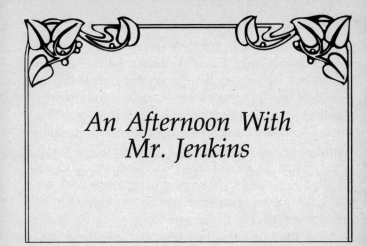

An Afternoon With Mr. Jenkins

Timothy yawned. If eight years knew anything about such a word Timothy was bored. Saturday was a rather stupid day at any time and he could not go down to the Glen. He was not allowed to go out of the home grounds when his aunts were away—not even to Ingleside to play with Jem Blythe. And lately his aunts had been more fussy than ever about this. Of course Jem could come up to his aunts' place as often as he pleased but Jem often had other fish to fry on Saturday afternoons and Timothy never was allowed away from home alone now at all. Surely a big boy of eight didn't need to be cooped up at home just because his aunts had gone to Charlottetown.

They had gone that morning on the early bus and Timothy felt sure they were worried. More than usual, that is, for they were always worried over something. Timothy didn't know what it was but he sensed it in everything they did or said of late. It hadn't been so years ago, Timothy reflected, with the air of an octogenarian recalling his youth. He could remember them as laughing and jolly, especially Aunt Edith, who was really very jolly for an old maid, as the boys in school called her. And they were great friends with the Ingleside people and thought Dr. and Mrs. Blythe the finest people in the world.

But they had laughed less and less these past two years and Timothy had an odd feeling that this was somehow connected with him, although he couldn't understand how that could be. He wasn't a bad boy. Not even Aunt Kathleen who, perhaps because she was a widow, thought rather poorly of boys, ever said he was a bad boy. And Jem Blythe had told him that Susan Baker had said he was really one of the best-behaved boys she knew, outside of the Ingleside group.

Now and then of course . . . but it was hard to be perfect. Why, then, did they worry so about him? Maybe just because they were women. Maybe women had to worry. But Mrs. Blythe seemed to worry very little and Susan Baker not much more. So why?

Men now . . . he never perceived that Dr. Blythe worried. If father had lived! But in that case he, Timothy, might not have been living with Aunt Edith in the little place the Glen St. Mary people called "The Corner." And Timothy loved The Corner. He felt sure he could never live anywhere else. But when he said this to Aunt Kathleen one day she had sighed and looked at Aunt Edith.

She hadn't said anything but Aunt Edith had replied passionately, "I can't believe God could be so unjust. Surely he—even *he*—couldn't be so heartless."

Were they talking about the God whom the Ingleside people said was Love? Even Susan Baker admitted that.

"S-sh," said Aunt Kathleen warningly.

"He'll have to know some time," said Aunt Edith bitterly.

Why, he knew about God now. Everybody he knew did. So why so much mystery?

"He'll have to know some time," went on Aunt Edith bitterly. "The ten years will soon be up— and probably shortened for good behaviour."

Aunt Edith's "he's" puzzled Timothy hopelessly. He knew now it was not God they were talking about. And what "he" would he have to know some time and in any case why should it all be "s-sh-ed" away? Aunt Edith immediately began talking about his music lessons and the possibility of securing Professor Harper of Lowbridge as a teacher. Now Timothy hated the very thought of music lessons. Jem Blythe laughed at the mere idea. Yet he knew he would have to take them. Nothing ever made Aunt Kathleen change her mind. Tim often felt aggrieved.

Aunt Edith had promised to take him to the

little lake that was a Lowbridge summer resort. They would go in the car; cars were very new things and Timothy loved riding in them. Dr. Blythe had one and often gave him a "lift" in it. And at the lake he would be let ride a horse on the merry-go-round, another thing he adored and very seldom got because Aunt Kathleen did not approve of it. But he knew Aunt Edith would.

But there had been a letter that morning for Aunt Kathleen. She had turned dreadfully pale when she read it. Then she had said something to Aunt Edith in a queer choking voice and Aunt Edith had turned pale, too, and they had gone out of the room. Timothy heard them having a long conversation with Dr. Blythe on the telephone. Was Aunt Kathleen sick?

After a little while Aunt Edith came back and told Timothy she was very sorry but she could not take him to the lake after all. She and Aunt Kathleen must go to Charlottetown on some very important business. Dr. Blythe was going to take them.

"Then one of you *is* sick?" said Timothy anxiously.

"No, neither of us is sick. It . . . it is worse than that," said Aunt Edith.

"You've been crying, Aunt Edith," said a troubled Timothy. He got up out of his chair and hugged her. "Just you wait till I grow up and when I'm a man nothing'll ever make you cry."

And then the tears welled up in Aunt Edith's sweet brown eyes again.

But Aunt Kathleen was not crying. She was pale and stern. And she told Timothy very shortly and unsympathetically that he must not go outside the gate until they returned.

"Can't I go down to Ingleside for a little stroll?" implored Timothy. He wanted to buy something for Aunt Edith's birthday tomorrow. He had a whole quarter saved out of his allowance and he meant to spend it all on her. There were pretty things in Lowbridge but Carter Flagg kept a glass case with some rather nice things in it. Timothy remembered a lace collar he admired.

But Aunt Kathleen was inexorable. Timothy did not sulk. He never sulked, which was more than could be said of even Jem Blythe, although you would have taken your life in your hands if you had said so to Susan Baker. But he put in a rather dismal forenoon. He ran races with Merrylegs. He counted and rearranged his birds' eggs, finding a little comfort in the thought that he had more than Jem had. He tried to jump from one gatepost to the other—and fell in the dust ignominiously. But he would do it some day. He had eaten all the lunch old Linda had set out for him. He also tried to talk to Linda, for Timothy was a sociable little soul. But Linda was grumpy, too. What was the matter with all the folks that day? Linda was usually good-natured, though he did not like her quite so well as Susan Baker at Ingleside. Timothy could not see how he was going to put in the afternoon.

Well, he would go down to the gate again and

watch the cars and buggies go by. That wasn't forbidden anyhow. He wished he had some raisins to eat. Every Sunday afternoon he was given a handful of big, juicy raisins to eat as "a Sunday treat."

But this was only Saturday and when Linda was grumpy there was no use asking her for anything. Though, if he had but known it, Linda would gladly have given him the raisins today.

"What are you thinking of, son?" asked a voice.

Timothy jumped. Where had the man come from? There hadn't been any sound, any footstep. Yet there he was, just outside the gate, looking down at him with a peculiar expression on a handsome, sulky, deep-lined face. He wasn't a tramp, he was too well-dressed for that. And Timothy, who was always feeling things he couldn't have explained, had an idea that he wasn't used to being so well-dressed.

The man's eyes were grey and smouldering, and Timothy felt, too, that he was cross about something—very cross—cross enough to do anything mean that occurred to him. This must certainly be what Mrs. Dr. Blythe called "a Jonah day."

And yet there was something about the man that Timothy liked.

"I was thinking what a splendid day it would have been for the lake at Lowbridge," he explained, rather stiffly, for he had always been warned not to talk to strangers.

"Oh, the lake! Yes, I remember what a fascinating spot it was for small boys—though it was not a resort then and a good many people called it the pond. Did you want to go there?"

"Yes. Aunt Edith was going to take me. Then she couldn't. She had to go to town on important business. Dr. Blythe took them."

"Dr. Blythe! Is he still in Glen St. Mary?"

"Yes. But they live at Ingleside now."

"Oh, and is your Aunt Kathleen at home?"

Timothy thawed. This man knew Aunt Kathleen, therefore it was allowable to talk to him.

"No, she went, too."

"When will they be back?"

"Not till the evening. They went to town to see a lawyer. I heard Linda say so."

"Oh." The man reflected a moment and then gave a queer inward chuckle. Timothy didn't like the sound of it particularly.

"Are you a friend of Aunt Kathleen?" he inquired politely.

The man laughed again. "A friend. Oh, yes, a very near and dear friend. I'm sure she'd have been delighted to see me."

"You must call again," said Timothy persuasively.

"It's quite likely I shall," said the man. He sat down on the big red boulder by the gate, lighted a cigarette with fingers that were strangely rough and callous, and looked Timothy over in a cool, appraising manner. A trim little lad . . . well set up . . . curly brown hair, dreamy eyes and a good chin.

"Whom do you look like, boy?" he said abruptly. "Your dad?"

Timothy shook his head. "No. I wish I did. But I don't know what he looked like. He's dead—and there isn't any picture."

"There wouldn't be," said the man. Again, Timothy didn't like it.

"My dad was a very brave man," he said quickly. "He was a soldier in the Boer War and he won the Distinguished Service Medal."

"Who told you that?"

"Aunt Edith. Aunt Kathleen won't talk of him ever. Aunt Edith won't either—much—but she told me that."

"Edith was always a bit of a good scout," muttered the man. "You don't look like your—your—mother either."

"No, I can see that. I have a picture of mother. She died when I was born. Aunt Edith says I look like Grandfather Norris, her father. I'm called after him."

"Are your aunts good to you?" asked the man.

"They are," said Timothy emphatically. He would have said the same thing if they had not been. Timothy had a fine sense of loyalty. "Of course, you know, they're bringing me up. I have to be scolded sometimes—and I have to take music lessons . . ."

"You don't like that?" said the man, amused.

"No. But I guess maybe it's good dis . . . cipline."

"You have a dog, I see," said the man, indicating Merrylegs. "Good breed, too. I thought Kathleen and Edith never liked dogs."

"They don't. But they let me have one because Dr. Blythe said every boy ought to have a dog. So my aunts gave in. They don't even say anything when he sleeps on my bed at nights. They don't approve of it, you know, but they let him stay. I'm glad because I don't like going to sleep in the dark."

"Do they make you do that?"

"Oh, it's all right," said Timothy quickly. He wasn't going to have anyone imagine that he was finding fault with his aunts. "I'm quite old enough to go to sleep in the dark. Only— only. . ."

"Yes?"

"It's only that when the light goes out I can't help imagining faces looking in at the window— awful faces—hateful faces. I heard Aunt Kathleen say once that she was always expecting to look at the window and 'see his face.' I don't know who she meant—but after that I began to see faces in the dark."

"Your mother was like that," said the man absently. "She hated the dark. They shouldn't make you sleep in it."

"They should," cried Timothy. "My aunts are bricks. I love them. And I wish they weren't so worried."

"Oh, so they're worried?"

"Terribly. I don't know what it is about. I can't think it's me—though they look at me sometimes. Do you see anything about me to worry them?"

"Not a thing. So your aunts are pretty good to you? Give you everything you want?"

"Almost everything," said Timothy cautiously. "Only—they won't have raisins in the rice pudding on Fridays. Aunt Edith would be willing but Aunt Kathleen says the Norrises have never put raisins in the rice pudding. Oh, are you going?"

"I'm going down to the lake," said the man. "Would you like to come with me?"

Timothy stared. "Do you want me to?"

"Very much. We'll ride on the ponies and eat hot dogs and drink pop—anything you like."

It was an irresistible temptation.

"But . . . but," stammered Timothy, "Aunt Kathleen said I wasn't to go off the grounds."

"Not alone," said the man. "She meant not alone. I'm sure she'd think it quite—lawful—to go with me."

"Are you quite sure?"

"Quite," said the man, and laughed again.

"About the money," faltered Timothy. "You see I've only ten cents. Of course I've got a quarter from my allowance but I can't spend it. I must get Aunt Edith a birthday present with it. But I can spend the ten cents—I've had it a long time. I found it on the road."

"This is my treat," said the man.

"I must go and shut Merrylegs up," said Timothy, relieved. "And wash my face and hands. You won't mind waiting a few minutes?"

"Not at all."

Timothy flew up the driveway and disposed rather regretfully of Merrylegs. Then he scrubbed himself, giving special attention to his ears. He hoped they were clean. Why couldn't ears have been made plain? When Jem Blythe asked Susan Baker the same question one day she told him it was the will of God.

"It would be more convenient if I knew your name," he hinted, as they walked along.

"You may call me Mr. Jenkins," said the man.

Timothy had a wonderful afternoon. A glorious afternoon. All the merry-go-rounds he wanted—and something better than hot dogs.

"I want a decent meal," said Mr. Jenkins. "I didn't have any lunch. Here's a restaurant. Shall we go in and eat?"

"It's an expensive place," said Timothy. "Can you afford it?"

"I think so," Mr. Jenkins laughed mirthlessly.

It was expensive—and exclusive. Mr. Jenkins told Timothy to order what he wanted and never think of expense. Timothy was in the seventh heaven of delight. It had been a glorious afternoon; Mr. Jenkins had been a very jolly comrade. And now to have a meal with a real man—to sit opposite him and order a meal from the bill of fare like a man himself. Timothy sighed with rapture.

"Tired, son?" asked Mr. Jenkins.

"Oh, no."

"You've had a good time?"

"Splendid. Only . . ."

"Yes—what?"

"I didn't feel as if you were having a good time," said Timothy slowly.

"Well," said Mr. Jenkins slowly, "I wasn't, if it comes to that. I kept thinking of—a friend of mine and it rather spoiled things for me."

"Isn't he well?"

"Quite well. Too well. Too likely to live. And, you see, he isn't happy."

"Why not?" asked Timothy.

"Well, you see, he was a fool—and worse. Oh, he was a very big fool. He took a lot of money that didn't belong to him."

"You mean he—stole it?" queried Timothy, rather shocked.

"Well, let's say embezzled. That sounds better. But the bank thought it bad any way you pronounced it. He was sent to prison for ten years. They let him out a little sooner—because he behaved rather well. And he found himself quite rich. An old uncle had died when he was in prison and left him a pot of money. But what good will it do him? He is branded."

"I'm sorry for your friend," said Timothy. "But ten years is a very long time. Haven't people forgotten?"

"Some people never forget. His wife's sisters for instance. They were very hard on him. How he hated them! He brooded all those years on getting square with them when he came out."

"How?"

"There is a way. He could take something from them that they want very much to keep. And he's lonely . . . he wants companionship . . . he's very lonely. I've been thinking about him all afternoon. But you mustn't think I haven't enjoyed myself. It's been something to remember for a long time. Now, I suppose you want to get back before your aunts come home?"

"Yes. But just so they won't get worried. I'm going to tell them about this, of course."

"Won't they scold you?"

"Likely they will. But scolding doesn't break any bones, as Linda says," remarked Timothy philosophically.

"I don't think they will scold you much—not if you get the head start of them with a message I'm sending them by you. You got that present for your aunt's birthday, didn't you?"

"Yes. But there is one thing. I've got that ten cents yet, you know. I'd like to buy some flowers with it and go over to the park and put them at the base of the soldier's monument. Because my father was a brave soldier, you know."

"Was he killed in South Africa?"

"Oh, no. He came back and married mother. He was in a bank, too. Then he died."

"Yes, he died," said Mr. Jenkins, when they had reached The Corner. "And," he added, "I fancy he'll stay dead."

Timothy was rather shocked. It seemed a queer

way to speak of anyone—what Aunt Kathleen would call flippant. Still he couldn't help liking Mr. Jenkins.

"Well, goodbye, son," said Mr. Jenkins.

"Won't I see you again?" asked Timothy wistfully. He felt that he would like to see Mr. Jenkins again.

"No, I'm afraid not. I'm going away—far away. That friend of mine—he's going far away—to some new land—and I think I'll go, too. He's lonely, you know. I must look after him a bit."

"Will you tell your friend I'm sorry he's lonely, and I hope he won't be always lonely?"

"I'll tell him. And will you give your aunts a message for me?"

"Can't you give it to them yourself? You said you were coming back to see them."

"I'm afraid I can't manage it after all. Tell them they are not to worry over that letter they got this morning. They needn't go to their lawyer again to see—if the person who wrote it has the power to do what he threatened to do. I know him quite well and he has changed his mind. Tell them he is going away and will never bother them again. You can remember that, can't you?"

"Oh, yes. And they won't be worried any more?"

"Not by that person. Only there's this . . . tell them they must cut out those music lessons and put raisins in the Friday pudding and let you have a light to go to sleep by. If they don't—that person might worry them again."

"I'll tell them about the music lessons and the pudding, but," said Timothy sturdily, "not about the light if it's all the same to that person. You see, I mustn't be a coward. My dad wasn't a coward. If you see that person will you please tell him that?"

"Well, perhaps you're right. Ask Dr. Blythe about it. I went to college with him and I fancy he knows what's what. And this is for your own ear, son. We've had a fine time today and it's all right as it happens. But take my advice and never go off with a stranger again."

Timothy squeezed Mr. Jenkins' hard hand. "But you aren't a stranger," he said wistfully.

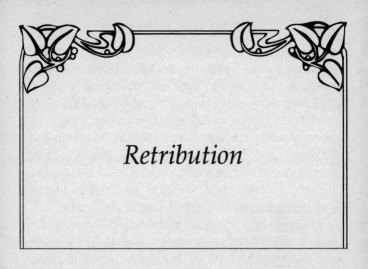

Retribution

Clarissa Wilcox was on her way to Lowbridge. She had heard that David Anderson was dying. Susan Baker of Ingleside had told her. Dr. Blythe of Glen St. Mary was David Anderson's doctor in spite of the fact that Dr. Parker lived in Lowbridge. But years ago David Anderson had quarrelled with Dr. Parker and would never have him again.

Clarissa Wilcox was determined to see David Anderson before he died. There were some things she must say to him. She had been waiting for forty years to say them—and her chance had come at last, thanks to Susan Baker whom she hated (there had been an age-old feud between the Bakers of Glen St. Mary and the Wilcoxes of Mowbray Narrows and she and Susan Baker never did more than nod coldly when they met). Besides, Susan Baker put on such ridiculous airs because she was the hired girl at Ingleside. As if that was any great thing! None of the Wilcoxes ever had to hire out to earn their living. They had been wealthy once and had looked down on the Bakers. That time had long since passed. They were poor now but still they looked down on the Bakers. Nevertheless she was grateful to Susan Baker for telling her about David Anderson.

He must be very close to death indeed or Susan Baker would not have mentioned it. They were a close-mouthed lot at Ingleside when it came to the doctor's patients. Susan was always being pumped but she was as bad as the rest of them— as if she belonged to the family, thought Clarissa scornfully. Such airs as some people gave them- selves! But what else would you expect of a Bak- er?

The main thing was that she had found out in time that David Anderson was really dying.

She had known this chance must come. Amid all the injustices of life this one monstrous injustice could never be permitted: that David Anderson, with whom she had danced in youth, should die without hearing what she had to tell him. Susan Baker had wondered at the strange flash that had come into Clarissa Wilcox's old, faded face when she had happened to mention his approaching death. Susan wondered uneasily if she should have mentioned it at all. Would the doctor be offended?

But everybody knew it. There was no secret about it. Susan decided that she was being over-scrupulous. None the less she was careful to mention it to Mrs. Dr. Blythe.

"Oh, yes," Mrs. Blythe had said carelessly. "The doctor says he may go out at any moment."

Which set Susan's conscience at rest.

Clarissa Wilcox knew that David Anderson could still hear her—so much gossip said. In fact, Dr. Blythe had said so. The sudden, unheralded stroke that had laid her hated enemy low (everybody in Lowbridge and Mowbray Narrows and Glen St. Mary had forgotten for generations that there was any enmity or cause of enmity between them but to Clarissa Wilcox it was still a thing of yesterday) . . . well, this stroke had robbed him of speech and movement, even of sight, since he could not lift his eyelids, but he could still hear and was quite conscious.

Clarissa was glad he could not see her, could not see the changes time had wrought in her once fair face. Yes, she *had* been good-looking once in spite of the Bakers' sneers—something few of the Bakers had ever been—certainly not poor Susan who, however, belonged to a younger generation. Yes, she could say what she liked to David Anderson without any risk of seeing the old laughing scorn in his eyes.

She would avenge Blanche at last . . . beautiful, beloved Blanche, dead in her dark young loveliness. Did anybody remember Blanche but her? Susan Baker's old aunt perhaps. Had Susan ever heard the story? Not likely. The matter had been hushed up.

Clarissa, as usual, was shrouded in black, and she was bent and unsmiling. She had worn black ever since Blanche died, a Wilcox peculiarity, so the Bakers said. Her heart-shaped face, with its intense unfaded blue eyes, was covered with minute wrinkles. Susan Baker had thought that afternoon how strange it was that old Clarissa Wilcox had kept her eyes so young when all her contemporaries' were sunken and faded.

"Mrs. Doctor, dear," said Susan, as they concocted a fruit cake together, "is it better to be beautiful when you are young and have it to remember always, even though it must be hard to see your good looks fade, than to be always plain and so have nothing much to regret when you grow old?"

"What strange questions you ask sometimes, Susan," said Anne, deftly snipping candied peel into slender strips. "For my own part, I think it would be nice to be beautiful when you were young and remember it."

"But then you were always beautiful, Mrs. Doctor, dear," said Susan with a sigh.

"Me beautiful—with my red hair and my freckles," laughed Anne. "You don't know how I longed to be beautiful, Susan. They tell me that old Miss Wilcox who called this afternoon was quite a beauty in her youth."

"The Wilcoxes all thought they were handsome," said Susan with a sniff. "I never thought

Clarissa was but I have been told that her sister Blanche was really handsome. However, though I am far from young, Mrs. Doctor, dear, I do not remember her."

"You Bakers have never seemed to be very friendly with the Wilcoxes, Susan," said Anne, curiously. "Some old family feud, I suppose?"

"I have been told so," answered Susan, "but to tell the plain truth, Mrs. Doctor, dear, I have never really known how it started. I only know that the Wilcoxes thought themselves much better than the Bakers."

"And I suppose the Bakers thought themselves much better than the Wilcoxes," teased the doctor who had come in.

"The Wilcoxes had more money," retorted Susan, "but I do not think they were any better than the Bakers for all that. This Clarissa, now, was said to have been quite a belle in her youth but she did not get a husband any more than some of the rest of us."

"Perhaps she was more particular," said the doctor. He knew that would enrage Susan, and it did. Without a word she picked up her pan of raisins and marched into the house.

"Why will you tease her so, Gilbert?" said Anne reproachfully.

"It's such fun," said the doctor. "Well, old David Anderson of Lowbridge is dying. I doubt if he will survive the night. They say he was a gay blade in his youth. You wouldn't think so to see him now."

"The things time does to us!" sighed Anne.

"You're a bit young to be thinking of that yet," said Gilbert. "Clarissa Wilcox looks rather young for her age. Those eyes—and hardly a thread of grey hair. Do you know who his wife was?"

"No . . . Rose Somebody. Of course I've seen it on her monument in the Lowbridge cemetery. And it seems to me that there was some scandal about David Anderson and this Clarissa's sister Blanche."

"Who is talking scandal now?" asked Gilbert.

"A thing that is so old ceases to be scandal and becomes history. Well, I must go and placate Susan and get this cake in the oven. It's for Kenneth Ford's birthday—they'll be at the House of Dreams Wednesday, you know."

"Have you become reconciled to exchanging the House of Dreams for Ingleside?"

"Long ago," said Anne. But she sighed. After all, there would never be any place for her quite like the House of Dreams.

Meanwhile Clarissa Wilcox walked along the red road south to Lowbridge with the step of a young girl. Her dark hair, as the doctor had said, had few grey hairs in it, but looked rather unnatural around her wrinkled face. It was covered by a crocheted fascinator, as it used to be called, which Blanche had made for her long ago. She seldom went anywhere so it had lasted well. She never cared—now—what she wore. She had a long, thin mouth and a dreadful smile when

she smiled at all. Very few people had ever seen
Clarissa Wilcox smile.

The magic light of a long, blue evening was
sifting in from the Four Winds Harbour but the
wind was rising rapidly. It sighed in the tall old
spruces along the road and it seemed to Clarissa
that ghostly years were calling to her in its voice.
It was not an ordinary wind—it was a wind of
death blowing for David Anderson. What if he
died before she got to him? She hurried faster
along the road to Lowbridge.

In the distance two ships were sailing out of
the Four Winds Harbour—likely *his* ships, she
thought, forgetting that David Anderson had
retired from business years ago. To be sure,
some nephews of his carried it on. Where were
they going? Ceylon . . . Singapore . . . Mandalay?
Once the names would have thrilled her; once she
had longed to see those alluring places.

But it was Rose who saw them with him . . .
Rose instead of Blanche as it should have been
. . . and Rose was dead, too. But the ships still
went out, although David Anderson, who had
been a shipbuilder and owner all his life, carrying
on trade in ports all over the world, had long
ceased to go in them.

He left that to his son. His son! Perhaps!

Clarissa did not even know that his son was
a ship-surgeon and was seldom ever seen in
Lowbridge.

Lowbridge was before her. There on Main Street
was David Anderson's rich, splendid house,

where Rose had queened it for years. It was still rich and splendid in Clarissa Wilcox's eyes, although the younger generation were beginning to call it old-fashioned and out-of-date. Little white cherry blossoms were fluttering down on the walks through the cool spring air.

The wide door was open and she went in unseen—across the hall—up the wide, velvet stairs where her footsteps made no sound. All about her were empty rooms. Dr. Blythe had just made his last call on David Anderson and now he was standing at the gate talking to the white-garbed nurse whom both he and Dr. Parker wanted at the same time.

"I really think I ought to go to Dr. Parker's case," she was saying slowly. She would much rather have taken on Dr. Blythe's. He was much more reasonable than Dr. Parker who, for instance, would have disapproved of her leaving David Anderson for a moment, as long as the breath was in his body. As if it made any difference now!

"Go to Parker's by all means," said Dr. Blythe. "I can get Lucy Marks who is on a visit with her mother over at Mowbray Narrows. You will not be needed here much longer," he added significantly.

Young fools, thought Clarissa. *She is trying to get up a flirtation with Dr. Blythe.*

To old Clarissa Wilcox both of them seemed mere children. But she did not care what they did. The only thing that mattered to her was to be alone with David Anderson—her longed-for chance had come at last, after years of waiting. All about her were empty rooms. The dead and the dying were soon forgotten, she reflected bitterly. Even the nurse had left the dying man alone. Blanche, she thought, should have reigned in those rooms. *She* would not have left her husband to die alone. It did not occur to Clarissa that Blanche might have died before him as Rose had done.

As she had come up the stairs she had glanced through the portières of dull gold velvet that hung in the library doorway. She saw the portrait of Rose hanging over the fire-place—where Blanche's should have hung.

Rose had been painted in her wedding gown of ivory satin. David Anderson had had the picture painted by a visiting artist and Clarissa well remembered the local sensation it had made in Lowbridge, which was just a small village then where even photographs were taken once in a lifetime. When it was painted and hung David Anderson had given a celebration party. It was talked of for months.

Although Clarissa saw nobody it seemed to her that whispers haunted the house. It was full of shadows . . . shadows that seemed to grasp at you. They must be shadows that had come to attend David Anderson into eternity. Rose and Blanche and Lloyd Norman—and who knew whom else. But she would not be daunted by them. She had things to say, things to say that would astonish them all except Blanche and perhaps—who knew?—Lloyd Norman. Time was getting short. At any moment that gossiping nurse might return.

Ah, here was his room at last—a long, feline room with a little fire at the end of it, like the red tongue of a cat. The room he had shared with Rose!

And there was nobody in it except the dying David Anderson. What a piece of good fortune! She had been afraid that the nurse might have called in the housekeeper to keep watch while she talked at the gate with Dr. Blythe. There was not even a light and the crowding trees outside made it dimmer still. Of course it did not matter to David who could no longer see, but still it gave Clarissa a feeling of horror she could not have explained. The ghosts would have it all their own way in the dimness. She knew people did not believe in ghosts nowadays. She had heard both Dr. Blythe and Dr. Parker telling ghost stories and laughing over them. When they reached her age they would be wiser. And what an assemblage of ghosts must be crowding about David Anderson's bed!

The perfume of the lilac hedge below came heavily up through the window. Clarissa had never liked the scent of lilac blossoms. They always made her think of some secret, too-sweet thing . . . perhaps like the love between David Anderson and Blanche Wilcox. Or . . . again, who knew, between Rose Anderson and Lloyd Norman. For the thousandth time, Clarissa

wished she knew the whole truth about that
matter.

There was a vase on the table full of some
white flowers that glimmered spectrally through
the dusk. *That* was amusing. David Anderson had
never cared for flowers. She supposed the nurse
had put them there. Or maybe somebody had
sent them in. She remembered a rose Blanche
had given him and which he had dropped carelessly on the garden walk. Had he cared more for
Rose's flowers? She, Clarissa, had picked up that
rose and had it somewhere yet—only she could
not remember where. In some old dusty, faded
volume of poems, she thought.

On the wall above the flowers hung a miniature
of Rose. It had been painted while they were away
on one of their visits. Clarissa hated the portrait
in the library but she hated the miniature still
more. It was so intimate and possessive, as if it
slyly flaunted its complete ownership of David
Anderson.

The frame was of gold with a golden bowknot
atop. Rose, she knew, had given it to David on one
of her birthdays—after she had begun carrying on
with Lloyd Norman, too. Well, Blanche would
have been true to him at least. The Wilcoxes
were always true to their husbands, even when
they hated them.

After all, Clarissa was glad the room was dim.
She did not want to say what she had to say to
David Anderson with Rose smiling down trium-
phantly at her.

His face on the pillow was a face of yellow
wax. His eyes—his smoky grey eyes, which had
been, so they said, an inheritance from his Irish
mother, were hidden under wrinkled lids. His
long-fingered, exquisite, rather cruel hands, were
lying on the spread. She remembered once, long
years ago, they had walked home from somewhere—she could not remember from where, but
she remembered the clasp of his hands. But that
was before Rose . . .

The deep dimple was still in his chin. Blanche
used to put her finger teasingly into that dimple.
No doubt a hundred other girls had, too. What
was that old saying about a sailor with a lass
in every port? Why, she had heard Dr. Blythe
quote it one day. How proverbs lived while people died!

But at least the dimple had not changed. His
magnificent white hair swept back from his brow.
He was an old man but he did not seem old even
as he lay there, dying.

And, thought Clarissa with a shudder, he still
gave you the feeling that he was doing you a
favour in allowing you to look at him. All the
Andersons had it, more or less, but it was most
strongly marked in David.

Clarissa sat down on a chair. Her breath came
as fast as if she had been running. Only a few sec-
onds had elapsed since she had entered the room
but she felt as if she had been there for a century.

And she was surprised, unpleasantly surprised,
to find that she was still afraid of him. She had

always been afraid of him—she admitted it at
last—but she had never dreamed that she would
be afraid of him, now that he was as good as dead.
She had not expected either that he would still be
able to make her feel crude, silly, always in the
wrong. As if the Andersons were so much above
the Wilcoxes! But he could—and did.

She found her thin, veined hands trembling.
She was furious. She had waited a lifetime for
this hour—and she would not be robbed of it.
If the nurse or the housekeeper came she would
slam the door in their faces.

She fought down her weakness. Her voice was
quite steady when finally she spoke—steady and
clear and quite young. Youth seemed to have
come back to her. She and David Anderson were
both young and it was all nonsense that he was
dying, just gossip somebody had started. But then
Rose must be young, too, and that she would not
have. No, they were all old and she must say
certain things quickly, or someone would come
in and she would lose her chance.

The old house seemed listening to the cold
poison of her words. At times the gusts of wind
died away, too, as if the whole world wanted to
listen. Dr. Blythe and the nurse were still talking
at the gate. Men were all alike. What would Mrs.
Blythe say if she knew?

"Tonight I shall rest well for the first time in
years, David Anderson. Rest as well as you who
will be dead. Dead, David Anderson. You never
thought you could die, did you? Perhaps you will

not rest . . . if it is true that the soul survives the body. But I shall rest . . . for I shall have told you what I have always wanted to tell you . . . what I have waited years to tell you.

"How I have hated you always—always! You won't believe that. You thought nobody could hate you. How I have looked forward to seeing you on your deathbed! My only fear in all these years has been that I might die before you. But I knew heaven would not allow such an injustice. The world is full of injustice but there are some things that are not permitted. This was one of them. You cannot see me, David Anderson, but you can hear me—at least Dr. Blythe says you can and he is one of the few honest men I know.

"You ruined and killed my sister Blanche. You knew she died—but you did not know that her child lived! Ah, if you could move I think you would start at that. Very few people ever knew it. We Wilcoxes had our pride as well as the proud Andersons. It was a boy, David Anderson. Perhaps your only son. Ah, that should make you flinch if you had any power of movement left! But you never mistrusted Rose, did you? In your eyes she was the perfect wife. And all the time—well, never mind. Gossip will be gossip, you know. Your son was called John Lovel. When he was seventeen he came back to Lowbridge and you gave him a job in your shipping office—a poor, underpaid job. Your son, David Anderson. Do you remember? I doubt it. I suppose you have forgotten him long ago.

"I think perhaps I was the only one who knew the secret. But some may have guessed it, for he was the image of you. When he had been with you two years he took some money from your safe. Your partner wanted to overlook his fault— he said he was so young—and our cousin had not troubled himself much about his bringing up. But you were relentless. Do you remember, David Anderson? Your son . . . *Your son* . . . went to jail and when he came out five years later he was a criminal. Your son, David Anderson!

"I can prove all this—and when you are dead I shall publish it. Everyone will know that you, the just, upright, censorious man . . . it was all so long ago that people have forgotten your wild youth. Why, you are even an elder in the church, aren't you?

"But when you are dead and buried—beside Rose, David Anderson—everyone will know that you were the lover of a girl you ruined and the father of an illegitimate son who is a jailbird. I have proof as I have told you, David Anderson.

"How will the minister feel when he is preaching your funeral sermon? And how I will be laughing to myself. For I will be there, David Anderson. Oh, yes, I will be there; I have not gone anywhere for years but I will go to your funeral. I would not miss it for anything. Think how people will talk. Even the young ones who have forgotten you, to whom you are only a name. They will talk about it for many a day. The Andersons will try to hush it up but they will not be able to. Oh, no, people love gossip too much, even when it is fifty years old or more.

"You will be buried in the Anderson plot—beside Rose. The vacant space is left on the gravestone for your name. Did it ever occur to you, David Anderson, that there was another name she might better have liked to have there? No, I don't think it did. There could be no higher honor than having the name of Anderson on your tombstone, could there? But it should be Blanche and not Rose, David Anderson.

"And when people pass your grave they will point it out and say, 'Old David Anderson is buried there. He was a hypocrite.' Oh, yes, they will. I will take care they shall not forget. Even the younger ones will not forget. For one person I shall tell is Susan Baker. And I shall enjoy telling her. She pretends not to like gossip—she likes to imitate that stuck-up Mrs. Blythe in every way she can. I could tell Mrs. Blythe a few things about Dr. Blythe and his nurses—yes, and about him and Mrs. Owen Ford if I wanted to. But it is nothing to me. My business is with you, David Anderson.

"Oh, how I shall laugh when I pass your grave! I go through the graveyard every Sunday, for I still go to church, David Anderson. Going to church seems to be going out of fashion but I go every Sunday I can, and I go by that little path through the graveyard. People think I am a very devoted daughter—if they think about it at all. But I go through it to laugh—quietly, to myself—knowing that if I opened my mouth, I could blacken that spotless reputation of which you were so proud. And now I shall laugh more than ever.

"You were a proud man always, David Anderson—proud even for an Anderson. Do you remember the time you would not sit beside my cousin in school because he was a Wilcox? And you were prouder as you grew older. Proud of your wife, of your big business, of your beautiful ships, proud of being Captain Anderson, proud of your rich, fine house— did it ever occur to you that Rose married you for your house?—proud of your handsome son.

"Are you sure he was your son, David Anderson?

"Ah, now we come to it. Other people were not quite so sure. Ask Susan Baker's grandfather when you meet him on the other side.

"Your beautiful Rose had a lover. You didn't know that, you never even suspected it. *I* knew it—perhaps I was the only one who knew it— but a good many suspected it. Why, even Susan Baker spoke of it when you had your stroke. She said her grandfather saw Rose and Lloyd Norman one night. And there were suspicions of you and Blanche, too, though you thought you were so careful.

"I've always meant to tell you before you died. I knew, somehow, I should live longer than you. Not just because I was so much younger—but,

well, I *knew*. You worshipped Rose, didn't you?
You put up a beautiful and costly stained glass
window to her memory in your Lowbridge
church. At night its light falls across her grave
and touches Lloyd Norman's.

"But he does not come to her now; her baby
face does not flush at his footsteps as I have seen
it flush, you blind David Anderson. Her cheek is
cold—the grave is a bitter lover, David Anderson.
But you know now; you know at last. And you
know all I have said is true. We do not tell lies
to the dying. At last you know your wife—your
beautiful Rose whom the winds of heaven must
not visit too roughly—was false to you. And you
know that many people suspected it, while you
were holding your head so high. Susan Baker says
her grandfather told his wife at the christening of
Rose's son, 'It's a wise child that knows its own
father.' "

Her passionate words sank into the silence as
into a deep well. She had wreaked her hatred
at last.

Not a moment too soon. Dr. Blythe had finished his conversation with the nurse and had
gone. The nurse was coming back to her patient.
There was a stir as if the housekeeper were coming up the back stairs. But she had done what
she had meant to do for years. Ah, revenge was
sweet.

Suddenly she knew that she was alone in the
room. With shaking hands she snatched up a
match and lighted a candle on the table. She held

it up—its faint, flickering light wavered over the face on the pillow.

David Anderson, once so tremendously alive, was dead. He had died while she was talking to him. And, lying dead, he smiled.

Clarissa had always hated his smile because one could never tell what it meant. Nor could she tell now. Was he mocking her because nothing mattered . . . any longer?

He had been the only one of the Andersons with such a smile. The Wilcoxes had hated all the others but not for their smile. She remembered that a schoolteacher had said that little David Anderson must have been to hell to learn a smile like that. The Andersons had him dismissed for the remark. But Susan Baker's grandfather had said it was only because David Anderson liked to cheat people out of their just dues. They said he ruled his crews by that smile alone. And Clarissa recalled that the Andersons had always had difficulty manning a ship if David was going on the voyage. She wondered if Rose had found out it meaning.

"I am an old maid," Susan Baker had said, "and I will be honest and admit that I have never had a chance to be anything else. But rather than marry a man with a smile like my grandfather said David Anderson had, I would live the lives of a hundred old maids."

Clarissa seemed to go limp like an old dress as the nurse hurried into the room.

"He is dead," she said. "We have been expecting it all day."

"He died when you were having your nice little flirtation with Dr. Blythe," said Clarissa venomously.

The nurse stared in amazement. She knew old Clarissa Wilcox was supposed to be "not quite all there," but the idea of flirting with Dr. Blythe!

Clarissa felt aged—worn out—foolish. The nurse was laughing at her, even in the presence of death. Quickly she went out of the room, leaving him smiling on the pillow, arrogant in death as in life. Noiselessly she went down and out and along the darkening evening street. The embers of sunset smouldered in the west. There were curling crests of ice-white foam on the harbour as if it were gnashing its teeth at her. She felt very cold.

"I wish I were dead," said Clarissa Wilcox aloud, quite careless of who might hear her. "I loved him so—oh, I always loved him so—from the time we were children at school. I hope he didn't hear me. Oh, God, grant that he didn't hear me! But I shall never know."

The
Twins Pretend

Jill and P.G.—alias Pig or Porky, according to
Jill's mood—were somewhat bored. This was not
a common occurrence with them, for the imaginations which had kept everybody wondering
during all their ten years of life as to what those
two young devils would be up to next, seldom
failed to make the world a most interesting and
intriguing place.

But something was wrong this particular morning at Half Moon Cove, which was situated about
halfway between Mowbray Narrows and Glen St.
Mary, and was only beginning to be what was
afterwards called "the summer colony."

Perhaps certain unlawful snacks in which they
had indulged the preceding night, when Aunt
Henrietta had had one of her bad spells and

Mums had been too busy to keep an eye on them, may have had something to do with it. Nan and Diana Blythe had been over from Glen St. Mary.

"And we *had* to give them a decent lunch, Mums."

"I don't see why they needed lunch at all," said Mums severely. "They had had their suppers and they were here only half an hour or so while their father made a sick call in the Upper Glen."

"I expect that old Susan Baker doesn't give them half enough to eat," said Jill. "Anyhow, they are lovely girls, Mums, and I wish we lived nearer to them."

"I have heard that the Blythe family are very nice," admitted Mums. "I know their father and mother are. But if they brew up as much mischief in a week as you two do in half an hour I pity the household and I think it might be better if this Susan Baker you talk of did not give them half as much to eat as rumour says she does. Did they tell you she did not give them enough to eat?"

"No, oh, no, they are too loyal," said Jill. "But I know by the look of her she would starve you if she could. I've seen her in church."

"Leaving Susan Baker and the Blythe twins entirely out of the question," said Mums, "who has been using Aunt Henrietta's new stewpan in such a way that it is hopelessly battered and dented?"

"Oh, we wanted something for a Roman helmet," said P.G. easily.

A little thing like that never worried P.G. Why, there were dozens of better stewpans in the store at Glen St. Mary.

At all events, there the twins were, digging their brown toes into the sand and scowling viciously at each other. As Jill said, you had to do something to break the monotony. Probably they would have quarrelled (and the twins' quarrels always made their tired, overworked little mother wonder why Fate had picked *her* for their upbringing), had not Anthony Lennox happened along.

But Anthony Lennox did happen along and Jill fell in love with him at sight. As she told Nan Blythe later on, he looked as if he had some dark secret on his conscience. Jill, like Nan, was at the stage when she adored villains. There was no surer passport to her favour than to look as if you were the wreck of a misspent life.

"Or a remorseful pirate," Nan had said.

"It would be better still for him to be an unremorseful one," said Diana.

Jill felt that she would die for an unremorseful pirate. It was then they discovered that Susan Baker did not approve of pirates. Of course a woman who did not approve of pirates would starve you if she got the chance.

"Oh, no," said Diana loyally, "Susan wouldn't starve anyone. Mother is always scolding her for giving us snacks after we go to bed. She would only say we would have more sense when we grew up."

"Isn't that the most maddening thing?" demanded Nan.

Jill agreed that it was.

Anthony Lennox looked gloomy enough to justify almost anything you could pretend about him. Just why the millionaire publisher of a Canada-wide string of magazines should look gloomy and discontented on such a morning the twins didn't know, any more than they knew why he was a millionaire (Susan Baker had told the Blythe twins that) or why, being a millionaire, he had selected this obscure, unknown Prince Edward Island retreat for his summer vacation.

Like the twins, Anthony was bored. But, unlike the twins, it was fast becoming a chronic state with him. Susan Baker had said you got that way when you didn't have to work hard enough for your money.

Anthony was tired of everything. He was tired of making money; of publishing magazines; of shaping public opinion; of being chased by women. He was ungallant enough to put it that way.

The whole world had gone stale.

And now he was tired of Half Moon Cove already though he had been there only a few days. What a fool he had been to come back there! He might have known—he had known— just how it would be. He strode over the shingle with the sting of the blowing wind in his face.

There was a blue sky above, a blue sea before; a great, dazzling, merciless blue world all around him. No place for ghosts one would think. And yet here he was, haunted. Confound it!

And worse than haunted—bored. It all came back to that. Ghosts and boredom were the two things Anthony Lennox couldn't endure. He had spent fifteen years trying to escape both. Of course his doctor had told him that he must go to a quiet place for the summer if he wanted his nerves to behave by the fall. But surely not a dead place.

He would leave that afternoon.

Just as he decided on this he reached the spot where Jill was sitting on a rock, with the air of a queen on a throne, and P.G. was lying flat on his stomach on the sand, too bored himself even to lift his head.

Anthony paused and looked at Jill—at her droll, impudent little face under her fringe of reddish brown hair; at her nose which was not the usual smudge of ten but a nose that stood on its own merits; at her long, new-moon mouth, now drooping at the corners.

And the soul of Anthony Lennox was at that moment knit to the soul of Jill, nevermore to be unknitted. But it was not the nose or the mouth or the impudence that won him. Diana Blythe whom he had met had all those, lacking a little of the impudence perhaps.

It was the eyes—the luminous, black-lashed eyes. They were like eyes he had once known, except that they were stormy and mutinous and grey, whereas the eyes he remembered had been blue and dreamy and yet somehow suggestive of all sorts of wild, secret, unfettered delights.

"Well," said Anthony.

"Well, yourself," retorted Jill, a bit sulkily.

"Now, what is the matter?" said Anthony. "Two kids like you ought to be merry as grigs on a morning like this."

"Matter! Matter!" Jill's wrongs surged up and overwhelmed her. "This is all Pig's fault!"

Pig grunted.

"Oh, yes, grunt. He won't do one thing this morning but grunt. He won't pretend, he simply won't. Just wallows there and grunts. If you never pretend . . ." Jill waxed dramatic, "how are you going to exist here?"

"How indeed!" agreed Anthony fervently.

"The Blythe girls asked us to visit them but we can't go there every day. It isn't . . ."—in one of her April changes Jill was almost tearful—"it isn't as if I was unreasonable. I told him I'd pretend whatever he wanted. It was my turn to choose— and there was one thing I did want. Nan Blythe said she and Walter often pretended it in Rainbow Valley, but I told him he could choose. I'd pretend anything—tortured Indians—or entertaining the King—or a prince's daughter imprisoned in a castle by the sea—or Edith Cavell at her execu- tion—or the land where wishes come true—the Blythe girls love that—or *anything*. And he *won't*. He says he's tired of everything."

Jill came to an end of breath and italics and poked P.G.'s shin savagely with her left foot.

P.G. rolled over on his back and revealed a face uncannily like Jill's, except for a pair of fine hazel eyes and more freckles.

"The land where wishes come true is the silliest pretend of all," he said scornfully, " 'cause wishes never do come true. Jill's got wheels in her head."

P.G. turned over again and gave Jill her chance of revenge.

"You didn't say that to Nan Blythe last night," she hissed. "You said you thought it the best game of all. And you'd better not lie on your stomach. You didn't wash behind your ears this morning!"

P.G. gave no sign of hearing but Jill knew the shot had gone home. P.G., for a boy, was fussy about cleanliness.

"What was it you wanted to pretend?" said Anthony.

"Oh, I wanted to pretend we were rich—we're really poor as snakes, you know—and that we bought Orchard Knob and brought it back to life. Diana says they often pretend that, too. Though they *could*, perhaps. Their father is a very successful doctor."

Anthony's brown eyes opened widely. "Where and what is Orchard Knob? And why and when did it die?"

"Tell him everything," jeered P.G. "Don't keep anything back. He'll be *so* interested."

"Oh, we just gave it that name after a place in a book. It's about half a mile back from the Cove and halfway between here and the Glen. It belongs to someone who went away years ago and never came back. It was a lovely place once. Nan says Susan Baker says it was even prettier than Ingleside though I don't believe *that*. Have you ever seen Ingleside?"

"Oh, yes, I've been there," said Anthony, skipping a stone over the water in a way that made P.G. green with envy. "But I don't know any place called Orchard Knob."

"I *told* you we just named it that ourselves. It would be lovely yet if anyone loved it a little. It's so out at elbows, as Nan says. The shingles are all curled up and the veranda roof is sagging and the shutters are all broken. And one of the chimneys has blown down and burdocks are growing over everything, and it's so lonely and heartbroken."

"You borrowed that speech from Nan Blythe," muttered P.G.

"I don't care—very likely she borrowed it from her mother. They say Mrs. Blythe writes stories. And anyhow I do want to cry every time I see it. It's awful to see a house so lonely."

"As if houses had any feelings!" scoffed P.G.

"They have," said Anthony. "But why has it never been bought?"

"Nobody will buy it. Diana says the heirs want too much for it and Susan Baker says she wouldn't take it as a gift. It would take a fortune to fix it up.

But I would buy it if I was rich. And so would Pig if he wasn't too sulky to say so."

"And what would you do with it?"

"Oh, I know. Pig and I have pretended so often that we know exactly. It isn't a bit like the Blythes would do it but they are more economical in their imaginations. But I say, when it is only imagination anyhow, what difference does it make how extravagant you are?"

"Agreed. But you haven't answered my question."

"Well, we'd shingle it—Nan Blythe would stucco it—and build up the chimney—we were all agreed on that; you ought to see the fireplace they have at Ingleside—and tear down the old veranda and put in a nice sunporch."

"You seem to forget that he has been at Ingleside," sneered P.G.

"And we'd make a rose garden in the burdock patch. Susan agrees with us there. You'd be surprised how much imagination Susan Baker has got when you come to know her well."

"Nothing about a woman would surprise me," said Anthony.

"Is that a cynical speech?" asked Jill, staring at him. "I've always wanted to hear a cynical speech."

"What would you do with the inside?" said Anthony. "I suppose it has gone to seed, too."

"Oh, we'd furnish it like a palace. I can tell you it's fun."

"Yes," sneered P.G., unable to keep silence any

longer. "That's why Jill likes to pretend about it. She loves to fuss with curtains and cushions and stuff. So do the Blythe girls. Though they have some sense. They'd do what I'd like to do."

"And what is that?"

"Being a man you ought to know. I'd put in a swimming pool and a tennis court and a rock garden—you ought to see the one they have at Ingleside."

"I thought you said he'd been at Ingleside," said Jill. "They dragged the stones up from the harbour shore themselves and Susan Baker helped them."

"It wouldn't cost much for a rock garden," said P.G. "Look at all the stones round here. But besides I'd have a boathouse on the river—there's a little river runs past Orchard Knob—and kennels for hundreds of dogs. Oh!" P.G. groaned. "The things one could do if one were rich!"

"But we aren't. And you know, Porky . . ." Jill was softening, "imagination doesn't cost anything."

"You bet it does—sometimes," said Anthony. "More than the richest man alive could afford to pay. But that idea of the rose garden gets me. I've always had a secret, starved ambition to grow roses."

"Well, why don't you?" said Jill. "Everyone says you are rich enough. The Blythe girls say their father says—"

"It isn't exactly a question of riches, Jill dear, but of time to enjoy it. What would be the use of a rose garden you saw only once in so many years? I might have to be in Turkestan when the roses were in bloom."

"But you'd know the roses were there," said Jill, "and somebody else might be enjoying them if you weren't."

"What a philosopher!" Anthony decided the thing in a flash just as he always decided things. "Suppose we do fix up this Orchard Knob of yours?"

Jill stared. P.G. concluded that the man was crazy. Nan Blythe had said Susan had said people said he was.

"Fix it up! Do you mean really? And how can we? Can you buy it?"

"I don't need to. It's mine already, though I've never laid eyes on it for fifteen years. And it was just the 'old Lennox place' then. At first I didn't know you were talking about it."

P.G. looked him over and concluded Nan was right. Jill did the same and concluded he was sane.

"And what do you mean," she said severely, "by going away and leaving that beautiful place to die? No wonder Susan Baker thinks—"

"Never mind what Susan Baker thinks. I'll tell you the whole story some time. Meanwhile, are you coming into partnership with me or are you not? I will furnish the cash and you will furnish the imagination. But the Blythe girls are not to know anything about it until it is finished."

"They're awfully nice girls," protested Jill dubiously.

"Of course they are nice. The daughters of Gilbert Blythe and Anne Shirley couldn't help being nice."

"They'd never tell if they promised not to," said P.G.

"They wouldn't mean to. But don't you think Susan Baker would pick it out of them in a wink?"

"Have you got plenty of money?" demanded Jill, coming down to practicalities. "If we make it like we pretended, it will cost—millions, I guess."

"No," said P.G. unexpectedly. "I've figured it all out lots of times. Thirty thousand will do it."

Anthony stared at him with a look which Jill took for dismay. "You haven't got so much? I knew nobody could have. Susan Baker says—"

"If you mention Susan Baker's name to me again I will pick out one of those nice round stones and go down to Ingleside and lay her out flat. And then do you think the Blythe girls will like you?"

"But you looked—"

"Oh, I suppose I looked a bit staggered," admitted Anthony, "but it was not by the amount. Don't worry, darling. There are quite a few shekels in my old stocking. Well, are you coming in with me?"

"You bet," said Jill and P.G. together.

It would have been incredible to anyone else, but nothing was ever incredible to the twins. They had sojourned so often in the land where wishes come true that nothing amazed them much or long.

"I suppose your parents won't object?" said Anthony. "I'll want you at this Orchard Knob a lot of the time you know."

"We've no parents," assured Jill. "Oh, there is Mums, of course, but she is so busy waiting on Aunt Henrietta that she doesn't bother much about us. She won't worry. Besides, you're respectable, aren't you?"

"Entirely so. But your father—is he . . ."

"Dead," said P.G. cheerfully. A father who had died three months after he and Jill had come into the world was only a name to him. "He didn't leave a cent, so Susan—people say, so Mums had to go to work. She teaches school when we are home. We live out west, you know."

"And she wasn't very well last year," said Jill, "so the board gave her a year's leave of absence—"

"With salary," interposed the financially minded P.G.

"And she came to Half Moon Cove for a rest."

"She rests waiting on Aunt Henrietta," said P.G. scornfully.

"It's a change of tribulation I suppose."

"I don't think we'd better tell her about this anyhow," said Jill, "because then she might think she ought to worry about us and she's got enough without that, so Susan—I mean people say. She'll just think we're prowling around the shore as usual as long as we're home for meals and bed. We are used to looking after ourselves, Mr.— Mr.—?"

"Lennox—Anthony Lennox, at your service."

"What will you do with Orchard Knob when you do fix it up? Live in it?"

"God forbid!" said Anthony Lennox.

There was that in his tone that forbade further questioning.

They went up to Orchard Knob that night. The twins were wild with excitement but Anthony felt like turning tail and running, as he unlocked the rusty iron gate with the key he had got from Lawyer Milton of Lowbridge.

"The very first thing to do," said Jill, "is to tear down this dreadful wall and gate. It's all holes anyway. Porky and I used to crawl through one behind the barns. We couldn't get into the house though. We couldn't even see into it. Susan—a lady we must not mention to you for fear you flatten her out with a stone—said it used to be a fine place long ago."

"Well, you'll see it now. We'll go all over it and then we'll sit down on the veranda and plan what we are going to do with it."

"Oh, I've got all that planned out long ago," said Jill airily. "Nan Blythe and I finished furnishing the sunroom last night. I suppose I can mention *her* name to you without her getting flattened out?"

"Well, yes. But she is not to know anything about this."

"We promised," said Jill, with dignified rebuke. "But if we are much at Orchard Knob the secret will soon get out."

"But not the fact that I am following your ideas," said Anthony.

Then he shrugged his shoulders resignedly. She should have her way. It would be fun of a sort to give her her head and see what she would make of the place. What earthly difference would it make to him? After Orchard Knob was renovated it would be easy to find a purchaser for it. Long ago it would have been almost impossible but summer tourists were coming to the Island now. In any case it meant nothing to him, nothing.

Nevertheless, his hand trembled oddly as he unlocked the door. He knew what he should see inside.

Yes, there it was: the big fireplace in the square hall and in it the ashes of its last fire beside which he had sat one unforgotten night, unforgettable night, fifteen years ago, and looked despair in the face before turning his back on the old place forever. Why hadn't the ashes been swept up? Milton was supposed to find a woman to keep the place in order.

Evidently he hadn't troubled much about it. Dust was thick on everything.

Jill sniffed.

"For goodness' sake leave the door open," she commanded. "This house smells awful. No wonder, poor thing. No sunshine for fifteen years. But we'll change all that. If Susan Baker saw this place—"

"Have you forgotten what I said?" demanded Anthony.

"Yes. You didn't mean it, you know. I'm going to speak about Susan and the Blythe twins whenever they come into my head. But I won't talk of your fixing up Orchard Knob with them, I give you my word of honour."

The next hour was one of wonder for the twins. They explored the house from attic to cellar and Jill went quite mad over its possibilities. Even P.G. waxed enthusiastic.

But one thing, Jill avowed, gave her the creeps—the dead clock on the stair landing, a tall grandfather clock pointing to twelve, very like the one she had seen at Ingleside.

"I stopped it there one night fifteen years ago," said Anthony, "long before the Blythes came to the Glen at all. I was on a sentimental orgy that night, you know. I thought time was ended for me."

They went out and sat down on the veranda steps. Anthony looked around him. What a beautiful, melancholy old place it was! And once it had been so gay.

How weedy was the garden his mother had loved! That far corner where nothing had been allowed to grow but violets was a jungle of burdocks. He felt the reproach of the house. It had once been full. Men and women had loved each other in it. There had been births and deaths; agony and joy; prayer; peace; shelter.

And yet it was not satisfied. It craved more life. It was a shame to have neglected it so long. He had loved it well once. And what a view there was from this front door, over a sea that was silver and sapphire and crimson. The view from Ingleside, over Four Winds Harbour, was justly renowned, but it could not compare with this, let good old Susan brag as she might.

"And now before we go home," said Jill, "you might as well tell us why you left Orchard Knob all alone. You promised, you know."

"I said I'd tell you some time," objected Anthony.

"This *is* some time," said Jill inexorably. "And you might as well begin at once because we must be home before it gets too dark or Mums might get worried."

In the end he told them. He had never told anybody before. For fifteen years he had held his tongue and brooded. Now he found a queer relief in telling these round-eyed youngsters all about it. They wouldn't understand, of course, but just to tell it sluiced some old bitterness out of his soul.

"There was a young fool once—"

"You?" demanded P.G.

"Hush! Have you no manners?" said Jill in a fierce whisper.

"Never mind manners. They don't come into this. Yes, I was the young fool. And I am not any wiser now. There was a girl—"

"Always a girl," muttered P.G. in disgust.

"Pig, hush!" ordered Jill terribly.

As he told them the story his eyes and his voice grew dreamy. He ceased, Jill reflected, to look like a pirate and began to look like a haunted poet.

He and this girl had been pals in childhood and then, as they grew older, lovers. When he had gone abroad for his education he had given her a little ring which she had promised to wear "as long as she cared for no one else."

On his return from England three years later she was not wearing the ring. That meant she didn't care for him any longer. He was too proud and hurt to ask her why.

"Just like a man," said Jill. "Why, there might have been some perfectly good reason. It might have got too loose and slipped off her hand when she was washing. Or it might have broken and she hadn't had time to have it fixed."

"Well, I had this place shut up—it was mine then as my parents had died—and left it to dust and decay."

"I don't think you managed a bit well," said Jill cruelly. "You should have asked her right out why she didn't wear the ring."

"I would have, you bet," said P.G. "No girl would ever put anything like that over on me. And, as Jill says, there might have been some perfectly simple explanation."

"There was. She was in love with another man. I soon found that out."

"How?"

"People told me."

"*She* didn't tell you. Maybe she was as proud as you were."

"Well, even if the story was true there was no sense in leaving Orchard Knob to die, was there?" asked P.G.

"Men are such selfish pigs," said Jill. "Susan Baker says Dr. Blythe is the most unselfish man she knows but even he, if anyone eats the slice of pie she leaves for him in the pantry when she goes to bed, raises Cain."

"Men in love are never sensible—and rarely unselfish, Jill. And, you see, I was terribly hurt."

"Yes, I know." Jill slipped her little brown paw into his and gave it a sympathetic squeeze. "It's rotten to have anyone let you down like that. What was she like?"

Ah, what had she been like! "Pale, shy, sweet. She laughed rarely but her laughter was exquisite. She was like—why, like a silver birch in moonlight. All the men were crazy over her." He had thought the other night that Mrs. Dr. Blythe of Glen St. Mary reminded him of her somewhat. Though they didn't look a bit alike. It must have been some soul resemblance. No wonder she wouldn't have him, a poor devil whose only patrimony was a small country estate.

"And her eyes—blue as the sea and bright as the stars. Why, a man might die for such eyes."

"Like Helen of Troy's," murmured Jill.

"Helen of—how much?"

"Of Troy. Surely you know who Helen of Troy was!"

"Of course. My ancient history has grown a little rusty, that's all. She was the lady men fought for ten years about. I wonder if the winner thought she was worth fighting for so long?"

"Susan Baker says no woman is or ever was," said P.G., "but then nobody ever fought about *her*."

"Never mind Susan Baker. Whom do you pretend is Helen of Troy?" asked Anthony.

"The artist who is boarding next door to Aunt Henrietta's for the summer. We don't know her name but she smiles so beautifully at us when we meet her. She has such sweet blue eyes—oh, she is transcendently lovely."

"She's a good-looking gal, not so young as she used to be," said P.G. who liked to pretend he was hard-boiled and who had heard Dr. Blythe say the same of someone.

"Oh, do shut up," said Jill furiously again. "Did she—I mean your girl—marry the other fellow?"

"I suppose so."

"You *suppose* so. Don't you *know*?"

"Well, her family moved out west next year. I don't know what became of her."

"And you never took the trouble to find out. Well, I guess Susan Baker has more sense than most women," said the disgusted Jill.

"Well, you see I was too sore ever to try to find out. Now, shall we call this a day? Helen of Troy will probably be anxious about you even if your mother isn't."

"Helen doesn't know us, and mother is very anxious about us as a rule," said P.G. indignantly.

"Only Aunt Henrietta is very exacting. She was our father's sister not Mum's. And Susan Baker says she is the worst crank on the Island. Even the doctor says—"

"P.G.," said Jill solemnly, "you are not to repeat gossip, not even if Diana Blythe tells you."

"Who is it he's stuck on?" whispered Anthony to Jill. "Nan or Diana?"

"Both," said Jill. "But now what about this house?"

"I'll run up to town tomorrow and by next week we can get started," said Anthony.

A few days later an army of workmen descended on Orchard Knob and Jill entered the seventh heaven. Never in all her life had she had such fun. She bossed the men to death, but as she had the technique of managing the sex at her fingers' ends, they never knew it and did exactly as she ordered. She let Anthony and P.G. run the out-of-doors alterations for the most part, but as far as the house was concerned she was supreme.

The old place had been asleep for many years but now it was wakened up with a vengeance. The chimney was built up, the roof shingled with lovely green and brown shingles, the house wired from top to bottom and fitted up with all kinds of mechanical gadgets.

Jill, for all her romantic tendencies, was surprisingly practical when it came to equipment. She insisted on a china closet being put in between the kitchen and the dining-room, and the lovely green and mauve and old-rose bathrooms—she had a colour scheme for every floor—ran up a bill that would have staggered Jill if she had ever seen it. When it came to refurnishing, her cup ran over. She was brimming with ideas. Anthony had to get a Chinese embroidery Jill liked for the hall walls and a dear little blue china cabinet with bouquets painted on its doors, and wonderful brocade curtains for the living room that were between spring-green and pale gold. Oh, Jill certainly had taste! Mirrors in all the closet doors; Persian rugs like velvet; brass andirons and silver candlesticks and a lace-like, wrought-copper lantern to hang in the new porch.

"Anyhow, you have your window," said P.G. comfortingly to Anthony.

As for that window, Jill and Anthony had had several pitched battles over it. He wanted one cut in the hall at the side of the living room door, so that a wonderful view of the sea, with Four Winds Harbour in the distance, could be seen, but Jill was sure it would spoil the wall.

Anthony proved surprisingly stubborn, said he didn't care if the wall was spoiled, and in the end they compromised. He was to have his window and Jill was to have the bedroom that had already been painted a robin's egg blue redecorated with a startling wallpaper spattered with parrots. Anthony thought it would be rather awful but as usual the result vindicated Jill's taste.

Finally the end came. The workmen had gone. All the disorder had been eliminated. Orchard

Knob lay in the late August sunshine, a beautiful, gracious place, inside and out.

Jill sighed. "It's been a heavenly summer," she said.

"I've enjoyed it myself," admitted Anthony. "I hear your friends, the Blythe girls, are home again. Perhaps you would like to have them see it."

"Oh, they were over here this afternoon," said Jill, "and we showed them everything. They thought it wonderful—I *will* admit they are not a bit jealous—but they *must* have thought Ingleside pretty small potatoes after this."

"Ingleside is a pretty nice place just the same," said P.G. who had been down there and found he liked Susan Baker's pies.

"But—" Jill looked at Anthony reproachfully, "this house wants to be *lived* in now. *That* is the advantage Ingleside has."

Anthony shrugged. "Well, someone will be living in it—in the summers at least. I've had a good offer already, from a New York millionaire. I think I'll close with it."

"Well . . ." Jill sighed and yielded to the inexorable logic of facts. Of course if Anthony had no intention of spending any more summers at Half Moon Cove somebody else might as well have Orchard Knob. "That is better than shutting it up again and leaving it. Anyhow, we must have a housewarming. I have it all planned out."

"You would have. Are you going to ask Susan Baker?"

"Don't be sarcastic, Anthony. We *must* have Dr. and Mrs. Blythe—but not a mob, you understand."

"Certainly the Blythes. I *would* like Mrs. Blythe to see this place before it belongs to anyone else."

"We're going to light a big fire in the fireplace. Nan Blythe says she knows where we can get all the driftwood we need. And we'll turn on all the lights in the house. Won't it look gorgeous from outside? And isn't it lucky the house is so near the river? We'll bring a lunch and have a jamboree. Mother said she would provide the eats. We told her all about everything last night. But she knew most of it before."

"It's a way mothers have."

"Will tomorrow night suit you?"

"Haven't you settled the night also?" scoffed Anthony. "Might as well, seeing you've planned everything else."

"But we must have a night that would suit you," said Jill. "It would never do for you not to be at your own housewarming. And we have to consider the Blythes, too."

"And make sure nobody has a baby too near the Glen that night," P.G. snorted.

"You need not be indelicate," said Jill.

"Is a baby indelicate?" asked P.G. "Then make sure you never have one."

"I'm going to have a half-dozen," said Jill coolly. "If that girl had still been wearing your ring, Mr. Lennox, how many babies do you think you would have had?"

"For heaven's sake, let us cut out this type of conversation," begged Anthony. "I am old-fashioned, I know, but it embarrasses me. Have your housewarming and plan it as you like. And don't blame me if Dr. Blythe has a baby that night."

They had planned something Anthony had not suspected. He knew they would bring their mother of course—Aunt Henrietta being willing—but he did not expect Mrs. Elmsley, the artist, whom, as it chanced, he had never happened to meet.

P.G. stared when Jill told him she had asked Mrs. Elmsley. "But why? She's a stranger to him."

"Don't be so stupid, Pig. She's dying of curiosity to see the place and she has to go back to Winnipeg very soon—too soon for Anthony to fall in love with her."

"Do you want him to fall in love with her?" P.G. felt all at sea.

"I do. She is so beautiful he can't help it."

"But she's a Mrs."

"She is a widow, Pig. I should think you would take that for granted when I want Anthony to fall in love with her. And don't you see? He wouldn't sell Orchard Knob then and they'd live here in the summers anyhow. And they'll have three children—two boys and a girl. And the girl will have the blue parrot room. Oh, how I hate to think of anyone, even Anthony's daughter, having that parrot room!"

"But we'll be out west. And I don't suppose we'll ever come east again. So you won't be harrowed seeing her in it," said P.G. with more sympathy than he usually displayed.

"But I'll always be seeing her in it in imagination. And I just wish the parrots would peck her eyes out."

The next night for the first time in fifteen years Orchard Knob blazed with light, and a fire of driftwood glowed in the hall fireplace. The walls blossomed with red candles like rose blooms.

Half the people in Glen St. Mary and Mowbray Narrows and Lowbridge drove or walked past the "old Lennox place" that night. Susan Baker was not among them but she heard all about it from the doctor and Anne next morning.

"I wonder what the widow thinks," she said. "Winnipeg may be a very fine place—I have a nephew there—but to think it could beat the Island!"

Jill was dancing on the rug before the fire.

"I'm pretending this is a magic rug," she cried. "Everyone who steps on it will forget every disagreeable thing in his life. Try it, Anthony."

Anthony got up from the chair where he had been sprawled by the fire and sauntered across to the window to look out on a night that was drowned in moonlight, and see if any of the guests were coming. The Blythes had phoned that they would be there but a little on the late side. Luckily no babies were expected but Jim Flagg had broken his leg.

"I'm getting jumpy. It's time Mrs. Elmsley was

here," whispered Jill anxiously to P.G. "I hope she hasn't forgotten. I've heard that artists aren't very dependable."

"What is the matter with Anthony?" whispered P.G.

Anthony, looking out of the new, magic window, was also wondering what was the matter with him.

Had he gone quite mad? Or was the window really the magic one of Jill's pretence?

For she was there, crossing the moonlit lawn with that light step that always made him think of Beatrice, "born under a dancing star." The next moment she was standing in the doorway. Behind her were dark trees and a purple night sky.

Her sweet face . . . her eyes . . . her dark wings of hair . . . unchanged . . . unchangeable.

"Betty!" cried Anthony.

"Mums!" cried the twins. "Where is Mrs. Elmsley? Isn't she coming?"

"God grant she isn't," muttered the doctor who was just behind Betty. He had got through with Jim's leg sooner than he expected and something in Anthony's face told him the whole tale. "At least not for a while. Anne, come out with me to the rose garden. No, not a word of objection. For once I am going to be obeyed."

Anthony was at the door. He had her hands in his.

"Betty—it's you! Do you mean to say you're their—you're their mother. Of course they told me their name but it's such a common one."

Mums began to laugh because, as Jill—who had lived a century in a moment—perfectly understood, she had either to laugh or cry. P.G., less quick at taking the heart out of a mystery, still continued to stand quiet, staring, with his mouth hanging open. "Anthony! I didn't know . . . I never dreamed. The children didn't tell me your name and I had never heard of an Orchard Knob. I've had to stick so close to Aunt Henrietta this summer I never went anywhere or heard any gossip. And they pretended you were—they called you—oh, I thought it was just some of their nonsense—oh—"

Everybody seemed to be so balled up that Jill had to come to the rescue. She had never seen anything as amazing as Anthony's face. Neither had Anne Blythe, who had deliberately disobeyed her husband and gone back to the front door.

"Mums, isn't Mrs. Elmsley coming? We thought—"

"No, she has one of her bad headaches. She asked me to tell you so with her apologies."

"Jill," said Anthony suddenly, "you have been ordering me around all summer. I'm going to have my turn at it now. Go out—go anywhere, you and P.G.—for half an hour. And, Mrs. Blythe, will you excuse me if I—"

"Ask the same thing? I will. I'll go and apologize to my husband."

"And as a reward you may tell Susan Baker everything tomorrow," said Anthony.

When they came back to say the supper was

ready in the dining room they found Anthony and Mums on the settee by the fireplace. Mums had been crying but she looked extraordinarily happy and prettier than they had ever seen her—all the sadness gone.

"Jill," said Anthony, "there is another chapter to that story I told you here one night."

"No decent person eavesdrops," said Dr. Blythe to his wife who had been drawn back to the sunroom steps.

"I am not a decent person then," said Anne, "and neither are you."

"It was all a dreadful mistake," went on Anthony.

"I knew it," said Jill triumphantly.

"She was still wearing my ring—on a chain round her neck—but she'd heard things about me . . . had she a title, Betty?"

"Not quite as bad as that," smiled Mums.

"Well, she thought I had forgotten our old compact, so she took the ring off her finger—and we were just two proud, hurt, silly young things . . ."

"I seemed to have only one object in life," murmured Mums, " . . . to keep people from thinking I cared."

"You succeeded," said Anthony a bit grimly.

How history repeats itself, thought Dr. Blythe to himself. *When I thought Anne was engaged to Roy Gardiner—*

Isn't that life? thought Anne. *When I thought Gilbert was engaged to Christine Stuart—*

"But why did you go and marry father?" demanded Jill reproachfully.

"I . . . I was lonely . . . and he was nice and good . . . and I was fond of him," faltered Mums.

"Shut up, Jill," said Anthony.

"If she hadn't, you and P.G. would never have been born," said Dr. Blythe, coming in with a smile.

"So you see," said P.G., "and what I want to know is this: is anybody going to have any eats tonight?"

"So you see it's all right now," said Anthony. "We're all going to live here and the parrot room will be yours, Jill. And we'll start up that old clock since time has begun to function for me again. Mrs. Blythe, will you do us the honour of setting it going?"

"Are you really going to be our dad?" demanded Jill, when she had got her breath.

"As soon as law and gospel can make me."

"Oh!" Jill gave a rapturous sigh. "That is what P.G. and I have been pretending right along!"

Fancy's Fool

Esmé did not want particularly to spend the weekend at Longmeadow, as the Barrys called their home on the outskirts of Charlottetown.

She would have preferred to wait until she had definitely decided to marry Allardyce before becoming a guest in his home. But Uncle Conrad and Aunt Helen both thought she should go and Esmé had been so used all her life to doing exactly what her uncles and aunts on both sides thought she should do that she ran true to form in this as in many other things.

Besides, it was all but settled that she would marry Allardyce. Dr. Blythe, out at Glen St. Mary, who knew the family well, though he had never had anything to do with them in a professional

way, told his wife it was a shame. He knew
something about Allardyce Barry.

Of course he was considered a great catch.
People thought he was a surprisingly great catch
for a misty little thing like Esmé to pick up. Even
her own clan was amazed.

Sometimes Esmé thought secretly—she had a
great many secret thoughts since she had no especial friend or confidant—that her luck was rather
too much for her. She liked Allardyce well enough
as a friend . . . but she did not know . . . exactly
. . . how she was going to like him as a husband.

Was there anyone else? Decidedly not. It was
folly to think about Francis. There never had been
any Francis—not really. Only—she could never
manage to feel quite sure. He had seemed so very
real in those lovely, long-ago, stolen moments at
Birkentrees in the moonlit garden.

Since her childhood she had never met Allardyce's mother. The Barrys had lived abroad since
the death of Allardyce's father. It was only six
months since they had come home and opened
up Longmeadow for the summer.

All the girls were "after" Allardyce—so Uncle
Conrad said. All except Esmé.

Perhaps that was why Allardyce had fallen in
love with her. Or perhaps it was just because she
was so different from anyone else. She was a pale,
lovely thing, delicate and reserved. Her relatives
always complained that they could "make nothing of her." She seemed like a child of twilight.

Grey things and starriness were of her. She moved gently and laughed seldom but her little air of sadness was beautiful and bewitching.

"She will never marry," Anne Blythe told her husband. "She is really too exquisite for the realities of earth."

"She will likely marry some brute who will misuse her," said Dr. Blythe. "That kind always do."

"Anyhow, he has very nice ears," said Susan Baker.

Men who met Esmé always wanted to make her laugh. Allardyce succeeded. That was why she liked him. He said so many whimsical things that one had to laugh.

And had not Francis, long ago, said whimsical things? She was almost sure he had although she could not remember them. She could only remember him.

"So the ugly duckling has turned out a swan," twinkled Mrs. Barry when they met—by way of setting Esmé at ease. But Esmé, had Mrs. Barry but known it, was not in any special need of that. She was always quite mistress of herself, under the fine aloofness which so many mistook for shyness—so many except Mrs. Dr. Blythe and she lived too far away for frequent meetings.

And Esmé did not quite like Mrs. Barry's implication that she had been a plain child who had unaccountably grown up into beauty. She had not been a very pretty child, perhaps, but she had never been accounted an ugly one. And had not Francis once told her . . .

Esmé shook herself. There was no Francis, never had been any Francis. She *must* remember that, if she were going to marry Allardyce Barry and be chatelaine of this beautiful Longmeadow, which was just a little too big and splendid and wonderful. Esmé felt she would have been much more at home in a smaller place—like Ingleside at Glen St. Mary for instance—or . . . Birkentrees. She felt suddenly homesick for Birkentrees.

But nobody lived there now. It had been shut up and left to ruin, ever since Uncle John Page's death, owing to some legal tangle she had never understood. She hadn't seen it for twelve years, although it was only three miles from Uncle Conrad's place. She really had never wanted to see it again. She knew it must be weed-grown and deserted. And she knew she was a little afraid to see it . . . without Aunt Hester.

Strange Aunt Hester! Esmé, recalling her, shivered. But she never shivered when she thought of Francis. Sometimes she could still feel her little childish hand in his big strong one. It frightened her a little. Suppose . . . suppose . . . she were to get like Aunt Hester!

She did not see the picture till the next afternoon. Then Allardyce showed her all over the house and when they came to what had been his father's den it was hanging on the wall in the shadows.

Esmé's cool, white face flushed to a warm rose

when she saw it and then turned whiter than ever.

"Who . . . who is that?" she said faintly—very much afraid of the answer.

"That?" said Allardyce carelessly. He was not much interested in old things and had already made up his mind that he and Esmé would not spend much of their time at Longmeadow. There was more fun to be had elsewhere. But it would be a very good place for his mother to spend her declining years. She had always been a little drag on Allardyce. Esmé wouldn't. She would do just as he told her, go just where he wanted to go. And if there were other . . . ladies . . . she would never believe tales about them or make a fuss if she did. Dr. Blythe of Glen St. Mary could have told him a different story but Allardyce did not know Dr. Blythe or would not have had much opinion of his views if he had. He had met Mrs. Blythe once—and tried to flirt with her—but he had not tried a second time and always shrugged his shoulders meaningly when he heard her name mentioned. He said red-headed women were his abomination.

"That," said Allardyce, "was my great-uncle Francis Barry—a dare-devil young sea captain of the eighteen-sixties. He was captain of a brigantine when he was only seventeen years old. Can you believe it? Took her down to Buenos Aires with a cargo of lumber and died there. They say it broke his mother's heart. He was the apple of her eye. Luckily hearts don't break so easily nowadays."

"Don't they?" said Esmé.

"Of course not, else how could anybody live? But she was a Dalley and there was always something a little queer about them, I've been told. Took things much harder than is good in this kind of a world. We've got to be hard-boiled or we go under. Uncle Francis was a dashing young blade by all accounts. But you'll have to go to mother if you want family history. She revels in it. But what is the matter, Esmé? You don't look just right, honey. It's too hot here. Let's go out where the air is fresh. This old house has got musty through the years. I told mother so when she took a notion to come here. Though I'm glad she did since I've met *you*."

Esmé let him lead her to a vine-screened corner of the veranda. She was relieved to feel a solid seat under her. She took hard hold of its arms for comfort. They at least were real; the grassy lawns around her were real; Allardyce was real— too real.

And Francis *was* real. Or had been real! She had just seen his picture. But he had died in the eighteen-sixties. And it was only fourteen years since she had danced with him in the little locked garden at Birkentrees!

She told Allardyce only the bare bones of it, but as she told her story she lived over everything again in detail.

She had been only eight. She was a child whose father and mother were dead and who lived around with various uncles and aunts. She had come to spend the summer at Birkentrees, the old homestead of the clan. Uncle John Dalley lived there, an oldish man, the oldest of the large family of which her father had been the youngest son.

Aunt Jane, who had never married, lived there, too, and Aunt Hester. Strange Aunt Hester! Aunt Jane was old—at least Esmé thought so—but Aunt Hester was not very old, no more than twenty-five.

She had been strange in all the summers that Esmé had spent at Birkentrees. Esmé heard somebody say—she was so quiet that she was always hearing people say things they would never have dreamed of saying before a more talkative child—that Aunt Hester's lover had died when she was twenty. So much Esmé, sitting on her little stool, her elbows on her chubby knees, her round chin cupped in her hands, had found out as the "grown-ups" laughed and gossiped. And Aunt Hester had never been "the same" since.

Most children were afraid of her but Esmé was not. She liked Aunt Hester, who had haunted, tragic eyes and did little but wander up and down the long birch lane of Birkentrees and talk to herself, or to someone she fancied was there with her. This, Esmé thought, was what made people call her "queer."

She had a dead white face and strange, jet-black hair, just as Esmé had. Only at that time

Esmé's hair always fell over her amber eyes in a neglected fringe, giving her a doggy sort of look.

Sometimes she even ventured to slip one of her little slender hands—even at eight Esmé had very beautiful hands—into Aunt Hester's cold one and walk silently with her.

"I wouldn't dare do that for a million dollars," one of the visiting cousins had said to her extravagantly.

But Aunt Hester did not seem to mind it at all, although as a rule she resented anyone's company. "I walk among the shadows," she told Esmé. "They are better company than I find in the sunlight. But you should like the sunlight. I liked it once."

"I do like the sunlight," said Esmé, "but there is something about the shadows that I like, too."

"Well, if you like the shadows, come with me when you want to," said Aunt Hester.

Esmé loved Birkentrees. And most of all she loved the little garden which she was never allowed to enter—which nobody, as far as she knew, ever entered. It was locked up. There was a high fence around it and a rusty padlock on the gate. Nobody would ever tell her why it was locked up but Esmé gathered that there was something strange about it. None of the servants would ever go near it after nightfall. Yet it looked harmless enough, as far as could be seen through the high fence screened with roses and vines running wild.

Esmé would have liked to explore it—or
thought she would. One summer twilight, when
she was lingering near it, she suddenly felt something strange in the air about her. She could not
have told what it was—could not have described
her sensations. But she felt as if the garden was
drawing her to it.

Her breath came in quick little gasps. She
wanted to yield but she was afraid to. Small fine
beads broke out on her forehead. She trembled.
There was no one in sight, not even queer Aunt
Hester. Esmé put her hands over her eyes and
ran blindly to the house.

"Whatever is the matter, Esmé?" asked tall,
grim, kind Aunt Jane, meeting her in the hall.

"The . . . the garden wants me," cried Esmé,
hardly knowing what she said—and certainly not
what she meant.

Aunt Jane looked a little grey. "You had better not play too near that—that place again,"
she said.

The warning was needless. Yet Esmé continued
to love it. Sally, one of the servants, told her it
was "haunted." Esmé did not then know what
"haunted" meant. When she asked Aunt Jane,
her aunt looked angrier than Esmé had ever seen
her look and told her she must not listen to the
foolish gossip of servants.

There came a summer when she found Aunt
Hester much changed. Esmé had expected this.
She had heard the older people say that Hester
was "much better," so much happier and more

contented. Perhaps, they said, she might "come
all right" yet.

Certainly Aunt Hester looked happier. She never walked in the birch lane now or talked to
herself. Instead, she sat most of the time by the
lily pool with the face of one who listened and
waited. Esmé felt at once that Aunt Hester was
simply waiting. For what?

But in her secret soul Esmé felt that the grown-
ups were all wrong. Aunt Hester *did* look happier
but she was not really any "better." But Esmé did
not say so to anyone. She knew her opinion did
not count for anything with anybody. She was
"only a child."

Before she had been very long at Birkentrees,
Esmé found out what it was for which Aunt
Hester was waiting.

One night she was out on the lawn when she
should have been asleep. But Aunt Jane was away
and old Mrs. Thompson, the housekeeper, was in
bed with a headache. So there was no one to look
after Esmé, who thought she was quite able to
look after herself.

There were people who did not agree with
her. Dr. and Mrs. Blythe, passing by on their
way home to Glen St. Mary from Charlottetown,
did not.

"They should not allow that child to associate so much with Hester Dalley," said the doctor.

"I've often felt that myself," said Anne Blythe,
"and yet why shouldn't she?"

"Minds act and react on each other," said the doctor rather shortly. "At least, some minds. It mightn't hurt Nan or Diana a mite . . . but the Dalleys are different. Most of them never know what is reality and what is imagination."

"People always told me that I had too much imagination," said Anne.

"This is a different kind of imagination. And Esmé Dalley is a very impressionable child—far too much so, indeed. If she were my daughter I confess I should feel a little anxious about her. But she has no parents to look after her and nobody appears to think there is any harm in letting her associate so much with her Aunt Hester."

"And is there?" asked Anne. "I had no parents to remember either, you know."

"But you had a good deal of common sense mixed up with your imagination, Anne-girl," said the doctor smiling at her—the smile that always made Anne's heart beat a little faster, in spite of years of wifehood and motherhood.

"Gilbert, is Hester Dalley really out of her mind?"

"Ask a psychiatrist, not me," smiled Gilbert. "I don't think she could be certified as insane. At least nobody has ever tried. Perhaps she is quite sane and it is the rest of the world who are insane. And some people hold that everyone is a little insane, on some point or other. Susan thinks lots of people crazy whom you and I regard as quite normal."

"Susan says Hester Dalley is 'cracked,'" said Anne.

"Well, we'll have to leave it at that, since we can't do anything about it," said Gilbert. "Only, I repeat my opinion that if Esmé Dalley were my niece or daughter, I would see to it that she was not too much with her Aunt Hester."

"Without being able to give a single good reason for such an opinion," taunted Anne.

"Exactly—just like a woman," riposted the doctor.

Meanwhile Esmé was thinking it would be wicked to sleep on such a beautiful night. It was a night that belonged to the fairies—a night drenched in the glimmer and glamour of a magnificent full moon. And while she sat alone by the lily pond, with old dog Gyp for company, Aunt Hester came gliding over the lawn.

She was wonderfully gowned in white and had pearls in her black hair. She looked, thought Esmé, like a bride she had once seen.

"Oh, Aunty, how beautiful you are!" cried Esmé, all at once realizing that Aunt Hester was still a young woman. "Why don't you always dress like that?"

"This was to have been my wedding dress," said Aunt Hester. "They keep it locked away from me. But I know how to get it when I want it."

"It is lovely, and so are you," said Esmé, to whom fashions as yet meant nothing.

"Am I lovely?" said Aunt Hester. "I am glad. I want to be beautiful tonight, little Esmé. If I share a secret with you, will you keep it very faithfully?"

Oh, wouldn't she! Esmé thought it would be wonderful to share a secret only they two knew.

"Come then." Aunt Hester held out her hand and Esmé took it. They went across the lawn and through the long moonlit lane of birches. Old Gyp followed them, but when they came to the locked gate of the little old garden he drew back with a growl. The hair on his back rose like bristles.

"Gyppy, come on," said Esmé. But Gyp drew back a little further.

"Why does he act like that?" asked Esmé.

Aunt Hester made no answer. She merely unlocked the padlock with a rusty old key that seemed to turn as easily as if it had never known rust.

Esmé drew back.

"Are we going in there?" she whispered timidly.

"Yes, why not?"

"I am . . . a little . . . afraid," confessed Esmé.

"You need not be afraid. Nothing will harm you."

"Then why do they keep the garden always locked?"

"Because they know no better," said Aunt Hester scornfully. "Long, long ago little Janet Dalley went in there and never came out again.

I suppose that is why they keep the garden locked. As if she couldn't have come out if she wanted to!"

"Why did she never come out again?" whispered Esmé.

"Who knows? Perhaps she liked the company she found there better than what she left behind."

Esmé thought this was just one of Aunt Hester's "queer" sayings.

"Perhaps she fell over the stone wall into the river," she said. "Only if that was so, why was her body never found?"

"No one has to stay in the garden against her will," said Aunt Hester impatiently. "You need not be afraid to come into the garden with me, Esmé."

Esmé *did* feel a little afraid still, but she would not admit it for worlds. She clung very closely to Aunt Hester as she opened the gate and went through. Gyp turned and ran. But Esmé forgot all about him. And she suddenly forgot all her fear too.

So this was the strange—the forbidden—garden! Why, there was nothing very terrible about it. In fact, nothing terrible at all. Why on earth did they keep it locked up and untended? Oh, yes, Esmé remembered that it was supposed to be "haunted." She was quite ready to call that nonsense now. Somehow she had a strange feeling that she had come home.

The garden was less overgrown than might have been expected. But it had a lonely look in the

moonlight, as if it, like Aunt Hester, were waiting—waiting. There were a great many weeds,
but along the south wall a row of tall lilies looked
like saints in the moonglow. There were some
young poplars on which the leaves were trembling and in one corner was a slim white birch
which Esmé knew—but could not have told how
she knew—that some long-ago bride had planted.

Here and there were dim paths on which lovers
of half a century ago had walked with their ladies.
One of the paths, flagged with thin sandstones
from the shore, ran through the middle of the
garden to the river shore, where there was no
fence, only a low stone wall to keep the garden
from running into the river.

There . . . why, there was someone in the garden. A young man was coming up the sandstone
path, with outstretched hands.

And Aunt Hester, who never smiled, was smiling.

"Geoffrey!" she said.

Then Esmé knew what "haunted" meant but
she was not in the least afraid. How foolish to
be afraid! She sat on the stone wall while Aunt
Hester and Geoffrey paced up and down the
walks and talked in low tones. Esmé could not
hear what they said and she did not want to. She
only knew that she would have liked to come
to the garden every night—and stay there. No
wonder Janet Dalley had not come back.

"Will you bring me here again?" she asked
Aunt Hester, when they finally left.

"Would you like to come?" asked Aunt Hester.

"Yes—oh, yes."

"Then you must never tell anyone you have been here," said Aunt Hester.

"Of course I won't if you don't want me to," said Esmé. "But why, Aunt Hester?"

"Because there are so few people who understand," said Aunt Hester. "I did not understand until this summer. But I do now—and I am very happy, Esmé. But we can go into the garden only on full moonlight nights. It is sometimes hard to wait so long. We must have some playmates for you next time. You understand now why Janet Dalley never came back, don't you?"

"But Janet Dalley went into the garden over sixty years ago," cried Esmé, some of her fear coming back.

"There is no time in the garden," said Aunt Hester, smiling tranquilly. "Janet could come back even now if she wanted to."

Esmé found it very hard to wait for the next full moon. Sometimes she thought she must have dreamed it all. The garden looked exactly the same by daylight as it always had. She did not know whether she hoped or feared it was a dream.

But the next full moon did come and again Esmé went with Aunt Hester to the little garden.

It was very different that night. It seemed to be full of people who came and went. Girls with laughing, dreamy eyes . . . slender women like pale flames . . . slim boys . . . twinkling children. None of them took any notice of Esmé except a little girl of about her own age, a little girl with golden hair cut low over her brow and great, wistful eyes.

Esmé could not have told how she knew the little girl's name was Janet but she did. Janet stopped as she was running by in pursuit of a silvery green moth and beckoned to Esmé. Esmé was on the point of following her—she often wondered what would have happened if she *had* followed—when Francis came.

She never understood either how she knew his name was Francis. But she did understand that she had always known him. He was tall and slender, with a boyish face on which an air of command sat strangely. He had thick brown hair, parted in the middle, and shining dark blue eyes. He took Esmé's hand in his and they walked about the garden and talked. She could never remember what they talked about but she knew he made her laugh.

When Esmé recollected Janet and turned to look for her, Janet had gone. Esmé never saw her again. She did not greatly care. Francis was so funny and wonderful, he was the best of comrades. Then they danced on the open grassy space around the old dried-up fountain where wild mint grew so thickly. It smelt so beautifully when they trod on it.

And the music to which they danced made Esmé tremble with delight—and something that was not quite delight. She could not understand where the music came from and Francis only laughed when she asked him. His laugh was more delightful than any music. Esmé had never heard anyone laugh so beautifully.

None of the other people who came and went spoke to them or took any notice of them. Aunt Hester never came near them. She was always with Geoffrey.

Aunt Jane was a little worried about Esmé those days. She thought the child was moping. She did not run about or play as usual, but sat, like Hester, on the lawn with a dreamy, waiting face.

"I wish we could go to the garden every night," Esmé said to Aunt Hester.

"They only come on the nights when the moon is full," said Aunt Hester. "Watch when the moon comes back. When it is full and casts a shadow on the birch lane, we will go again."

Dr. Blythe happened to call at Birkentrees that day and the next time he saw Conrad Page he told him to take his niece away from Birkentrees as soon as possible.

But the problem was solved in a different way. When the August moon was near fullness Aunt Hester was dead. She had died very quietly in her sleep, and her face was young and smiling and happy. The doctor said her heart had been affected for some time.

She lay with flowers clasped in her pale, beautiful hands and her clan came and looked at her, and the women cried a little, and all felt secretly relieved that the problem of "poor Hester" had been so decently and effectively solved.

Esmé was the only one who cried very much. *She has gone to be with Geoffrey for always*, thought Esmé, *but I shall never see Francis again.*

At first the thought seemed more than she could bear. She had never gone back to Birkentrees after that summer. Uncle John had died and Aunt Jane had moved to Charlottetown.

But Esmé had never quite forgotten. She always came to the conclusion that she had dreamed it all. And just as often as she concluded this she knew, somehow, she hadn't.

"And that picture of your great-uncle, Allardyce. He was the Francis I saw in the garden— the Francis I never saw in life. Was Sally right when she said the garden was haunted? I think she must have been."

Allardyce gave a roar of laughter and squeezed her hand. Esmé shivered. She wished Allardyce wouldn't laugh like that, wouldn't look at her with that ready, easy, meaningless—yes, it *was* meaningless—smile of his. She suddenly felt that he was a stranger.

He had a ready common-sensible explanation. "Sal was nothing but a superstitious goose," he said. "Your Aunt Hester was quite—well, to put it plainly—out of her mind. Oh, I've heard all about her. She just imagined she saw people in the garden, and somehow she made you see them, too, or think you saw them. You are such a sensitive, impressionable little thing, you know. And I daresay you imagined a good bit of it yourself. Children do, you know. They haven't the power to distinguish between what is real and what is imagination. You just ask my mother the queer things I used to tell her."

"Aunt Hester never saw your Great-uncle Francis nor did I," said Esmé. "How could we have imagined him?"

"She must have seen his picture. She was often at Longmeadow when she was a girl. It was here she met Geoffrey Gordon, you know—a sap, if ever there was one. But she was wild about him. For that matter, you may have been here yourself when you were too young to remember, and seen the picture. Now, don't think any more about this, honey-child. It's foolish to monkey with spooks. They're interesting things but dangerous. So irresponsible, you see. I don't deny I like a good ghost yarn myself once in a while, but for a steady thing they're not good diet."

"All the same . . . I can't marry you . . . ever," said Esmé.

Allardyce stared at her.

"Esmé—you're joking!"

But Esmé was not joking. She had a hard time to make Allardyce believe she was in earnest but she finally succeeded. He went off in a tremendous huff, trying to make himself believe that it was just as well not to marry anyone with Dalley blood in them. His mother was furious—and relieved. She had always wanted a more brilliant match for Allardyce. Why, there was an Italian princess who was crazy about him, as everybody knew. And that insignificant little Esmé Dalley had actually turned him down!

Esmé had a very hard time of it with Uncle Conrad and Aunt Helen. It was impossible to make them understand. They and the whole clan thought she was an utter little idiot.

The only ones who really approved her action were Dr. and Mrs. Blythe. But as Esmé never knew they did, it did not comfort her much.

"A bad egg that same Allardyce Barry," said the doctor.

"Not having met him very often, I take your word for it," said Anne.

"I never believed a word about that yarn about the Rooshian princess," said Susan.

One early October evening, Esmé found herself alone. Everyone had gone out. It was going to be a moonlit evening with a full moon.

It made her think of the old garden at Birkentrees—and strange Aunt Hester—angry Allardyce Barry—and all the trouble of that dreadful time, for which Esmé knew she had never been forgiven. The clan only tolerated her now.

She found herself trembling a little with the thought and the desire that suddenly came to her: the thought of the little locked garden by the river shore and the desire to see it once more. Who knew what dim, lovely things waited there for her still?

Well, why shouldn't she? It was only three miles to Birkentrees by a cross-country cut and

Esmé had always been a good walker in spite of her ethereal looks.

An hour later she was at Birkentrees. The old house came out darkly against the sunset sky. Its grim shadow lay across the lawn and the spruce wood beyond it had turned black. There was an air of neglect over everything. Disputes among the heirs had prevented a sale.

But Esmé was not interested in the house. She had come to walk on the secret paths of her enchanted garden once more and she hurried to the birch lane that led to it.

Dr. Gilbert Blythe, whizzing by in his car, saw her and recognized her.

What on earth is that girl doing alone at that forsaken old place? he wondered a little uneasily. He had heard tales that summer that Esmé Dalley was "getting queer" like her Aunt Hester. These tales emanated mostly from people who had said Allardyce Barry had "jilted" her.

Dr. Blythe wondered if he should stop and go over and offer her a drive home. But he had a serious case waiting for him in the Glen—and, besides, he had a feeling that Esmé would not come. Anne always said that Esmé Dalley had an iron will under all her sweetness and the doctor had a great deal of respect for the intuition of his wife.

Whatever Esmé had come to Birkentrees for, she would carry out her intention. So he went on. In after days he boasted that he had at least made one match by leaving things alone.

The gate to the garden was no longer locked

but hung open slackly. It all seemed smaller than Esmé remembered it. There were only withered leaves and frosted stalks where she had danced with Francis—where she had imagined or dreamed she had danced with Francis.

But it was still beautiful and eerie, full of the strange, deep shadows that come with the rising of the hunter's moon. There was no sound but the sigh of the wind in the remote pointed firs that had grown up of their own accord among the still golden maples in a corner.

Esmé felt lonelier than she had ever felt in her life as she went down the grass-grown path to the river shore.

"There isn't any *you*," she whispered piteously, thinking of Francis. "There never was any you. What a little fool I have been! I suppose I shouldn't have used Allardyce so. No wonder they were all so cross with me. No wonder Mrs. Barry was glad."

For Esmé had never heard the tales about Allardyce's foreign life and the Italian or Russian princesses. To her, Allardyce was still the man who made her laugh a little as Francis had—the Francis who had never existed.

She wondered a little what had become of the picture of Great-uncle Francis when the Barrys had closed Longmeadow and gone abroad again, this time, it was said, for good. Mrs. Barry had reported, so rumour ran, that they did not mean to return to Canada. Everything was so crude here—and all the girls pursued Allardyce. She was afraid he would make some silly match. Esmé Dalley had almost hooked him but, thank the Lord, she had failed. Allardyce had come to his senses in time.

Esmé was thinking of the picture. Somehow, she would have liked to have it—even if it were only the picture of a dream.

But when she got to the old stone wall—most of which had fallen down—she saw him coming up the steps from the river. The steps were very loose and some were missing altogether, so that he was picking his way a bit carefully. But he was just the same as she remembered him—a little taller, perhaps, and dressed in a more modern fashion, but with the same thick brown hair and the same adventurous light in his blue, eagle eyes. (In the future he and Jem Blythe were to share a German prison, but nobody dreamed anything about that then.)

The long, dim river and the deserted garden and the pointed firs whirled around Esmé.

She threw out her hands and would have fallen if he had not caught her as he sprang over the crumbling wall.

"Francis!" gasped Esmé.

"Francis is my middle name, but my friends call me Stephen," he said, smiling, the same frank, friendly, pleasant smile she remembered so well.

Esmé recovered herself a little and drew away, but she was still trembling so violently that he kept his arm around her, just as Francis had done.

"I am afraid I have frightened you," he said

gently. "I'm sorry my appearance was so abrupt. I know I'm not handsome but I didn't think I was so ugly that I would scare a girl into nearly fainting."

"It's—it's not that," said Esmé, quite conscious now that she had made an awful fool of herself. Perhaps she *was* queer, like Aunt Hester.

"Perhaps I'm trespassing, but the place looked so deserted, and they told me I could take this short cut. Please forgive me for frightening you."

"Who are you?" cried Esmé wildly. Nothing mattered but that.

"A very humble individual: Stephen Francis Barry, at your service. My home is at the coast but I came east a few days ago to take charge of the new biological station down at the harbour. I knew I had—or once had—some distant cousins over this way at a place called Longmeadow, so I thought I'd come over this evening and hunt them up if they were still here. Somebody else told me they had gone abroad. 'What is truth?'—as Pilate once said."

Esmé knew now who he was: a western third cousin she had heard Allardyce mention, contemptuously enough.

"He works," Allardyce had said, as if that were something shameful. "I've never seen him—none of the family have ever been east—too busy studying bugs, I suppose."

Esmé drew a little further away still, looking gravely at him. She had no idea how exquisitely lovely she looked in the velvet and shadow of the moonlight, but Stephen Barry had. He stood and looked at her as if he could never get enough of looking.

"It was not your sudden appearance that startled me," said Esmé gravely. "It was because you looked so much like somebody I once saw—no, like somebody I dreamed I saw. A picture of Captain Francis Barry that used to be at Longmeadow."

"Great-uncle Frank? Granddad always told me I looked like him. Do I really look as much like this Francis as all that?"

"You look exactly like him."

"Then no wonder you took me for a ghost. And you? I think I must have dreamed you years ago. You have just stepped out of my dream. Won't you be unconventional and tell me who you are?"

"I am Esmé Dalley."

Even in the moonlight she could see his face fall.

"Esmé Dalley! Oh, I've heard—Allardyce's young lady!"

"No, no, no!" Esmé cried it almost violently. "And there is nobody at Longmeadow. It is shut up and is for sale. Allardyce and his mother have gone abroad for good, I believe."

"You believe? Don't you know? Aren't you his—his fiancée?"

"No," cried Esmé again. For some mysterious reason she could not bear to have him think that. "There is no truth in that report. Allardyce and I are nothing but friends—hardly even that," she added, in her desire to be strictly truthful, and recalling her last interview with Allardyce. "Besides, as I have told you, he and his mother have gone to Europe and are not expected to return."

"Too bad," said Stephen quite cheerfully. "I had counted on seeing them. I'm to be here a couple of months, and relations liven up things a bit. Still, there are compensations. I've seen you, 'moving in moonlight through a haunted hour' to me. Are you quite sure you are not a ghost, little Esmé Dalley?"

Esmé laughed—delightful laughter. "Quite sure. But I came here to meet a ghost. I'll tell you all about it sometime."

She felt quite sure he would not laugh as Allardyce had done. And he would not try to explain it away. Besides, somehow or other, it no longer mattered whether it could be explained away or not. They would just forget it together.

"Let's sit down here on this old stone wall and you can tell me all about it now," said Stephen.

It was just about that time that Dr. Blythe was saying to his wife, "I met Stephen Barry for a moment today. He is to be in Charlottetown for a few months. He is really a splendid fellow. I wish he and Esmé Dalley would meet and fall in love. They would just suit each other."

"Who is matchmaking now?" asked Anne sleepily.

"Trust a woman to have the last word," retorted the doctor.

A Dream Come True

When Anthony Fingold left home on Saturday evening, he intended merely to go down to the store at Glen St. Mary to get the bottle of liniment Clara wanted. Then he would come back and go to bed.

There would be nothing else to do, he sadly reflected. Get up in the morning; work all day; eat three meals; and go to bed at half-past nine. What a life!

Clara didn't seem to mind it. None of his neighbours in the Upper Glen seemed to mind it. Apparently they never got tired of the old routine. They hadn't enough imagination to realize what they were missing, probably.

He remarked gloomily at the supper table—it couldn't be denied that Clara cooked excellent suppers, though it never entered Anthony's head to tell her so—"There ain't been anything exciting in this part of the Island this summer—not even a funeral."

Clara had calmly reminded him that the Barnard washing at Mowbray Narrows had been stolen three weeks before and that there had been a robbery at Carter Flagg's store at Glen St. Mary several weeks before, and then she passed him the ginger cookies.

Did she think ginger cookies a substitute for impassioned longings and mad, wild, glamorous adventures?

Then she added insult to injury by remembering that Carter Flagg was offering bargains in pyjamas!

It was the one source of difference between him and Clara that she wanted him to wear pyjamas and he was determined he would never wear anything but nightshirts.

"Dr. Blythe wears pyjamas," Clara would say mournfully.

Anthony thought there was nobody on earth worth mentioning in the same breath with Dr. Blythe. Even his wife was a rather intelligent woman. As for Susan Baker, maid-of-all-work at Ingleside, he had been at feud with her for years. He always suspected that she put Clara up to the pyjama idea. In which he did them both a grievous wrong.

As for the Mowbray Narrows washing, of course it would have to be at Mowbray Narrows! No such good fortune for the Upper Glen or the Fingolds. And what did the robbery at Carter Flagg's store matter? Carter had lost only ten dollars and a roll of flannel. Why, it wasn't worth mentioning. And yet people had talked about it for days.

Susan Baker had been up one evening and she and Clara had talked of nothing else—unless the whispered conversation on the doorstep when Susan took her departure had to do with pyjamas. Anthony strongly suspected it had. He had seen the doctor buying a pair in Carter Flagg's store not long ago.

Anthony had never done anything more adventurous in his life than climb a tree or throw a stone at a strange dog. But that was Fate's fault, not his. Given anything of a chance, he felt that he had it in him to be William Tell or Richard Coeur-de-Lion or any other of the world's gallant adventurers. But he had been born a Fingold of the Upper Glen in Prince Edward Island, so he had no chance of being a hero. It was all very well for Dr. Blythe to say that the graveyards were full of men who had been greater heroes than any mentioned in history, but everyone knew the doctor's wife was romantic.

And had William Tell ever worn pyjamas? Not very likely. What *did* he wear? Why did books never tell you the things you really wanted to know? What a boon it would be if he could show Clara in a printed book that some great hero of history or romance had worn a nightshirt!

He had asked somebody once, and the some-body—he had forgotten who he was—had said he didn't think they wore anything in those days.

But that was indecent. He couldn't tell anything like that to Clara.

Sometimes he thought it would have been a great thing even to have been a highwayman. Yes, with any luck he could have been a highwayman. Prowling all night as they did, they might not need either nightshirts or pyjamas.

Of course a great many of them got hanged, but at least they had *lived* before death. And he could have been as bold and bad as he wanted to be, dancing courantes on moonlit heaths with scores of voluptuous, enticing ladies—they might as well be princesses while they were about it—and, naturally, he would return their jewels or gold for the dance. Oh, what life might have been! The Methodist minister in Lowbridge had preached once on "Dreams of What We Might Have Been." Though he and Clara were rigid Presbyterians they happened to be visiting Methodist friends, so went with them.

Clara thought the sermon a very fine one. As if she ever had dreams! Unless it was of seeing him decked out in pyjamas! She was perfectly content-ed with her narrow existence. So was everybody he knew, or so he thought.

Well, Anthony sighed, it all came to this. He was only little, thin, pepper-and-salt Anthony Fingold, general handyman of the Glen, and the only excitement that ever came his way was

stealing cream for the cat. Clara found out about
his stealing it but not until the cat had lapped it.
She never scolded him, although he had a horrid
conviction that she told Susan Baker the whole
story. What else would they be laughing about?
He found himself hoping Susan would not tell
Dr. or Mrs. Blythe. It was so paltry. And they
might not think it was the proper thing for a
church elder.

But he resented Clara's calm acceptance of his
crime. All she said was, "That cat is as fat as
butter now. And you could have all the cream
you wanted for him if you had asked for it."

"She won't even quarrel with me," thought
Anthony in exasperation. "If she'd only get mad
once in a while things wouldn't be so tame. They
say Tom Crossbee and his wife fight every day—
and that scratch he had on his face last Sunday
was one she gave him. Even that would be something. But the only thing that riles Clara is that I
won't wear pyjamas. And even then she doesn't
say much except that they are more up to date.
Well, I must endure my life as everyone else does.
'God pity us all, who vainly the dreams of our
youth recall.' "

Anthony couldn't remember where he had
heard or learned those lines. But they certainly
hit the mark. He sighed. He met nobody but a
tramp on his way to the store. The tramp had
boots—of a sort—but no socks. His bare skin
showed through the holes in his shirt. He was
smoking and looked very contented and happy.

Anthony envied him. Why, this man could sleep out all night if he wanted to. Likely he did. With the whole sky for a roof. Nobody would pester him to wear pyjamas. How delightful it must be not to have any idea where you were going to sleep at night!

They would never have elected him elder, he reflected, as he trotted along the village street, if they had known what a desperate fellow he was in reality. They never dreamed of the wild adventures and glorious deeds he was constantly having and performing in imagination.

But his dreams, though they satisfied some dramatic urge in him, left him always with a mournful conviction that he had missed the best in life. Dreams would never make Caroline Wilkes look at him admiringly. And that was, and always had been, the master dream of Anthony Fingold's life, the one he could never have spoken about to anyone: to make Caroline Wilkes, née Caroline Mallard, look at him admiringly. All poor Clara's years of devotion were as nothing compared to that never-seen, never-to-be-seen admiration in Caroline's eyes.

Anthony heard a bit of news at the store which made him decide to return to the Upper Glen by the lower road. It was much longer than the upper road and much less interesting, there being no houses along it, except Westlea, the new summer home the Wilkes family had built for themselves.

But Carter Flagg said the Wilkes were already at

Westlea, coming early on account of the old lady's health. When Anthony anxiously inquired what was the matter with her, Carter Flagg said carelessly he had heard it was some kind of attacks— a heart condition, so Susan Baker had been heard to say—and this year, said Carter Flagg, she must be worse than common for they had brought a nurse with them and it was rumoured Dr. Blythe had been there more than once. He added that old lady Wilkes had always thought there was no one like Dr. Blythe, though she had been to specialists all over the world.

Anthony thought that if he went home by the lower road, he might get a glimpse of Caroline if she happened to be about the grounds.

It was, he reflected sadly, a long time since he had seen her. She had not been in any of the churches around there for years. For the last two summers she had never been seen outside of Westlea—that is, since it had been built.

When she had grown up and, naturally, moved in a far higher circle of society—she was the leading merchant's daughter—he still worshipped her from afar. Never did the slightest idea of trying to "court" her enter his head, save in romantic dreams. He knew he might as well aspire to a king's daughter.

He suffered secret agonies when she married one of the wealthy Wilkes of Montreal—whose people were really furious because he had stooped so low—and he did not think Ned Wilkes worthy to tie her shoelaces.

But then, who would be? He went on worshipping her just the same. He saw her rarely, only when she came home to visit her people in Lowbridge. She always made it a point to be in Lowbridge church those Sundays.

He read everything he could find in the papers about her. His family thought him crazy and extravagant because he insisted on taking a weekly Montreal paper that ran a society column.

There was often something: she was entertaining a foreign nobleman or going to Europe or having a baby. She never seemed to grow old. In her photographs, as in his recollections of her, she was always stately and beautiful, seemingly untouched by time or trouble.

Yet she had her troubles, if rumour spoke truly. Ned Wilkes had hit the high spots in life, according to all accounts. But he had been dead for years and all her children were married—two of them to English lords—and she must be close on sixty now to all the world, except Anthony Fingold, who still thought himself quite a young man.

In between times Anthony had courted and married Clara Bryant—whose people thought she was throwing herself away. Anthony was very fond of Clara. She had always been a good, if unexciting, wife and in her youth she had been plump and pretty.

But his secret homage had always been given to Caroline Mallard—Caroline Mallard of the sea-blue eyes and proud, cold, queen-like face. At least, that was how he recalled her. Most people thought her a good-looking girl who had been lucky enough to catch a rich husband.

But to Anthony she was a grand lady if ever there was one. An aristocrat to her backbone. It was a privilege to have loved her, even hopelessly; a privilege to dream of serving her. He pitied the other boys who had loved and forgotten her. *He* had been faithful. He often told himself he would be willing to die any death you could think of if he could but once have touched her beautiful hand.

He never dared ask himself the question: Would he have been willing to have worn pyjamas for her sake? Of course Ned Wilkes must have worn them. But then Ned Wilkes would do anything.

Anthony would have been not a little amazed if he had realized that Clara knew all about his passion for Caroline Wilkes—and did not care. *She* knew all that it amounted to. Just one of those crazy fancies of his. And *she* knew what Caroline Wilkes was like now and what ailed her. And why the Wilkes family had come to Prince Edward Island that year so early. Everyone knew.

When Anthony stopped by the Westlea gates, for a sentimental look at the house which held his divinity, Abe Saunders came scurrying down the driveway. Abe was the general caretaker at Westlea, while his wife looked after the house. The Wilkes really spent very little time there. Abe and Anthony had never been on really friendly terms, partly because of some obscure old feud dating back to schooldays (neither of them could have told you how it began) and partly because Abe had once wanted Clara Bryant himself. He had forgotten that, too, being very well satisfied with the wife he had, but the feeling was there, and both knew it.

So Anthony was much surprised when Abe buttonholed him rather distractedly and exclaimed, "Tony, will you do me a favour? The wife and I have just got word that our girl over at the Narrows has been hurt in a car accident—broke her leg, so they say—and we've got to go over and see her. They are going to take her to the Charlottetown Hospital and Dr. Blythe is looking after her. But still, when it's your own flesh and blood! Will you set in the house till Mr. Norman Wilkes comes home? He ought to be along any time now. He's motoring out from Charlottetown. The old lady is in bed asleep—or pretending to be—but that scalawag of a George has disappeared and we don't dast leave the house with no one in it."

"Ain't there a nurse?" gasped Anthony in amazement.

"She's got the evening off. Gave the old lady a hypo. That's all right—Dr. Blythe's orders. All you'll have to do will be just to set in the sun porch till somebody comes. Most likely George will soon turn up—if he hasn't gone to see some girl down at the village. But for pity's sake don't take all evening making up your mind."

"But what if she . . . if Mrs. Wilkes . . . takes one of her sinking spells?" gasped Anthony.

"She don't have sinking spells," said Abe impatiently. "It's—it's something quite different. I ain't allowed to talk. But she won't have any kind of a spell after the hypo. It puts her to sleep." (*If that goose of a nurse didn't forget to give it to her*, he reflected, but was not going to say so to Anthony.) "She'll sleep like a log till the morning, always does. Will you or won't you? I didn't think you were the man to hesitate when a friend was in trouble. They may have whisked Lula off to the hospital before we get there."

Hesitate! When Abe and a distracted Mrs. Abe—what if Clara went into hysterics like that?—had whirled away in their wheezy old car, Anthony Fingold was sitting in the sunroom in a dream of bliss. He could hardly believe it was not all a dream.

Here he was in the same house with his long-worshipped Caroline—on guard while she slumbered. Could anything be more romantic? Of course it would be just as well if Clara never heard of it—and she would hear of it most likely. But he would have had the enjoyment of it, in any case. How he blessed George, who was the orphan son of a poor cousin of the Mallards, for disappearing! He hoped nobody would come home for hours. Smoke a pipe! Perish the irreverent thought! Nobody but a Saunders would think of suggesting such a thing. He would just sit there and try to remember all the poetry he knew. Clara would think he was at the store so she wouldn't be worried. Somehow he didn't want Clara to be worried in spite of his happiness.

"What are you doing there, little man?"

Anthony Fingold sprang up as if he had been shot, and gazed in absolute consternation at the object standing in the sunroom doorway!

It couldn't be—it couldn't be his Caroline, his beautiful, romantic, glamorous adored Caroline. In the last photograph of her he had seen in a Montreal paper she had been almost as young and handsome as ever.

But, if it was not Caroline, who was it, this raddled old dame in a flannel nightdress—a nightdress not half so pretty as the ones Clara wore—which did not conceal her bony ankles? Thin grey hair hung in wisps about her wrinkled face, and her mouth was drawn inward over toothless gums. Fancy Clara appearing before anyone without her false teeth. She would have died first.

There was a weird light in her sunken blue eyes and she was looking at him in a way that made his skin crinkle. And in one hand she held an implement which couldn't be anything but a dagger. Anthony had never seen a dagger but he had seen pictures of them and a thousand times he had imagined himself carrying one and running people through with it. But the reality was very different.

"Well, now, if it isn't little Anthony Fingold who used to be so much in love with me!" said the apparition, brandishing her dagger. "Do you remember those good old days, Anthony? If I'd had the sense of a cat, I'd have married you instead of Ned Wilkes. But we never have sense when we are young. Of course, you will say you never asked me. But I could have easily made you. Every woman knows that. And how is Clara? How jealous she used to be of me!"

It *was*—it must be—Caroline. Poor Anthony put a hand to his head. When all your dreams come tumbling about you in one fell swoop, it is hard to bear. He still hoped he was in a nightmare and that Clara would have sense enough to wake him.

"What are you doing here?" demanded Caroline again. "Tell me at once or—" she brandished the dagger.

"I'm here . . . I'm . . . Abe Saunders asked me to stay till him and his wife got back," stammered Anthony. "They had to go . . . his daughter had been in an accident and was going to the hospital . . . and he didn't like to leave you alone."

"Who said his daughter had to go to the hospital?"

"Dr. Blythe, I believe . . . I . . ."

"Then she probably had to go. Dr. Blythe is the only man with any sense on Prince Edward Island. As for me, poor old Abe needn't have been worried. Nobody could have run off with the house, and don't you think this would keep any robber at bay?"

Anthony looked at the gleaming dagger and thought it would.

"That gadabout of a nurse is out—on the trail of some man," said Caroline. "Oh, I know their tricks! You men are so easily fooled."

"And George . . ."

"Oh, I've hung George in the closet," said Caroline. She suddenly shook with laughter. "I've always had a hankering to kill a man and at last I've done it. It's a sensation, Anthony Fingold. Did *you* ever kill anybody?"

"No . . . no . . ."

"Ah, you don't know what you've missed! It's fun, Anthony, great fun. You should have seen George kicking. And do you mean to tell me that you've never wanted to kill Clara? Especially when she begged you to wear pyjamas?"

So everybody knew it! Susan Baker, of course. But it didn't matter. Nothing mattered now. Suppose Caroline, having done away with George and wanting to repeat the sensation, attacked him, Anthony, with that dagger!

But Caroline was laughing.

"Why don't you kiss me, little man?" she demanded. "People always kiss me. And you know very well you would have given your soul for a kiss from me a hundred years ago."

Yes, Anthony knew it. Only it wasn't a hundred years. How he had dreamed of kissing Caroline—of snatching her up in his manly arms and covering her lovely face with kisses. He remembered with shame amid all his horror that when he used to kiss Clara he was wont to shut his eyes and imagine it was Caroline.

"Well, come and kiss me," said Caroline, pointing the dagger at him. "I'd rather like it, you know. I always would have."

"I . . . I . . . it wouldn't be proper," stammered Anthony.

The nightmare was getting worse. Why didn't somebody have the sense to wake him up. Kiss *that* . . . even without taking the dagger and the murdered George into account! Was *this* how dreams came true?

"Who cares for propriety at our age?" asked Caroline, polishing her dagger on the tail of her nightdress. "Please don't think this is *my* nightdress, Anthony. They had locked up all my clothes and I had spilled some tea on the blue silk one I had on, so I borrowed one of Mrs. Abe's. Well, if you won't kiss me—you were always a stubborn little devil, all the Fingolds were—I'll have to kiss you."

She came across the sunroom and kissed him. Anthony staggered back. Was this how dreams came true? But he had the oddest sense of relief that the nightdress didn't belong to Caroline.

"Stop staring, Anthony darling," said Caroline. "Did Clara ever kiss you like that?"

No, thank God, she never had, never would. Clara didn't go about with daggers, kissing men.

"I must be getting home," gasped Anthony, forgetting all about his promise to Abe.

He was filled with terror. Caroline Wilkes was out of her mind. *That* was what was the matter with her, not sinking spells. And she might become violent at any moment; no doubt that was what her "spells" meant. Confound Abe Saunders! He'd get square with him yet. Abe must have known perfectly well what ailed her. And Dr. Blythe, too. Even Clara. They were all in the plot to have him murdered.

"And leave me alone in this big house with a murdered boy in my closet?" said Caroline, glaring at him, and flourishing her dagger in his very face.

"*He* won't hurt you if he is dead, and you say you killed him yourself," said Anthony, gathering courage from the extremity of fear.

"How do you know what dead people can or cannot do?" demanded Caroline. "Were *you* ever dead, Anthony Fingold?"

"No," said Anthony, wondering how soon he might be.

"Then stop talking about something you know nothing of," said Caroline. "You are not going home until Abe Saunders comes back. But you can go to bed if you want to. Yes, that will be the best plan, from every point of view. Clara won't worry. She knows she can trust her little Anthony. Go to bed in the north gable."

"I'd . . . rather . . . not. . . ." said Anthony feebly.

"I am accustomed to being obeyed," said Caroline, putting on the high and mighty manner she could always assume like a garment. How well he remembered it! It had gone admirably with silk dresses and marcelled hair and jewels—but with dingy old flannel nightgowns! And daggers!

"Do you see this dagger?" continued Caroline, holding it up in a hand bonier than her ankles, if that were possible. Anthony thought of Clara's plump, pink, if somewhat work-worn hands.

"It is a poisoned dagger from Ned's collection," said Caroline. "One tiny prick and you are a dead man. I'll stick it into you if you don't go up to the north gable at once."

Anthony Fingold skipped up the stairs and into the north gable and stood not upon the order of his skipping. He only wanted to get a door shut between himself and Caroline. If there would only be a key in it! But to his horror she followed him and yanked open a bureau drawer.

"Here is a pair of my son's pyjamas," she said, tossing them into his arms. "Put them on and get into bed and sleep like a Christian. I'll look in presently to see if you've done as you're told. Clara has always given you too much of your own way. If you had married me you would have worn pyjamas from the start."

"How . . . how did you hear about Clara wanting me to wear pyjamas?" stammered Anthony, his curiosity getting the better of his terror.

"I hear about everything," returned Caroline. "Get into bed now. Set to watch me, indeed! I'll show them. If there's any watching to be done I'll do it. I'm not a child yet."

Caroline took the key out of the door, to poor Anthony's deep disappointment.

"I suppose you know the earth is flat?" she said, lifting the dagger.

"Of course it is flat," agreed Anthony, hastily.

"Perfectly flat?"

"P . . . perfectly."

"What liars you men are!" said Caroline. "There are hills on it." She disappeared with a horrible soundless chuckle.

Anthony allowed himself a breath of relief as the door closed. He lost no time in getting into the pyjamas. Clara had been at him for years to wear pyjamas, and had never prevailed. But then Clara did not go about pointing poisoned daggers at you. Anthony felt that he had lived a hundred years since his casual visit to the Glen St. Mary store.

Anthony crawled in between the sheets and lay there quaking. What if Caroline took a notion to return to see if he had obeyed her? Was there a telephone in the house? No, he remembered there wasn't.

Oh, if he were only at home in his own bed and nightshirt, with the cat sleeping across his legs and a hot water bottle at his feet! Confound nurses who gadded and women who got their legs broken in car accidents and Georges who disappeared! Could she really have hung George in the closet? It sounded incredible—but an insane person might do anything—anything!

And what closet? Why, it might be the one of the room he was in! At the thought Anthony broke out in a cold perspiration.

What Caroline did do next was something the unhappy Anthony had never dreamed of. She came back, stalking in without anything so conventional as a knock. He heard her footsteps coming up the stairs and quivered with agony. He drew the bedclothes up to his chin and peered at her in dismay.

She had put on a dress, a rather handsome one of grey silk, and a pair of shell-rimmed glasses. She had her teeth in but her head was bare, her hair still floated in elf locks around her shoulders, and she still wore the old felt bedroom slippers she had worn on her first appearance. Likely Mrs. Abe's too. *And* she still carried the dagger. Anthony gave himself up for lost.

He would never see Clara again; never join in the local gossip in Carter Flagg's store of an evening; never wear a nightshirt. But there was not so much comfort in *that* thought as he would have expected. Were shrouds so much better? He wished he had humoured Clara. It would have been something for her to remember when he was gone.

"Get up," said Caroline. "We are going for a drive."

Anthony broke into another cold perspiration.

"I . . . I'd rather not . . . it's too late . . . and I'm very comfortable here."

"I said get up." Caroline pointed with the dagger.

Anthony got up. You had to humour them. What on earth had become of Abe? Had he gone all the way to Charlottetown with his daughter? Or had that crazy old car of his broken down? He caught sight of himself in the mirror and had to admit that pyjamas did look—well, more manly than a nightshirt. Only he did not admire Norman Wilkes' taste in colours.

"Never mind your clothes," said Caroline. "I'm in a hurry. Somebody may come home at any moment. I haven't had a chance like this for years."

"I . . . I . . . I can't go out in these things," stammered Anthony, gazing in horror at the violent orange and purple pyjamas.

"Why not? They cover you all up and that is more than can be said of a nightshirt. Can you fancy me, Caroline Wilkes, driving with a man in a nightshirt? Don't be a moron."

Anthony hadn't the least idea what a moron was but he did know that a poisoned dagger was a poisoned dagger.

Meekly he preceded Caroline down the stairs, out of the house, and across the lawn to the garage. The big Wilkes car was outside and Anthony, still at the dagger's point, got in.

"*Now* we'll step on the gas," said Caroline with a fiendish chuckle, as she laid the dagger on the seat beside her and took the wheel.

A faint hope came into Anthony's heart that he might at least get possession of the dagger. But Caroline seemed to have eyes all over her head.

"Leave that alone, little man," she said, "or I'll stick it clean through you. Do you think I am

going to be left without a weapon of defence
when driving with such a desperate character as
you? Now rig-a-jig-jig and away we go! Oh, we'll
have a merry drive. It is a long time since I had
a chance to drive a car. And once I was the best
driver in Montreal. Where would you like to go,
little man?"

"I . . . think I'd better go home," chattered Anthony.

"Home! Nonsense! A body can go home when
they can't go anywhere else. Clara won't be worried. She knows you too well, little man."

Yes, of course it was a nightmare. It couldn't
be anything else. He couldn't be flying along the
highway at nine o'clock at night in a car with
Caroline Wilkes as driver. Once such a thought
would have seemed to him unalloyed bliss! And
Clara *would* be worried. Like all women, she was
in the habit of worrying over nothing. He had
developed a sudden anxiety in regard to Clara's
feelings.

"We're . . . we're going rather fast, ain't we?"
said the poor buccaneer, wondering if anyone had
ever died of sheer terror.

"Why, this is nothing to what I can do," laughed
the cheerful old ghoul beside him.

Then she proceeded to show what she could do.
She spun off into a corkscrew side road on two
wheels; she went slap through the spruce hedge
that was the pride of Nathan MacAllister's heart;
through a wide brook and a field of potatoes; up
a muddy narrow lane; through John Peterson's

backyard; through another hedge—and finally out to the highway, which, on this especial night, seemed crowded with traffic. There were really not many cars, though a considerable number of horses and buggies, but to poor Anthony's eyes there seemed no room anywhere.

Finally they struck a cow who had imprudently ambled out of a side road. The animal promptly disappeared in the most unaccountable fashion. In truth she was only slightly grazed and hurried back to her side road. But Anthony thought she must have been scared into that "fourth dimension" that he had heard Dr. Blythe and Dr. Parker joking about. Anthony hadn't the slightest idea what the fourth dimension was but he had gathered that anyone or anything that went there was not seen again. Well, *he* would not be seen again, but his dead body would—clad in Norman Wilkes' pyjamas. And Tom Thaxter had always wanted Clara. Even in the horror of the moment, Anthony felt for the first time a pang of jealousy of Clara.

"We saved ten minutes by that short cut," Caroline was chortling. "Nothing like short cuts, I've taken them all my life. Got ten times more fun than most women. Now for a clear road to Charlottetown. We'll teach these country bumpkins what joy-riding really means. They haven't the slightest idea you know. Clara ever go joy-riding?"

Anthony had been supported through that terrible "short cut" by the conviction that somewhere or other he had heard or read that nothing ever happened to a lunatic.

But now he gave himself up for lost. Not even a lunatic could negotiate the night traffic on the Charlottetown highway at the rate that tiger cat of a Caroline was going.

On Saturday nights every boy in the country took his best girl to a show in town and everyone who boasted possession of a Ford was out showing off.

Besides, there were three railroad crossings.

His only remaining hope was that death might not be too terrible. The idea of dying in bed was no longer so unattractive as it had once seemed. Even if you were wearing pyjamas.

Then a dreadful thought occurred to Anthony. They would have to pass through Lowbridge. And hadn't he heard poor Clara say there was to be a community dance and street parade in Lowbridge that night?

She had spoken disapprovingly and—Anthony had thought—narrow-mindedly. It was the first thing of its kind that had ever been heard of in that part of the country, but it sounded romantic.

Everybody in Lowbridge knew him, of course. And any number of Clara's relations lived there—people who had never approved of Clara "taking" him.

Suppose they saw him—tearing through the town in pyjamas with Caroline Wilkes! And of course they would see him. Everybody would be out.

"And me an elder in the church!" groaned Anthony.

He knew now how he had prized that eldership, although he had affected to despise Clara's pride and Susan Baker's increased, though veiled, respect. What was an eldership to the heroes of his dreams?

But he knew now. And of course it would be taken from him. He didn't know how such things were done but of course there was a way. It wouldn't be the slightest use to point out that pyjamas were more respectable things than nightshirts in which to drive about with ladies. Nobody would see the necessity of either.

Everybody would think he was drunk—that was it, drunk. Jerry Cox had been fined ten dollars and costs for driving a car when drunk. Jim Flagg had to spend ten days in jail. Suppose he, Anthony Fingold, was sent to jail!

And what if Old Maid Bradley heard of this escapade—as of course she would—and wrote it up for that scoundrelly *Enterprise* of hers that hadn't six words of truth in it from one year's end to the other?

Poor, poor Clara! She would never lift her head again. And how Dr. Parker would roar! How Susan Baker would smile and say she had always expected it! How he would lose the respect of everybody! Welcome death! It would be far better than such a fate.

"I never thought the like of this would happen to me on this side of the grave," groaned

Anthony. "I've never done anything very bad—except in imagination. But I suppose you are punished for that. What was the sermon Mr. Meredith preached last year that everyone talked of? 'As a man thinketh in his heart so is he.' " By that rule he, Anthony Fingold, was wicked beyond description.

Perhaps he even deserved this. But it was very bitter.

"I wonder if they'll find the axe," said Caroline.

"What axe?" asked Anthony through chattering teeth.

"Why, you old fool, the one I chopped George up with. I dropped it under the loose boards in the back porch floor. I suppose you'll blazon that all over the country. Men can never hold their tongues."

"You told me you hung him in the closet," yelled Anthony, to whom, for some inexplicable reason, this change in George's fate seemed the last straw. "You couldn't have both hung and chopped him up."

"Why not, little man? I hung him first, then I cut him down and carved him up. You don't suppose I'd leave his body there to be found, do you? None of the men I've murdered have ever been found. Did you ever have the fun of murdering anyone, Anthony?"

"I never wanted to murder anyone," said Anthony rashly and falsely. "And I don't believe— yes, you can stick the dagger in me if you like—I'm not altogether a worm—you carved George up."

"A Mallard can do anything," said Caroline superbly.

It seemed as if a Mallard could. Caroline flew along that highway at a terrible rate, cutting out, cutting in, and never dreaming of slowing down at curves. It might have been some small comfort to Anthony if he had known they were going so fast that no one they met or passed had the slightest idea what he was wearing. They only recognized the Wilkes car and cursed the driver thereof. Even Dr. Blythe told Anne when he got home that something really ought to be done about that Wilkes man. "He'll kill someone yet."

Caroline's grey hair streamed behind her and her eyes blazed. A score of times Anthony shut his eyes in expectation of the inevitable collision, and a score of times it did not take place. Perhaps there was some truth after all in the old belief that nothing ever happened to a lunatic. Surely Caroline would stop when they got to Charlottetown. A policeman—but would Caroline pay any attention to a policeman?

And then, about a mile out of town, Caroline suddenly turned and shot down a side road.

"The car that has just turned in there is after no good," she deigned to explain. "I've been keeping my eye on it for some time."

To Anthony the car seemed like any other car. To be sure, it was going at an awful rate for a narrow side road full of S-bends. Even Caroline couldn't catch up with it, though she kept it in sight. On and on they went, twisting and turning until Anthony lost all sense of direction and all sense of time. To him it seemed that they must have been driving for hours.

But they were in an uninhabited country now, all scrub spruce. It must be blueberry barrens. In his despair, Anthony looked back.

"We are being followed ourselves," he gasped. "Hadn't we better stop?"

"Why?" said Caroline. "We have as good a right to the road as anyone. Let them follow. I tell you, Anthony Fingold, I am going to catch those fellows ahead. They've been up to no good. Would they be driving at such a rate on this kind of a road if they weren't trying to get away from the police? Answer me that question if you have any brains? You used to have some at school. You could always beat me in arithmetic. You were in love with me then, you know—and I was quite gone on you—though I would have died rather than admit it. What fools we are when we are young, aren't we, Anthony?"

Caroline Mallard was calmly admitting to him that she had been "gone" on him when they went to school together, when he had thought she was hardly aware of his existence, and now the only word of her speech that made much impression on him was "police."

He looked at the car behind. He was sure the driver was in uniform. And no one but police or lunatics would be driving at such a rate. The police were after him and Caroline. He did not know whether the thought was a comfort or a torture. And what would happen? Caroline, he felt sure, would not stop for a policeman or anything else. Oh, what a story for the *Enterprise*! What a tale for the Glens! He would never dare to show his face in Carter Flagg's store again. As for Clara, she might and probably would leave him. In Prince Edward Island, people did not get divorces—but they "separated." He was sure Clara's Aunt Ellen had "left" her husband.

"A-ha, we're gaining on them," said Caroline exultantly.

The car ahead had slowed down as they spun around a hairpin curve and saw it crossing a creek bridge ahead of them. It *had* slowed down a little and Anthony could see plainly, by the light of a moth-eaten old moon that was just rising above the horizon, that someone in it threw a bag over the railing of the bridge as they whirled across it. Perhaps the remains of the chopped-up George were in it. By this time Anthony had so nearly lost his own reason that any wild idea seemed plausible to him.

Caroline saw the bag go over, too. In her excitement, she pushed heavily on the accelerator, and Anthony's long awaited catastrophe came. The Wilkes car banked into the decrepit old railing; the railing gave way—and they went over.

To the last day of his life, Anthony Fingold firmly believed in the truth of the adage that no harm could befall a lunatic.

The big car was smashed to bits, but he crawled out of the wreck unharmed, to find himself standing in the middle of a shallow, muddy, deep-banked stream. Caroline was already beside him. Behind them, the third car had stopped at the edge of a cowpath that led down to the brook. Two men and a woman were scrambling down it, one of them in a chauffeur's uniform which Anthony had mistaken and still mistook for a policeman's. All three, even the chauffeur, smelled to high heaven of what Clara would have called "grog."

"Now you'll catch it for kidnapping me," said Caroline. "You might have drowned me. And where did you get my son's pyjamas? You are a thief, that is what *you* are, Anthony Fingold. And look what you have done to my car!"

She came threateningly towards him with that infernal dagger still in her hand. Anthony quaked with terror. He caught up the first protective thing that came to hand: a bag that was lying high and dry on the edge of a log—a bag that rustled oddly as he struck blindly at Caroline's uplifted arm.

The poisoned dagger—it was really an old paper cutter—flew from her grasp and spun away into the darkness.

"Upon my word, the little fellow has spunk after all," said Caroline admiringly.

But Anthony did not see that long-desired admiration. Nor would he have cared if he had. It no longer mattered to him, never would matter again, what Caroline Wilkes thought of him.

He was scrambling up the opposite bank of the brook, still keeping an unconscious hold on the bag. They should not catch him; he would *not* be arrested for kidnapping a crazy old woman who ought to be in the asylum.

As he disappeared in the shadows of the trees, the other people gave their attention to Carolyn Wilkes, whom they knew slightly, and took her home. She went meekly enough, her "spell" being over.

Poor Anthony had run for the best part of a mile before he realized that no one was pursuing him. Then he pulled up, quite out of breath, and gazed around him, hardly daring to believe his good fortune. For such it certainly seemed, after the horrors of the preceding hours.

He was in the blueberry barrens behind the Upper Glen. In all that wild racing and chasing along side roads, they must have doubled back until he was within five miles of home. Home! Never had the word seemed so sweet to Anthony Fingold—if, indeed, he still had a home! He had read of men spending what they thought was a few hours somewhere and finding that a hundred years had passed. He felt that it would not surprise him to find that a century had elapsed since he had gone to Carter Flagg's store to get that liniment for Clara.

Beloved Clara! Worth a hundred Caroline Mallards. Of course, he would get a scolding from her, but he felt he deserved it. He wished he might appear before her clad in something else than Norman Wilkes' pyjamas. But there were no houses in the Barrens and he would not have had the spunk to call at them if there had been. Besides, the fewer times he had to tell the tale, the better.

An hour later, a weary, aching Anthony, still clad in wet orange and purple pyjamas, crept into his own kitchen. He was very tired. His heart might be as young as it used to be, but he had discovered that his legs were not.

He had hoped that Clara would be asleep, but Clara was not asleep. The tasty little snack she had always left for Anthony when he was out late was spread on the kitchen table, but it was untouched. For the first time in their married life, he found Clara—calm, placid, Clara—on the verge of hysterics.

The story had reached her over the telephone that Anthony had been seen driving at a terrific rate with old Caroline Wilkes, who was not right in her head, as everybody knew. A distracted Abe Saunders had telephoned. A distracted George Mallard had called. Clara had practically spent the evening at the telephone, making or answering calls. Everybody at Ingleside seemed away, as she could get no answer from them, or she might have had some comfort. She had just decided to get the neighbours out searching when Anthony shambled in.

He did not know what she would say. He was prepared for a real scolding—the first one she had ever administered to him, he reflected. But anything she might say was well deserved. He had never appreciated her.

Clara whirled from the telephone and said the last thing Anthony expected her to say—did the last thing Anthony expected her to do. Clara, who never indulged in any outward display of feeling, suddenly broke into a fit of wild tears.

"That woman," she sobbed, "has been able to get you to wear pyjamas when I never could. And after all the years I've tried to be a good wife to you! Oh, such an evening as I have spent! Didn't you know she has been out of her head for years?"

"You never told me that!" cried Anthony.

"Tell you! I'd have died before I mentioned her name to you. I've always known it was her you wanted. But I thought someone else would have told you. It's common knowledge. And now you've been spending the whole evening with her—and come home in pyjamas. I won't stand for it. I'll get a divorce. I'll—"

"Clara, please listen to me," implored Anthony. "I'll tell you the whole story. I swear every word of it is true. But let me get into some dry things first. You wouldn't want me to die of pneumonia, would you? Though I know I deserve it."

Beloved Clara! Never did any man have such a wife. She was worth a million of what he had believed Caroline Mallard to be. Without another word she wiped her eyes, brought him a warm dressing gown, rubbed his sprained back, anointed his bruises, and made him a cup of hot tea. In short, she almost restored his self-respect.

Then he told her the whole story. And Clara believed every word of it. Would any other woman in the world have done so?

Finally, they thought of the bag, which was lying on the floor.

"Might as well see what's in it," said Clara, her own calm, composed self once more. Men were men and you couldn't make them into anything else. And it really hadn't been Anthony's fault. Caroline Wilkes could always do as she liked with them. The old harridan!

When they saw what was in the bag, they stared at each other in amazement, aghast.

"There . . . there's sixty thousand dollars if there is a cent," gasped Anthony. "Clara, what are we to do?"

"Susan Baker phoned up from Ingleside just after you left that the Bank of Nova Scotia in Charlottetown had been robbed," said Clara. "I guess the robbers thought you and Caroline were after them and they'd better get rid of their loot. They must have been out of ammunition. There's a reward offered for the capture of the bandits or the recovery of the money. Maybe we'll get it, Anthony. They couldn't give it to the Wilkes gang. It was you who found and brought home the money. We'll see what Dr. Blythe has to say about it."

Anthony was too tired to feel excited over the prospect of a reward.

"It's too late to phone anyone about it tonight,"

he said. "I'll bury it under the pile of potatoes in the cellar."

"It'll be safe enough locked up in the spare room closet," said Clara. "And now the wisest thing for us to do is to go to bed. I'm sure you need a rest."

Anthony stretched himself in bed until his still cold toes were cosy against the hot water bottle. Beside him was a rosy, comely Clara, in the crimpers he had often despised but which was certainly a thousandfold more beautiful than Caroline Wilkes' elf locks.

The very next day he would start making that herbaceous border she had so long wanted. She deserved it if ever a woman did. And he had seen some blue and white striped flannel in Carter Flagg's store that would make very tasty pyjamas. Yes, Clara was a jewel among women. She had never turned a hair over some parts of that wild yarn of his which any woman might have been excused for disbelieving. He supposed the Wilkes gang would send his clothes home. Of course, it would get out everywhere that he had been seen joy-riding in pyjamas with old Caroline. But there were some humiliating things no one would ever know. He could trust his Clara. If Caroline Wilkes told anyone she kissed him, no one would believe her. Well, there would be a few humiliating weeks and then people would forget it. And the reward the bank offered might ease them up. He might even be thought a hero instead of a— well, a dod-gasted fool.

But no more adventures for me, thought Anthony Fingold as he drifted into sleep. *Enough's enough. I was never really in love with Caroline Mallard. It was just a case of calf love. Clara has really been the only woman in my life.*

He honestly believed it. And perhaps it was true.

Penelope Struts
Her Theories

Penelope Craig went home early from Mrs. Elston's bridge party. She had the notes to prepare for her lecture on child psychology that evening, and there were several pressing problems demanding her attention, especially the drafting of a child's diet with the proper number of vitamins in it. The other ladies were sorry to see her go, for Penelope was popular with her friends, but that did not prevent them from laughing a little after she had gone.

"The idea," said Mrs. Collins, "of Penelope Craig adopting a child."

"But why not?" asked Mrs. Dr. Blythe, who was visiting friends in town. "Isn't she a recognized authority on child training?"

"Oh, yes, of course. And she is also president

of our S.P.C.A. and convenor of our child welfare committee and lecturer for the National Association of Women's Clubs, and in spite of it all, she's the sweetest thing that ever breathed. But *still* I say . . . the idea of her adopting a child."

"But why?" said the persistent Mrs. Blythe who had once been an adopted child herself and knew that people thought Marilla Cuthbert at old Green Gables stark crazy for taking her.

"Why!" Mrs. Collins threw out her hands expressively. "If you had known Penelope Craig as long as we have, Mrs. Blythe, you'd understand. She is full of theories but when it comes to putting them into practice—and with a boy at that!"

Anne remembered that the Cuthberts had sent for a boy in the first place. She found herself wondering how Marilla would have got along with a boy.

"She *might* manage a girl. After all, there's probably something in all those theories and it's easier to experiment with girls," continued Mrs. Collins. "But a boy! *Just* fancy Penelope Craig bringing up a boy!"

"How old is he?" asked Anne.

"About eight, I'm told. He's really no relation to Penelope. He's merely the son of an old school friend of hers who died recently. His father died soon after he was born, and the boy has never had any contacts with men, so Penelope says."

"Which is an advantage in her eyes, of course," laughed Mrs. Crosby.

"Does Miss Craig dislike men?" It was Mrs. Blythe again.

"Oh, I wouldn't go as far as to say she dislikes them. No, not actually dislikes them. I would rather put it that she can't be bothered with them. Dr. Galbraith could tell you that. Poor Dr. Galbraith! I suppose your husband knows him."

"I think I've heard him speak of him. He's very clever, isn't he? And is he in love with Miss Craig?"

What an outspoken person this Mrs. Blythe was! On her part she was thinking how hard it was to find out simple things. People took it so for granted that you must know all they did.

"I should say so. He's been proposing to Penelope off and on for—it must be ten years or so. Let me see, yes, it's thirteen years since his wife died."

"He must be a very persistent man," smiled Mrs. Blythe.

"I should say so. The Galbraiths never give up. And Penelope just goes on refusing him so sweetly that he's sure she'll relent next time."

"And don't you suppose she will . . . sometime?" Mrs. Blythe smiled, recalling some incidents of her own romance.

"I don't think there's a chance. Penelope will never marry Roger Galbraith or anybody else."

Roger Galbraith, thought Anne. *Yes, that is the man. I remember Gilbert saying that when he set his mind on anything there was no moving it.*

"They are the best of friends," said Mrs. Loree. "And friends they will remain, nothing more."

"Sometimes you find out that what was thought was friendship is really love," said Mrs. Blythe. "She's very handsome," recalling Miss Craig's beautiful blue-black hair in little dark curls around her wide, low, cream-white brow. Anne had never grown really reconciled to her own ruddy tresses.

"Handsome and clever and competent," agreed Mrs. Collins. "That is why she has no patience with men."

"I suppose she thinks she doesn't need them," said Anne.

"Likely that is the reason. But I confess it annoys me to see a man like Roger Galbraith dangling after her for ten years when there is any number of lovely girls he could get. Why, half the unmarried women in Charlottetown would jump at him."

"How old is Miss Craig?"

"Thirty-five, though she doesn't look it, does she? She has never had a worry in her life—or any sorrow, for her mother died when she was born, so she has never missed her. Since then she has lived in that apartment with old Marta, a third or fourth cousin or something like that. Marta worships her, and she devotes her time to club work of all kinds. Oh, she's clever and competent, as I've said, but she's going to find that bringing up a child in practice is a very different thing from bringing it up in theory."

"Oh, theories!" Mrs. Tweed laughed, as the

successful mother of six children felt she had a right to. "Penelope has theories in abundance. Do you remember that talk she gave us last year on 'patterns' in child training?"

Anne recalled Marilla and Mrs. Lynde. What would they have said to such talk?

"One point she stressed," continued Mrs. Tweed, "was that children should be trained to go ahead and take the consequences. They shouldn't be forbidden to do anything. 'I believe in letting children find out things for themselves,' she said."

"Up to a point she's right," said Mrs. Blythe. "But when that point is reached—"

"She said that children should be allowed to express their individuality," said Mrs. Parker reminiscently.

"Most of them do," laughed Mrs. Blythe. "Does Miss Craig *like* children? It seems to me that that is a very important point."

"I asked her that once," said Mrs. Collins, "and all she said was, 'My dear Nora, why don't you ask me if I like grown-up people?' Now, what do you make out of that?"

"Well, she was right," said Mrs. Fulton. "Some children are likeable and some aren't."

A memory of Josie Pye drifted across Anne's mind. "We all know that," she said. "In spite of sentimental piffle."

"*Could* anybody like that fat, dribbly Paxton child?" demanded Mrs. MacKenzie.

"His mother probably thinks him the most beautiful thing on earth," said Anne, smiling.

"You wouldn't say that if you knew the whalings she gives him," said Mrs. Lawrence bluntly. "*She* doesn't believe in sparing the rod and spoiling the child."

"I've lived on buttermilk for five weeks and I've gained four pounds," said Mrs. Williams bitterly. She thought it was time the subject was changed. After all, Mrs. Blythe was a B.A. even if she did live in some out-of-the-way place in the country.

But the others ignored her. Who cared if Mrs. Williams were fat or lean? What was diet compared to the fact of Penelope Craig adopting a boy?

"I've heard her say no child should ever be whipped," said Mrs. Rennie.

She and Susan would find themselves kindred spirits, thought Anne amusedly.

"I agree with her there," said Mrs. Fulton.

"H'mm!" said Mrs. Tweed, pursing her lips. "Five of my children I never whipped. But Johnny . . . I found a sound spanking was necessary about once in so long if we were to live with him. What do you think about it, Mrs. Blythe?"

Anne, recalling Anthony Pye, was spared the embarrassment of a reply by Mrs. Gaynor, who had hitherto said not a word, and thought it high time she asserted herself. "Fancy Penelope Craig spanking a child," she said.

Nobody could fancy it, so they returned to their game.

Dr. Roger Galbraith was in Penelope's living room when she reached home and Marta, who adored him, was giving him tea, with some of her big fat doughnuts.

"What's this I hear about your adopting a boy, Penny? All the town seems to be talking about it."

"I have begged her not to adopt a *boy*," said Marta, in a tone which implied she had done it on her knees.

"I did not happen to have any choice in the matter of sex," retorted Penelope, in her soft, lovely voice which made even impatience seem charming. "Poor Ella's child could not be left to the care of strangers. She wrote to me on her deathbed. I regard it as a sacred trust, though I *am* sorry he is not a girl."

"Do you think this is any place to bring up a boy?" said Dr. Galbraith, looking around the dainty little room and running his fingers dubiously through his mop of tawny hair.

"Of course not, Mr. Medicine Man," said Penelope, coolly. "I realize quite as clearly as you do how very important the background of a child's life is. So I have bought a story book cottage over at Keppoch. I mean to call it Willow Run. It's a delightful spot. Even Marta admits that."

"Plenty of skunks, I suppose," said Dr. Galbraith, "and mosquitoes."

"There is a large summer colony of boarders there," said Penelope, ignoring his reference to skunks. "Lionel will have plenty of companions.

There are some drawbacks to every place, but I think it is as nearly an ideal place for children as can be found: plenty of sunshine and fresh air; room to play; room to develop individuality; a sleeping porch for Lionel, looking out on a hill of spruce."

"Lionel!"

"Yes, of course it is an absurd name, but Ella was rather given to romance."

"He'll be a regular sissy with such a name. But he'd be that anyway, pampered and petted by a widowed mother," said Dr. Galbraith, getting up. His six feet of lean muscle did seem far too big for the little room. "Will you take me out and let me see this Willow Run of yours? What is the sanitation like?"

"Excellent. Did you suppose I would overlook that?"

"And the water? You get it from a well, I suppose? There was a lot of typhoid at Keppoch one summer a few years ago."

"I'm sure it's all right now. Perhaps you'd better come out and look it over."

Penelope was slightly meeker. She knew all about bringing up these glad, simple little creatures, children, but typhoid was a different matter, for this was before the days of its comparative conquest. A doctor was not without his legitimate uses.

Dr. Galbraith came along in his car the next afternoon, and they went out to Willow Run.

"I met a Mrs. Blythe at Mrs. Elston's yesterday,"

said Penelope. "Her husband is a doctor, I believe. Do you know him?"

"Gilbert Blythe? Of course I do. One of the best. And his wife is a most charming person."

"Oh . . . well, I didn't see much of her, of course," said Penelope, wondering why Dr. Galbraith's evident approval of Mrs. Blythe rather grated on her. As if it mattered a pin's worth! But then she had never fancied red-haired women.

Dr. Galbraith approved the well and almost everything else about Willow Run. It was impossible to deny that it was charming. Penelope was nobody's fool when it came to buying a place. There was a quaint old roomy house, surrounded by maples and willows, with a rose-trellis entrance to the garden and a stone walk, bordered with white quahog shells where daffodils bloomed all the spring. Now and then a break in the trees gave a glimpse of the blue bay. There was a white gate in the surrounding red brick wall, with blooming apple trees branching over it.

"Almost as beautiful as Ingleside," said Dr. Galbraith.

"Ingleside?"

"That is what the Blythes call their place out at Glen St. Mary. I like the fashion of giving names to places. It seems to confer an individuality on them."

"Oh!" Again, Penelope's soft voice seemed a trifle cold. She seemed to be running up against those Blythes at every moment now. And she did not believe that this what-do-you-call-it—

Ingle-something—could be as beautiful as Willow Run.

The interior of the house was equally charming.

"It should develop the right sort of attitude in Lionel, I think," said Penelope complacently. "A child's attitude towards his home is very important. I want Lionel to love his home. I am glad the dining room looks out on the delphinium walk. Fancy sitting and eating and gazing out at delphiniums."

"Perhaps a boy would rather look at something else—though Walter Blythe—"

"Look at those squirrels," said Penelope hastily. For some unknown reason she felt that she would scream if Dr. Galbraith mentioned any of the Blythes again. "They are quite tame. Surely a boy would like squirrels."

"You can never tell what they'll like. But it is probable he will, if it is only as something to set the cat chasing."

"I shall not have a cat. I don't like them."

"Talking of cats, a queer thing happened at Ingleside. They had a black—"

"I can hardly wait to move out," interrupted Penelope rather rudely. "I can't imagine how I could have existed, cooped up in that apartment so long. And now with Willow Run and a child of my own—"

"Don't forget he isn't really a child of your own, Penny. And if he were, there would be problems too."

Dr. Galbraith looked up at her as she stood on the step above him. His good-natured, black-grey eyes had suddenly grown very tender. "It's such a glorious day, Penny, that I can't help proposing to you again," he said lightly. "You needn't refuse me unless you want to."

Penelope's lips curled at the corners, a bit mockingly, but kindly. "I could like you so much if you didn't want me to love you, Roger. Our friendship is so pleasant. Why will you persist in trying to spoil it? Once and for all, there is no place for men in my life." Then, for no reason she could ever give, even to herself, she added, "It's such a pity Mrs. Blythe isn't a widow."

"I shouldn't have thought *you* capable of saying such a thing, Penny," said Roger quietly. "If Mrs. Blythe were a widow, it wouldn't matter a sixpence to me in *that* way. I've never cared for red-haired women."

"Mrs. Blythe's hair isn't red. It's a most charming auburn," protested Penelope, suddenly feeling that Mrs. Blythe was a delightful creature.

"Well, call it any shade you like, Penny," Dr. Galbraith's tone was several degrees lighter. He believed that Penny had really felt jealous of Mrs. Blythe—and where there is jealousy, there is hope. But he was more silent than usual on the way back, while Penelope discoursed blithely about the child mind, the wisdom of letting a child do what he wanted to do—"exhibiting his ego," she summed it up—and the importance of seeing that he ate enough spinach.

"Mrs. Blythe has given up trying to make Jem eat spinach," said the doctor on purpose.

But Penelope no longer cared what Mrs. Blythe did or didn't do. She condescended, however, to ask the doctor what he thought about the power of suggestion, especially when a child was asleep.

"If a child was asleep, I'd let him sleep. Most mothers are only too glad when a child does go to sleep."

"Oh, most mothers! I don't mean for you to waken him up, of course. You just sit beside him and very quietly and calmly, in a low controlled tone, suggest what you want to impress on his mind."

"I don't," said Dr. Galbraith.

Penelope could have bitten her tongue out. How could she have forgotten that Roger's wife had died in childbirth?

"There may be something in it," said Dr. Galbraith, who had once remarked rather cynically to Dr. Blythe that the secret of any success he might have had was due to the fact that he always advised people to do what he knew they really wanted to do.

"It will be wonderful to watch his little mind develop," said Penelope dreamily.

"He's eight, so you tell me," said Dr. Galbraith drily. "Probably his mind has already developed to a considerable extent. You know what the Roman Catholic church says of a child: The first seven years, etc. However, it is never forbidden to hope."

"You lose so much out of life by being cynical, Roger," rebuked Penelope, gently.

Though Penelope would not have admitted it, even to herself, she was glad that Dr. Galbraith was away when Lionel came. He had gone for a vacation and would be gone several weeks. Long before he came back she would have become used to Lionel and all the problems would have been worked out. For, of course, there would be problems. Penelope did not blink on that. But she was quite sure that, given patience and understanding, both of which she felt she possessed in abundance, they would be easily solved.

The first sight of Lionel, when she went to the station in the early morning to take him over from the man who had brought him from Winnipeg, was a bit of a shock. She had somehow been expecting to see Ella's golden curls and baby-blue eyes and willowy grace in miniature. Lionel must look like the father she had never seen. He was short and stocky, with thick black hair and unchildishly thick black eyebrows, almost meeting across his nose. His eyes were black and smouldering, and his mouth was set in an obstinate line which broke into no smile at her affectionate greeting.

"I am your Aunt Penelope, darling."

"No, you ain't," said Lionel. "We ain't no relation."

"Well . . ." Penelope was slightly taken aback. ". . . Not really an aunt, of course, but won't it be nice to call me that? I was your mother's dearest friend. Did you have a nice trip, dear?"

"Nope," said Lionel.

He got into the runabout beside her and looked neither to the right nor to the left on the road to Willow Run.

"Are you tired, dear?"

"Nope."

"Hungry, then? Marta will—"

"I ain't hungry."

Penelope gave up. There was a good deal in child psychology about letting children alone. She would let Lionel alone, since he evidently did not want to talk. They covered the distance in silence, but Lionel broke it just as Penelope brought her car to a halt before the door where Marta was waiting.

"Who is that ugly old woman?" he asked distinctly.

"Why . . . why . . . darling, that's Marta, my cousin who lives with me. You can call her Aunty, too. You'll like her when you know her."

"I won't," said Lionel.

"And you mustn't—" Penelope remembered just in time that you must never say "must not" to children. It does something to their ego. "Please don't call her ugly."

"Why not?" asked Lionel.

"Why . . . why . . . oh, because you don't want to hurt her feelings, do you? Nobody likes to be called ugly, you know, darling. *You* wouldn't, would you?"

"But I ain't ugly," said Lionel.

This was true enough. In his own way, he was rather a handsome child.

Marta came forward grimly and held out her hand. Lionel put his hand behind his back.

"Shake hands with Aunt Marta, darling."

"Nope," said Lionel, and added, "She ain't my aunt."

Penelope felt something she had never felt before in her life: a desire to shake somebody. It was *so* important that he should make a good impression on Marta. But just in time she remembered her patterns.

"Let us have some breakfast, dear," she said brightly. "We'll all feel better afterwards."

"I ain't sick," said Lionel, and added, "I ain't going to be called 'dear.' "

There was orange juice and a coddled egg for Lionel. He looked at it with aversion. "Gimme some sausages," he said.

As there were no sausages, Lionel couldn't have any. That being the case he would not have anything else. Penelope again decided to leave him alone. "A little wholesome neglect sometimes does a child good," she said, remembering her books on the bringing up of children. But when lunch hour came and Lionel still demanded sausages, a dreadful feeling of helplessness crept over her. Lionel had spent the entire morning sitting on the front porch, staring straight ahead of him. Since Dr. Roger's departure, she had paid a visit to Ingleside at Glen St. Mary and she could not help recalling the different behaviour of the Ingleside youngsters.

After lunch Lionel still stubbornly refused to eat anything because there were still no sausages, and went back to the steps.

"I suppose he has no appetite," said Penelope, anxiously. "I wonder if he needs a pill."

"He doesn't need a pill. What he needs—and needs bad—is a good spanking," said Marta. Her expression indicated that she would enjoy being the spanker.

Had it come to this so soon? Lionel had been at Willow Run only six hours, and Marta was calling for spanks. Penelope lifted her head proudly.

"Do you suppose, Marta, I could ever spank poor Ella's child?"

"I'd attend to it for you," said Marta, with undoubted relish.

"Nonsense. The poor child is likely very tired and homesick. When he gets adjusted he will eat what he should. We'll just stick to our policy of leaving him alone, Marta."

"Best thing to do, since you won't spank him," agreed Marta. "He's a stubborn one. I saw that the first moment I laid eyes on him. Will I order some sausages for his dinner?"

Penelope would not dip her colours.

"No," she said shortly. "Sausages are most unwholesome for children."

"I et plenty of them when I was a child," said Marta shortly, "and they never did me any harm."

Lionel, who had probably not slept very well

on the train, fell asleep so soundly that he did not waken when Penelope lifted him in unaccustomed arms and carried him to a couch in the sunroom. His face was rosy and in sleep looked child-like. His close-shut lips had parted and Penelope saw that one front tooth was missing. After all, he was only a little fellow.

"He must be five pounds overweight," she thought anxiously. "I daresay it won't do him a bit of harm to go without food for a little while. He's very different from what I expected him to be, but in spite of everything there is something attractive about him. Poor Ella didn't know anything about child psychology. I suppose she never really found the right approach to him."

For dinner there was a delicious roasted chicken, with spinach for Lionel, and ice cream.

"Sausages," said Lionel.

Penelope was in despair. It was all very well to say let a child alone, let him learn for himself the consequences of certain acts, but you couldn't let him starve to death. That might be learning consequences too late.

"I'll . . . there'll be some sausages for your breakfast, darling. Try a bit of this nice chicken."

"Sausages," said Lionel. "And my name ain't darling. The boys at home called me Bumps."

Marta went out and brought in a platter of sausages, with a defiant glance at Penelope.

"I got 'em just to be on the safe side," she said. "My cousin's wife, Mary Peters, out at Mowbray

Narrows made them. They're of good clean pork. You couldn't let him go with an empty stomach all night. He might come down sick."

Lionel fell to on the sausages and ate every one of them. He accepted a helping of peas but said "Nope" to the spinach.

"I'll give you a nickel if you'll eat your spinach," said Marta to Penelope's horror. Bribing a child to do right!

"Make it a dime," said Lionel.

He got the dime and he ate the spinach—every scrap of it. At least Lionel believed in fulfilling his part of the contract. He did well by his ice cream but reverted to sulks when Penelope refused to give him coffee.

"I've always had coffee," he said.

"Coffee is not good for little boys, darling," she said, and stuck to it. But she did not enjoy her own. Especially as Lionel said, "You must be awful old. You can't seem to remember that my name isn't darling."

Penelope never forgot those first two weeks of Lionel's existence at Willow Run. By dint of giving him some bacon with his egg he was induced to refrain from demanding sausages and, apart from that, his appetite seemed normal enough. He even ate his spinach without being bribed.

But the problem of his meals being partially solved, there remained the problem of amusing him. For it had come to that. He would not make friends with any of the neighbouring youngsters and he sat on the porch steps and stared into vacancy or wandered idly around the grounds of Willow Run. Penelope took him out to Ingleside one day and he seemed to hit it off with Jem Blythe, whom he called a "good bean," but you couldn't go to Ingleside every day. He never looked at the squirrels, and the swing which Penelope had erected for him in the backyard he disdained. He would not play with the mechanical donkey or the electric train or the toy airplane she bought him. Only once he threw a stone. Unluckily he picked the exact time when Mrs. Raynor, the wife of the Anglican minister, was coming in at the gate. It just missed her nose by an inch.

"You mustn't throw stones at people, dar— Lionel," said Penelope miserably (forgetting that you mustn't say "mustn't"), after the very stately lady had gone.

"I didn't throw it at her," said Lionel dourly. "I just threw it. It wasn't my fault she was there."

Penelope took to going into the sleeping porch every night (Lionel refused to sleep anywhere else) and "suggesting." Marta thought that it was some kind of witchcraft: Penelope "suggested" that Lionel should feel happy; should not want sausages or coffee; should like spinach; should realize they loved him.

"Old Marta doesn't," said Lionel one night suddenly, when she had supposed him sound asleep.

"He won't *let* us love him," said Penelope despairingly. "And as for letting him do what he wants to do, he doesn't want to do *anything*.

He doesn't want to go driving, he won't play with his toys, and he doesn't laugh enough. He doesn't laugh *at all*, Marta. Do you notice that?"

"Well, some kids don't," said Marta. "What that kind want is a man to bring them up. They don't take to women."

Penelope disdained to reply. But it was after this she suggested a dog. She had always rather hankered for a dog herself, but her father had not liked dogs. Neither did Marta and an apartment was really no place for a dog. Surely Lionel would like a dog; a boy should have a dog.

"I'm going to get you a dog, dar—Lionel."

She hoped to see Lionel's face light up for once, but he only looked at her out of lack-lustre black eyes.

"A dog? Who wants a dog?" he said sulkily.

"I thought all boys liked dogs," faltered Penelope.

"I don't. A dog bit me once. I'd like a kitten," said Lionel. "They have heaps of kittens at Ingleside."

Neither Penelope nor Marta liked cats but this was the first thing Lionel had wanted, apart from the sausages. Penelope was afraid it would not do to thwart him.

If you thwart a child you don't know what kind of a fixation you may set up, she remembered.

The kitten was procured. Mrs. Blythe sent one in from Ingleside, and Lionel announced that he would call it George.

"But dar—Lionel, it's a lady kitten," faltered Penelope. "Susan Baker told me so."

"Susan Baker thought Jack Frost was a tom," said Lionel who had heard more than Penelope ever imagined during his visit at Ingleside.

"Better call it Fluffy," suggested Penelope. "Its fur is so soft; or Topsy."

"Its name is George," said Lionel.

Lionel kept George by him and took her to bed with him, much to Penelope's horror, but he still prowled darkly about Willow Run and refused to enjoy himself. They had got used to his silence— evidently he was a taciturn child by nature—but Penelope could not get used to his smouldering discontent. She felt it to the marrow of her bones. Suggestion seemed of no avail. Ella's child was not happy. She had tried everything. She had tried amusing him, she had tried leaving him alone.

"When he begins to go to school it will be better," she told Marta hopefully. "He will mingle with other boys then and have playmates. He seemed quite different that day we spent at Ingleside."

"The doctor and Mrs. Blythe have no theories, I'm told," said Marta.

"They must have some. Their children are very well behaved, I admit that. I'd have had some boys in before, but the children hereabouts have some kind of spots. I don't know if it's catching but I thought it best not to expose Lionel to it. I . . . wish Roger were back."

"There are plenty other doctors in town," said Marta. "And you can't keep a child wrapped up in cotton wool all his life. I may be an old maid, but I know *that*. Anyhow, it's two months yet till school opens."

Marta was taking things easily. Marta rather approved of Lionel, in spite of his calling her an ugly old woman.

He didn't get into mischief and he didn't say impolite things to you if you left him alone. He had to be bribed to drink his nightly glass of milk sometimes—Marta did that more often than Penelope had any idea of—but he hoarded the dimes he got.

Once he asked Marta how much a ticket to Winnipeg cost and would not eat any lunch after he had been told. That night he told Marta he was "through with guzzling milk."

"I ain't a baby," he said.

"What will your Aunt Penelope say?" admonished Marta.

"Do you think I care?" said Lionel.

"You ought to care. She is very good to you," said Marta.

Penelope came to a certain decision on the day Lionel came in with a bad bruise on his knee. Not that he made any fuss over it, but when he was asked how he got hurt, he said the church steeple fell on him.

"Oh, but Lionel, that isn't true," said Penelope, horrified. "You couldn't expect us to believe that."

"I know it ain't true. When Walter Blythe says

things that ain't true, his mother calls it imagination."

"But there is a difference. He doesn't expect her to believe them."

"I didn't expect you either," said Lionel. "But nothing ever happens here. You've just got to pretend things happen."

Penelope gave up the argument. She bathed and disinfected the knee. She was conscious as she did so of a queer desire to kiss it. It was such an adorable fat brown little knee. But she was afraid if she did, Lionel would look at her with that fine trickle of disdain which sometimes appeared so disconcertingly in his expression.

He refused to let her put a bandage on it, although Penelope felt sure it should be done to prevent possible infection.

"I'll rub some toad-spit on it," said Lionel.

"Where did you hear of such a thing?" exclaimed Penelope in horror.

"Jem Blythe told me. But he wouldn't tell his father," added Lionel. "His father had some queer notions just like you and Marta."

If only Roger were here! came unbidden and unwelcomed into Penelope's mind.

She thought hard that afternoon and announced the result to Marta at night, after Lionel and George were in bed.

"Marta, I have come to the conclusion that what Lionel needs is a companion: a chum, a pal. All boys should have one. The Ingleside boys are all too far away. And really, after what Jem told

Lionel about toad-spit—but you know they say a child with no one but grown-ups around him will have an inferiority complex. Or do I mean a superiority complex?"

"*I* think you don't know what you mean yourself," said Marta. "Have a talk with Mrs. Blythe. She is in town, I hear."

"Mrs. Blythe is a B.A. but I have never heard that she was an authority on child psychology."

"Her children are the best behaved I've ever seen," said Marta.

"Well, anyhow I have decided that Lionel needs a companion."

"You don't mean that you are going to adopt another boy!" said Marta in a tone of consternation.

"Not *adopt* exactly. Oh, dear me no, not adopt, Marta. But I simply mean to get one for the summer, till school opens. Mrs. Elwood was talking about one yesterday. I think his name is Theodore Wells."

"Jim Wells' nephew! Why, Penelope Craig! Wasn't his mother an actress or something?"

"Yes, Sandra Valdez. Jim Wells' brother married her ten years ago in New York or London or somewhere. They soon parted and Sidney came home with his boy. He died at Jim's farm. Jim has looked after the boy but you know he died last month and his wife says she has enough to do to look after her own."

"He was never very welcome there, from all I've heard," muttered Marta.

"She wants to find a home for him until she can get in touch with Sandra Valdez, and I feel it is providential, Marta."

"I feel the old Scratch has had more to do with it," said Marta.

"Marta, Marta, you really mustn't. Mrs. Elwood says he is a dear little chap, looks like an angel."

"Mrs. Elwood would say anything. She is a sister of Mrs. Jim Wells. Penelope, you don't know what that child is like—or what he may teach Lionel."

"Mrs. Elwood says the Wells children are all well behaved and well brought up."

"Oh, she said that, did she? Well, they're her own nephews and nieces. She ought to know."

"Suppose he *is* a little mischievous."

"Oh, she admitted that, did she? Well, children should be mischievous. I may be an old maid but I know that. They say those Blythe youngsters you're so fond of quoting—"

"I very seldom mention them, Marta! But Dr. Galbraith—well that is one thing that worried me about Lionel. He isn't half mischievous enough. In fact, he is not mischievous at all. It isn't normal. When Theodore comes—"

"Theodore! That is even worse than Lionel."

"Now, Marta be nice," said Penelope pleadingly. "You *know* I'm right."

"If you had a husband, Penelope, I wouldn't care how many children you adopted. But for two old maids to start bringing up boys—"

"That will do, Marta. A woman who has made a study of child psychology, as I have, knows more about bringing up children than many a mother. My mind is made up."

Oh, how I wish Dr. Roger was home! groaned Marta to herself. *Not that I suppose he would have the slightest influence either.*

Theodore looked as Lionel should have looked. He was slender and had delicate features, with red-gold hair and astonishingly lustrous gray eyes.

"So this is Theodore," said Pentelope graciously.

"Yes'm," said Theodore with a charming smile. There was evidently nothing of Lionel's gruffness about him.

"And this is Lionel," smiled Penelope.

"I've heard about him," said Theodore. "Hello, Bumps!"

"Hello, Red," condescended Lionel.

"Suppose you go out into the garden and get acquainted before dinner," suggested Penelope, still smiling. Things were going much better than she had dared hope.

Marta sniffed. She knew something about Theodore Wells.

A few minutes later, blood-curdling howls came from the backyard. Penelope and Marta both rushed out in dismay to find the two boys in a furious clinch on the gravelled walk, kicking, clawing and yelling. Penelope and Marta dragged them apart with difficulty. Their faces were covered with dirt. Theodore had a cut lip and another of Lionel's teeth was missing. George was up on a maple tree, apparently wondering if her tail really belonged to her.

"Oh, darlings, darlings," cried Penelope distractedly. "This is dreadful. You musn't fight—you *musn't*."

It was evident that for the moment, at least, Penelope had forgotten the rules of child psychology.

"He pulled George's tail," snarled Lionel. "Nobody ain't going to pull *my* cat's tail."

"How did I know it was your cat?" demanded Red. "You hit first. Look at my lip, Miss Craig."

"It's bleeding," said Penelope with a shudder. She could never endure the sight of blood. It turned her sick.

"It's only a scratch," said Marta. "I'll put some vaseline on it."

"Kiss the place and make it well," jeered Theodore.

Lionel said nothing. He was busy hunting for his lost tooth.

At least he isn't a cry-baby, Penelope comforted herself. *Neither of them is a cry-baby.*

Marta took Lionel to the kitchen. He went willingly because he had found his tooth. Penelope took Theodore to the bathroom where she washed his face, much against his will, and discovered that his neck and body were in deplorable need of attention also. A bath was indicated.

"Gee, I'd hate to be as clean as you all the time," said Theodore, looking himself over afterwards. "Do you wash yourself all over every day?"

"Of course, dear."

"*All* over?"

"Of course."

"If I wash my face at the pump once a week—thorrerly, won't that be enough?" demanded Theodore. "And can I call you Momma? You smell nice."

"I think Aunty would be much better," faltered Penelope.

"I've got all the aunts I want," retorted Theodore. "But I ain't got no Momma. Just as you say, though. Say, that tooth of Bumps was ready to come out anyhow. What are cats' tails for if they ain't to be pulled?"

"But you don't want to hurt poor little animals, do you? If you were a kitten and had a tail, would you like to have it pulled?"

"If I was a kitten and had a tail," sang Theodore. He really sang it, in a delightfully clear, true sweet voice. Lionel could sing, too, it appeared. The two sat on the steps after dinner and sang all kinds of songs together. Some of the songs Penelope thought rather terrible for small boys, but it was such a comfort to find Lionel taking an interest in something at last. She had been right. All Lionel really needed was a companion.

"Did you hear how they ended up that bee-i-ee-i-ee song?" demanded Marta. "They *didn't* end it with 'way down yonder in the field.' What if Mrs. Raynor had heard them?"

Mrs. Raynor had not heard. But a certain Mrs. Embree who was passing at that moment had. It was all over the neighbourhood by next day. Someone telephoned it to Penelope. Did she really think Theodore Wells a fit companion for her nephew?

By now Penelope, who had screwed the truth out of Marta, was wondering herself. Marta had found the two boys at the pump before lunch.

"What's the matter?" demanded Marta, looking at Lionel's face.

"Nothing," said Lionel.

Penelope came running out. *"What is the matter?"*

"Red was chewing beetroot and he spit on me," growled Lionel.

"Oh, Theodore! Theodore!"

"Well, you told me I mustn't fight," yelled Theodore, who seemed in a towering rage. "There wasn't nothing I could do but spit."

"But why—why spit?" said Penelope weakly.

"He said he bet his father could swear worse'n my father could if they were alive. I ain't going to let anybody run down my relations. I've got more guts than that. If I can't fight, I'm going to spit—spit *hard*. But I forgot about the beetroot," he added frankly.

"There's just one of two things you can do, Penelope," said Marta, after Lionel's face had been purified. "You can send this Theodore young one back to his aunt."

"I can't do that, Marta. It would look so—so— it would be a confession of defeat. And think how Roger would laugh at me."

So Roger's opinion is beginning to have some weight with you, thought Marta with satisfaction.

"And really, Lionel is a changed boy even in so short a time," protested Penelope. "I mean he's taking an interest in things."

"Then you can let them fight it out when they want to fight," said Marta. "It don't hurt boys to fight. They get a lot of divilment out of their systems in that way. Look at them two now, out behind the garage, digging for worms, as good friends as if they'd never fought or spit. No, don't quote the Ingleside gang to me. They've got a different lot of parents altogether and a different bringing up."

"And of course frustration *is* about the worst thing possible for a child," murmured poor Penelope, still holding a few illusions about her, like tattered rags.

There was no more frustration with Lionel and Theodore. As far as fighting was concerned. They had another set-to that day, but they also had a trout-fishing excursion up the brook and came home triumphantly with a string of very decent little trout which Marta fried for their dinners. Perhaps it would be better to let them fight when they yearned to. But Penelope confessed to herself in dire humiliation that she would be letting them fight more because she felt powerless to stop them, than because she felt really convinced about the frustration problem. And she wondered what Mrs. Elwood's conception of a well-trained boy was. It was not, of course, possible that Mrs. Elwood was—

Still, amid all her distraction of mind, in the ensuing weeks there was the faint comfort that one problem regarding Lionel had ceased to be. He was amused. From early morn to dewy eve, he and Theodore were "up to something," as Marta put it. They fought frequently and Penelope was sure the whole countryside must hear their wild howls and think they were being shamefully whipped or something of the sort. But Lionel condescended to explain to Penelope that "it had been awful lonesome before Red came with no one to fight with."

Theodore had an explosive temper which vanished as soon as it had exploded. Between times, even Marta admitted his charm. After all, Penelope tried to convince herself, their mischief was really no more than normal. Likely, if one only knew, the Ingleside boys did precisely the same things.

That snake on the laundry floor—of course, poor Marta *had* got a nasty fright.

"He's a *good* snake," Theodore had protested. "He wouldn't hurt you."

It really was a harmless garter snake. But still, a snake was a snake.

And how charmingly he had assured Mrs. Peabody that her hat would come all right if she steamed it. Theodore hadn't meant to sit on it.

Penelope wished she felt quite sure of that, but she knew how both boys hated Mrs. Peabody, and really, Mrs. Peabody had been rather disagreeable. Why had she left her hat on the garden seat anyhow? She had declared it was a Paris hat, but Penelope had seen Mrs. Dr. Blythe wearing a much smarter one at a Charlottetown tea a few days before and she had bought it from a Charlottetown milliner.

Of course, Lionel shouldn't have turned the hose on the baker's boy, and the living room *was* a terrible sight after their pillow fight. Unfortunately, one of the pillows had burst and of course Mrs. Raynor had to bring the Bishop and his family to call at that very moment. They had all been very nice about it and the Bishop had told of some much worse things *he* had done when a boy. To be sure, his wife had reminded him that his father had given him some terrible whippings for his kididoes. But the Bishop had replied that times were changed and children were treated very differently now. Mrs. Raynor looked as if the whole thing had been planned as an insult to her.

But Penelope really couldn't see why everyone blamed the boys so much the night she and Marta thought they were lost. It was all her own fault that she hadn't looked in the sleeping porch. They had simply gone to bed after supper without saying a word to anyone and were sleeping soundly and sweetly, with George purring between them, when the summer colony was searching for them, and there was talk of calling over the Charlottetown police. Penelope for the first time in her life was on the verge of hysterics because someone was sure she had seen them in an automobile with a very suspicious-looking man just at dark.

Finally someone had suggested looking in the sleeping porch and then people had said, so Penelope was informed, "Just what you would expect of those two young demons," when the poor tired little creatures had simply gone to bed. Even Marta was indignant. She said Jem Blythe out at Ingleside had done almost exactly the same thing one night and nobody ever thought of punishing him. Susan Baker had told her all about it and just seemed thankful no worse had happened to him.

But Theodore really had to be punished when he cut his initials in the new dining room table the afternoon Penelope was over in town at a meeting of the Child Welfare Committee. Marta had spanked him before Penelope got home, and Theodore had said scornfully when it was over, "*That* didn't hurt. *You* don't know anything about spanking. If you'd taken some lessons from Aunt Ella now!"

There are times, thought Marta bitterly, *when a man would be comforting.*

Penelope, looking at her once beautiful table, almost agreed with her.

Penelope was soon driven almost mad with telephone calls. People had discovered that Miss

Craig was inclined to be a little on her dignity when anything was said to her about those two young Satans she had adopted, and it was easier to say it on the telephone and hang up when you had finished.

"Will you be good enough to look after your boys, Miss Craig? They have been playing at harpooning elephants and have harpooned our cow."

"Miss Craig, I think your boys are digging out a skunk in Mr. Dowling's wood lot."

"Miss Craig, one of your boys has been most impertinent to me. He called me an old owl when I warned him off my flowerbeds."

"Miss Craig, I'm sorry but I really cannot allow my children to play with those boys of yours any longer. They use such dreadful language. One of them threatened to kick Robina on the *bottom*."

"She said I was a brat you'd picked out of the gutter, Aunt Penelope," explained Theodore that night, "and I didn't kick her bum. I only said I'd do it if she didn't shut up."

"Miss Craig, perhaps you don't know that your boys are gorging themselves with green apples in that old deserted orchard of the Carsons."

Penelope knew it that night for she had to be up with them till the grey dawn. She would *not* send for Roger, as Marta wished.

"I wonder what it would be like to sleep—really sleep—again," she said. Then she shuddered. Was her voice getting actually querulous?

Gone forever were the peace and quiet she

loved. The only times she ever felt at ease about the boys were when they were asleep or singing together out in the twilit orchard. They really did sound like young angels then. And *why* were people so hard on them? Marta had told her that she had heard from a friend in Glen St. Mary that the Ingleside boys had tied another boy to the stake and set him on fire. Yet everyone seemed to think the Ingleside family a model one.

I suppose they expect more of mine because I have always been known as an expert on child psychology, she thought wearily. *Of course they expect them to be perfect on that account.*

Once Lionel smiled at her—suddenly—spontaneously—a dear little smile with two teeth missing. It transfigured his whole face. Penelope found herself smiling back at him.

"It's only two weeks till school opens," she told Marta. "Things will be better then."

"Or worse," said Marta dourly. "It'll be a woman teacher. What they need is a man."

"The Blythe family have a father, but the stories one hears—"

"I've heard you say yourself it doesn't do to believe half you hear," retorted Marta. "Besides, people expect more of your boys. You've been talking for years about how to bring up children. Mrs. Blythe just minds her own business."

"Don't quote Mrs. Blythe to me again," said Penelope, with sudden passion. "I don't believe her children are a bit better than other people's children."

"I never heard her claim they were," retorted Marta. "It is Susan Baker who does the bragging."

"How is the family coming on?" bantered Dr. Galbraith on his first call after his return.

"Splendidly," said Penelope gallantly. They *were*, she told herself. It was *not* a lie. They were perfectly healthy, happy, normal boys. Roger Galbraith should *never* suspect that she lay awake at nights worrying about them and the downfall of her theories, or what a horrid feeling came over her whenever she heard the telephone ring.

"*You* aren't coming on splendidly, Penny," said Dr. Galbraith with real concern in his face and tone. "You're thin, and your eyes have a strained look."

"It is the heat," said Penelope, knowing with another shudder that she was telling a lie. "It's been a frightfully hot summer."

Well, it had. And she was very tired. She seemed to realize it all at once. And yet the last time she had seen Mrs. Blythe—Penelope seemed to be running up against her almost continually now, she had so many friends among the summer colony and cars made the distance between town and Glen St. Mary almost as nothing now. And Mrs. Blythe had five children. Penelope would never have admitted it but she was really coming to hate Mrs. Blythe—she, Penelope Craig, who had never hated anyone in her life. And yet what had Mrs. Blythe ever done to her? Nothing but have a family whom everyone praised. Penelope would never dream of admitting she was jealous—she, Penelope Craig. Besides, she had heard plenty of tales, whether true or not.

Well, she wouldn't make any dates for fall or winter lectures. Mrs. Blythe never went about the country talking. That woman again! But, anyhow, you couldn't be expected to go careering about the country telling other women how to train their children when you had two boys of your own to look after. She would be as stay-at-home and domestic as Mrs. Blythe herself.

That woman is becoming an obsession with me, thought Penelope, desperately. *I must stop thinking about her. Her children have had advantages mine have not. I wish Roger wasn't so chummy with Dr. Blythe. Of course, the man brags about his children, all men do. And Theodore and Lionel never tried to burn anybody at the stake—while Mrs. Blythe was an orphan from goodness knows where. She has simply got on my nerves because Marta is always quoting something that Susan Baker, whoever she is, has said. I don't care if the Ingleside family is perfect. Perhaps Mrs. Blythe has been at some of my lectures.*

The thought was cheering and removed from Penelope's mind the fear that she was going insane. Besides, Roger was back. There *was* a comfort in the thought, though Penelope would never have admitted it.

"Please, Aunt Penelope," said Lionel—who had begun calling her "Aunt" quite naturally after

Theodore came—"Red has jumped off the roof of the garage and he's lying on the stones. I think he's dead. He said he'd jump off if I wouldn't buy his dead rat for George. I knew George wouldn't eat a dead rat. And I wouldn't—and he did. Does a funeral cost much?"

This was probably the longest speech Lionel had ever made in his life, at least to a grown-up person.

Before it was finished, Penelope and Marta were running like mad creatures across the yard to the garage.

Theodore was lying face downwards in a horrible, huddled little heap on the cruel-looking stones.

"Every bone of him is broken," groaned Marta.

Penelope wrung her hands. "Telephone for Roger. Quick, Marta, quick."

Marta was quick. As she disappeared into the house, a lady in a flowered chiffon, with very golden hair and a very brilliant complexion and very red lips, came floating across the yard to where Penelope was standing in a trance of horror, not daring to touch Theodore.

"Miss Craig, I presume? I am Sandra Valdez. I came—is that MY CHILD?"

With a piercing shriek, the newcomer threw herself in the dust beside the limp body of the dishevelled Theodore.

Penelope seized her by the arm. "Don't touch him, don't dare to touch him—you may do him harm. The doctor will be here any moment."

"Is *this* how I find my darling?" wailed the lady of the scarlet lips, which had not paled in the least, any more than her cheeks. "My own, only little son! What have you done to him? Miss Craig, *I ask you, what have you done to him?*"

"Nothing, nothing. He did it himself."

Oh, life was too terrible! Would Roger never come? Suppose he was out on another case! There were other doctors, of course, but she did not trust them. Nobody but Roger would do.

"See if Red can wriggle his toes," said Lionel. "If he can, his back ain't broke. Ask him to wriggle his toes, Aunt Penelope."

"Oh, my son, my son, my poor little son!" moaned Miss Valdez, rocking backward and forward over her son's apparently unconscious body. "I should never have left you to the care of others, I should have taken you with me."

"What's all this?"

Dr. Galbraith had dropped in for a call while Marta was still trying frantically to locate him. It did not matter to Penelope that Dr. Blythe of Glen St. Mary was with him. They were on their way to a consultation. Nothing mattered but Theodore. Penelope almost flung herself on his breast.

"Oh, Roger! Theodore jumped from the roof. I think he's dead—and this woman—oh, can you do anything?"

"Not if he's dead of course," said Dr. Galbraith sceptically. He seemed very cool above it all.

"IS HE DEAD?" demanded Sandra Valdez

in capitals, springing up and confronting Dr.
Galbraith, like a tragedy queen.

"I don't think so," said Dr. Galbraith, still coolly. Dr. Blythe seemed trying to hide a smile.

Dr. Galbraith stooped and tried Theodore's
pulse. His lips tightened ominously, and he
turned him callously over.

Theodore's blue eyes opened.

"My son!" breathed Miss Valdez. "Oh, tell me
you are living! Just tell me that."

Then she gave a shriek as the doctor unhere-
moniously grasped Theodore's shoulder and
pulled him to his feet.

"You brute! Oh, you brute! Miss Craig, please
tell me what you mean by calling such a
man? Surely there are doctors in Charlottetown
capable—"

"Dr. Galbraith is one of the best doctors on the
Island," said Marta indignantly.

"What does this mean?" said Dr. Galbraith, in a
tone which Theodore understood. Dr. Blythe was
actually laughing.

"I just wanted to scare them all," said Theodore
with unaccustomed meekness. "I—I didn't jump
from the roof. I just told Bumps I would, to scare
him. And when his back was turned, I just run
round here and yelled and flopped. That's all,
honest."

Dr. Galbraith turned to Penelope. "I am going
to teach this young man a lesson he won't forget
in a hurry. And you are going to marry me inside
of three weeks. I'm not asking you. I'm telling

you. And no interference! It's time somebody did something. Child psychology is all very well, but you've lost fifteen pounds since I've been away—and I'm at the end of my patience."

"Congratulations," said that abominable Dr. Blythe.

"Don't you dast touch Red," yelled Lionel. "This ain't any of your business. Aunt Penelope is bringing us up. If you do, I'll bite you. I'll—"

Dr. Blythe took Lionel by the scruff of the neck and set him on the gate-post. "That will be enough out of you, my lad. You stay there until Dr. Galbraith says you can come down."

A few minutes later certain sounds from the interior of the barn indicated that Theodore was not so indifferent to Dr. Galbraith's punishment as he had been to Marta's.

"He's killing him," gasped Sandra Valdez with another shriek.

"Oh, his life is safe enough," said Dr. Blythe, still laughing.

But it was Penelope who stepped in front of Sandra Valdez. Penelope, of all people. "Don't you interfere. Theodore has a spanking coming to him. Dr. Blythe, you have a right to laugh."

"I wasn't laughing at you, Miss Craig," said Dr. Blythe apologetically. "I was laughing at the trick Theodore had played. I knew the moment we drove in at the gate it was only a trick. So did Galbraith."

"After this is over, you may have him, Miss

Valdez," said Penelope. "Bumps is enough for me."

Miss Valdez was suddenly meek—and natural. "I—I don't want him. I can't be bothered with a child in my career. You must realize that, Miss Craig. I only wanted to be sure he had a good home and was well treated."

"He has—he is—"

"And had a mother, a loving mother."

"He will. And," added Penelope, "a father, too. Laugh away, Dr. Blythe. I suppose your own children are so perfect."

"They are very far from being perfect," said Dr. Blythe, who had stopped laughing. "In fact, they—the boys at least—are very much like Lionel and Theodore in many ways. But they have three people to correct them. So we keep them in fair order. When a spanking is indicated, we wait till Susan Baker is out of the house. And—will you let me say it? I am very glad you have made up your mind to marry Dr. Galbraith at last."

"Who told you I had?" blushed Penelope.

"I heard what he said. And I knew it when you forbad Miss Valdez to interfere. We doctors are wise old fellows. And I am not running down your studies in child psychology, Miss Craig. There is a wonderful lot of wisdom in them. Mrs. Blythe has a bookcase full of volumes about it. But every once in so long—"

"Something else is required," admitted Penelope. "I've been a perfect idiot, Dr. Blythe. I hope you and Mrs. Blythe will come to Willow Run the next time you are in town. I—I should like to become better acquainted with her."

"I can't answer for myself, I generally come in on professional business only. But I'm sure Mrs. Blythe will be delighted. She was charmed with you the day she met you at Mrs. Elston's party."

"Really?" said Penelope, wondering why she should feel so highly gratified. "I'm sure we have many things in common."

The sounds in the garage had ceased.

"Will Dr. Galbraith whip us often?" inquired Lionel, curiously.

"I am sure he will not," said Dr. Blythe. "For one thing, you will not require it. For another, I am sure your Aunt Penelope would not allow it."

"As if she could stop him when he had made up his mind," said Lionel. "I'll bet Mrs. Blythe couldn't stop you."

"Oh, couldn't she! You don't know as much about matrimony now as you will some day, my lad. But I recommend it, for all that. And I'm sure you'll like Dr. Galbraith for an uncle."

"I've always liked him—and I think Aunt Penelope should have married him long ago," said Lionel.

"How did you know he wanted to marry me?" cried Penelope.

"Red told me. 'Sides, everyone knows it. I like a man round. He'll keep Marta in her place."

"Oh, you mustn't talk of your Aunt Marta like that, Lionel."

"I'll bet he won't call me Lionel."

"Why don't you like Lionel?" inquired Penelope curiously.

"It's such a sissy name," said Lionel.

"It was the name your dear mother chose for you," said Penelope reproachfully. "Of course, she may have been a wee bit romantic—"

"Don't you dast say a word against my mother," said Lionel.

Penelope could never have told why, but this pleased her. And Red and Dr. Galbraith were looking as if they were quite good friends. After all, the thrashing had not likely been a very severe one. Roger was not that kind of a man. And even Mrs. Blythe studied books on child culture. The world was not such a bad place after all. And Red and Bumps were not worse than other boys after all. She would wager they were just about as good as the Ingleside boys—only the latter had had the advantages of a father. Well, Red and Bumps. . . .

The
Reconciliation

Miss Shelley was going over to Lowbridge to forgive Lisle Stephens for stealing Ronald Evans from her thirty years ago.

She had had a hard struggle to bring herself to do it. Night after night she had wrestled with herself. She looked so pale and wan that her niece secretly consulted Dr. Blythe about her and got the tonic he recommended.

But Miss Shelley would not take the tonic. The struggle continued. Yet morning after morning she confessed herself defeated. And she knew quite well that she could not look the Reverend Mr. Meredith in the face until she had won the battle.

"We must forgive. We must not cherish old

bitternesses and grievances and wrongs," he had said, looking like an inspired prophet.

The Presbyterians of Glen St. Mary worshipped him, especially Miss Shelley. He was a widower and had a family but she would not let herself remember that. Neither did she think any the more highly of Mrs. Dr. Blythe after hearing her say to her husband as they came down the church steps, "I suppose I'll have to forgive Josie Pye after that sermon."

Miss Shelley had no idea who Josie Pye was or what had been the nature of the quarrel between her and Mrs. Blythe. But it could never have been as bitter as the one between her and Lisle Stephens.

Miss Shelley could not conceive of Mrs. Blythe cherishing bitterness for thirty years. She liked her but she thought her too shallow for that. She had been heard to say that it was a pity Dr. Blythe had not selected a woman of deeper nature for his wife.

Miss Shelley's neighbours had said that she thought he ought to have waited for her niece. But Miss Shelley did not know that and in due time she came to like Mrs. Blythe very well.

And at last she had brought herself to forgive Lisle and not only to forgive her but to go and tell her she forgave her.

She felt indescribably uplifted over her victory. If only Mr. Meredith might know of it! But there was no chance of that. She could never tell him and she was very sure Lisle would not. She drew her shabby fur coat around her withered throat and looked at all travellers who passed her with condescending pity. It was not likely one of them knew the triumph of thus conquering their baser selves.

Lisle Stephens and she had been friends all through childhood and girlhood. Lisle had no end of beaux, but she, Myrtle Shelley, a little, thin, red-haired girl with large blue eyes, never had any until Ronald Evans came. Lisle had been away then on a visit to her aunt in Toronto. It was apparently love at first sight with them both. Ronald was handsome, slim-waisted and lean-hipped, with sleek, dark hair and dark, heavy-lidded eyes. There had never been anyone just like him in Glen St. Mary. Then came the barn dance.

Grey Myrtle Shelley recalled that dance as of yesterday. She had looked forward to it so eagerly. It would be the first time she had danced with Ronald. They would go home together beneath the moon which seemed waiting for the miracle. Perhaps he would kiss her. She knew the Glen St. Mary girls were often kissed by the boys—she had even heard some of them boast of it—but she, Myrtle Shelley, had never been kissed.

She remembered the gown she had worn to the dance. Her mother thought it very frivolous. It was of pale green nun's veiling with a red belt. She thought it became her. Ronald had once

told her her skin was like a flower. That had
been vanity, but it was pleasant to hear. She
had not had a great many compliments in her
life.

When she reached the barn, the first thing she
had seen was Ronald dancing with Lisle, who
had returned home that day. Ronald waved his
hand to Myrtle but he did not ask her to dance.
He danced with Lisle most of the evening and
when they weren't dancing, they were sitting out
in one of the buggies behind the barn.

He ate supper with her and after supper they
disappeared. He never even looked at Myrtle
with his handsome careless eyes.

She came face to face with them later under
the gay Chinese lanterns strung outside the barn.
Lisle was flushed and excited. Her thick wheat-
hued hair was tied close to her head with a fillet of
blue ribbon. Her tilted, golden-brown eyes were
shining. What chance had anyone against eyes
like that?

"Hello, darling," she said to Myrtle, breezily.
"I just got home today. What have you been doing
with yourself while I was away? Busy as a bee as
usual, I suppose, you industrious little creature.
Mr. Evans, have you met my friend, Miss Shelley?
We've always been great chums."

Myrtle had lifted her hand and slapped Lisle
across her smiling face.

"What on earth do you mean, Myrtle Shelley?"
Lisle had exclaimed indignantly. To do Lisle jus-

tice, she had not the faintest idea why she had been slapped. She had never heard that Ronald Evans was "beauing" Myrtle Shelley—though it might not have made much difference if she had!

Myrtle said nothing; had simply turned her back and gone home.

"Well, of all the jealous creatures!" Lisle had exclaimed when Ronald had made some lame explanation.

Lisle had flaunted Ronald for several weeks after that, then dropped him before he went away. She said he had nothing in either his head or his pocket. She tried to make up with Myrtle but was icily repulsed.

The next spring Lisle had married Justin Rogers, a Lowbridge merchant, who had been "after her" for years, and she had gone to Lowbridge to live. Myrtle Shelley had never seen her since, though she had heard ten years ago of Justin Rogers' death.

It was quite a distance from the Glen to Lowbridge, and Miss Shelley refused all offers of a "lift." Her feet ached and the nipping wind brought tears into her faded blue eyes. She also knew that the tip of her nose was red. But she kept on resolutely.

Lisle's house was a trim, well-groomed one. It was said Justin Rogers had left his widow well provided for. The bay window was full of very fine geraniums and begonias. Miss Shelley had never had any luck with begonias, though Susan

Baker had given her slips from the finest plants at Ingleside.

Lisle came to the door. Miss Shelley knew her at once. The same sleek curves, the same tilted eyes, the same golden hair, with hardly a thread of gray in it.

Just as flippant as ever, thought Myrtle virtuously. *Lipstick! And her fifty!*

But she noted that Lisle was beginning to have pouches under her eyes. There was some satisfaction in that—until she remembered Mr. Meredith.

"I . . . I feel that I *should* know that face," said Lisle. Her voice had not changed. It was still smooth and creamy.

"I am Myrtle Shelley."

"Myrtle, darling! Why, I'd never have known you! How many years is it since I've seen you? Of course I hardly ever leave home but I *am* glad to see you again. We used to be such chums, didn't we? Come right in. You don't mean to tell me you've walked all the way here from the Glen! You poor lamb! Aren't you just dead? Surely somebody might have given you a lift. I always say people are getting more selfish all the time."

"I didn't want a lift," said Myrtle.

"You were always so independent—and a good walker too. Do you remember the long walks we used to take together around the harbour?"

"Yes, I remember them," said Myrtle. "And I remember another walk I took—alone."

"Oh, take *this* chair," said Lisle, wondering what on earth Myrtle meant, "you'll find it heaps more comfortable. Why, you are shivering. A good cup of tea will warm you up in a trice. Do you remember how we used to laugh at the old ladies with their cups of tea? Fifty seemed to us very vulnerable then, didn't it?"

"I didn't come for a cup of tea," said Myrtle.

"Of course not. But we'll have one all the same. It won't be a mite of trouble. And we'll have a gabfest over old times. Nothing better than a good gossip over a cup of tea, I always say, is there, darling? We just have a million things to talk over. Didn't we have some silly old quarrel years ago? What *did* we fight about, anyhow?"

Miss Shelley had not intended to sit down in Lisle Rogers' house but she accepted the offered chair because she felt a little queer.

"You . . . you took Ronald Evans away from me at the Clark barn dance," she said stonily.

Lisle Rogers stared for a moment. Then her plump shoulders shook.

"Who on earth was Ronald Evans? I seem to remember the name. Was *that* what we squabbled over? Weren't we a pair of idiots? I *was* a terror to the boys in those days. I had only to *look* at them. It was my eyes. Folks used to say there was something about them—sort of come-hither really. Even yet, there are some old widowers and bachelors—but I've had enough of the men. They are all alike, blaming every mistake they make on the women. I don't know but you were wise never to marry. I remember Ronald now. Whatever became of him? He was a perfect clown to dance with, in spite of his good looks. Stepped all over my toes. I could never wear those slippers again. But he could pay compliments. It all comes back to me, though I haven't thought of him for years. Aren't men funny? Put your feet up on this hot fender."

"Do you remember that I slapped your face?" persisted Miss Shelley.

Lisle Rogers burst out laughing as she measured the tea into the teapot.

"Did you really? Yes, I believe you did. I'd forgotten about that part of it. Well, never mind sitting on the mourner's bench now about it, honey. Forgive and forget has always been my motto. Now we'll have a real nice visit together and never think of all our old foolishness. We were only children anyhow. People *do* quarrel over such simple things, don't they?"

To be forgiven when you came to forgive!

Myrtle Shelley stood up. Her face had turned a dull crimson. Her faded blue eyes flashed fire. Deliberately she slapped Lisle Rogers across her smiling face—a hard, no-nonsense-about-it, tingling slap.

"You didn't remember that first slap," she said. "Perhaps you will remember this one."

Miss Shelley walked back to Glen St. Mary, minding neither cold wind nor fallen arches, after that satisfying slap. She did not even care what the Reverend Mr. Meredith might think about it. She had seldom done anything that gave her such a sense of not having lived in vain. Yes, Lisle would remember *that* slap.

The
Cheated Child

Uncle Stephen Brewster's funeral was over—the house part at least. Everybody had gone to the cemetery, or home—everybody except Patrick, who wanted to be called Pat and never got anything but Patrick, save from Walter Blythe out at Glen St. Mary. And he seldom saw Walter. Uncle Stephen did not like the Blythes. He said he did not like educated women; it spoiled them for their duties in life. So it was only the Brewster boys who ever called Patrick Pat. And they mostly called him Patty and laughed at him because they knew he hated it.

But he was glad they had not taken him to the cemetery. Graveyards always frightened him, though he could not tell why. The father he did not remember at all and the mother he remem-

bered so dimly had been swallowed up in a graveyard.

But all at once the loneliness of the big house
overwhelmed him. Loneliness is a terrible thing
for anyone and most of all when you are only eight
and nobody likes you. Patrick knew quite well
that nobody liked him. Nobody ever had liked
him—unless it was Walter Blythe, with whom he
had felt a strange kinship the few times they had
met. Walter was like himself: quiet and dreamy
and sensitive, and did not seem to mind owning
up that he was afraid of some things.

Patrick thought that he, himself, was afraid of
everything. Perhaps that was why Uncle Stephen
had never liked him. Uncle Stephen liked boys
to be robust and aggressive—real "he boys"—or
said he did. As a matter of fact, he did not like
any kind of a boy. Patrick knew he did not know
very much, but he knew *that*, though people were
always telling him how good his uncle was to him
and how grateful he ought to be to him.

The maids, in their stiff, starched uniforms,
were busy restoring the rooms to order, and talking in low voices of how young Master Patrick
seemed to feel the death of his uncle. Patrick went
into the library, where he could escape hearing
them and the sense of guilt they gave him—
because he knew quite well that what they were
saying was not true and his uncle's death did not
really matter much to him. It ought to have. He
felt that, but there was no use in pretending to
oneself.

The house had never liked him either. In his few brief visits to Ingleside (there was some distant relationship between Dr. Blythe's mother and Uncle Stephen or they would not have been permitted, he felt quite sure) he had felt, without any telling, that the house loved all the people in it. "Because *we* love it," Walter had explained to him. But Oaklands was always watching him— resenting him. Perhaps it was because it was so big and splendid it had no use at all for a little boy who felt lost and insignificant in its magnificence, who did not do it no credit. Perhaps it liked people to be afraid of it, just as Uncle Stephen had liked people to be afraid of him. Patrick knew *that*, too, though he could never have told how he knew it. Walter Blythe even could not explain it. Walter owned up to being afraid of many things but he could not understand being afraid of your own relations. But then Walter's relations were very different. Patrick would never have been afraid of Dr. or Mrs. Blythe either.

It was very strange to think of Uncle Stephen being dead. In fact, it was impossible. Patrick could see him plainly still, as plainly as when he was alive, sitting over there in his high-backed chair, wearing his heavy brocaded dressing gown, and looking as if he had never been young.

He did not look old, although he had been silver-haired as long as Patrick could remember. He had some heart ailment and Dr. Galbraith came often to see him. Sometimes Dr. Blythe came in from Glen St. Mary for a consultation.

Patrick always had a queer feeling of shame on these occasions, much as he liked Dr. Blythe. Uncle Stephen was always so rude to him. But Dr. Blythe never seemed to mind. He could sometimes hear him and Dr. Galbraith laughing as they drove away from the house, as if at some exquisite joke. He loved Dr. Blythe and Mrs. Blythe but he was very careful never to let Uncle Stephen suspect it. He had a secret feeling that if he did he would never be allowed to go to Glen St. Mary again.

Uncle Stephen was usually very sarcastic and remote. But he could be affable and amusing when he liked to be. At least other people thought him amusing. Patrick didn't. He remembered that he had never heard his uncle laugh. Why? Ingleside rang with laughter. Even old Susan Baker laughed upon occasion. He wondered what it would be like to live with a person who laughed sometimes.

He wondered, too, what would become of him, now that Uncle Stephen was dead. Would he just go on living in this unfriendly house, with Miss Sperry giving him lessons and glaring at him through her glasses when he made a spelling mistake? The prospect filled him with horror. If he could only escape—get away anywhere—hop on that bus which had just gone tearing past the big gates.

Patrick had always longed to ride on a bus. The Ingleside children often did. He never could, of course. When Patrick went out he went in the big car driven by Henry. He didn't like the big car and he knew Henry thought him a dumb kid. He had heard him tell the housekeeper so.

If he could only have one single ride on a bus! Or, as he and Walter Blythe had planned, fly across the country on a black courser—Walter's choice was a white one and his mother didn't laugh when he told her. Taking fences and everything as a matter of course! That would be glorious. He did that in his other world. But just now that other world seemed too far away. He could not get into it.

As long as Patrick could remember he had lived at Oaklands with Uncle Stephen. At first, like a dim dream, there had been a mother, and, like a dimmer dream still, the memory of being with that mother in a lovely place—a place something like Ingleside—in a house that smiled at you on a hill; in a garden where the walks were bordered with crimson geraniums and big white shells. And far down, over long, still fields, sand dunes lying in a strange, golden magic of sunshine, with white gulls soaring over them. There was a flock of white ducks in the yard and somebody gave him a slice of bread with honey on it. He had, he remembered, felt so near his other world then— so near that a step would have taken him into it forever. And somebody like Dr. Blythe, only younger, carried him about on his shoulder and called him Pat.

Mother was nowhere soon after that. Some people told him she had gone to heaven but

Patrick believed she had just stepped into his other world. Uncle Stephen had told him she was dead—Patrick did not know what that meant—and had said he didn't like squalling brats. So Patrick had not cried much except when he was in bed at night.

He did not cry now. In fact, he felt no inclination to cry which perhaps was why the housekeeper said he was the most unfeeling child she had ever known. But he wished he had a dog. Uncle Stephen had hated dogs and he knew Miss Sperry would never let him have one. She said dogs were unsanitary. Yet they had dogs at Ingleside and Dr. Blythe was a doctor.

There were dogs in his other world, and slim little deer racing through vast forests; horses with shining skins and dainty hoofs; squirrels so tame they fed from your hands; and lions splendidly maned. And all the animals were very friendly.

And there was a little girl in a scarlet dress! Not one of the Ingleside girls, much as he liked them. He had never even told Walter about *her*. But she was always there, ready to play with him and talk with him, and ready to stick her tongue out so saucily at him, like little Rilla out at Ingleside, only she wasn't really a bit like Rilla.

What would Miss Sperry say if she knew about her? Likely, in a voice as cold as rain, "Control your imagination, Patrick. It is this world with which we are concerned at present. Your answer to this multiplication sum is WRONG."

Just like that, in capitals. Just as Susan Baker

would have spoken if she had been a teacher and a pupil had brought her a sum with a wrong answer. Only Susan was not a teacher and he rather liked her except when she scolded Walter for writing poetry.

When they came back from the cemetery they all came into the library to hear Uncle Stephen's will read. Lawyer Atkins had asked them all to be present. Not that any of them had much interest in it. The money would go to Patrick, Stephen had told them so often enough. It had come from his mother, not from theirs. He was only their half-brother, while Patrick's father was his full brother. Still, there was the matter of a guardian. There would have to be one. Likely Lawyer Atkins, but you could never tell, with an eccentric creature like Stephen.

Patrick watched them filing in. They had all been pretending to cry. Aune Melanie Hall, Uncle John Brewster and Aunt Elizabeth Brewster, Uncle Frederick Brewster and Aunt Fanny Brewster, Aunt Lilian Brewster and her cousin who lived with her, Miss Cynthia Adams. He was afraid of every one of them. They were always finding fault with him. As his eye caught Aunt Lilian's he nervously unwrapped his legs from the chair rungs.

Her very look said, "Sit properly at once."

Strange. When he was at Ingleside, Susan Baker was always scolding the children for that very thing. And he never minded her but tried to obey her.

Lawyer Atkins followed them with a paper in his hand. The tortoise shell-rimmed glasses on his big handsome face made Patrick think of an owl, an owl that had pounced on a poor trembling mouse, which did Lawyer Atkins a great injustice. He was an honest man who had had a hard time of it with his client, Stephen Brewster, and did not approve of the will at all.

It was short and to the point. Even Patrick understood it.

Oaklands was to be sold. He was glad of that. At least, he would not have to live *there*. Lawyer Atkins was appointed his legal guardian, but Patrick was to live with an uncle or aunt until he was twenty-one when a sum of money so enormous that it had no meaning for Patrick was to be his. Only he felt sure it would be enough to buy a place like Ingleside. He was to choose for himself the relative with whom he preferred to live. Having made his choice, there could be no change, unless the chosen one died. But in order that he might know what he was doing, he was first to live with each uncle and aunt for three months. When he had done this he was to make his permanent choice. The sum of two thousand a year was to be paid to the temporary guardian until Patrick was twenty-one, as compensation for his board, lodging and care generally.

Patrick desperately wrapped his legs around the chair rungs again. Aunt Lilian might look her eyes out, he thought, but he had to do something to steady his body.

He didn't want to live with any of them. If he could only go to Glen St. Mary now, and live at Ingleside! The very thought seemed like heaven. But, alas, the Ingleside people were not related to him, except so distantly it didn't count.

And he didn't want to live with any who were. He hated the very thought—hated it bitterly, as he knew Uncle Stephen had known very well.

Aunt Melanie Hall was a widow. She was big, capable and patronizing. She patronized everybody. He had heard Dr. Blythe say once she would patronize God.

Uncle John Brewster always thumped him on the back and Aunt Elizabeth Brewster had such an extraordinarily long face: long forehead, long nose, long upper lip and long chin. Patrick could never bear to look at her.

Live with that face for years and years! He just couldn't.

Uncle Frederick Brewster was a thin, beaten little man of no importance. But Aunt Fanny was every inch an aunt. He had heard Uncle Stephen say she wore the breeches. Patrick didn't know what it meant, but he did know he didn't want to live with Aunt Fanny.

Aunt Lilian was not married and neither was Cynthia Adams. They pretended not to care but Patrick knew somehow that they *did* care. Uncle Stephen would never see Aunt Lilian and Cynthia Adams at the same time. "I can stand only one old maid at once," he used to say.

"Wouldn't you know Stephen would make a

crazy will like that!" Aunt Fanny was saying in a disgusted tone. "I see Dr. Blythe is one of the witnesses. I shouldn't wonder a mite if he put him up to it."

She was thinking, *I should have him. He should live with other children. He always seemed so different for a while after he came back from one of those Ingleside visits. I never cared for either Dr. Blythe or his wife—but they have a family—and Patrick never seemed so odd for a while. But I suppose he won't choose me. I've always felt he never liked me. I suppose Stephen poisoned his mind against me. Still, there's three months . . . It might be possible to win his affection if we were all very nice to him. That two thousand—it would take care of our boy's education— otherwise, I don't see how we can ever manage it. And Frederick and I could have a holiday. I wish I'd made more of him, but he's always been such a strange shy child, more like that little Walter Blythe at Ingleside than any of his own kin. And I know I'll have trouble with the boys, they do love to tease. I don't seem to have any influence over them. Ah, children are not what they were in my young days. They listened to their parents then.*

It would provide for Amy's wedding, Aunt Elizabeth was thinking. *He'll never be happy with those awful boys of Fanny's. They are really young demons. And the very idea of an old maid like Lilian having him is laughable. That chinchilla cape—Melanie couldn't put on any more airs about her moleskin coat. I saw the most marvellous lace tablecloth at Moore and Stebbins. Of course, I know*

*Patrick doesn't like me—Stephen knew it, too, but in
three months—*

He should come to me, thought Aunt Lilian.
*Stephen knew that perfectly well. I need the money
more than any of them. I'm tired of scrimping and
pinching and if I had money perhaps George Imlay
. . . Of course, it's rather dreadful to think of having
a boy in the house, especially when he begins to grow
up. And he's frightened of me. He's never tried to hide
that—but in three months—only Cynthia is so very
uncertain. She may pretend to like him, but he'll be
sure to see through her. I don't see how anyone can
really like children anyhow. They may pretend to—
that Mrs. Dr. Blythe makes me sick . . .*

"Well, we'll all start from scratch," said Uncle
John with his great hearty guffaw that always
startled Patrick. It was not a laugh, just a guffaw. He thumped Patrick's thin little back with
his large, fat hand.

Patrick didn't like fat hands.

"Which one of us are you going to pick for first
go, my boy?"

Patrick wasn't doing any picking. He looked
from one to the other of them with the gaze of
a trapped animal in his big grey eyes under their
level brows. Aunt Lilian wondered if he were
really half-witted. Some people said that Walter
Blythe was, but there was no relationship, except
distantly, and she remembered the time she had
hinted such a thing to Susan Baker.

"What's to be done?" asked Uncle Frederick
feebly.

"We'd better draw lots," said Aunt Melanie briskly. "That will be the fairest way—in fact the only way—if anything about this whole business is fair. Lawyer Atkins, I am surprised you didn't advise Stephen—"

"Mr. Brewster was not a man who was fond of taking advice," said Lawyer Atkins drily. They all knew that as well as he did.

"I'm sure somebody put the idea into his head. Dr. Blythe—"

"Dr. Blythe happened to call that day and I asked him to be a witness. That is all *he* had to do with it."

"Well, luckily we all live close together, so there'll be no trouble about changing his school every three months."

So he would be going to school! Patrick rather liked this idea. Anything would be better than Miss Sperry. And the Ingleside boys went to school and thought it lots of fun. At least, he knew Jem did. He was not quite so sure about Walter.

"Poor lamb!" said Aunt Lilian sentimentally.

That finished Patrick. He got himself out of the room. Let them draw their lots! He didn't care who got him, first or last or in between.

And yet a sudden memory came to him of the time he had cut his finger at Ingleside and Susan Baker had said, "Poor lamb!"

He had liked it. Oh, things were very puzzling in this queer world.

"A problem child decidedly," said Aunt Elizabeth. "But it is our duty . . ."

"Oh no, *I* wouldn't call him a problem child," said Aunt Fanny who made it a rule never to agree with Elizabeth. "A little odd, unchildlike, you might say. Is it any wonder, living with Stephen? And his mother—no family, no background, and his father made his money in a mine out west. But Patrick would soon become quite normal if he lived with other children, and get over that nonsense of his about the other world."

"What other world? I'm sure Stephen—"

"Oh, *I* don't know. Just one of his silly fancies. Miss Sperry found out about it somehow. She's a gimlet, that woman. *I* think she overheard Patrick and Walter Blythe talking about it. I never did approve of Stephen's intimacy with that family. But he would never listen to me, of course. Miss Sperry was worried about it. I told her not to mind, he would outgrow it. So few people understand the child mind. You'd think to hear Mrs. Dr. Galbraith—"

"Oh, we all know she is a little off when it comes to bringing up children—though I will say that since her marriage . . ."

"Come, come, we're not getting anywhere," boomed Uncle John.

"That was just what Stephen wanted," said Aunt Fanny. "He thought he'd set us all fighting. *I* know his mind. Well, since we have to go through this absurd performance . . ."

"How else could we settle it?" asked Aunt Lilian.

"I am not going to quarrel with you, Lilian. We

are each to have him three months, so much is perfectly clear. After that, it is up to him to make his choice. He will have to make it, whether he likes it or not. There will be no drawing of lots then."

Patrick fell to Aunt Elizabeth for September, October and November. He was called in and came reluctantly, and Aunt Elizabeth kissed him when she told him the result. He didn't like her kiss because he didn't like her. Yet he had always liked Mrs. Blythe's kisses.

When he was taken to Aunt Elizabeth's house— leaving Oaklands with no sense of regret what- ever—his cousin Amy kissed him, too. Amy was a very grown-up young lady, with blood-red finger nails. He remembered how Dr. Blythe laughed at painted finger nails. He did not see much of Amy nor of his cousin Oscar either, who never said anything to him except "Hello, kid!" when they happened to meet and always seemed sulky about something.

Neither, to his relief, did he see a great deal of Aunt Elizabeth. She was always so busy, arrang- ing club bridges, giving and attending all sorts of social functions. Mealtimes were almost the only times he saw her, when her long face spoiled what little appetite he had and her never forgotten kiss took away the rest. If she only wouldn't kiss him!

But they were all exceedingly kind to him. He felt that they worked very hard being kind to him. Every wish would have been gratified if he had ever expressed any wishes. He did only once.

On a Saturday afternoon in October, he timidly asked Aunt Elizabeth if he might go for a ride on the bus. Just a short weeny teeny ride.

Aunt Elizabeth was so horrified that her long face grew longer than ever—something which Patrick had not believed possible.

"Darling, you wouldn't like it at all. Any time you want a drive, Amy or Oscar or I will take you in the car anywhere you want to go—any-where."

But it appeared that Patrick didn't want to go anywhere, unless it was to Glen St. Mary and he knew very well he would not be allowed to go there. Aunt Elizabeth did not like the Blythes.

Patrick never spoke about the bus again. They showered gifts on him, very few of which he wanted. Uncle John boomed at him and thumped him and gave him candy every day. Uncle John really thought this must be a pleasant change for a boy after living for years with that sardonic nut, Stephen. *He*, John Brewster, knew how to handle boys. He didn't know that Patrick didn't care much for candy and gave most of it away to the laundress for her children.

Uncle John drove him to school in the mornings, joking him about something all the way. Most of the jokes Patrick couldn't understand at all. Amy or Aunt Elizabeth called for him at night. He did not make many friends at school. Aunt Fanny's boys went to the same school and they told everybody he was a sissy. The other boys took to calling him Missy. But he preferred the school to Miss Sperry.

At home—that is, in Aunt Elizabeth's house—he spent much of his time curled up on a window seat on the stair landing. Through a gap in the houses he could see a distant hill with violet-grey woods about it.

There was a house on it, a house that seemed lifted above everything. Patrick often wondered who lived there. He knew it could not be the Ingleside people; he knew Glen St. Mary must be much further away than that. But there was something about it that vaguely reminded him of Ingleside, he could not tell just what.

When late November came and the cold kiss of the snowflakes was on the window, he looked across the wintry roofs in the early dusk to that house, from which a star now shone through the wild, white weather and thought that perhaps it was in his other world.

Perhaps the little girl in the scarlet dress lived there. As long as he could see the light shining to him across the far distance he did not feel so lonely and unwanted.

Because none of them really wanted him. It was only the money they wanted. Patrick could not have told you how he knew that, but know it he did.

"I'm afraid I'll never be able to understand him," sighed Aunt Elizabeth to Uncle John—who was quite sure he understood Patrick perfectly and who had never had the least doubt that they would be the chosen ones in the end.

"We've done *everything* but we can't thaw him."

"Oh, well, some boys are like that—naturally quiet."

"But he just seems to draw into a shell."

"I told you you shouldn't have let him go on that visit to Glen St. Mary," said Uncle John, who had never said a word against it but now felt he must lay the blame on his wife. Ah, well, hers was a hard lot, but there was nothing to do but bear it. Men were like that.

"Amy says he makes her nervous."

"It doesn't take much to do that," said Uncle John. "Now if she were like Mrs. Dr. Blythe—"

"I don't want to hear anything about Mrs. Blythe," said Aunt Elizabeth haughtily. "I have long been aware that she is the only perfect woman in the world in your eyes."

"Now, Elizabeth—"

"I am not going to quarrel with you. I simply refuse to quarrel; I thought we were talking about Patrick."

"Well, what about Patrick? He seems quite happy and contented, I'm sure. You women are always making mountains out of molehills. You'll see he'll pick us in the end."

"His eyes aren't normal. Even you, John Brewster, must see that."

"I've never noticed anything wrong with his eyes. Why don't you take him to an oculist?"

"They seem to be looking through you, looking for something he can't find," said Aunt Elizabeth, with a rare flash of insight. "Do you really suppose he'll choose us when the time comes, John?"

"Not a doubt of it. Those boys of Fanny's will torment him to death. Melanie and Lilian have no earthly idea how to handle a boy. Don't worry. He'll be mighty glad to come back to us for keeps when the time comes, or I miss my guess."

Aunt Elizabeth was by no means so sure. She wished she dared ask Patrick to promise to come back to them. But somehow she dared not. There was *something* about the child. John might be as sure as he liked, but he really knew nothing about children. Why, she had had all the care of Amy and Oscar when they were little.

"Darling, if you find your cousins at Aunt Fanny's a little trying, you can always come over here for a bit of peace and quiet," was as far as she dared go.

"Oh, I don't think I'll mind them," was all that Patrick said.

They would have to be pretty bad, he thought, to drive him back to Aunt Elizabeth's. If he could only go to Glen St. Mary for a visit first!

But everybody vetoed that, although Mrs. Blythe had sent a most cordial invitation. Patrick often wondered why, but he never dared ask any questions about it.

Aunt Fanny's boys *were* pretty bad. They teased the life out of him—on the sly, when Aunt Fanny and Uncle Frederick were not about. Yet they pretended to be very polite to him, "because you have to be polite to girls," said Joe.

When Bill broke Aunt Fanny's Chinese tea-cup—the five-clawed one that had been part of the loot of the Summer Palace, so she claimed—Bill coolly told his mother that Patrick had broken it. Patrick got off with a very mild rebuke, whereas if Aunt Fanny had known the truth some terrible punishment would have been meted out to Bill.

"We're always going to blame things on you because you won't be punished," Joe said. "Mother wants to make sure of you choosing us for keeps when the time comes. Don't do it. She's got the temper of the devil."

Patrick could do anything and there would never be a word of scolding. How they hated him for that! And they would never have believed that Patrick hated it too. He knew if he had done all those things, he should be scolded for them. And he knew Joe and Bill resented his immunity even when they took advantage of it.

He couldn't see the house on the hill from any window in Aunt Fanny's house and he missed it. But at least Aunt Fanny didn't kiss him and he rather liked Uncle Frederick. Though Uncle Frederick didn't count for much in Aunt Fanny's house. It was a very well-run house, so people said. So well-run that it was depressing. A book out of place, a rug crooked, a sweater left lying around, were unforgiveable crimes in anyone except Patrick. Patrick was not very tidy, and

Aunt Fanny had to put great restraint on herself. She never dreamed that Patrick saw through it, but when the time came for him to go to Aunt Lilian's, Aunt Fanny felt anything but sure that he would ever come back.

"He has had a real home here," she told Uncle Frederick, "and I don't believe he appreciates it at all. Such care as I have taken with his balanced meals! Dear knows what Lilian will give him to eat! She knows nothing whatever about bringing up children."

"He is a cheated child," said Uncle Frederick. "He has been cheated all his life."

Aunt Fanny paid no attention to him. Cheated? What absurdity! The trouble was Patrick had been too much indulged all his life. Every wish fulfilled. She wished she could do for her boys what had been done for Patrick.

March and April and May were Aunt Lilian's. Aunt Lilian "my-lambed" him and fussed over his clothes until Patrick thought he would go crazy. He had to go to bed at night up a gloomy stair and along a gloomy hall. There never was any light in the hall. Aunt Lilian nearly had a fit if anyone left an unnecessary bulb burning. She said she had to keep down her bills, she was not rich as his Uncle Stephen had been, and she held that the light in the lower hall lighted the upper one quite sufficiently. Patrick was always forgetting to turn the lights off.

As for Miss Adams, she generally looked at him as if he were some kind of obnoxious black beetle and her skinny Persian cat would have nothing to do with him. Patrick tried to make friends with it because he was so hungry for any kind of a pet, but it was no use. Miss Adams had no particular motive for winning his affections. She knew quite well she would be no better off if Lilian did get him finally and she hated children.

Patrick had not been especially fond of either Uncle John or Uncle Frederick, but this manless house was very terrible. Yet why need it have been? He thought he would not have been unhappy living alone with Susan Baker.

It was a bit better at Aunt Melanie's, patronizing and all as she was. For one thing, she neither kissed him nor "my-lambed" him. For another, she had a dog, a coach dog who did nice doggish things, like the dogs at Ingleside, such as rolling over in the pansy bed and bringing bones into the house. His black spots were adorable. His name was Spunk and he seemed really to like Patrick.

If Aunt Melanie had not been so constantly praising him and quoting him, Patrick would have been almost contented. But he grew afraid to open his mouth because she would admiringly tell what he had said to the next caller.

And she had insisted on his sleeping in the large, airy front bedroom, when he had wanted to sleep in the little back room at the end of the hall. He slipped into it whenever he could because he could see the house on the hill from it. There it was, far away across valleys full of the palest purple shadows. Sometimes summer fogs

came up into the valleys but they never reached
as high as the house on the hill. It was always
serenely above them, living a secret, remote life
of its own. At least, that was his fancy.

Patrick was less unhappy at Aunt Melanie's
than he had been anywhere else. Nobody said
sarcastic things to him. There were no boys to
tease him. But he was not happy. Soon the time
would come when he must choose with whom
he must live for the next twelve years.

Day by day it drew inexorably nearer. Lawyer
Atkins had already informed him of the date
upon which the choice must be made.

And he didn't want to live with any of them.
Nay, more, he hated the very thought of it. They
had all been very nice to him. Too nice, too fussy,
too overdone. An Ingleside scolding, now, would
be much pleasanter.

And they had all, some skilfully, some clum-
sily, tried slowly to poison his mind against the
others.

He wanted to live with someone he liked,
someone who liked him. Liked him for himself,
not because he meant two thousand dollars a
year for his guardian. He felt that if Uncle
Stephen were alive, he would be smiling over
his predicament.

When Patrick's ninth birthday approached,
Aunt Melanie asked him how he would like
to celebrate it. Patrick asked if he could go out
to Glen St. Mary and spend it with the Blythes
at Ingleside.

Aunt Melanie frowned. She said he had not been invited. Patrick knew that did not matter in the least, but he knew he would not be allowed to go.

Then he said he would like to go for a ride on the bus. This time Aunt Melanie laughed instead of frowning and said carelessly, "I don't think *that* would be much of a celebration, darling. Don't you think a party would be nicer? You'd like a party, wouldn't you? And ask all the boys at school you like. You'd like a party, wouldn't you?"

Patrick knew it didn't matter whether he liked it or not. A party there would be. He wouldn't know what to do or say. Still, he supposed he could put up with it. He could even say "thank you" for the expensive gifts his uncles and aunts would give him and which he didn't want at all.

"Can I invite Walter Blythe?" he asked.

Again Aunt Melanie frowned. She could never understand his hankering for those Blythes. They might be all right in their way, but—

"They live too far away, darling," she explained. "I don't think he would be able to come. Besides, he is only a country boy, not the kind you will be expected to associate with a few years from now."

"He is the nicest boy I know," said Patrick indignantly.

"Our tastes change as we grow older," said Aunt Melanie indulgently. "They tell me he is a sissy, and not over-brave into the bargain."

"That isn't true," cried Patrick indignantly. "He is nice—*nice*. They all are. Mrs. Blythe is the nicest woman I ever knew."

"But you haven't known many women, darling," said Aunt Melanie. "Certainly Miss Sperry was a poor example. You don't mean to say that Mrs. Blythe is nicer than—well, than me, or even Aunt Fanny or Aunt Lilian?"

Patrick felt he dared not say yes.

On the morning of his birthday Spunk was killed by a passing truck. Aunt Melanie didn't mind much. A dog was a sort of safeguard against burglars, but one was as good as another. Besides, Spunk had been very tiresome with his bones. All the maids complained about them. And it was very mortifying to have a caller shown into the living room and see a large, well-gnawed bone reposing on the chesterfield. Not to speak of hairs on the carpet. Aunt Melanie made up her mind she would get a Pekinese. They were so cute, with such darling faces. Patrick would love a Pekinese. Why hadn't she thought of it before?

Patrick stood by the gate in dumb misery after the body of poor Spunk had been taken away. He was seething with hot rebellion. The idea of a birthday party when the only thing he cared for in the world had been killed! It wasn't to be endured—and he wouldn't endure it!

The bus came along, the big red and yellow bus. Patrick felt in his pocket. He had fifty cents. He ran to the bus stop and told the driver he wanted to go as far as fifty cents would take him.

"I suppose it wouldn't go as far as Glen St. Mary?"

"Well, no, not quite," said the driver, who had a certain soft spot in his heart for boys. "That would be twenty miles further. Besides, it's on another route. But I'll tell you. It will take you as far as Westbridge. Hop on."

At first Patrick was too unhappy about Spunk to enjoy this longed-for ride. A chow and a Great Dane, trotting companionably along the road, made his heart ache worse than ever. But by and by pleasure crept in. He imagined that Walter Blythe was with him and that they talked over everything they saw.

The red road, climbing gradually upward, was beautiful. Spruce woods; gipsy brooks; great rolling meadows like those around Glen St. Mary; gardens full of gay hollyhocks and perennial phlox and marigolds, like Susan Baker's own private plot at Ingleside. And the air was so clear and sparkling. He saw something of interest in every place he passed. A big striped cat sitting on the steps of a house. An old man painting his well-house a bright yellow. A stone wall with a door in it. A door that might—should—open into that other world. He pictured what he and Walter might find there.

Riding in a bus was jolly, just what he had expected it to be. In this one thing at least there was no disappointment. And he even laughed a little to himself when he pictured the consternation at Aunt Melanie's and the frenzied search that must even then be going on.

Then he saw it. The road had climbed until it had finally reached the top of the far hills you saw from the town.

And there it was—unbelievably, there it was. The house he had loved so long. In spite of the fact that he had never seen it save from far away, he recognized it at once. It was in a corner where two roads met. He sprang up and asked the driver to let him off. The driver did so, obligingly, in spite of the fact that he did not feel altogether easy about the boy. There was something . . . well, a little odd about him . . . some difference the good man could not have explained, between him and other boys.

Patrick saw the bus roll away without any regret or any wonderment about how he was to get back to town. He didn't care if he never got back. Let them hunt for him until they found him. He looked about him devouringly.

There was a gate with arched rustic lettering over it: "Sometyme Farm." Sometyme! What a delightful name! The house beyond was a white clapboarded one and it looked friendly. There was something about it that reminded him of Ingleside, though Ingleside was of brick and this of lumber.

The woods that had seemed so near to it when he had looked up from the town were really quite a distance away, but there were trees all about it, great-armed maples and birches like slim silver ghosts, and spruces everywhere, little rows of them running along the fences. It looked just like one of the Glen St. Mary farms.

The funny thing was that when you were looking south at it, you didn't seem to be on a hill at all. Before you was a long level land of farms and orchards. It was only when you turned north and looked away down, away over the town, over the sea, that you realized how very high up in the world you were.

Patrick had the strangest sensation of having seen it all before. Perhaps in that other world that was daily becoming more real to him. Even the name seemed familiar to him.

A young man was leaning over the gate, whittling out a little wooden peg. A dog was sitting by him, a lemon-and-white setter, with beautiful eyes. The young man was tall and lean and sunburned with bright blue eyes and a rather untidy mane of red-gold hair.

He had a smile Patrick liked—a real smile.

"Hello, stranger," he said. "What do you think of the weather?"

His voice was as nice as everything else about him. It was, somehow, a voice you knew. Yet, as far as Patrick knew, he had never seen him before.

"The weather is all right," said Patrick.

"Meaning that it is about the only thing that is all right?" said the young man. "I am inclined to agree with you. But isn't the view something. Strangers are always raving about it. You can see for twenty miles from here. You can see as far as the harbour at Glen St. Mary. Four Winds, they call it." Patrick looked eagerly in the direction indicated.

"That is where Walter Blythe lives," he said. "Do you know the Blythes?"

"Who doesn't?" said the young man. "But, apart from the weather and the view, I perceive that, like everyone else on this misbegotten planet, you have troubles of your own."

Patrick was moved to confide. It was a strange feeling. He had never before experienced it, save at Ingleside.

"Our dog was killed this morning, and I just had to come away for the day. Aunt Melanie was having a birthday party for me, but I couldn't stay for it."

"Of course you couldn't! Who would expect you to? The things people do! May I ask your name, now?"

"I'm Pat Brewster."

The young man had dropped the wooden peg and fumbled a little before he found it.

"Oh . . . ah . . . yes. Well, mine is Bernard Andrews or, if you would prefer it, Barney. How does it strike you?"

"I like it," said Pat, who wondered why Barney was looking at him so intently. Also, why he had again that queer feeling of having seen Barney before. He was sure he couldn't have.

After a moment, the intentness faded out of Barney's expression and the twinkle reappeared. He opened the gate.

"If you left Charlottetown on the eleven o'clock bus, you must be hungry," he said. "Won't you come in and have a bite of dinner with us?"

"Won't it inconvenience you?" asked Pat politely. He knew how Aunt Melanie regarded unexpected company, no matter how sweet she was to their faces.

"Not a bit. Unexpected company never rattles us. We just put some more water in the soup."

Pat went in joyfully. Barney dropped the new peg into the slot and turned to see Pat caressing the dog.

"Don't pet Jiggs till after dinner, please," said Barney, quite seriously. "He was mean. He went and ate up all the poor cat's morning rations. He's done it several times. And her with seven children depending on her. If you pat him he'll think he's forgiven too soon. He'll soon learn that he mustn't do it—he's fond of being petted. You have to use different methods with different dogs, you know. How did you discipline Spunk?"

"He was never disciplined," said Pat.

Barney shook his head. "Ah, that's a mistake. Every dog needs some disciplining, and most of them need their own special form. But after dinner you may pet him all you like."

They went towards the house through a garden that had run a little wild and yet had a lovely something about it that seemed to tell of children who had once played there and played no more. The walk was edged with geraniums and quahogs, just like Susan Baker's garden at Ingleside. In fact, there was something curiously like Ingleside about the whole place. And yet they were really not a bit alike. Ingleside was a rather stately brick house while this was just a common farmhouse.

In the grassy front yard was an old boat full of gay petunias and they walked on a row of smooth, worn old stepping stones that looked as if they had been there for a hundred years. There was another house just opposite across the side road, a friendly house, too, with a dot of scarlet in the yard.

And, coming around the house, was a long lovely line of snow-white ducks.

"I *have* been here before," cried Pat. "Long ago, when I was very small. I remember it! I remember ducks just like that."

"I shouldn't wonder," said Barney composedly. "We have always kept ducks, white ducks. And lots of people come here. We sell eggs."

Pat was so shaken by his discovery that he could hardly speak to the cat who said *Meow* very politely to him in the porch, beside a basketful of kittens. She was a fine corpulent cat, in spite of Jiggs.

"Do you happen to want a kitten?" asked Barney. "We are fond of cats here, but eight are rather too many, even for Sometyme. Walter down at Ingleside has bespoken one, much to Susan's indignation."

"Oh, do you know the Ingleside people?" cried

Pat, feeling that here was another link between them.

"I know the young fry well. They come here for eggs sometimes, for all it is so far away. And here's Aunt Holly," added Barney, opening the brown kitchen door. "Don't be afraid of her. All good fellows are friends of hers."

Pat wasn't in the least afraid of her. She was a frail old woman with a lined face. He liked the pleasant kindliness of her eyes.

She ushered him into a little bedroom off the kitchen and left him there to wash his hands. Pat thought the bedroom was old and gentle, just like the house, just like Aunt Holly. There was a clean, threadbare carpet on the floor, and a pitcher and basin of clouded blue ware.

There was a door opening right into the garden, held back by a pink conch shell. Now, where had he seen a big conch shell like that before? Suddenly he remembered. Susan Baker at Ingleside had one at her bedroom door. She said her uncle, who had been a sailor, had brought it to her from the West Indies.

Pat thought it would be delightful to creep into that bed at night, under the gay patchwork quilt, leaving the door open so he could see the hollyhocks and stars through it, just like they could from the sleeping porch at Ingleside. But he knew it was vain to hope it. Long before night, Aunt Melanie would have found him, if she had to call out the police.

"Will you have your dinner now or wait till you

get it?" demanded Barney with a grin, when Pat had returned to the kitchen, with hands scrubbed as clean as hands could be.

"I'll have it now, please and thank you," grinned Pat in return. It was really the first time in his life he had ever grinned, though he had been trained to smile very politely.

There did not seem to be any soup after all, but there was abundance of cold ham and scalloped potatoes. Barney passed him a heaping plateful.

"I expect boys' appetites haven't changed much since I was a lad," he said. "I know Susan Baker is always complaining that she can never get the Ingleside boys filled up. Girls, now, seem different."

Pat discovered that he was very hungry and nothing had ever tasted so good to him. Nobody talked much. Barney seemed absorbed in some reflections which Pat had an idea were not happy ones, though he could not understand how anyone could live at Sometyme Farm and not be happy.

Jiggs sat beside Pat and occasionally thumped his tail placatingly on the floor. Once he went out to the porch, licked the cat's head and returned. The time of his discipline was not yet up, but Pat slipped him an occasional bit of ham while Barney pretended not to notice.

They had apple pie with thick cream for dessert. And besides all that, Pat felt somehow that he was eating the very bread of life.

"How are you going to spend the afternoon,

Pat?" asked Barney, when nobody could eat any more. To be sure, Aunt Holly hadn't eaten much but she kept pecking, and Barney didn't seem to have as much appetite as you would expect from his inches.

"Please, may I spend it here?" said Pat.

"The word is with you," said Barney. "I've got to fix the fence behind the barn. Would you like to come and help me?"

Pat knew Barney was only being polite. There was really nothing he could do to help but he wanted to go. Barney held out his hand and Pat took it.

"Think your folks won't be worrying about you?" asked Barney. "Who do you live with—at present, anyhow?"

Pat told him.

"Well, I'll tell you. I'll telephone them you are spending the afternoon at Sometyme Farm and that you'll be back this evening," said Barney. "How will that do?"

"I suppose it would be the best way," said Pat dolefully. He hated the thought of going back to Aunt Melanie's, but of course he had to.

"I wish I could live here forever," he said wistfully.

Barney ignored the wish.

"Come along," he said, holding out his hand. Pat took it.

"I'm glad he hasn't a fat hand," thought Pat. "I like the feel of a nice, lean, cool hand like Dr. Blythe's."

And he liked to feel, too, that Barney liked him, really liked him for himself. He knew somehow that he did.

Pat sat on a big mossy stone on the shady side of the spruce wood behind the barn while Barney worked at the fence. Sometimes it occurred to him that Barney hadn't really much interest in the fence. But that must be nonsense. Anyone would be interested in such an adorable fence, built of rails, a snake fence, though Pat didn't know the name, with all sorts of wild things growing in its corners.

Far, far down the sea laughed beyond the golden dunes, just as it did at Ingleside, only so much further away. It was all just as he remembered it. The memory was becoming clearer every instant.

There were drifts of filmy cloud over the tree tops and a smell of sun-warm grasses all about him. A deep, wonderful content pervaded his entire being. He had never, even at Ingleside, imagined it possible to feel so happy.

He wanted to stay here forever, Aunt Melanie and the rest of them were millions of years, millions of miles away. He knew that at night he would have to go back to Aunt Melanie's ugly foursquare house in town and be forgiven. But the afternoon was his. Sometyme Farm was his! It knew him as he knew it.

In the late afternoon, Aunt Holly brought him out a big slice of bread, spread with butter and brown sugar. Just as Susan did at Ingleside. He was amazed to find how hungry he was again and how good the simple fare tasted.

Barney came and sat down beside him while he ate it.

"What does it feel like to own all those fields?" asked Pat.

"I'd know what it was like if I did own them," said Barney bitterly. "In a word—heaven."

He spoke so bitterly that Pat did not dare to ask any more questions. But who owned Sometyme if Barney didn't? Pat felt quite certain, though he could not have told why, that Barney was not a hired man.

He *should* own Sometyme. What was wrong?

When Pat had finished his slice of bread and sugar, they went back to the yard. As they entered it Pat felt Barney's hand tighten on his own slightly.

A girl was coming across the road from the house on the other side. She had a blue scarf wound around curls that were just the colour of Rilla Blythe's at Ingleside, and she had gay, hazel eyes in a fresh, wind-blown face.

She had slim golden arms and walked as if she would just as soon fly. The girls at Ingleside walked like that, and so did Mrs. Blythe, although she was so much older. Pat thought she was just like the spicy geraniums and the fresh new bread and those far away, golden dunes. Beside her trotted a little girl in a dress of Turkey red print.

"Why here are Barbara Anne and the Squaw

Baby!" said Barney, pretending to be surprised. Pat wondered why he pretended it. He knew quite well that Barney had seen them coming.

But Pat had caught a certain look in Barney's eyes. For his own part, he was more interested in the little girl with the red dress. He liked Rilla Blythe, but she never made him feel like that. Besides, he was quite sure Rilla would never stick her tongue out at anybody. She was too well brought up, and what a tongue-lashing Susan Baker would have given her if she had ever caught her at it. Even Mrs. Blythe would have disapproved.

"Whom have we here?" asked Barbara Anne. Her voice was like her looks—gay and fresh. Yet Pat felt that it was not very far from tears.

"This is Pat Brewster," said Barney, when they went through the side gate, a gate that looked as if it had been used a good deal.

"You've heard of Patrick Brewster, of course?" said Barney carelessly.

For just a moment a queer look came into Barbara Anne's hazel eyes. Pat had an odd feeling that she knew a good deal about him. That was impossible, of course. But had not the whole day been full of queer feelings? What did one more or less matter? Pat had almost concluded that he was in a dream.

Barbara Anne's gay eyes—but were they so gay after all?—glimmered at Pat and a wide, lovely smile came over her face, a smile like Mrs. Blythe's. Why in the world did everything at

Sometyme Farm remind him of Ingleside? Really, the two places were not a bit alike, nor were the people.

But Pat felt that he had known Barbara Anne for years. He wouldn't mind a bit if she called him "my lamb." He even felt he could stand being kissed by her.

"And this is Squaw Baby," said Barney.

Incredible things did happen. Here was the little girl in scarlet. And she was sticking out her tongue at him! Of course, it was a dream. But what a lovely dream! Pat hoped it would be a long time before he would wake up.

The Squaw Baby, seemingly quite unmindful of Barbara Anne's shaking, stuck out her tongue at him again. It was such a pretty little red tongue, as red as her lips and her dress.

She pirouetted three times on her bare toes and sat down on a big grey granite stone by the gate. Pat would have liked to sit beside her, but he was too shy. So he sat on an upturned milk pail instead and they stared at each other on the sly while Barbara Anne and Barney talked, looking at each other as if they were saying things with their eyes entirely different from what their tongues said. Pat wondered again how he knew this. But anything was possible in a dream.

They spoke low and seemed to have no idea that Pat could hear them. But Pat had amazing ears.

"I've decided on the western trip," said Barbara Anne lightly.

"What's the matter with the Hill?" asked Barney, just as lightly.

"Oh, nothing, nothing at all." Barbara Anne's voice conveyed to Pat that something very terrible was the matter with it and Pat felt hotly indignant with her.

"But one gets tired of the same old place, you know."

As if anyone could ever get tired of Sometyme!

"I don't like *you*," said the Squaw Baby. But just then that didn't matter. The Squaw Baby was so indignant that she gave up sticking her tongue out at him and devoted her attention to Jiggs.

"Sometyme Farm *is* very dull," said Barney.

"And living with an ever-so-nice brother and his wife—even with an entirely adorable Squaw Baby thrown in—gets a bit monotonous," continued Barbara Anne, lifting the cat and squeezing purrs out of her. "And then when you feel you are not needed! Can the Squaw Baby have one of the kittens?"

"All of them if she wants them," said Barney, "except of course the one I've promised to the Blythes."

"You don't mean to say they want more cats there! I thought Susan Baker—"

"Susan doesn't rule the roost at Ingleside, though so many people think she does. And so you're really going west?"

Again Pat felt that some tremendous issue hung upon the answer. He tried to divert the attention of the Squaw Baby from Jiggs, but entirely in vain.

"Will you be gone long?" asked Barney indifferently.

"Well, Aunt Ella wants me to stay the winter with her anyhow." Barbara Anne set the cat carefully down and made as if to go.

"And probably longer," said Barney.

"Quite probably," agreed Barbara Anne.

"In fact you think it probable that you will remain there?" said Barney.

"Well, you know there are opportunities in the west," said Barbara Anne. "Come, Squaw Baby. It's time we were going. We've taken up too much of these people's valuable time as it is."

"I don't want to go," said Squaw Baby. "I want to stay and play with Pat."

"Well," said Barney. Pat, in spite of the exultation which had filled him when the Squaw Baby said that, had another of his queer feelings that it cost Barney, who was suddenly looking ten years older, much more than he could afford, to say that "well" so lightly. Pat had had so many queer feelings that day that he felt he must be ten years older himself. "You'll likely have a wonderful time. I'd miss you . . . if I were going to be much longer on the Hill myself. But I'm going, too."

An immeasurable feeling of desolation swept over Pat. For the first time he wished he might waken. The dream had ceased to be beautiful.

Barbara Anne only said, "Oh?"

The Squaw Baby, finding her advances thrown away, returned to Jiggs.

"Yes. The mortgage is coming home to roost at last."

"Oh!" said Barbara Anne again. Pat wished the cat would stop purring. The sound did not seem in harmony with things at all.

"Yes. It's a way mortgages have, you know."

"But perhaps—"

"No, there is no doubt of it any longer. Pursey delivered his ultimatum yesterday."

"Oh!"

Barbara Anne's gay eyes clouded, darkened, misted. Pat felt that if she had been alone she would have cried. But why? There were too many mysteries in dreams. Even the Squaw Baby was full of them. Why, for instance, did she pretend to be so wrapped up in Jiggs when he, Pat, knew perfectly well that she was dying to stick her tongue out at him?

"It's a shame, a shame!" Barbara Anne was saying indignantly.

Why should she care, wondered Pat?

"Four generations of you at Sometyme! And after you've worked so hard!"

The Squaw Baby turned from Jiggs and tried to get the cat. But Pat wouldn't let her. Perhaps if he wouldn't she might stick her tongue out at him again.

"If you hadn't had to spend so much money on Aunt Holly's operations!" Barbara seemed to be getting more indignant all the time.

The Squaw Baby was trying to get a thistle out of one of her bare toes. Pat wished he dared offer to help her—to hold one of those dusty sunburned little toes in his hand—but . . .

"And now she is quite well and you might catch up, he forecloses!"

What did "foreclose" mean? The Squaw Baby had got the thistle out by herself and was gazing at the far-off sea. Pat did not think he liked such self-reliant women.

"I don't blame Pursey," Barney was saying. "He has been very patient really. Not a cent of interest for over two years! Even yet, if I could show him any reasonable prospect of ever catching up—but I never can now. Oh, I know when I'm beaten."

"What are you going to do?" Barbara Anne's voice had suddenly grown very gentle.

"Oh, Aunt Holly and I won't starve. I've been offered a job on a fox ranch. It'll be enough for Aunty and me to exist on sparingly."

"You on a fox ranch," said Barbara Anne scorchingly.

"One must eat, you know. But I confess I don't feel very enthusiastic over the thought of looking after caged creatures."

The bitterness in Barney's voice was terrible. It made Pat forget even the Squaw Baby and her tongue. Yes, it was certainly time to wake up.

Barbara Anne loosened her blue scarf as if it choked her. She dropped her voice even lower, but Pat still heard her. Of course in dreams you heard everything. And what on earth was she saying? Pat really did forget the Squaw Baby this time.

"If—if you had put in your claim when Stephen Brewster died! You have just as much claim on the boy as those others in town. More—more! They're only half-relatives. You'd have been able to pay the mortgage then. I wanted you to. You know I wanted you to! But men will never listen to women!"

What on earth was she talking about? Dreams *were* the queerest things. The Squaw Baby had found another thistle but just then Pat did not care a hoot if her toes were full of thistles. What did Barbara Anne know about Uncle Stephen? And what had Barney to do with him?

"I couldn't qualify, Barbara Anne. This old, out-of-the-way farm—" He *couldn't* be talking of Sometyme, thought Pat. "Only a district school to attend—" Wasn't it only a district school at Ingleside? thought the dazed Pat. "And only old Aunt Holly to look after him. It wouldn't have been fair to the kid."

"A good deal fairer than you have any notion of," said Barbara Anne indignantly. "Men are the stupidest creatures."

The Squaw Baby looked as if she agreed entirely with her.

"And then my pride—"

"Oh, yes, your pride!" said Barbara Anne, so violently that even the Squaw Baby jumped and Jiggs looked around for a possible stranger dog. "You needn't tell me anything about your pride. I know all about it. You'd sacrifice anything— anybody—to it!"

Pat felt he ought not to let her say such things to Barney. But how could he stop her? And he *must* know what Uncle Stephen Brewster had to do with it, even if the Squaw Baby never stuck her tongue out at him again. She did not look as if she wanted to. She was interested only in thistles. Let her be, then.

"Not quite," said Barney. "But I'm not exactly a worm. All the Brewsters looked down on my sister when Pat's father married her, as if she were a sort of insect. You know that as well as anybody."

"What were the Brewsters?" asked Barbara Anne scornfully. "Everyone knows how *they* made their money. And they had nothing to boast of. Two generations against the Andrews' six."

"Well, I wasn't going to crawl to them," said Barney stubbornly. "And, anyhow, they wouldn't have let me have him."

"Didn't Lawyer Atkins notify you?"

"Oh, yes."

"And they couldn't have stopped him if he'd wanted to come. Lawyer Atkins is a fair man. And everybody knows about Stephen Brewster's will."

"He made it on purpose to mortify me," said Barney bitterly. "He thought I'd put in my claim and the boy would laugh at me. As he would have. Do you suppose a boy brought up at Oaklands would choose *this*?"

Barney waved his hand at the sagging gate and at the old clapboard house that needed paint so badly and at an outmoded reaper in the yard. But to Pat, he seemed to be waving at the boatload of petunias and Jiggs and the bedroom with the garden door, at the long, level meadows beyond and at an unseen school where he would be "Pat" among the boys and the Squaw Baby would be sitting where she could stick her tongue out at him whenever she wanted to. If she ever did want to again.

Pat stood up shakily and went over to Barney. He didn't know whether he would be able to speak, but he must try. There were things that had to be said and it seemed that he was the only one who could—or would—say them. The Squaw Baby left her thistles alone and looked after him with a peculiar expression. Jiggs wagged his tail as if he knew something was coming.

"You are my uncle," he said, his grey eyes looking up into Barney's blue ones—Barney's blue eyes that were so full of pain. How strange that he had not before seen the pain behind the laughter!

Barney started. Could the kid have overheard them? Barbara Anne started too. So did the Squaw Baby, but that may have been because of a very large thistle. Jiggs began wagging his tail harder than ever. The cat seemed to purr twice as loudly. And all the ducks started quacking at once.

"Yes," said Barney slowly, "I'm your mother's youngest brother. I was only a kid when she married your father. This was her old home."

"I . . . I think I must have known it," said Pat, "though I don't see how I could."

"You *felt* it if you didn't know it," said Barbara Anne. "People so often *feel* things they can't possibly know. I went to school with your mother. She was older than me, of course, but she was the sweetest thing."

"I've often wanted to see you, Pat," said Barney. "I saw you just once when you were five. She brought you here one day when Stephen Brewster was away."

"I remember it," cried Pat. "I *knew* I'd been here before."

"But your father's people would never let you come again," said Barney. "And when she died— I thought it wasn't any use. I went to Ingleside when I heard you were there on a visit. But I was just a day too late. You had gone—home."

"Home!" said Pat. And "Home!" said the Squaw Baby, just for the fun of mimicking and making him mad and making him take some notice of her.

Then he brushed everything aside. There was only one thing that really mattered.

"Since you are my uncle, I want to live with you," he said. "*You* wouldn't be taking me because of the money I brought, would you?"

"I'd be glad to have you if you hadn't a cent," said Barney honestly.

"You'd just take me because I am *me*?" said Pat.

"Yes. But I'm going to be honest with you, Pat. The money would mean an awful lot to me."

"It would mean Sometyme Farm," said Pat shrewdly.

"Yes, but how did you know that?"

"I don't know; I just *knew* it. And you'll scold me when I deserve it?"

"If I'm allowed to," said Barney, with a peculiar glance at Barbara Anne, who wouldn't look at him, but seemed completely taken up with Jiggs. The Squaw Baby was still occupied with her thistles.

Pat was puzzled. Who would or would not "allow" him to be scolded? Surely Aunt Holly wouldn't interfere? But the great question was not settled yet.

"I *must* live with you," he said determinedly. "I can, you know. I can choose the one I'm to live with."

"Could you be happy here, Pat?"

"Happy? Here?" Pat looked at the Sometyme farmhouse, at Barbara Anne and at the Squaw Baby, who at once stuck her tongue out at him and seemed to forget all about thistles. "Oh, Uncle Barney! Uncle Barney!"

"What do you say, Barbara Anne?" asked Barney.

"I'm sure it's no business of mine," said Barbara Anne.

Of course it wasn't, thought Pat, and wondered why Barney suddenly laughed—real laughter, young, hopeful laughter. So unlike the laughter Pat had already heard from him.

What a lovely colour was flooding Barbara Anne's cheeks. What a pity she was going away! Pat felt that he would like to have her round. But at least she wasn't going to take the Squaw Baby. And why, oh why, didn't Barney answer his question? After all, that was the only important thing.

"Miracles do happen it seems," Barney said at last. "Well, here's looking at you, Pat. There'll be a jolly old fight."

"Why need there be any fight?" asked Pat. "They'll all be glad to be rid of me. None of them like me."

"Perhaps not—but they like—however, never mind that. You and I are the same breed it seems. Sometyme is ready for you."

Pat sat down on the pail again. He knew his legs wouldn't have borne him up another minute. He couldn't understand what Barney meant about a fight, but he knew Barney would win. And what was the matter with Barbara Anne? Surely she couldn't be crying?

He was glad when the Squaw Baby stuck her tongue out at him. It made things more real. After all it couldn't be—

"This isn't a dream, is it?" he asked anxiously.

"No, though it seems like one to me," said Barney. "It's all real enough. You were right, Barbara Anne. I should have claimed him long ago."

"Miracles do happen," mimicked Barbara Anne. "A man owning up that he was wrong!"

"Thank you, Uncle Barney," he said. "It's awfully good of you to take me in."

"Awfully," agreed Barney. He was laughing

again, and Barbara Anne was laughing through her tears. Even the Squaw Baby—what was her name anyhow? He must find out as soon as possible. She would never let a stranger call her Squaw Baby. And what would he call Barbara Anne? Not that it mattered. She was going away. Was that why she was crying?

"I . . . I wish . . . I wish you weren't going west," Pat said politely. He did wish it, too, with all his heart.

"Oh!" Barney laughed again. Long, low infectious laughter. Pat felt it would make anybody laugh. Even Uncle Stephen. Or Miss Cynthia Adams. Which, Pat felt, would be the biggest miracle of all this miraculous day. What a birthday it had been!

And *what* was Barney saying?

"Oh," said Barney, still laughing, "Barbara Anne won't be going west now."

"Where will she be going?" asked Pat.

"Ah, that is the question. Where will you be going, Barbara Anne?"

Barbara Anne's face was very red. "I . . . might move across the road," she said. "What . . . what do you think of that idea, Barney?"

"I think it is a very good one," said Barney, "since you honour me by asking my advice."

"I think I will take it—for once," said Barbara Anne saucily.

Pat had a feeling that both Barney and Barbara Anne wished he and the Squaw Baby were miles away. And, strangely enough, he did not resent it.

But there was one thing he *must* find out first. Then he would ask the Squaw Baby if she would like to go and see the kittens.

"Where is Barbara Anne going?" he persisted. "There is no place across the road but Sometyme."

Both Barney and Barbara Anne fairly shouted with laughter.

"We'll have to let her live here, with us, at Sometyme, I suppose," said Barney. "Would you be willing to have her here?"

"I'd love it," said Pat gravely. "Will the Squaw Baby come too?"

"I'm afraid her father and mother would not want to give her up," said Barney. "But I think you will see enough of her for all that—too much perhaps."

"Nonsense!" said Pat.

He had never dared to say "nonsense" to anyone in his life before. But one could say things at Sometyme. And what was the Squaw Baby saying?

"Let's go and have a look at the kittens," she said. "Perhaps Momma will let me have one though Walter Blythe has been promised the prettiest. I don't like Walter Blythe, do you?"

"Why don't you like him?" asked Pat, feeling that he loved Walter Blythe with all his heart.

"He doesn't care whether I stick my tongue out at him or not," said the Squaw Baby.

They went to see the kittens, leaving Barney and Barbara looking at each other—at least as long as they were in sight.

"What a fight you'll have with the Brewsters!" said Barbara Anne.

"I can fight the whole world and lick it now," said Barney.

Fool's Errand

Lincoln Burns had put up a sign at his road gate, telling people they were welcome to an apple from his big orchard. That showed you what sort of a man he was, as Anne Blythe said.

And everybody agreed he had been good to his mother. Not many sons would have put up with her as patiently as he had. He had waited on her for years and done most of the housework into the bargain, for no "girl" would ever stay long. Couldn't stand the old lady's tongue. But then he had always been easy-going, "the late Lincoln Burns" as he was called, because he was never on time for anything, and had an amiable habit of ambling into church just as the sermon was over. He had never been known to be "put out" over anything. Hadn't enough snap to get mad, Susan Baker of Ingleside used to say.

And now Mrs. Burns had died, to the surprise of everybody. One really couldn't expect her to do anything so decisive as dying. For the last ten years she had hung between life and death, a peevish, unreasonable, fretful invalid. People said Dr. Blythe must have made a fortune out of her.

Now she was lying in state in the old parlour, while the white flakes of a late, unseasonable spring snow were coming softly down outside, veiling with misty loveliness the unlovely landscape of early spring. Their beauty pleased Lincoln who liked those sort of things. He was feeling very lonely, although few except Dr. and Mrs. Blythe would have believed it. Everybody, including his mother, thought this death would have been a relief to him.

"You'll soon be shed of the trouble I'm making you, as Susan Baker says," she said to him the night before she died, as she had said it off and on for ten years—and as Susan Baker had never said. "Knowing the creature too well, Mrs. Doctor, dear," she said, "she'll live to ninety."

But Susan was wrong. And Lincoln was glad he had said, "Now, Ma, you know I don't think it any trouble to do anything I can for you."

Yes, he realized that he was going to be very lonely. Ma had given a sort of meaning and purpose to his life: now that she was gone he felt frightfully adrift and rudderless. And Helen would be at him soon to get married. He knew she would. Ma had protected him from Helen, although she had always pretended to think that he was wild to get married.

"You're just waiting till I'm dead to do it," she used to reproach him.

It was quite useless for Lincoln to assure her earnestly that he had no notion of marrying.

"Who'd have an old bachelor like me?" he used to say, trying to be jocular.

"There's lots would jump at you," snapped Mrs. Burns. "And when I'm gone one of them will pounce on you. Dr. Blythe has changed my medicine again. Sometimes I think he's longing to get me off his hands—and maybe get Susan Baker off, too. They say Mrs. Blythe is a renowned matchmaker."

"I'm not young," said Lincoln, with a laugh, "but Susan Baker is a bit old for me."

"She's only fifteen years older. She thinks I don't know her age but I do. And you're so easygoing you'd marry anyone that up and asked you, jest to be rid of the trouble of refusing her."

"Ma looks nice, don't she?" he said to Helen who had come in.

Mrs. Marsh had been crying—why, nobody knew. She thought Lincoln very unfeeling because he had not cried.

"Beautiful," she sobbed. "Beautiful, and so natural."

Lincoln did not think his mother looked natural. Her face was too smooth and peaceful for that. But he thought she looked curiously young.

As long as he could remember she had looked old and wrinkled and cross. For the first time he understood why his father married her. She had been really ill and she had really suffered. Even Susan Baker admitted that and Dr. Blythe knew it.

Lincoln sighed. Yes, life was going to be dull without Ma. And difficult.

"What are you going to do now, Lincoln?" asked his sister.

Lincoln thought Helen might have waited a little before bringing such a matter up. But Helen was never one to put things off. There was nothing easy-going about her. "I guess I'll have to do as they do up in Avonlea," he said mildly.

Helen bit. "What do they do up in Avonlea?"

"They do the best they can," said Lincoln still more mildly.

"Oh, do grow up," said Helen stiffly. "I don't think it is decent to be joking like that before Ma is cold in her grave."

"I didn't mean it for a joke," said Lincoln. He had meant it for a snub. And it wasn't original either. He had heard Dr. Blythe say it more than once.

"But you never had any feeling, Lincoln. And it's no joke the way you're left. I don't know of anyone you could get as housekeeper. Lincoln, you've just *got* to marry. You ought to have been married these ten years."

"Who'd have come in with Ma?"

"Lots would. You've just made Ma an excuse

for being too lazy to go courting. I know you, Lincoln."

Lincoln did not think she knew him at all, in spite of relationship and neighbourhood. But then they had always taken different views of the business of living. Helen wanted to make the business prosperous. Lincoln wanted to make it beautiful. To him it did not matter so much if the wheat crop failed as long as the autumn brought asters and golden rod.

"Lena Mills would have you," went on Helen, "or Jen Craig—though she is cross-eyed—or even Sara Viles might. She's none too young. But you can't afford to be particular. Just take my advice, Lincoln. Start right out and get yourself a wife. It will make a new man of you."

"But I don't want to be made a new man of," protested Lincoln plaintively. "It might be inconvenient, as Dr. Blythe says."

Helen ignored him. That was the only way to do with Lincoln. If you gave him a chance he would talk nonsense by the hour: about his garden, or the partridges that came every winter evening to the same apple tree, and senseless things like that, instead of market prices and potato bugs.

"You must get married and that is all there is to it, Lincoln. I don't care who it is as long as she's respectable. You can't go on farming and cooking your own meals. It's made an old man of you already. Think of the comfort of coming in tired to a good meal and a tidy house."

Yes, Lincoln sometimes had thought of it. He admitted to himself that the idea was attractive enough. But there were other things than comfort and a tidy house, as Dr. Blythe had once warned him, when some gossip had got around.

And these things Helen knew nothing about. He remembered driving past Ingleside on a cool autumn night. A delicious odour of frying meat floated out. No doubt Susan Baker was preparing the doctor's supper. No meal he had ever really eaten had given him as much pleasure as that odour—that banquet of fancy.

And, as Mrs. Blythe had once said in his hearing, there was never any aftermath of satiety or indigestion. "You may tire of reality, but you never tire of dreams," Mrs. Blythe had said.

That night Lincoln paced up and down between his barn and his house, through the mild spring night, until late. He envied Dr. Blythe.

He always liked to be out in the night. To stand on his hill and watch the stars in a beautiful aloneness. To pace up and down under dim stately trees that were of some kin to him. To enjoy the beauty of darkness or the fine blue crystal of moonlight.

If he married any of the women he knew, would he be able to do this? And he was terribly afraid he would have to marry. Helen had made up her mind to it and would give him no peace. She would contrive it in some way.

Suddenly into his mind came a memory of a

dim yesterday that everybody but he had forgotten.

He had been ten or eleven and had gone with Ma on a visit to Uncle Charlie Taprell who lived at Mowbray Narrows. The visit had been an agony to the shy lad. He had sat stiffly on the edge of a hard chair in an ugly room. Such an ugly room! The mantelpiece was crowded with ugly vases and the walls were covered with ugly chromos and the furniture was cluttered with ugly roses. And Ma had admired everything sincerely.

His three cousins, Lily and Edith and Maggie, had all sat together on the sofa and laughed at him. They were not ugly. They were considered very pretty girls, with round, rosy cheeks and round bright eyes. But Lincoln did not admire them; he was afraid of them and kept his eyes resolutely fixed on a huge purple rose at his feet.

"Oh, ain't you the bashful one!" giggled Edith.

"Which of us girls are you going to marry when you grow up?" asked Lily. Then they all giggled and the grown-ups roared.

"I'm going to get Ma's tape measure and measure his mouth," said Maggie.

"Why don't you talk to your cousins, Lincoln?" said his mother fretfully. "They'll all think you've got no manners at all."

"Maybe the cat's got his tongue," giggled Lily.

Lincoln stood up desperate, hunted. "I'd like to go out, Ma," he said. "This place is too fine for me."

"You can go to the shore if you like," said his Aunt Sophy, who rather liked him. "Now, Catherine, what could happen to him? He ain't a baby. My girls are too fond of teasing. I often tell them so. They don't understand."

That was the matter with all the world, nobody understood. Lincoln never changed his opinion.

He drew a long breath of relief when he got out of the house. Between it and the cove was a grove of ragged old spruces and beyond it a field where all the buttercups in the world seemed to be blowing. Halfway through it, Lincoln met her—a little girl, perhaps a year or so younger than himself—who looked at him shyly out of soft grey-blue eyes, the colour of the harbour on a golden-cloudy day, but who did not laugh at him.

Lincoln, who was afraid of all little girls, did not feel in the least afraid of her. They went down to the sandshore, shyly but happily and made sand-pies. He could not even remember whether she was pretty or not but she had a soft, sweet little voice and beautiful slim brown hands. He found out that her name was Janet and that she lived in the little white house at the other side of the spruce grove.

He had given her a blue bead and promised her that the next time he came he would bring her a West Indian shell that he had at home. He also promised that when he grew up he would come back and marry her. She had seemed quite pleased at that.

"Mind you wait for me," Lincoln had urged. "It'll be an awful long time before I'm grown up. You won't get tired of waiting, will you?"

She shook her head. She was not a talkative little girl. Lincoln couldn't remember much she had said. When Ma came to the buttercup field and called him from there, he had left her stirring her pebble raisins into her big sand-pie. He had looked back before a dune hid her from his sight and waved his hand to her.

He had never seen her since. She would be middle-aged and married now, of course. But he suddenly felt that he would like to make perfectly sure of that. And how? He did not even know her last name.

The memory of her dogged him all summer. This was curious, he had not thought of her for years. He supposed it was Helen's confounded mewling about marriage that had brought it all back. He did not want to marry; but he thought he would not mind very much if he could find somebody like Mrs. Dr. Blythe or—or if he could find that little girl of the sandshore and discover she was not married.

One night, waking from a horrible dream of finding himself married to Lena and Jen and Sara all at once, with Susan Baker thrown in, he made up his mind that he would try to find out.

With a promptness very surprising in Lincoln, he started off the next day, despite the fact that in a recent chat Dr. Blythe had said, "Don't marry till you find the right woman, Lincoln, no matter how much your female relatives nag you."

"*You* were lucky enough to find yours in youth," said Lincoln. "At my age, it's take what you can get."

He got out his horse and buggy and trotted over the long miles between his place and Uncle Charlie's, with dread and a queer hope mingled in his heart. He knew that he was going on a fool's errand but what of that? Nobody else need know of his folly. There was nothing strange in a fellow going to see his uncle.

And he remembered hearing Mrs. Blythe say that there were times it made one happy to be a fool. It made you feel that you were driving straight back into the past.

He had actually never been to Uncle Charlie's since that long-ago afternoon. It would be different now. His teasing cousins were married and gone, and there would be only old Uncle Charlie and Aunt Sophy. But they made him welcome. The parlour was just as ugly as ever. Lincoln wondered how such ugliness could have lasted all these years. One would think, as Mrs. Blythe said, that God must have got tired of it long ago.

"Life can't be all beauty, Anne-girl," the doctor had said soberly. He had seen a good deal of pain and ugliness and suffering. "But there's a lot of beauty in the world for all that. Think of Lover's Lane."

"And the moon coming up over the trees in the Haunted Wood," agreed Anne.

But the very sameness gave him a comfortable feeling of having really got back into the past. Luckily they had supper in the sunny old kitchen, where things were not "too fine" and Lincoln found no difficulty in talking to Uncle Charlie. He even, after many false starts, contrived to ask who lived in the quaint old white house at the other side of the spruce grove.

"The Harvey Blakes," said Uncle Charlie.

"And Janet," quavered Aunt Sophy.

"Oh, yes, Janet," said Uncle Charlie vaguely, as if Janet didn't count for much.

Lincoln found his hand trembling as he set down his cup of tea. He shook his head when Aunt Sophy passed him the cake. Nothing more for him.

"So . . . Janet . . . is still there?" he found himself saying.

"And likely to be," said Uncle Charlie, with the unconscious scorn men feel for all old maids.

"Janet's a lovely girl," protested Aunt Sophy.

"Too quiet," said Uncle Charlie. "Far too quiet. The boys like someone with more pep. Like Mrs. Dr. Blythe now. There's a woman for you. And I never met her till Sophy had pneumonia last winter. She did more good than the doctor, I'll swear."

Lincoln admired Mrs. Blythe as much as anyone, but after all the years of his mother's ceaseless chatter, he felt that quietness in a woman was not a liability. He got up.

"I think I'll take a walk to the shore," he said.

He meant to go to the white house, but his courage failed him. After all, what could he say? She wouldn't remember him. He would have a look at the cove and then go home.

He went down through the field that had been a glory of buttercups so long ago and was a pasture now, dotted over with clumps of young clover. He was not surprised to see a woman standing at the end of the sandy road, looking out over the sea. Somehow, it all fitted in, as if it had been planned ages ago. He was quite close to her before she turned.

He thought he would have known her anywhere. The same soft grey-blue eyes and the same beautiful hands. She looked at him a little wonderingly, as if she thought she was looking at no stranger but couldn't be quite sure.

"Is the sand-pie done?" said Lincoln.

It was a crazy thing to say of course, but wasn't everything a little crazy today? Not quite normal, anyhow. Recognition trembled into her eyes.

"Is it—can you be—Lincoln Burns?"

Lincoln nodded. "So you do remember me and the afternoon we made sand-pies here?"

Janet smiled. It made her face look strangely young and wonderful.

"Of course I remember," she said, as if it were quite impossible she should have forgotten.

They found themselves walking along the shore. They did not talk at first. Lincoln was glad. Talk was a commonplace that did not belong to this enchanted time and place. A big moon was rising over the cove. The wind rustled in the dune grasses and the waves washed softly on the shore.

Soon they would have to turn back. The rock shore was ahead. The big light at the mouth of Four Winds Harbour was flashing.

Lincoln felt that something must be settled before they turned, but he didn't know how on earth he was going to settle it. It would be absurd to say, "Do you think you could marry me?" to a woman he had not seen for twenty-five years. But it was the only thing that came into his head and presently he said it, badly and flatly.

"Now, I've done it," he thought, quaking.

Janet looked at him. In the moonlight, her eyes were demure and mischievous.

"I've waited for you a long time," she said. "You promised you'd come back, you know."

Lincoln laughed. He was suddenly fearless and confident. He would not be afraid to marry Janet. She would understand why he put up that notice about the orchard and why the little fields back in the woods meant so much to him. He pulled her close to him and kissed her.

"Well, you know, I'm never on time," he said. "They call me the late Lincoln Burns. But better late than never, Janet darling."

"I've got the blue bead yet," she said, "and where is the West Indian shell you promised me?"

"At home on the parlour mantel," said Lincoln, "waiting for you."

The Pot
and the Kettle

Phyllis Christine opened her eyes, very large, very dark-brown eyes, whose lashes had lain all night on her creamy cheeks like silken fans—well, if not all night, at least all that was left of it after the barn dance at Glen St. Mary—and smiled her prettiest smile at Aunty Clack, who was standing by her bed with a tray, looking just as much like a ripe, rosy apple, sound and wholesome, as she had looked in the far away years when Chrissie was a little girl and "Chrissie" only to Clack.

She was Phyllis to every one else, and how she hated it!

"Clack darling, you shouldn't! I meant to get up. You should have called me, I really like to get up in the mornings, the earlier the better, though no one will ever believe me. You'd be amazed if

I told you how many sunrises I've seen. I'd slip out, you know, and then slip back to bed again. But I don't want or expect trays here. Dad didn't send me here to be pampered; he sent me here to be disciplined. You mustn't do this again."

"I dunno's I will, lamb," said Mrs. Claxton comfortably. "But I thought you'd be tired after that barn dance." Clack's voice betrayed considerable disapproval in the intonation of the words "barn dance." She had not thought Chrissie should go to a barn dance. The Clarks of Ashburn had never gone to barn dances. Of course, Nan and Diana and perhaps Rilla Blythe would be there, though they were young for that sort of thing. But Dr. Blythe had to curry favour with people, and anyhow they said Kenneth Ford was "gone" on Rilla Blythe, though they were mere children.

But Chrissie had been determined to go, and when Chrissie had been determined on a thing, nobody but old Mrs. Clark could stop her—and she not always, as Mrs. Claxton secretly reflected, with concealed satisfaction.

She had not only gone, but she had taken a pie with her to be put up at auction, a pie she had made herself. Such was the custom. Goodness knew what country bumpkin would have bought it and devoured it in company with Phyllis Christine Dunbar Clark—so named after two grandmothers, both of whom would have died of horror at the very idea of a descendant of theirs eating a pie with a come-by-chance partner at a barn dance.

It would not have been quite so bad if Kenneth Ford had been the buyer or Jem Blythe. But they had to take their chance like all the rest. And everyone knew that Jem Blythe and Faith Somebody-or-other were sweet on each other, though they were far too young for anything like that yet. It seemed that mere children were in love with each other nowadays. It wasn't so in her young days, Clack reflected with a sigh.

But old Mrs. Clark, Chrissie's great-aunt who had brought her up when her mother died at her birth, was still very much alive. Brought her up, indeed! Clack had her own opinion about that.

But why in the world had she let Chrissie come down to Memory for a whole month when she had never been allowed to visit her old nurse before?

It was a puzzle indeed. Old Mrs. Clark and Mrs. Claxton had hated each other very quietly and determinedly during all the years the latter had been at Ashburn. Mrs. Clark had hated Clack because Phyllis Christine loved her best and didn't love Mrs. Clark at all, no matter how many gifts were showered on her.

But she had power and had seen to it that there was no visiting back and forth when Polly Claxton's uncle had left her some money and a little down-country house at some out-of-the-way place named Mowbray Narrows. It had the lovely incredible name of Memory and Polly had gone to live there, leaving the eminently correct and landscaped estate of Ashburn, situated near Charlottetown, with bitter regret over parting from her lamb, mingled with satisfaction over escaping from old Mrs. Clark's thumb.

Clack—she would always be Aunty Clack to Chrissie—pulled up the blind, and Chrissie—she would always be Chrissie at Memory, never, *never* Phyllis—raised herself on one round elbow and looked out on a tiny river like a gleaming blue snake winding itself around a purple hill. Right below the house was a field white as snow with daisies, and the shadow of the huge maple tree that bent over the little house fell lacily across it. Far beyond were the white crests of Four Winds Harbour and a long range of sun-washed dunes and red cliffs.

Such peace and calm and beauty didn't seem real. And Dad had sent her here, though Chrissie knew very well that Aunty had put the idea into his head, in order that the dullness of this drowsy, remote end of the world might reduce her to obedience. Chrissie smiled at the thought.

And when Chrissie smiled, everybody in the world, except Adam Clark and Aunty Clack, laid down their arms.

Even Clack thought that, after all, you couldn't say a well-conducted barn dance wasn't respectable enough, and the Clarks *were* too proud and had too high a conceit of themselves. She was really thinking of old Mrs. Clark, though she would have died before she would have admitted it. Or that old Mrs. Clark would get her way somehow, whatever her motive was in sending Chrissie to Memory. For Clack knew perfectly well that it was old Mrs. Clark's doings. She had not lived with her for years for nothing. She always got her way.

She picked up the flowered daffodil chiffon that Chrissie had worn to the barn dance and hung it tenderly in the closet, secretly delighted that she could do that once more for her darling. She knew old Mrs. Clark thought girls should hang up their own dresses. Susan Baker at Ingleside had told her the Blythe girls had to. But, after all, one had to admit that the Blythes were not the Clarks.

Her lamb must have looked lovely in it. With those little golden-brown curls of hers bunched behind her pretty ears.

Clack did not know—and would be horrified to know—that the dress had cost Adam Clark seventy dollars. It was pretty, but not any prettier than those the Blythe girls wore, and Susan Baker had told her they made all their own dresses. The only consolation Clack would have had was that it must have horrified penurious old Mrs. Clark, who thought it sinful to spend money on dresses, when it should have been given to missions. Clack would have forgiven old Adam Clark anything for that.

"Clack darling! Salt-rising bread and butter— I've never tasted any since you left. Aunty thinks it isn't wholesome."

"Neither is it—at least Dr. Blythe says so."

"You all seem to swear by Dr. Blythe around here."

"For a man, he will do," said Clack cautiously, who would have died for any of the Ingleside family. "But a bit of salt-rising bread, once in a while, is not going to hurt anybody. Susan Baker makes it now and then and Mrs. Blythe winks at it and the doctor says, 'What good bread this is, Susan.' Oh, you have to learn how to manage the men!"

"And wild strawberries!"

"I picked them strawberries in the back orchard this morning. They're fresh as fresh."

"And Jersey cream in that lovely little old jug with the verse of poetry on it! Aunty used to want you to sell it to her, you remember?"

"When I am dead and gone, lamb, you are to have that jug. I have left it to you in my will. Don't forget that."

"Don't talk about wills and death on such a morning, Clack, darling. Look at those gold and purple pansies! Did you grow them yourself?"

"Susan Baker brought them up to me," acknowledged Clack reluctantly. "Mrs. Blythe is a great one to grow pansies. Were her girls at the barn dance last night, Chrissie?"

"Of course they were. Why, everybody was there! Why were you so opposed to my going, Clack darling?"

"I thought—I thought—"

"You thought they were beneath the Clarks. Be honest, Clack. Or else you were afraid of Aunty."

"I was never afraid of your aunt. But I am quite sure she was the means of sending you here—and she always gets her own way."

"It wasn't Aunty, it was Dad."

"She put him up to it. But it is of no use to argue with you, lamb. Are you hungry?"

"Am I hungry! I've had nothing to eat except a slice of pie since your incomparable supper last night. I couldn't eat more than a slice, whereat my partner was highly offended. Of course, Kenneth Ford bought Rilla Blythe's—that baby. I don't know how he knew it was hers, but he evidently did."

"Susan Baker has a special way of crimping the edges of her pies," explained Clack. "Oh, there are tricks in all trades, my lamb—even carpenters sometimes drive nails with a screwdriver. And mostly at a barn dance the boys know whose pie is being auctioned off. Though the Blythe girls are rather young to be going to dances. However, it is their own business. I suppose all the Blythe girls had dozens after their pies?"

"Oh, yes, they seem very popular. Or else it was Susan's crimps. My partner couldn't have any such an arrangement. Probably he was a stranger. He only ate one slice, too. I hope he didn't think it was *my* pie. I didn't do much dancing after it, I can tell you."

"Who bought your pie?" asked Clack, with affected carelessness, as she put shoe trees into a pair of slippers with ridiculous heels.

"A young man by the name of Don Glynne. He said he was the new gardener at Miss Merrion's."

"I heard Miss Merrion had one," said Clack, concealing her horror over Chrissie's eating a pie with a gardener. After all, a gardener was much better than some lout of a hired man. "He came about a week ago. I hear she is very well satisfied with him, so he must be some gardener, for she is awful hard to please. She has had five in a year. You know she has a place just outside Lowbridge. It is becoming celebrated for its rock and water gardens. She only came there to live a few years ago, and she makes a sort of hobby of her gardens."

"So he told me. We talked and danced a good deal. You see, leaving out the Blythes and the Fords, he was really the only possible man there."

"So I would suppose," said Clack, as sarcastically as it was possible for Clack to speak. But she found herself wishing old Mrs. Clark might know of it.

"I liked him, Clack darling. I felt acquainted with him as soon as we were introduced. I liked him because he was tall and had good shoulders and sleek black hair and eyebrows that flew up at the corners with cloudy blue-black eyes under them. He was the best-looking man there except Jem Blythe. And they say he is as good as engaged to the minister's daughter."

"But that is absurd, my lamb."

"What is absurd, darling Clack? Jem Blythe being good-looking, or his being engaged to Faith Meredith?"

"Neither. Jem is a very handsome boy, and Faith Meredith will make him a very suitable wife when the time comes. After all, they are only children yet and Jem has to get through college. He is going to be a doctor like his father. I hope he will be half as good a one."

"How you people round here worship the Blythes! Of course, they are a nice family—"

"I should not be living today if it were not for Dr. Blythe," said Clack.

"Then I owe him an eternal debt of gratitude. But let us return to our argument. What do you consider so absurd?"

"Why, liking a man just because he has cloudy blue-black eyes. The worst rascal I ever knew had eyes something like that. He is in jail now."

"You couldn't have a better reason, Aunty darling. I feel sure that George has prominent, gooseberry-green eyes."

Clack tingled. She felt that she was on the verge of the secret, the real reason why old Mrs. Clark had allowed Chrissie to come to Memory. But she remained outwardly calm.

"Who is George?" she asked, lifting the tray off Chrissie's bed and affecting indifference.

" 'Who is George?' says she. To think anyone doesn't know there is a George!"

"I know a dozen Georges," said Clack patiently.

"Well. I might as well tell you the story, now as any other time. Then you'll know why I was sent here. That is, if you are interested, Clack. If not, there is no use boring you."

"Oh, you know I am not bored," said the diplomatic Clack. "And anyhow I know quite well that your Aunt is behind it all."

"I have some such suspicion myself, Clack. I

feel sure Dad would never have thought it out for himself."

"If your aunt is behind it, you might as well give in at once," said Clack. "She'll get her way, never fear."

"She shall not, Clack. She will not, Clack. Well, if you must know . . . it's to be a secret, mind you . . . you're not to tell even Susan Baker."

"I don't tell Susan Baker or anyone else secrets that belong to other people," said Clack indignantly.

"Well, his whole name is George Fraser, and he is the man Dad and Aunty are determined I shall marry. There, you have the deadly truth at last, Clack darling."

Polly Claxton felt more bewildered than ever.

"Then why don't you know what colour his eyes are?"

Though as she spoke, Clack remembered that *she* could not quite remember what colour her own husband's eyes had been. She had an impression that they were a greyish blue.

"Because I have never seen him, darling Clack."

"Never seen him! And yet you are going to marry him!" Clack was more bewildered than ever. *What* was old Mrs. Clark up to?

"Never," said Chrissie energetically, "and I hope I never shall see him. Though I have my qualms. You know what Aunty is for getting her own way by hook or by crook. And, of course, she has Dad on her side this time."

Yes, Clack knew very well. But why in the

world did both old Mrs. Clark and Adam Clark
want Chrissie to marry this George if she didn't
want to? Adam Clark usually took Chrissie's
side, though, as Clack reflected somewhat venomously, it seldom did any good. In the end,
old Mrs. Clark had her way. There must be
money in the matter. Clack knew very well
that Adam Clark was by no means as rich as
rumour reported him.

"But she is going to find her match in me,"
Chrissie was saying energetically. "I *won't* marry
George, Clack. I simply won't."

"Have you fallen in love with anybody else?"
asked Clack anxiously. *That* would be a compli-
cation indeed. Clack knew Chrissie had the Clark
will, too. "Why do they want you to marry him?
And how does it come you have never seen him?"

"Because he is only a third cousin or something. And he has always lived at the coast. You
know all the Clarks think it isn't really proper
to marry anyone totally unrelated to you."

"Yes, I know. It is a family tradition," nodded
Clack. "And without money."

"Oh, this George is simply rolling."

Ah, thought Clack, *that explains a good many
things*. But she was prudent enough not to say it.

"Well, my Great-uncle Edward died about a
year ago. He was disgustingly rich."

"There are worse things than money," said
Clack wisely. "You can do a lot of good with it."

"I'm sure Uncle Edward never did anything
good with his. He just delighted in accumulating

it. But we didn't expect to get any of his billions—
you know the old quarrel?"

Yes, Clack knew of it. Adam Clark had told
her once when he had a glass too much, as Clack
charitably put it. Old Mrs. Clark would have died
before she told it to a servant.

"Well, of course that was another moth-eaten
tradition that had to be honoured. So we were
all amazed, Clack, when we heard about his will.
Wills are horrid things, aren't they, Clack?"

"They generally make a lot of trouble," said
Clack, "but still how could things go along without them? And may I ask what was the matter
with your Uncle Edward's will?"

"You may ask anything you like, darling."

"Did he leave his money to you?"

"No such good luck—at least, not exactly. He
left it all to this detestable George Fraser and me if
we married each other before I was twenty-one—
just another year. Did you ever, Clack, darling,
hear of anything more horribly, hopelessly Victorian than that? I ask you."

"Things might be worse," said Clack. "I've
heard of many queer wills in my time." Clack
hadn't the least idea what Victorian meant, but
she knew Chrissie did not like the will and she
did not blame her. It would not be a pleasant
thing for anybody to have to marry someone
she had never seen. But she understood Adam
Clark and old Mrs. Clark a little more clearly now.
They worshipped money, as she very well knew.
Chrissie must have got her disposition from her

dead mother. There wasn't an ounce of Clark in her. But then she had never known poverty.

"What if you don't marry him—or he doesn't want to marry you?" Though Clack could not conceive this possible. Still, he might already be in love with some other girl. Clack shuddered. It was a dreadful tangle. As for a month at Memory curing Chrissie of her obstinacy, that was sheer nonsense. No, old lady Clark had something up her sleeve.

"Then it all goes to some hospital. And of course I said I wouldn't marry him. That was why I was banished here. Though you can't imagine how glad I was to be banished, darling."

"You couldn't be any gladder than I was to have you come," said Polly Claxton truthfully.

"And—imagine it, Clack—this George actually wrote father, telling him that he couldn't get away from his business this summer, but would try to come in the fall. So it seems the creature actually works."

"Well, he is none the worse for that, darling," said Clack wisely.

"I'm not saying he is. I like people who work. But he might have been interested enough—however, that is beside the question. He didn't want to come, that was all."

"Perhaps he didn't like the idea of marrying someone he had never seen, any more than you did," suggested Clack.

"But at least he could have come and seen me and we could have talked the matter over. But he wouldn't, and Dad—prompted, as I am quite as well aware as you are, Clack, by Aunty—conceived the idea of going to the coast and taking me with him. Fancy, Clack, darling, just fancy."

"It was a silly idea," conceded Clack, who thought it worse than silly.

"Being trotted out there to see if I'd do! They were so afraid those millions would slip through their fingers yet. As they will!"

"Hmm," said Clack.

"They are afraid George might fall in love with somebody else. Perhaps he is in love with her already. Clack, I never thought of that."

"It is quite likely," agreed Clack. "Remember, he has never seen you."

"Perhaps that is why he couldn't leave his horrid business to come and see me. But he could have told us. Well, if that is the case I'm even up with him for I said no and stuck to it. We had ructions."

"I should think it likely," said Clack, remembering her own ructions with old Mrs. Clark, in which it was a good deal of satisfaction to recall that old Mrs. Clark had not *always* been the victor.

"You know you can never convince Aunty that anything she does not believe can be true."

"I know it too well, darling lamb."

"You don't know how nice it is to be called 'lamb' again! Well, of course she couldn't believe that anyone would turn down five millions."

"It *is* a lot of money," said Clack meditatively.

"Darling Clack, don't sound so mercenary.

You are not, really. Do you mean to tell me you would marry anyone you had never seen for his money?"

"No, lamb—but I'd have a look at him first."

"Even if he wouldn't come to see you?"

"No—but I'd manage it some way."

"Clack, I believe you've gone over to the enemy."

"Never, my lamb. You know me better than that. But I just wanted you to look at both sides of the question."

"There was only one side. Well, finally I was sent here—or, rather, I was given my choice of coming here or going to the coast. I didn't take a split second to decide. 'You are making a mistake,' said Aunty icily."

"I know just how she would say it," reflected Clack.

"I have a right to make my own mistakes, I said."

So have we all, thought Clack, *but we haven't the right to blame the consequences on somebody else. Though most of us do it,* she added honestly. Aloud, "And what did your aunt say?"

"Oh, just 'Indeed!' Like that! You know quite well how she would say it. And you know when Aunt says 'Indeed!' I usually wilt. But I didn't wilt this time, Clack. I was so glad to get away . . . and relieved."

For the time being, thought Clack.

"You know I had such an uneasy feeling that Aunt always gets her way in the end."

So she does, thought Clack.

"But she isn't going to get it this time."

"George may be very nice, my lamb."

"Clack, he's fat. I'm sure he's fat. All the Georges I know are fat."

"George Mallard is as thin as a lathe."

"He is the exception that proves the rule then. Besides, there is a picture of George Fraser at home, one his mother sent Aunt when he was a baby. His mother had some sense, she didn't hold with old feuds and traditions. He was a little fat baby with his mouth open."

"But babies change so, lamb. Some of the thinnest men I know were fat as dumplings when they were babies."

"I feel quite sure George hasn't changed. I know that he is a little fat man with a moon face. I can't bear a pudgy man with a moon face. And who could marry a moon face, Clack?"

"Anyhow, you are not going to marry anyone you don't want to marry as long as you are under *my* roof, lamb," said Clack loyally.

"There, I've eaten all the berries. They were delicious. I can't remember when I've had wild strawberries before. I even licked the dish when you were retrieving my comb from the wastebasket."

"Oh, no, you didn't lamb. A Clark would never do that."

"Do you think Nan Blythe would?"

"I would think it very unlikely. She has been better brought up. Susan Baker says—"

"Never mind what Susan Baker says. I don't care a hoot for her opinion or the Blythes' either. Though I do think the Blythes a nice family—and I wish Jem Blythe was a few years older. He won't be fat, and his name isn't George."

"What are you going to do today, my lamb?"

"Why, I'm going to *live* it, darling Clack. It is so long since I have had a chance to live a day. You know, we don't *live* at Ashburn. We just exist. As for today, I'm going to town with Don in the afternoon."

"Don? Who is Don?"

"Clack darling, have you forgotten so soon? Why, the boy who bought my pie and ate it with another girl. I wonder what became of the rest of the pie my partner bought. You didn't hear of anybody's dog dying, did you?"

"Not Don Glynne—not the gardener at Miss Merrion's?"

"Who else? There aren't two Don Glynne's hereabouts, are there? He has got to get a sod-edger and some special kind of snails for the new cement garden pool he is making for Miss Merrion."

Clack sat down. She really had to. And she felt that she must register a protest. "My lamb, don't you think you should be more . . . fastidious? He's only a gardener—really a hired servant."

"I'm sure he is an excellent gardener, if all you've told me of Miss Merrion is true. She's a crank, Don says, but she knows about gardens."

"Do you call him Don?"

"Naturally, Clacky. Would you have me call a

gardener 'Mr.'? And he calls me Chrissie. I told him my name was Christine Dunbar. Now darling, don't look like that. It isn't deceit, it's just protective colouration. He'd never come near me if he found out I was Adam Clark's daughter."

"I should think not," said Clack, with all the dignity she could muster.

"And he thinks I'm your niece. I called you Aunty, you see. You aren't ashamed of having me for a niece, are you?"

"Lamb," said Clack reproachfully.

"And I *think* he got the impression, Clack—I didn't tell him, I really didn't—that I was a nursery governess back in town. I only said that the life of a nursery governess was rather dull and hard."

"I'm sure Mrs. Blythe would never allow any of her girls to go riding with a . . . a servant."

"Clack, if you quote any of the Blythes to me again I'll throw something at you. And he gave my pie a word of praise, though he didn't know it was mine. And tonight we are going for a moonlit swim down at Four Winds Harbour. Don't look like that, darling. There will be a whole lot of others there. Don't worry, dearest of Clacks. This is just a bit of adventure. There isn't any danger of my falling in love with Miss Merrion's gardener, if that is what you are afraid of."

"It isn't. You couldn't forget you are a Clark of Ashburn."

"He is more intelligent than most of the young men I know back home. *He* would not have refused to come east to see what kind of a wife

his great-uncle had picked out for him. He would
have packed a grip and taken the first train."

"How do you know he would—or could,
lamb?"

"Wait till you see his eyes, Clack. You can
always read a man's character by his eyes."

"Not always, lamb," murmured Clack. "One
of the best men I ever knew had what you
call gooseberry-green eyes—and they bulged
besides."

"Well, I told you there were always exceptions.
Clack, am I a spoiled baggage?"

"Of course you are not," said Clack indignantly.

"Aunt says I am. And so does Dad. Might as
well have the game as the name. Besides, in the
end, I suppose I will really marry this George."

"You'd never marry a man you didn't love,
lamb."

"Well, we've always been a bit pinched for
money, according to our standards of living, in
spite of our Clarkism, and it's not nice, Clack, it
really isn't."

"It's better than marrying a man with gooseberry-green eyes," said Clack, swinging around
easily.

"Oh, he may not have gooseberry eyes. He may
be as handsome as a god. Aunt told me once
I wasn't capable of anything but tissue-paper
emotions!"

"Then she told a fib," said Clack indignantly.

"Well, it may be true, Clack. You are biased

in my favour, you know. Anyhow, if it is true, I
might as well make the best market I can."

"I don't like to hear you talk like that, lamb,"
said Clack uncomfortably. "It doesn't sound like
you."

"That, as I've told you, darling, is because
you have idealized me. I'm really just like
other girls, and I am full of Clark contrariness.
If Dad and Aunt had been opposed to the
marriage, I'd have been all for it. Anyhow,
I've got this free, wonderful month before I
have to decide, so don't spoil it, Clackest of
Clacks."

"You were born that way," said Clack resignedly. Apparently she washed her hands of things.
Anyway, she knew Chrissie would do as she
wanted to with everyone, except old Mrs. Clark.

She had to go on washing her hands. There
didn't seem anything else she could do. It wasn't
any earthly use talking to Chrissie. She even had
to snub poor Susan Baker who ventured to hint
that it wasn't quite the thing for a Clark of
Ashburn to be running everywhere with Miss
Merrion's gardener.

Besides, she could not help liking Don Glynne
himself, hard as she tried to hate him. He *was*
very likeable and his eyes did things to you. Even
when he wore overalls. For it was in overalls and
the rackety Ford Miss Merrion kept for her hired
help that he came to take Chrissie to town that
afternoon.

Clack could only stand up to it by picturing old

Mrs. Clark's face if she could have seen them as they whirled away. Chrissie, cool and delicious in blue linen, beside the faded overalls.

"Do you like me as well today as you did last night?" Don was asking, rather impudently.

The appalling thing was that she did, in spite of all the nonsense she had talked to Clack. She had thought the magic of the night before would vanish in broad daylight.

But he seemed even nicer in his overalls than in his party togs. As for magic—why, magic seemed everywhere. It spilled all around them as they tore through the golden afternoon in the open car.

Chrissie's curls blew back from her little face and stars came into her eyes. A cluster of roses from some part of Miss Merrion's garden lay on her lap, and their perfume seemed to go to her head.

Don Glynne hadn't believed she could be as pretty as he had thought her at the dance—and she was even prettier. They drove to town and Don got his sod-edger and ordered his special snails for the water garden and then they drove home more slowly by a winding, woodsy road under dark spruces. Don told her he liked his work and loved gardens.

"Some day I'm going to have a garden of my own—a secret garden that very few people will see—or criticize—or admire."

"Why?"

"Because they always admire the wrong things.

The only people who have admired the right things in Miss Merrion's gardens since I've been there were Dr. Blythe and his wife. They *did* seem to understand."

Again, Chrissie's heart was torn by a pang of jealousy. "Won't you let anybody see it?" she asked wistfully. "I mean . . . anybody you are sure will admire the right things."

Don looked sidewise at her.

"Oh, I can always tell the right kind. It's a sort of instinct. But there will be no mobs. I'm fed up with sightseers at Miss Merrion's in the short time I've been there. The tourists come there in shoals. Of course, they've been told Miss Merrion's gardens are one of the sights of the Island. I'd like to drown them in some of the pools. Miss Merrion likes it, though. Sometimes I think that is all she has a garden for, for people to squeal over."

"Miss Merrion *must* love some of her flowers," said Chrissie hastily.

"Oh, she likes a bouquet for the dining room table, especially when she has company. But she doesn't care a hoot for the garden itself. As Mrs. Blythe says, you have to work in a garden yourself or you miss its meaning. Will you come over and see it some day?"

"But I might admire the wrong things, too."

"I'll take a chance on that. I believe you'll love all the right things and pass by the wrong things, just as the Blythes did."

"I suppose it takes a great deal of money to have a garden like that?"

"Scads. But it's well spent. How could I make an honest living otherwise? And Miss Merrion is rolling, so they tell me. That is why she never married; she told me she was afraid all her suitors were after her money. I daresay they were, too. Have you ever seen Miss Merrion?"

"No."

"Well, she could have been no beauty at her best and youngest."

"It must be abominable to be married for your money," said Chrissie hotly.

"Rotten," agreed Don. "Or to marry for money."

"M . . . m . . . m . . ." said Chrissie. "Only— do you think it is as bad in a woman as a man?"

"Just as bad in either," said Don. "Of course long ago there wasn't anything a woman could do. But now there is no excuse for her."

"But if she hasn't been brought up to do anything useful?"

"Then her parents or guardians ought to be soundly spanked," said Don. "In my mind, there is one valid reason for marrying: genuine, earnest love."

"But sometimes people mistake infatuation for love," said Chrissie.

"Ah, that is the tragedy of life," said Don with a sigh. "It *is* hard to tell which is which. But if you would be willing to be poor—horribly poor— together, I think you might take the chance. And now we've got to get back because I have to spray the roses before dinner. Miss Merrion is very particular about that. And a good servant must please his employer if he wants to hold his job. Do you still want to go for that evening swim?"

"Yes, of course—if you do."

In the evening they went for the swim, much to Clack's silent but evident disapproval.

Afterwards, they sat on an old upturned dory and watched the moon make patterns on the water. The wind rustled in the dune grasses and there was a thin, silvery wash of little waves on the shore. Far up Four Winds Harbour were mists like dancing witches.

Who could suppose that Ashburn was so short a distance away? It seemed in another planet.

Don had told her there would be nothing to look at but sunsets. Sunsets! Why, there was Don's profile to look at. And his slim, sloping shoulders and long, steel-muscled golden-brown arms.

She thought of George's awful, plump white body in a bathing suit and shuddered.

"I wonder what would happen if I tried to hold your hand," said Don.

Nothing happened—at least nothing that anyone could see. Chrissie shuddered again to imagine what Clack would say if she saw. As for Aunt Clark—Well, she just would not think about *that*.

But she knew that the touch of Don's fingers was sending little thrills up her arm like the waves of some delicate spirit fire. She wondered if other girls felt like that when their friends touched them. It seemed impossible. No one but Don could make anyone feel like that. And yet she had met him only the night before.

In the weeks that followed Clack sometimes feared Chrissie had forgotten she was a Clark. But she could only fall back on her belief that her lamb could do no wrong. She had to have some amusement, hadn't she? Mowbray Narrows was a very quiet place.

Don Glynne and Chrissie went swimming together every evening, and soon every morning. There were no more breakfast trays. Don used to come and whistle outside her window, which Clack thought indelicate, to say the least of it. What business had he to know which was her window?

Then they were off to the sandshore, which was all pale golden in the thin, translucent glow of the sunrise.

Clack thought it was worse going swimming in the morning than in the evening. The other young folks of Glen St. Mary and the Upper Glen and a few from Mowbray Narrows went in the evening, and Clack had got resigned to it; but she could not resign herself to the morning expeditions. Nobody else went swimming in the morning except some of the summer colony, but they were not Clarks. Clack's only consolation was what old Mrs. Clark would say if she knew.

But she did not know. Or did she? Clack could

not lose her belief that you could not get ahead of old Mrs. Clark, no matter what you did. As for Adam, he was as easily fooled as any other man.

Sometimes Chrissie brought Don into breakfast with her, and Clack could not help being civil to him—could not help liking him. She knew Miss Merrion said she had never had a gardener like him, one who really seemed to take an interest in his work.

After breakfast Don and Chrissie used to go into the garden and eat red currants until it was time for him to show up at Miss Merrion's, when all the other servants would be just getting up. Don declared the cook was worried because he didn't seem to be hungry some mornings. "How could I eat two breakfasts?" he asked Clack.

He and Chrissie did a great deal of laughing and talking as they ate red currents. Clack often wondered what it was all about, but she was too well-bred to listen. Old Mrs. Clark would have listened without scruple, she knew. But she was not going to imitate her.

They went on picnics on his afternoons off, rattling away in the old Ford to some lonely place among the hills. These picnics worried Clack more than the swimming expeditions. Now and then she warned Chrissie who only laughed at her warnings.

"You say Aunt will be sure to get her way and if so I'll have to marry George," she would say.

"I am thinking of the poor young man,"

Clack would say, with all the dignity she could muster.

So was Chrissie, although she would never have admitted it. She knew quite well that Don Glynne was in love with her and that it was the real thing. She knew she ought to break with him at once, but, to her dismay, she found she could not do it. And yet she could never marry him.

"I couldn't have believed the Clark pride was so strong in me," she reflected miserably. "I'm really as bad as Aunt. Well, suppose I give them all the shock of their lives—including darling Clack— and marry Don? I *can* make him ask me to—easily. He thinks I am only a nursery governess. I believe I could do it, anyhow. And a fig for George!"

Sometimes they dug for clams at low tide and Clack made the most elegant chowders, and enjoyed seeing them eat them, unhappy as she was. For this month, to which she had looked forward so happily, was very unhappy for her. Her only consolation was that old Mrs. Clark always got her own way.

To think I should have come to finding comfort in that, she reflected miserably.

Why, Don and Chrissie even went to the dances at the Walk Inn—the summer colony dance house—and Clack knew, through Susan Baker, that often as not they never went inside but danced alone out under the trees to the music that drifted out from the Inn, while the moonlight sifted down on them. The moons that summer were simply wonderful. At least, Don and Chrissie would have told you so. To other people they seemed much like ordinary moons.

Once poor Clack heard a wild tale from a neighbour that Chrissie had been seen helping Don mow the Merrion lawns, but she refused to believe it—or even ask Susan Baker about it.

She might as well have believed it because it was true. And, whatever happened, the roses had to be sprayed. Also Chrissie helped Don with his weeding and learned a good deal about gardening as well as about other things. There was no doubt that Don understood his trade. She didn't know another thing about him—and never tried to find out—but she gathered that he had an uncle somewhere who was a farmer or an apple-grower or something like that, and no other relatives worth mentioning.

Poor Clack was the most unhappy woman in the world just then. She tried to find out something about Don Glynne but nobody seemed to know anything about him, not even Susan Baker. And what Susan Baker didn't know about anybody within a radius of thirty miles was not worth knowing, as Dr. Blythe was in the habit of saying. He had even been known to accuse his wife—good humouredly, of course—of listening to Susan.

Don Glynne seemed to know all about the gardens of history and romance and legend in the world, from Eden down. He told Chrissie much about them as they weeded or picnicked or chased night moths in the orchard. Once Chrissie stumbled over a root, and Don caught her. She knew he held her a little longer than was necessary—and she knew she liked it—and she knew that he knew she liked it. And she knew she would *never* marry George.

Which would not have comforted Clack much if she had known it. It *would* be a triumph to get the better of old Mrs. Clark for once; but she did not want Chrissie to marry Miss Merrion's gardener.

It is no use looking forward to anything, thought poor Polly Claxton. *I looked forward to this month with Chrissie so much, and see how it has turned out! I wonder if I ought to warn Adam Clark. But no. I will not play into old Mrs. Clark's hands like that. I haven't the least doubt she knows as much about it as I do anyway.*

Once Chrissie heard herself referred to as "Don Glynne's girl" and was horrified to find that it thrilled instead of annoyed her. Clack heard a similar reference—several of them, in fact—and it gave her a very bad quarter of an hour. But, after all, Chrissie was a Clark, and Clarks didn't marry gardeners. It was impossible, no matter how cloudy their blue eyes were or how tall and broad-shouldered their figures.

Of course anybody could see that Don Glynne was crazy about her, but Clack fell back on the assurance that the men ought to be able to look after themselves. The best of them, she felt, needed a lesson quite frequently.

When she saw Don offering Chrissie the quarter of an apple on the point of his garden knife one day, she felt much more at ease. It was a pity such a nice fellow should have such manners. And him looking so much like a gentleman, too!

Chrissie thought the apple was the most delicious she had ever tasted. She knew the knife was clean as Don had washed it in the brook before he carved up the apple.

But it was not until Don kissed her for the first time, that night on the shore, and just for one second was the centre of her universe, that she knew something else.

"From now on you are mine," he said, between his set teeth.

Chrissie knew there was only one way of escape, and she took it.

"Let us be sane," she said, lightly as wave-froth on the sand. "You know this can't go on. I've liked you very much—for the summer. But I must have a different beau for the winter time: Really."

"So . . . that is how it is?" said Don.

"You knew it, didn't you?"

"I suppose I ought to have known it," said Don. He laughed. "Life is a joke," he explained, "and what is a joke for but to be laughed at?"

He looked at Chrissie. She wore a silvery dress and looked like a mermaid just slipped out of the sea.

She knew he thought her the loveliest thing in the world. This is one of the things a woman knows without being told.

"Suppose I just said," went on Don, "you have got to marry me, and no more nonsense about it?"

"You wouldn't like it," said Chrissie still more frothily. She knew by his face that she would have to tell the lie she had hoped to escape telling.

"You see—I like you as a friend, but I don't care anything about you in any other way."

"And that," said Don, "is that."

They went back through the scented moonshine in a very dreadful silence. But at the corner of spruce where the road branched off to Miss Merrion's, Don spoke again.

"I think you were lying when you said you didn't love me. The real reason is that you think a gardener is not good enough for a governess."

"Don't be absurd, Don."

"So many true things are absurd."

"Well, I am going to tell you the truth at last. I have been acting a lie all summer. Oh, yes, I'm ashamed of it, but that doesn't make matters any better now. I am not a governess. I don't know how you ever got the idea that I was."

"I think you know very well—and I think you intended me to think you were."

"You could have easily found out by asking somebody."

"Do you think I was going to discuss you with the people around here?"

"Well, I am not Chrissie Dunbar either—at least, I am Christine Phyllis Dunbar, the daughter of Adam Clark of Ashburn, though that may not mean anything to you."

"Oh, yes, it means something," said Don, slowly and icily. "I know who Adam Clark is—and what the Clarks are. I seem to have been nicely fooled all round. But then I am so easily fooled. I believe in people so readily. I even believed Mrs. Blythe when she told me—"

"What did she tell you?" cried Chrissie jealously.

"Never mind. Merely a harmless answer to a harmless question I asked her. Anyone could have told me. It is common knowledge. It all comes back to the fact that I have been made an easy fool of. So easy. It really couldn't have been easier, Miss Clark."

"I am going away tomorrow," said Chrissie coldly, her ignorance of what Mrs. Blythe could have told him still rankling in her heart. Not that it could have made any difference.

"So this is good-bye?"

"Yes."

"Good-bye, Miss Clark."

He was gone—actually gone. At first she couldn't believe it. Then she lied again in saying, "Thank Heaven."

She went to her room and made up her mind that she would cry till ten o'clock and then put Don Glynne out of her mind forever.

She cried for the specified time. Very softly into her pillow, so that Clack wouldn't hear her.

Then she got up and picked up a very hideous cow that Clack, for some unknown reason had always kept on the dressing table—some unknown sweetheart of her youth had given it to her—and threw it out of the window. It made a satisfying crash on the stones of the walk.

Chrissie felt much better.

"In about twenty years or so, I'll be pretty well over it," she said.

In a cool green dawn Chrissie packed her trunk. She was all ready to go when an amazed Clack came in.

"I've stayed out my month, dearest, and now I'm going back to Ashburn. Don't deny that, under your grief, you are feeling secretly relieved. You've been worrying about Don and me. You needn't have—oh, if you knew how much you needn't have! I hate Don Glynne—hate him."

I wonder, thought Clack. Then she added, "Are you going to marry George?"

"No, I am not going to marry George. Aunt and Dad may—and will—spill emotions and rage over everything, but nothing will induce me to marry George."

I wonder, thought Clack again.

When Phyllis—it had to be Phyllis again—got back to Asburn, Aunt Clark looked at her critically.

"You look very washed out, my dear. I suppose you had a deadly dull time at Memory. If

you had done as your father wished, this wouldn't
have happened."

"I had a lovely time at Memory," said Phyllis.
"And such peace and quiet. And I may as well
tell you, Aunt dear, that I am not going to marry George Fraser and you are not to mention
his name to me again. I am not going to marry
anybody."

"Very well, dear," said Aunt Clark, so meekly
that Phyllis looked at her in alarm. Wasn't the
old dear feeling well?

Phyllis went to town and bought a gorgeous
new dress, a divine thing, really, of black net with
rows upon rows of tiny pleated frills around the
skirt and a huge red rose on its breast—red as
the roses she had helped to spray in the Merrion
gardens.

She did not notice that the clerk looked
a little queer when she told him to charge
it.

She wore it that night to the dinner party
Adam Clark was giving some important visiting Englishman, and sparkled impudently all
through the meal.

"My daughter has just been spending a month
with her old nurse in the country," apologized
Adam Clark, who thought she was really going
too far. "This is . . . ahem . . . her reaction against
its monotony."

Monotony! Peace and quiet! Ashburn seemed
horribly dull, Phyllis reflected at her room window that night. Horribly peaceful, horribly quiet.

with a ghostly abominable moon looking down at you!

That moon would be shining somewhere on Don. What was he doing? Dancing at the Walk Inn with some other girl, probably. Remembering her only with scorn and hatred because she had deceived him.

Well, did it matter? Not at all.

The Memory interlude was over. Definitely over. And George was just as definitely disposed of. Horrible fat George!

She would never see tall, lean Don again, but at least she wouldn't have to marry pudgy George. As far as Uncle Edward's millions—

"I'd rather keep boarders to help Don out than spend millions with George," she thought violently and ridiculously.

But it was absurd to think of marrying a gardener. Besides, she had no longer the chance of doing it. Aunt Clark and Dad must have resigned themselves to her refusal of George. Neither of them had mentioned his name or the trip to the coast since her return. Then she heard it—Don's whistle—just as she heard it so often in the mornings at Memory!

It came from the shrubbery at the back of Ashburn. Don was there! She hadn't the least doubt of it. Hate her he might; despise her he might; but he was there, calling her—calling the heart out of her body.

Of course she had lied when she said she didn't love him. And he hadn't believed her either. Thank God, he hadn't believed her. Love him! She'd show him whether she loved him or not. He might just be trying to get even with her, but that didn't matter. Nothing mattered but that he was there.

And in the midst of it all, how she wished she hadn't broken poor, dear Aunt Polly's china cow.

She flew downstairs and out of the side door and across the dew-wet lawn, her dress trailing in the grass. But it didn't matter about dresses. As a gardener's wife, she wouldn't need dinner dresses—or would she? Perhaps even gardeners had parties of their own. But that didn't matter either. She would be happy in a dinnerless desert with Don and wretched in paradise without him.

They didn't say a word when they met—not for a long time. They were otherwise occupied. And they were the only two real people in the world.

But at last . . .

"So you *were* lying," said Don.

"Yes," said Chrissie—always Chrissie now. Never again Phyllis. "And I think you knew it."

"After I cooled down I did," said Don. "Do you know where little girls go who tell lies?"

"Yes—to heaven. Because that's where I am now."

"If I hadn't come what would you have done?"

"Gone back to Memory. Oh, that Englishman! He was so dull. Even gooseberry George would have been better."

"Do you think you will ever be sorry you didn't marry George?"

"Never."

There was another interlude.

"I'll always be sure of a job as a gardener," said Don. "But how will your family feel about it?"

"They may never forgive me—at least Aunty—but that doesn't matter."

"Oh, I think they'll forgive you," said Don. "I'm not really worrying over their forgiveness. The question that bothers me is, will *you* forgive me?"

"Forgive you! For what?"

"What I want you to forgive me for is deceiving you shamelessly."

"Deceiving me? What on earth do you mean?"

"Chrissy, darling, put your head down on my shoulder . . . so . . . and don't look at me or say one word until I'm finished, I'm not Don Glynne."

"Not Don Glynne!" gasped Chrissie, disobeying him from the beginning. "Then who are you?"

"Well . . . at least . . . my mother's name was Glynne . . . no . . . keep still. I came east to see—to see someone in these parts. I arrived here just as you got into the car to drive away. Your lashes keeled me over. I . . . I decided then and there to follow you . . . and I did."

"How did you know where I was going?"

"Oh, I asked questions. I was lucky enough to get the job at Miss Merrion's. I *am* a good gardener. It has always been my hobby. My old uncle had the finest garden at the coast. And besides I took a course in gardening at the university."

"Don Glynne—"

"Wait . . . wait . . . you haven't heard the worst yet. And I asked you to keep still until you had."

"You are not married to anyone else? Or even engaged?"

"Not I. I've been waiting for my ideal. Well, I took the All-America cup for a bowl of roses at the Flower Show last year. So you see I am not wholly an impostor."

"Don, what *do* you mean?"

"I see that girls can't hold their tongues. I asked you to remain silent until I had told my tale."

"But you are so mysterious. And *what* am I to forgive you for?"

"Deception. Base deception."

"I could forgive you for anything."

"Some day," said Don irrelevantly, "I am going to have gardens that will make Miss Merrion's seem like a cottage plot. You'll help me weed them, won't you darling?"

"Of course I will. But what—"

"No, not yet. A moment longer. Because I know you won't forgive me."

"I suppose you have been divorced—"

"Not I. It is far worse. And yet you *must* forgive me. After all, I did just what you did yourself."

"I?"

"Yes. And you've heard the old proverb that the pot shouldn't call the kettle black. *Now!*"

Chrissie snuggled a bit closer if that was possible.

"Things like this simply can't *happen*," she said.

"They *must* be arranged by Providence. Don't you think so, Don?"

"Yes, everything is foreordained. I am a good Presbyterian."

"But it is rather odious, really, to think what Aunt will say."

"I think I can promise you she won't say much. Even dear old Aunt Polly won't say much. But she will have the satisfaction of being a true prophetess."

"Don, if you don't stop being so mysterious! Did anyone know?"

"Nobody knew except Miss Merrion and Mrs. Clark."

"Aunt Clark!"

"I knew you wouldn't forgive me. Your very tone implies it."

Don kissed her hair, and the tips of her ears. He thought he would be forgiven for it in time, but he knew Chrissie would cast it up to him for the rest of his life.

But she was worth it!

"My whole name is George Donald Fraser," he said as composedly as possible. "I—I didn't want to marry for money any more than you did. Stop wriggling. You have got to marry me now, whether you want to or not."

He kissed her hair—her lovely hair—again. He knew he was already forgiven, but it would be some time before she let him know it.

"Well, I might as well tell you and get it over. Chrissie, darling, I'm George Donald

Glynne Fraser. That coast idea was all a farce, Chrissie."

"I'm so glad you are not fat and haven't gooseberry eyes," she said. It was all she said—then!

"Did Clack know it? And how did you find where I was?"

Don kissed her again.

"No. Clack had no suspicion. That was why she was so worried. But I think the Blythes suspected. It is pretty hard to fool Dr. Blythe. He knows how to hold his tongue, however. That is partly why he is such a successful doctor."

There was another long kiss. But there was one thing she would never forgive. No woman could be expected to forgive it.

He *had* told a fib. He must never tell her he had gone into Ashburn after she had driven away and that the whole plot was a concoction of her aunt's, with her father's consent. Old Mrs. Clark had been a school friend of Jane Merrion's.

Clack had been quite correct in her estimate of old Mrs. Clark.

Here Comes
the Bride

The old church at Glen St. Mary was crowded. Somehow this particular wedding seemed unusual. It was not often there was a church wedding in Glen St. Mary, and still less often one of the summer boarders. Somebody from Charlottetown was playing the "Wedding March" very faintly and softly, and the two families most concerned stood in small clusters or alone, the collective reverberence of their words rising and falling in soft waves of sound.

A bored reporter from the *Daily Enterprise* was scribbling in a notebook in a back pew:

The old church at Glen St. Mary was thronged with guests this afternoon for the marriage of Evelyn, daughter of Mr. and Mrs. James

March, who are spending their summer in Glen St. Mary, to Dr. Darcy Phillips, Professor of Biology of McGill and son of Mrs. F.W. Phillips and the late Frederick Phillips of Mowbray Narrows.

The church was beautifully decorated with white 'mums by the teen-age girls' class of Glen St. Mary, and the lovely bride was given away by her father. She wore ivory satin, fashioned with a mid-Victorian line, and a halo of seed pearls held in place her wedding veil of rare old lace.

Miss Marnie March was maid of honour for her sister, and the three bridesmaids, Miss Rhea Bailey, Miss Rilla Blythe and Miss Janet Small, wore period gowns of silver cloth and picture hats of periwinkle blue with bouquets of blue iris. Mr. So-and-So was best man and the ushers, etc. etc. etc.

The reception afterwards was held at Merestead, the beautiful new summer home of the Marches at Glen St. Mary, where glowing roses made an attractive decor for the glowing rooms. The bride's table was centred with the handsome wedding cake made by Mary Hamilton who has been with the Marches thirty years as cook, nurse and beloved member of the household.

Mrs. March received her guests in a modish gown of grey, with a slight train, smart hat of black straw, and corsage of deep purple Princess violets.

Mrs. Frederick Phillips was in blue chiffon with matching hat, and corsage of yellow rosebuds. Mrs. Dr. Blythe, one of the guests, looked very charming in pale green chiffon.

Later the bride and groom left to spend their honeymoon at the groom's camp, Juniper Island, Muskoka, Ontario. The bride's going away ensemble etc. etc. etc.

Among the guests present were Mrs. Helen Bailey, Miss Prue Davis, Mrs. Barbara Morse, Mr. Douglas March (great-uncle of the bride, a hearty octogenarian of Mowbray Narrows), Mrs. Jem Blythe, etc.

Aunt Helen Bailey, sister of the bride's father and the mother of three unwedded and unbespoken daughters, among them one of the bridesmaids, thought:

So Amy has really got Evelyn off her hands at last. What a relief it must be to her! A girl like Evelyn—past her first youth. With one of those skins that age early—not like Mrs. Blythe's. Will that woman ever grow old! And that affair with Elmer Owen—it's really quite a triumph to get her married, even to a poor young professor like Darcy Phillips. I can remember him running barefoot round Glen St. Mary and cutting up didoes with the Ingleside boys.

Amy was simply heart-broken when the engagement to Elmer was broken off. She tried to brazen it off but everyone knew, of course, Evelyn never cared a scrap for him; it was his money she was after. That girl hasn't a particle of heart, she couldn't love anyone.

I wonder what really went wrong between her and Elmer. Nobody knows, though that silly Mrs. Blythe looks so wise when it is spoken of. Of course his parents never approved of it, but at one time he seemed quite taken with her. Amy certainly thought she had him trussed and skewered. How she used to purr over it! Such a ring! It must almost have killed Evelyn to give it back. It will be a long time before Darcy Phillips will be able to give her a square-cut emerald.

It was really indelicate the way she snapped Darcy up the moment Elmer threw her over. But it's easy to get a man if you don't care what you do. My poor girls haven't the audacity necessary for today. They're sweet and well-bred and womanly, but that doesn't count any longer. It's all very well for Dr. Blythe to say girls are the same in all ages. A lot he knows! No, nowadays you've got to stalk your man.

Why don't they come? The seats in these country churches are always so hard. Look at that mosquito on Morton Gray's fat jowl! Doesn't the man feel it? No, he's probably to thick-skinned to feel anything. I wish I could give it a slap—my nerves are getting jumpy.

What a lot of guests! And all the yokels from Glen St. Mary and Mowbray Narrows. I suppose a fashionable wedding is a treat to them. Prue Davis has a new dress and is trying to look as if it were an ordinary occasion. Poor Prue! Barbara Morse is making nasty remarks about everyone. I know by the look on her face. Ah, Mrs. Blythe has just snubbed her. I can tell by the look on her face. But it won't cure Barbara. The ruling passion! She'd gossip at a funeral, so why not at a fashionable wedding, where everyone knows the bride is taking the groom as a consolation prize and he is taking her, heaven knows why—probably because she just went after him. It's all nonsense of Mrs. Blythe to say they have always been in love. Everybody knows they fought like cat and dog all their lives. Evelyn has an indomitable will under all that surface sugar, just like Mrs. Blythe. I wonder if Dr. Blythe is as happy as he pretends to be. No, no man could be.

Is that really Jim's old Uncle Douglas there? I suppose they can have all their country cousins since the groom is only Darcy and the wedding in Glen St. Mary. But if it had been Elmer, at some fashionable church in town, they'd have been kept in the background. Uncle Douglas is evidently enjoying himself. A wedding feast is a wedding feast no matter how it comes about. He'll have something to talk about for years. What is Rose Osgood wearing? She must simply have put her hand in the family rag-bag and pulled out the first thing she grabbed. I wonder how Mrs. Blythe, living in Glen St. Mary, always contrives to look so up-to-date. Well, I suppose her daughters—

There goes Wagner at last, thank goodness. Here they come. Four ushers; four bridesmaids; two flower girls and a page. Humph! Well, I hope everything's paid for. Those white mums must have cost Jim a small fortune. I don't believe for a moment they came from the Ingleside garden. How could anyone grow mums like that in a little country place like Glen St. Mary? Where Jim finds the money I'm sure I can't imagine.

Evelyn's looking well, but she shouldn't have her dress cut that way. It gives her sway back away—

lordosis is the name nowadays, I believe. Evelyn is positively triumphant—no shrinking violets about her. I remember the day Amy gave the coming-out tea for her debutante daughter. And was she awkward! But of course seven seasons should give anyone poise.

Darcy isn't much to look at—his face is too long— but poor Rhea looks quite as well as the other bridesmaids. That shade of blue is so trying; probably Evelyn selected it for that reason. Marnie looks like a gypsy as usual—only gypsies aren't quite so plump. Amy will find it even harder to get her settled than Evelyn. Rilla Blythe looks rather well. There really is something about those Blythe girls—though I'd never admit it to their mother.

"I will"—oh, my dear, you needn't shout it. Everyone knows you will only too willingly. Even in Glen St. Mary they all know that Darcy was your last chance. It's odd how things get around! Of course, the Blythes may have lots of friends in Montreal and Toronto. And Mrs. Blythe may have the reputation of not being a gossip but she contrives to get things told—clever woman. Well, as for Evelyn, a professor's salary is better than an old maid's pension, no doubt. They're off to the vestry. Mrs. Darcy Phillips! You can see it sticking out all over her. Look at Rilla Blythe making eyes at Kenneth Ford. And yet they say the Blythe girls never flirt! I doubt if she'll be able to rope him in, for all her mother's fine tactics. However, that is none of my business. I'm sure I hope poor Evelyn will be happy. But it doesn't seem to me that anyone can be very happy when she's simply marrying one man to save *her face because another jilted her. Is anyone really happy in this mad world? They say the Blythes—but who knows what goes on behind the scenes? Not even old Susan Baker, I'll bet my hat. Besides, she is too loyal to admit it.*

Now for the reception and the presents—and the usual silly remarks—and then the trip to Muskoka in Darcy's new flivver. I wonder if The Enterprise will mention that the car is a flivver! Some difference between that and Elmer's fifteen-thousand-dollar streamliner—or even Jim's old Packard. But Evelyn will have to come down to a good many things. Jim always spoiled his family. There they come—quite a procession.

Prue Davis, a bit passé and envious of all brides in general, was thinking also, *It seems so funny that Evelyn is marrying Darcy Phillips after all, when she has used him so abominably for years. He's only a poor young professor. But of course any port in a storm. She's twenty-five—and looks it—more, I should say. Is that why she picked such young bridesmaids? Rilla Blythe looks sweet. Somehow, those Blythe girls are the only girls I ever met I really liked, and their mother is the only woman I ever felt I could love. If I'd had a mother like her! Well, we have to take what's handed out to us in this world, parents and children alike. Darcy is nice and clever—there was a time when I might have caught him on the rebound— after one of the worst of their quarrels. But I always drop my bread butter side down. I've always been a fool and missed my chances. Of course, the minute Evelyn crooked her finger he came to heel. Nobody else had any chance then. It's just a way she has of looking up under her eyelids. The Blythe girls all have it, too. I've noticed—well, some people have all the luck.*

I hope I won't get this dress spotted—receptions are such horrible things for that—for heaven knows when I'll get another. There they come. Evelyn looks well. She always knows how to wear her clothes, I'll say that for her. It's born in you. Look at Rilla Blythe. I'll bet that dress of hers didn't cost a tenth as much as the others did. I believe I heard a rumour she had it made in Charlottetown while the others came from Montreal, and yet look at it. Her hair, too. I never liked Evelyn's ash-blonde hair. Heigh-ho! I found a grey hair today. We Davises all turn grey young. Oh, things are so beastly cruel. "How do you do, Mrs. Blythe? A lovely wedding, wasn't it?"

Now, Prue Davis, haven't you any pride! Throw back your head and look as if you were sitting on the top of the world.

Thank heaven, that's over. I don't think any more people will speak to me. I don't know many of the country folks here except the Blythes and they've gone. I wish the reception was over, too. I'm beginning to hate going to such things. "What, Prue Davis still! When are we going to attend your wedding?" *Apart from remarks like that, nobody ever talks to me except old married men. My looks are going and it's no use having brains. When I say a clever thing to people they look startled and uncomfortable. I should just like to be quiet for years and years, and not to have to go on pretending to be bright and happy and quite,*

quite *satisfied. But I suppose most people have to do it. Only sometimes I think Mrs. Blythe—*

Oh, here's someone else. "How do you do, Mrs. Thompson? Oh, a lovely wedding! And such a charming bride! Oh, *me*! I'm not so easy to please as some girls you know. And independence is *very* sweet, Mrs. Thompson."

Of course she doesn't believe for a moment I think that way, but one must keep one's head up. Now for it.

Cousin Barbara Morse said to a friend, "This is what I've come all the way from Toronto for! These family ties—they're really all hooey. But I always liked Jim, and a trip to P.E.I. is always worth the money.

"It seems to me I've been here for hours. But you have to come early if you want an aisle seat, and you can't see much if you have any other one. Besides, it's really fun looking at everybody as they come in. Not that there's much to look at here. Most of the people are country folks. The Blythes of Ingleside seem to be the only ones who can pretend to any culture. I thought Mrs. Blythe a very charming woman. The doctor, like all the men, thinks he knows it all. But they have a charming family—at least, those I've met.

"The bridal party will be late, of course, none of Jim's family were ever known to be on time. *Everybody* seems to have been invited—and to have come. Of course, it's just the time of year when a trip to P.E.I. has a special charm. I must come again. Oh, so you come every summer? So I suppose you know most of the people well. Oh,

you have a summer cottage at Avonlea? That was
Dr. Blythe's old home, wasn't it? Isn't it strange
that a man of his ability should have chosen
to settle in a place like Glen St. Mary? Well, I
suppose it is predestination.

"*Why* doesn't Mattie Powell get those terrible
moles removed? Electrolysis does it so nicely.
Really, some people don't seem to care how they
look. How fat Mabel Mattingly is getting. But I
shouldn't talk. I never get weighed now. It simply
won't do. I'm blue for a week afterwards. Jane
Morris of Toronto told me she took four inches
off her hips, living just on buttermilk. I wonder—
but I'd never have the grit to do it. I'm too fond
of a good bite. I hope they'll give us something
eatable at the house. But Amy never was much
of a housewife. Of course, Mary Hamilton is a
good cook. I suppose that is why they bring her
with them every summer when they come to
Merestead. Oh, of course I know she's just like one
of the family. Amy always spoiled her servants.

"Look at Carry Ware—that stringy old chiffon!
You'd have thought she'd have got something
new for a wedding at least. Even Min Carstairs
has a new dress. I hear the Carstairs have come
into some money. They live in Charlottetown,
you know. And Andrew Carstairs is as mean
as skim milk. Of course that rose and silver is
far too young for her. What's that? Do you mean
to tell me she is only as old as Mrs. Blythe?
Well, city women always age more rapidly than
countrywomen. I agree with you, Mrs. Blythe is

the best dressed woman here. At least she gives that impression. And yet they say she gets all her clothes made in Charlottetown. But some people have a knack."

"Talking of ages, can *you* tell me how Sue MacKenzie contrives to look thirty-five when she is forty-seven? I'm not uncharitable, heaven knows, but one can't help wondering. When *she* was married—so the story goes—her father made her go back upstairs and wash the powder off her face. If he could see her now! No, they tell me Mrs. Blythe never makes up. But country people are so easily fooled. She couldn't look like that without a little make up. As for Sue's father—he was *such* an odd man, my dear—the queer things he would do when he got mad! Said nothing, but burned rugs and sawed up chairs!

"Prue Davis wears well, but she must be getting on. I always feel so sorry for the girls who are on the shelf at a time like this. They must feel it.

"Yes, that is one of the Blythe girls. But it can't be Rilla, she is one of the bridesmaids. The idea of having four bridesmaids at a quiet country wedding! But Amy always had very large ideas.

"There's old Mary Hamilton at the back of the church. Of course the eats are all in the hands of the Charlottetown caterers, worse luck, I'd rather take a chance with old Mary any day. But they say she made the wedding cake—she and Susan Baker of Ingleside between them. Susan has a recipe I'm told she won't give to anyone.

"Yes, Jim's family have always made an absurd

fuss over Mary, or Mollie as they call her some-times. Why, when Jim got his first car, nothing would do Mary but she must learn to drive it, too. And they actually let her! I'm told she's been fined for speeding times out of number. Oh yes, Irish for a thousand years! It's amazing how she took up with Susan Baker. You couldn't imagine two people more unlike. She's devoted to the bride and all that. At least people say so. But Mary knows on which side her bread is buttered—and to those of us who know a little about Evelyn's temper! Just look at her staring at everybody and gabbing to Susan Baker. I'll bet there are some queer tales being told.

"If they don't come soon I'll be carried out screaming, it's ten minutes past the time now. Perhaps Evelyn has changed her mind! Or maybe Darcy has faded out of the picture like Elmer. You can say what you like, but I'll never believe he really cares much about Evelyn. *Look* at the Walter Starrocks! Will you ever forget the day *they* were married and him standing there with his coat-tails all over cat hairs? Walter is getting pouches under his eyes. Yes, it's true we're all getting on. But I fancy the life Ella Starrocks leads him—you don't mean to tell me you've never heard! Well, just remind me some day.

"There they come at last. I don't care for those halo veils but Evelyn always must have the very latest fad. How is she going to indulge her expensive tastes on Darcy's salary? That shade certainly doesn't become Marnie. Rilla

Blythe looks very well in it, though. As for Rhea—well, it doesn't matter what *she* wears, only it's a pity to have the harmony spoiled, isn't it? Marnie is the plain sister so she'll make the best match, take my word for it. I don't know why it is, but you'll always see it. I suppose they're not so particular.

"Darcy looks as if he's carried Evelyn off from a hundred rivals instead of being Hobson's choice. But of course he doesn't know *that*. He's positively ugly, I think, except for his eyes, but I believe the women with the ugly husbands have the best of it. They don't have to be everlastingly scheming how to hold their men.

"Well, it really went off very well. I'm glad for Amy's sake. She's so fussy over small things. No doubt she has been praying for fine weather every night for a month. I hear that Mrs. Blythe says she believes in prayer. Did you ever hear anything so funny in this day and age?"

Uncle Douglas March was thinking, *Lot of lean women here. Never see anything of fine figures nowadays. That was back in the days when girls wore bangs and balloon sleeves. And were the same girls underneath, as Dr. Blythe says. His wife is the best-looking woman here. Looks like a woman. The church is dolled up all right. I must take in all the fixings to tell Ma. Too bad she couldn't have come. But rheumatiz is rheumatiz, as Dr. Blythe says.*

Some difference between this and my father's wedding. His dad gave him a fourteen-year-old horse and a two-year-old colt, a set of harness, a bobsled, and some provisions. He paid twenty dollars for his clothes, the minister and license, bought some chairs, a table and an old stove. Her dad gave her twenty-five dollars and a cow. Well, well, what do we work and slave for if it isn't to give the kids something better than the old folks had? And yet they don't seem any happier than we did. It's a queer old world.

Here they come. Evelyn fills the eye all right. When she ain't in sight I can never believe she is as pretty as I remember her. That's Jim's nose. A chip off the old block. Just as well, though Amy is a nice old puss— always liked her. Nice-looking boy Evelyn's got, too. Not too handsome but sort of dependable looking. Some dress! Ma was married in nun's veiling. Does anybody ever wear nun's veiling now? Such a pretty name— and pretty stuff. Ah, it's times like this makes a body realize that he's no longer young. My day's over, but I've had it—I've had it.

If there ain't old Mollie Hamilton back there, grinning like the frisky old girl she always was. She was a russet-haired jade when Amy got her, one time when she was visiting the Island. Mary's grey as a badger now. They must have treated her well, the way she's stuck to them. They don't hatch her breed of cats nowadays. She always declared she would never marry—you couldn't trust any man, she said. Well, she's kept her word. Don't know but she was wise. There's mighty few men you can trust, even if I'm a man myself. Except Dr. Blythe, now. I'd trust that man with my wife.

Now for the spread. Though they don't have the wedding suppers we had in the good old days. "Don't *eat things you can't digest, Pa," Ma told me. "You can digest anything if you have the courage to, Ma," I told her. I heard Dr. Blythe say that once, but Ma didn't know it. Doesn't hurt a woman to think her man can say smart things. A pretty wedding—yes, a pretty wedding. And a happy bride! I've lived long enough to know the real thing when I see it. By gum, I have. They'll stay married. Ma will have to read up about the wedding in* The Enterprise. *I couldn't ever do justice to it. Between* The Enterprise *and Mrs. Blythe, she'll get a pretty good idea of it. Only I must warn Mrs. Blythe not to tell Ma she saw me eating indigestible things. It's lucky she's a woman you can trust. They're few and far between. Dr. Blythe's a lucky man.*

A cynical guest said to herself, *H'mmm—white mums and palms. They've done it very well, though I did hear the mums came from the little Ingleside conservatory. And everybody is here who should be. No end of relations, and of course all the curious folks of the Glen and surrounding districts. I hope the groom won't be kissed to death, though there's not so much of that nowadays, thank whatever gods there be. They've even got old Uncle Douglas from Mowbray Narrows. He's inside the ribbon so he's a guest. How they must have hated having him—at least, Amy! Jim always had a bit of family feeling, but I doubt if Amy has any. Of course, he's Jim's uncle, not hers, but it would have been all the same. Poor Prue Davis—smiling with her lips but not her eyes— hope deferred maketh the heart sick. Odd, I learned that verse in Sunday school fifty years ago. If only*

Prue knew how well off she was! Moth balls! Who in the world is smelling of moth balls this time of year? Here they come—Evelyn looks well—her profile and eyelashes always carried her. Off with the old love and on with the new. Engaged to Elmer Owen two months ago, and now marrying a man she has hated all her life. Poor Darcy! I suppose all this flummery was really planned out for her wedding with Elmer, even to the dress. Amy looks worried. Well, I had to see both my daughters marry the wrong man.

Marnie's quite sparkling. She has twice the pep Evelyn has, but nobody ever looks at her when Evelyn is around. Maybe she'll have a chance, now that Evelyn is going.

Jim is doing everything very correctly—a well-trained husband. He was crazy about me before he met Amy. If I'd married him he'd have been more successful from a business point of view—but would he have been so happy? I doubt it. I couldn't have made him believe himself the wonder Amy has done. My sense of humour would have prevented it. We would likely have ended up in the divorce court.

Does that minister spin out his sermons like that? He seems to have perfected the art of talking for fifty minutes and saying nothing. Not that I'm an authority on sermons, goodness knows. They say the Blythes go every Sunday. Habit is powerful. But they say there is some engagement between the families. I suppose they want to keep on good terms with each other.

That stately old dowager in blue chiffon, with the old-fashioned pearls, must be Darcy's mother. They say she has devoted her life to him—and now she must hand him over to a chit of a girl. How she must hate Evelyn! Osler was right when he said everybody should be chloroformed at forty—or was it sixty? Women, anyhow. And isn't it odd how women hate to give their sons up when they are always so glad to get their girls well married off?

What a sight Rhea Bailey is! Those big gaunt girls should never wear flimsy dresses. But of course in this case she had no choice. It wouldn't have mattered anyhow. Those Bailey girls never had any taste in dress.

"For better, for worse." That sounds wonderful. But is there really such a thing as love in the world? We all believe it until we are twenty. Why, I used to believe it. Before I married Ramsay I used to lie awake at nights to think about him. Well, I did it after we were married too, but not for the same reason. It was to wonder what woman he was with. I wonder how his new marriage is turning out. Sometimes I think I was a fool to divorce him. A home and position means a good deal.

Well, it is over. Miss Evelyn March is Mrs. Darcy Phillips. I give them three years before the divorce— or at least before they want one. Of course, Darcy's bringing-up may prevent it. I don't suppose the farmers of Mowbray Narrows get divorces very often. But I wonder how many, even of them, would marry the same woman over again. Dr. Blythe would—I really do believe. But as for the rest! It's just as that queer old Susan Baker says, "If you don't get married you wish you had—and if you do, you wish you hadn't." But one likes to have had the chance.

The mother of the bride, thought rather discon-

nectedly, I won't *cry*—*I've always said I wouldn't
cry when my girls got married*—*but what are we going
to do without darling Evelyn? Thank goodness, Jim
hasn't got in the wrong place*—*Evie does look rather
pale*—*I told her she should make up a little*—*but
neither Jim nor Darcy like it. I remember I was a
dreadful brick red when I was married*—*of course, a
bride who made up in those days would have been
beyond the pale*—*Marnie looks very well*—*happiness
becomes the child.

How wonderfully everything has turned out! I never
liked Evie's engagement to Elmer*—*though he is such a
dear boy. I always felt somehow that her heart wasn't
in it*—*mothers do feel these things. But Marnie really
loves him. It's too bad he couldn't have been here, but
of course it would have looked queer*—*nobody would
have understood*—*and it would never do to announce
the engagement yet.

I've always loved Darcy. He isn't rich but they won't
be any poorer than Jim and I when we started out. And
Evie's a famous little cook and manager, thanks to
dear Mary. It seems like yesterday that we had Evie's
coming-out tea. How sweet she was*—*everybody said
so*—*just shy enough to seem really like a bud, as they
called them then.

Patricia Miller and that artist son of hers are here
after all. I do hope he won't be annoyed because we
didn't hang the picture he sent as a gift. But nobody
could really tell which side was up. They do paint such
extraordinary pictures nowadays.

I hope the reception will go off nicely. I hope nobody
will notice the worn place in the hall carpet. And I

hope the bills won't be too terrible. It was sweet of the Blythes to give us the mums, but I didn't want all those roses in the reception room. But Jim was so determined his daughter should have a nice wedding. Dear Jim, he's always worshipped his girls. We've been very happy, he and I, though we've had our ups and downs, even our quarrels. They say Dr. Blythe and his wife have never had a single quarrel, but I don't believe that. Tiffs anyhow. Everyone does.

He's pronouncing them man and wife . . . I won't cry . . . I won't. It's bad enough to see Jim with tears in his eyes. I suppose people will think I've no feeling—

The mother of the groom reflected, *My darling boy! How well he looks! I don't know if she is just the one I would have chosen for him—she's been brought up as a rich man's daughter—but if he is happy, what does it matter? Susan Baker told me Mary Hamilton told her there was nothing she couldn't do. If his dear father could have lived to see this day! I'm glad I decided on that Dutch walnut design in the dining room for my present. I had only one bridesmaid when I was married. She wore a picture hat of white lace with a drooping brim. Rilla Blythe is the prettiest of all the bridesmaids. Darcy is kissing his wife— his wife—how strange that sounds! My little baby married! She has a sweet face. She does love him—I feel sure of that—in spite of that engagement to Elmer Owen. There was something I didn't understand—I never will, I suppose—but Darcy seems quite satisfied about it, so I'm sure it's all right. Oh, what would the world be without youth? And yet it passes so quickly.*

We are old before we know it. We never believe it. And then some day we wake up and discover we are old. Ah me! But Darcy is happy. That is all that matters now. And I believe it will last. Strange how they used to quarrel, though. Ever since the Marches began coming to Glen St. Mary, long before they built Merestead. Darcy's father and I never quarrelled. But then we didn't meet until we were grown up, and it was love at first sight. Things are *different nowadays, let them say what they will. I have no son now—but if he is happy . . .*

The father of the bride was thinking, *My little girl looks very beautiful. A trifle pale—but I never like a made-up bride. Thank heaven, decent skirts are in again. It doesn't seem long since Amy and I were standing like that. Evie isn't so pretty a bride as her mother was, after all. That dress becomes Amy. She looks as young as any of them . . . a wonderful woman. If I had to choose over again I'd make the same choice. There's no one I could compare her to. I suppose we'll soon have to face the loss of Marnie, too. Well, mother and I were alone once and I guess we can stand being alone again. Only . . . we were young then . . . that makes all the difference. But if the girls are happy—*

The best man was thinking, *You'll never see me in a scrape like this—though that little bridesmaid is cute—slant eyes like a fairy's—twinkling like a little dark star—but he travels the fastest who travels alone. The Blythe bridesmaid is a bit of a beauty but they tell me she's bespoken. Bride looks a bit icy, rather like a cool white nun. Wonder why Darcy's so goofy about her. Seems to me I've heard something about another engagement. Hope he's not just a consolation prize. The gods grant my shoes don't creak when I'm going down the aisle like Hal Crowder's did and that I won't drop the wedding ring like Joe Raynor; it rolled to the very feet of the girl the groom had jilted. They've done the decorations rather well for a country church. It's over. Darcy's sewed up—poor Darcy!*

Maid of honour, Marnie March, was thinking, *How lonesome it's going to be without darling Evie! She's always been so sweet to me. But I'll have Elmer and that means all the world. I can't understand how Evelyn could ever have preferred Darcy to him, how thankful I am she did. I wish he wasn't so rich. People will say I'm marrying him for his money. Why, I'd jump at him if he hadn't a cent in his pocket. Darcy's a good egg. I think I'll like him for a brother-in-law, though I never could bear the way he laughs. He sounds so sneery. But I don't think he means it. I wish Elmer could see me now. This periwinkle blue becomes me. Not so well as it does Rilla Blythe, though. It needs lighter hair than mine, I wonder if she really is engaged to Kenneth Ford and if she loves him as I love Elmer. No, that is impossible.*

Oh, it's dreadful—and wonderful—and heavenly—to love anyone as I love Elmer. We Marches care so horribly when we do care! Those awful weeks when I thought he was going to marry Evie! And to think I ever called him a magazine-ad man! Oh, I hope I won't get any fatter! I'll take nothing but orange juice for breakfast after this. That must make some difference. Yet those Blythe girls eat anything they like and are always as slim as reeds. It must be predestination.

What a bombshell it would be if Elmer and I were getting married today, too, as he wanted. Of course, it would never have done. People would have talked their heads off. It's queer we can never do anything we really want to in this world for fear of what people will say! But anyway I wanted to get my breath after finding myself engaged to him. We won't have a fuss like this, anyway—I'm determined on that. Oh, how frightfully solemn the service is! "Until death do us part." We'll mean it. Does that make me thrill. Oh, Elmer!

The groom thought, *Will she really come after the beastly way I've always treated her? From the time we were kids and they had that little cottage at the end of our farm at the Narrows. I was just a jealous young idiot! I suppose Mollie's somewhere back there. God bless her. When I think what would have happened without her! She's coming! And I have to stand here like a stick instead of rushing to meet her and clasping her in my arms! How beautiful Evie is! God help me to make her happy . . . make me worthy of her . . . I wish I'd been a better man . . . it's over . . . she's my wife . . .* my wife!

Thought the bride, *Is this just some wonderful dream? Will I wake up presently and find I've got to marry Elmer? Oh, if anything were to happen yet to prevent it . . . the minister dropping dead . . . he doesn't look very robust. And to think Darcy always loved me when I thought he hated me! And the way I treated him! Oh, just suppose Mollie hadn't caught him!*

Marnie looks so sweet. I hope she'll be almost as happy a bride as I am. She couldn't be quite so happy, of course, nobody could.

How beautifully solemn this is! Oh, his voice saying, "I will." There, I hope everybody heard me. No bride in the world ever said it more gladly . . . I am his wife.

Reverend John Meredith thought, *I don't know why it is, but I have a feeling that these two people I've just married are perfectly happy. What a pity one has this feeling so seldom. Well, I only hope they'll be as happy as Rosamond and I are.*

Mary Hamilton said to her crony, Susan Baker, in a back seat, "Sure, Susan me dear, and one great advantage av the back sate is ye can be seeing iverybody and iverything without getting a crick in your neck. Evie, bless her heart, did be wanting me to sit up front wid the guests. There niver was any false pride about *her*. But I know me place better than that.

"There come the doctor and Mrs. Blythe. She do be looking like a girl for all her years."

"She's a girl at heart," sighed Susan, "but she's never been the same woman since Walter's death."

"Well, he died in a glorious cause. Me own nephew went, too. It's the proud and happy woman I am today, Susan Baker."

"I'm not wondering at that, if all I've heard is true. But you can't believe all you hear."

"No, nor one tinth av it. Well, I'll be telling you the truth, Susan, if you promise me solemnly niver to breathe a word av it to a living soul. They told me that av you whin I began coming here—how minny years ago?"

"Never mind," said Susan, who didn't care to be reminded of her age. "Just get on with your story before they come."

"Well, Susan Baker, I've been seeing a miracle happen—siveral av them in fact."

"It's a miracle to be seeing Evie marry Darcy Phillips," conceded Susan. "Everyone has always thought they detested each other."

"Not iveryone, Susan. Not me. I always did be guessing the truth. As for the miracle like iverything else they do be going by threes. Have ye iver noticed that?"

"To be sure I have."

"Well, it's little I was expecting innything like this two months ago, wid me pet going to marry the wrong man and Marnie breaking her heart about it and iverything so criss-cross I couldn't even belave the Good Man Himsilf could be straightening it out."

"So she *was* engaged to Elmer Owen? I heard it from several, but no one seemed sure."

"Av coorse she was—but you'll niver breathe a word av this Susan?"

"If Mrs. Doctor dear asks right out," said Susan doubtfully.

"Well, I wouldn't mind her knowing, it'd be better than her hearing a whole lot of gossip. And they tell me she's one that can hold her tongue."

"No one tighter," said Susan, "when anything

important is at stake. She never told a soul about me and Whiskers-on-the-Moon."

"She mightn't have, but it got out somehow."

"Oh well, you know what gossip is. And of course Whiskers couldn't hold his tongue. He's been abusing me ever since."

"What could you ixpect av a man? Well, to get back to me story. There niver was innyone but Evie for Darcy and don't let innyone tell ye different, Susan Baker!"

"I won't. But it is true they were always fighting from the time they were tads."

"And didn't ye be telling me that Rilla and Kenneth Ford used to fight like cats and dogs when they were small?"

"That was different," said Susan hastily.

"Not a mite av difference. Kids always do be fighting. They've been in love wid each ither iver since they grew up, only they didn't be knowing it. That's some folks' way av coorting. They wouldn't be fighting if they didn't be caring.

"They begun it the first day they iver met, whin he was tin and she was siven and they were stopping at the Phillipses till the cottage was ready for thim. She flung a big gob av mud at him bekase he was took up wid a liddle cousin av his that did be making eyes at him."

"They begun it young in those days," sighed Susan. "Maybe if my ma hadn't said I must behave myself when the boys were round . . . but it's too late now . . . and I'm content with my lot, as long as I can work."

"Sure and they didn't begin inny younger then than now. But if ye kape on interrupting me, Susan Baker—"

"Go on. It's only—well, did ever a decent man ask you to marry him, Mary Hamilton?"

"Millions av thim. At inny rate that's what I always do be telling people who ask impertinent questions."

"I was brought up to tell the truth," said Susan proudly.

"Well, if ye don't be wanting to hear me story—"

"Go on," said Susan resignedly.

"Well, he did be turning the hose on her in return for the gob. Oh, oh, the tithery'i's we did be having wid both mothers scolding! And ivery summer the same whin we come to the Narrows. The way they did be fighting come to be a family joke. Thin her ma forbid her going up to the Phillips—"

"Folks said she was too proud to associate with the country people, I remember," interjected Susan.

"There's a sample av lies for ye. There ain't a woman on this airth that's got less pride than Mrs. March."

"Except Mrs. Doctor dear," murmured Susan under her breath.

"Darcy used to spile her mud pies, just bekase he did be thinking she was more interested in thim than in him, as I knew very well—and her

knocking over his sand-castles for the same rason,
though she didn't know it herself, the darlint.

"And no better whin they did be growing up—"

"Kenneth and Rilla had more sense then," murmured Susan. But she had learned not to interrupt
Mary—and she wanted to hear the rights of the
story before the bridal party arrived.

"It was worse if innything, with her mocking
and twitting him and him sneering at her, both
av thim going white with jealousy whiniver ather
av thim looked at innybody ilse. The tantrums
they'd be taking! They wouldn't be spaking to
each other for wakes. Iverybody thought they
hated aitch other—iverybody excipt ould Mollie
Hamilton, cooking in the kitchen and fading thim
up whin they crept in for a snack whin they was
on fair terms."

Just like Kenneth and Rilla, thought Susan.

"Didn't I be seeing how it was? Ould Mollie
Hamilton isn't blind aven yet, Susan Baker. Him
crazy mad about her, and her up to her pretty
eyes in love wid him, and thinking she was the
last girl he'd iver look at. But thinks I to mesilf,
'They're young and it'll all come right in the ind,'
and in the manetime better a clane fight than the
moonlighting and flirting and 'petting,' as they
called it that wint on wid the rist av the summer
fry. Sure and I used to laugh at the spitting and
snarling av thim so much that I didn't be nading
a dose av medicine once a year."

"Folks are made different," reflected Susan.

"When any of the Ingleside children had a fight with the Fords or the Merediths, I'd lie awake at night, worrying over it. It was well the doctor and his wife had more sense. Mrs. Doctor dear used to say to me, 'Children have been spatting like that all down through the ages.' And I'm guessing she was right. Not that there was much of it in our crowd. But I remember how Darcy Phillips and Evelyn March used to fight. *They* tore up the turf when they went at it all right."

"But in the ind, Susan, me dear, it didn't be inny laughing matter: for they did have a terrible quarrel, though I niver found out what it was about. And Darcy wint off to college widhout thim making it up. He niver come home for two years and it's worried I was. For the time was passing and though he couldn't go to the war bekase av his short sight, there was always heaps av ither boys round. And Darcy sich a gr-and young man by this time wid them smoke-grey eyes av his. Evie hild her head high and pretinded she didn't care, but it's me that did be knowing. And the years did be slipping, and her friends marrying off, and the world getting big and lonely."

It's well I know that *sensation*, thought Susan. *I don't know whatever would have become of me if I hadn't got in with the Ingleside folks. The doctor likes to tease me about old Whiskers, but now I've got over being mad at the old fool I can at least be saying there was one man wanted to marry me, whatever his reason was.*

"Thin last winter she ups and goes to Montreal

for a visit and comes home ingaged to Elmer
Owen."

*Ah, now I'm going to hear the truth about that at
last,* thought Susan triumphantly. *The yarns that
have been going round would make you dizzy, some
saying she wasn't and some she was, and Mrs. Doctor
dear telling me it wasn't anybody's business but their
own. Maybe not, but a body likes to know the truth.*

"Ye could have knocked me down wid a feath-
er," said Mary. "For I did be knowing only too
well that she didn't love him. And it wasn't for
his money ather, Susan Baker. 'He's my choice,
Mollie,' she says grand-like."

As I'd have said if I'd taken Whiskers, thought
Susan.

" 'Oh, oh, if ye have to choose him he's not the
right man for you,' ses I 'There's no choosing wid
the right man,' ses I. 'Ye just *belong*'—like Darcy
and yersilf, I'd have liked to add, but dassn't.

"Av coorse iveryone begun saying she was taking Elmer becase he was a millionaire and talking
av it as a wonderful match for her. Maybe ye
heard some av the gossip, Susan Baker."

"Some of it," said Susan cautiously, who had
heard it and believed it. "But they always say
that when a girl marries a man with money."

"I could have died wid rage and spite, Susan
Baker. I was all built up to hate me fine Elmer
whin he come in June. But I couldn't kape it up,
for he was a rale nice liddle chap in spite av his
money."

"Mrs. Doctor dear said he was one of the nicest

men she had ever met and she thought Evelyn March was a very lucky girl."

"Ah, well, she weren't to blame, not knowing. We all liked him—aven Evie. Marnie hild off a bit at first—ah, there's the gr-r-and girl for ye, Susan Baker."

"I always liked her, what little I've seen of her," admitted Susan, adding in thought, *She didn't put on the airs Evelyn did.*

"Evie is by way av being my fav'rite bekase I looked after her whin she was a baby and her mother so sick."

Just like me and Shirley, thought Susan.

"So she's always seemed like me own. But Marnie's a swate thing and whin she took to moping it worried me, Susan Baker."

"When Shirley had the scarlet fever I was like to have gone clean out of my head," said Susan. "But I always like to think I didn't fail Mrs. Doctor dear for all that. Night after night, Mary Hamilton—"

"Marnie couldn't bear the talk av the wedding, and me thinking it was bekase she felt so bad over Evie's going and maybe a bit sore at Elmer bekase he said, 'Hello gypsy,' whin Evie introduced thim. 'Hello, magazine-ad-man,' said Marnie. Sure and she was niver at a loss of an answer, whin people did be tasing her. It's the blind thing I was, Susan Baker, but whin ye look back on things, ye can see thim as ye couldn't whin they was under yer nose."

"You never spoke a truer word in your life,

Mary Hamilton," agreed Susan, wondering if Mary would ever come to the point of her story.

"Though I couldn't be putting me finger on what was missing. Innyway, iverything was smooth as crame on top and they got all their plans made and Elmer went back to Montreal. And after he was gone, I wint into Marnie's room to swape, thinking she was out, and there she was sitting, crying, Susan Baker—crying so pretty—no noise—only just the big tears rolling down her nice liddle brown chakes."

The way Mrs. Doctor dear cries, thought Susan. *It's the real way of crying. I remember when Shirley— and Walter—*

" 'Darlint, what do be the matter?' ses I in a bit av a panic. It was such an uncommon thing to see Marnie cry. 'Oh, nothing much,' ses she, 'only I'm in love with the man me sister is going to marry. And I'm to be her maid av honour. And I wish I was dead,' ses she. Was I tuk aback, Susan Baker!"

Like I was when Rilla brought the baby home in the soup tureen, thought Susan. *Will I ever be forgetting that day!*

"Nothing," continued Mary, "could I think av saying only stupid-like, 'There's a lot av min in the world, me darlint. Why be getting in such a pother over one?'

" 'Bekase he's the only one for me,' ses me poor Marnie."

"Old maid as I am I could have told you she would say that," said Susan.

" 'But ye nadn't worry,' ses Marnie—as if a body could help worrying. 'Evelyn isn't going to know this, or aven suspect it. Oh, oh Mollie,' ses she, getting reckless-like, 'whin I first saw him I said, 'Magazine-ad-man,' and now I could kiss his shoes. But no one'll iver know it excipt you, Mollie, and if you iver tell I'll slaughter you in cold blood.' So I shouldn't be telling you, Susan Baker and me conscience—"

"Now, never be minding your conscience, Mary Hamilton. Marnie was meaning her own class and anyhow everything has changed since then. She wouldn't be minding now," said Susan rather guiltily, but consoling herself by reflecting that she would never breathe a word of it to a living soul.

"Tell, was it?" Mary Hamilton was too wrapped up in her tale to listen to Susan Baker's interruptions. "If I could have done inny good telling I'd have shouted it from the housetops. But I couldn't, so I hild me tongue. And thin, on top of all that, as soon as the engagemint was announced, comes me fine Darcy, raging mad, as I could very well be telling, but as cold as ice.

"I did be hearing it all as they fought it out on the verandy. Not that I did be listening av purpose, Susan Baker, but whin people are as close to ye as they were to me, ye can't be hilping hearing what they do be saying.

"Short and swate it was.

" 'Are ye going to sell yersilf for money? I'll

not belave it till I hear it from yer own lips,' ses
he. 'I'm going to marry Elmer Owen,' ses Evelyn
politely, 'and I happen to love him, Mr. Phillips.'
'Ye lie,' said Darcy—not over-polite now, was it
Susan Baker? And Evie ses, icier than himsilf
and white wid rage, 'Git out av me sight, Darcy
Phillips, and stay out av it.' "

*When the upper crust get quarrelling, there isn't
much difference between us*, thought Susan. *That
sounds just like something Whiskers-on-the-Moon
might have said in one of his tantrums.*

" 'I'll take ye at yer word,' ses Darcy. 'I'm
going to New York tonight'—he was interning
there for a year, whativer that may mean—'and
ye'll niver see me again, Evelyn March.' Did ye
iver be hearing the like?"

"Many's the time," said Susan.

"Well, wid that he wint. And me poor pet
comes inty me kitchen and looks at me, still holding her head high, but wid a face like death. 'He's
gone, Mollie,' she said, 'and he'll niver come back.
And I wish I was dead.'

" 'Do ye be wanting him to come back?' ses I.
'No lies, now, me pet. A lie do be a refuge I'm not
blaming inny woman for taking betimes, but this
be too serious for it. Iverything's snarled up and
I'm going to straighten it out wid a jerk, but I'm
wanting to know where I stand first.'

" 'I *do* want him back, and he's the only one
I've iver loved or iver will love,' ses she—as if
I didn't know that and always had been know-
ing av it! 'There's the truth for ye at last. But

it's too late, his train leaves in fifteen minutes. I wudn't give in—me pride wudn't let me. And he's gone—he's gone! And innyhow he's always hated me!'

"I'd picked that day to clane me oil stove, Susan Baker, and was I be way av being a sight! But I had no time to change inty me latest from Paris. Out I wint to the garage. Thank hiven the little runabout was there!

"I tuk a pace off the garage door as I backed out, and just shaved the lily pond. But me only worry was cud I be getting to the station afore the train wint. Niver cud I do it by the highway, but there did be a witch's road I knew av."

The short cut by the Narrow road, thought Susan. *It hasn't been used for years. I thought it was closed up. But to a woman like Mary Hamilton—*

"Down the highway I wint at the rate av no man's business—"

The doctor said he'd met her and never had such a narrow escape from a head-on collision in his life, thought Susan.

"Didn't I be thanking hiven there wasn't any speed cops in this part av the Island—and niver before did I be having the satisfaction av hitting it up to siventy. Just afore I rached me side cut what did I be seeing but a big black cat, looking as if he intinded to cross the road and me heart stood still. I do be supposing ye think I'm a superstitious ould fool, Susan Baker."

"Not me," said Susan, "I don't know that I hold much with black cats, though I remember one crossed my path the evening before we heard of Walter's death. But never mind that. Dreams, now, are different. While the Great War was going on there was a Miss Oliver boarding at Ingleside—and the dreams that girl would have! And every one came true. Even the doctor—but as for the cats we can all be having our own opinion of them. Did I ever tell you the story of our Jack Frost?"

"Yis—but I did be thinking it was my story ye was wanting to hear."

"Yes, yes. Go on," said Susan repentantly.

"Well, ather luck was wid me or the Ould Scratch had business for him somewhere for he turned around and wint back and I slewed round inty me cut.

"Twas be way av being a grand ride, Susan Baker. Niver will I be knowing the like again, I'm thinking. I skimmed over a ploughed field and tore through a brook and up a muddy lane and through the backyard av the Wilson farmhouse. I'm swearing I motored slap inty a cow though where she wint whin I struck her I'll never be telling ye—"

"I can be telling you," said Susan. "She wasn't much hurt except for a bit of skin or two, but she went clean off her milk and if the doctor hadn't talked Joe Wilson round—or even then if the Wilson's bill had ever been paid—he'd have made all the trouble he could for you."

"I slipped through the haystacks and I wint right over an acre of sparrow grass wid no bumps to spake av—and thin up looms a spruce hedge

and a wire fince beyant it. And I did be knowing
I had a few minutes to spare.

"I mint to stop and run for it—the station was
just on the other side—but I was a bit ixcited
like—and did be putting me foot on the accelerator instid av the brake."

*Thank the Good Man Above, I've resisted all
temptation to learn to drive a car*, thought Susan
piously.

"I wint slap through the hedge—"

"Sam Carter vowed he never saw such a sight
in his life," said Susan.

"—and the fince, and bang inty the ind av the
station. But the hedge and the fince had slowed
me up a bit and no rale harm was done to the
station.

"Darcy was just stipping on the train—"

Ah, now we're coming to the exciting part, thought
Susan. *Everybody has been wondering what she said
to him.*

"I grabbed him by the arm and I ses—"

Both arms, thought Susan.

" 'Darcy Phillips, Evelyn do be breaking her
liddle heart for you and ye get straight back to
her—and if I iver hear av inny more jawing and
fighting betwane ye, I'll give ye both a good
spanking, for it's clane tired I am av yer nonsense and misunderstanding. It's time ye both
grew up.' "

Do people ever grow up, reflected Susan. *The doctor and Mrs. Blythe are the only people I know of who
really seem to have grown up. Certainly Whiskers-on-*

the-Moon didn't. How he run. And Susan reflected with considerable satisfaction upon a certain pot of boiling dye which the said Whiskers-on-the-Moon had once narrowly escaped.

" 'Not a yap out av ye,' ses I, wid considerable severity."

They say she nearly shook the bones out of his skin, thought Susan. *Though nobody had any idea why.*

" 'Just be doing as you're told,' ses I.

"Well, Susan Baker, ye can be seeing for yersilf today what come av it. The insurance company was rale rasonable."

And lucky for poor Jim March they were, thought Susan.

"But ye haven't heard the whole wonder. When Evie told Elmer she couldn't iver be marrying him bekase she was going to marry Darcy Phillips, didn't we be looking for a tither-i! But he tuk it cool as a cowcumber and ses, ses he—what do ye be thinking he said, Susan Baker?"

"I could never be guessing what any man said or thought," said Susan, "but I think I hear them coming—"

"Well, he did be saying, 'He's the brother-in-law I'd have picked.' She didn't know what he was maning. But he turned up the nixt wake wid his fine blue car and its shining wire wheels. And I've been hearing that the moment he did be seeing Marnie, whin he come to plan the widding wid Evie, he knew he'd made a mistake, but he was too much av a gintleman to let on. He'd have gone through it widout moving a single hair if he'd had to."

"Maybe not if he'd known that Marnie had fell in love with him, too," said Susan. "It *is* them—well, I'm obliged to you for telling me the rights of the affair, Mary, and if there's anything you'd like to know—if it doesn't concern the family at Ingleside—I'll be right glad to tell you."

"Here they come, Susan Baker. Sure and me pet lights up the church, doesn't she? It'll be long afore it sees a prettier bride."

That depends on how long it is before Rilla and Kenneth Ford get married, thought Susan. *Though Rilla always declares she'll never be married in the church. The Ingleside lawn for her, she says. I'm thinking she's right. There's too much chance for gossip at these church weddings.*

"And now we'll shut up our yap, Susan Baker, until they are married safe and sound. That do be a load lifted from me mind. Will ye be coming home wid me, Susan, and having a cup av tay in me kitchen? And I'll see ye get a sight av the prisents. They're elegant beyant words. Did ye iver see a prettier bride? It's mesilf that's knowing there niver was a happier one."

I'd like anyone to say that to Mrs. Doctor Blythe, thought Susan. Aloud, "He's a bit poor, I hear."

"Poor is it? Have sinse, Susan Baker. I'm telling ye they're rich beyant the drames av avarice."

"An old maid like myself is not supposed to know much about such things," said Susan with dignity. "But maybe you're right, Mary Hamilton, maybe you're right. One can learn a good deal from observation in this world, as Rebecca Dew used to say. And the doctor and Mrs. Blythe were poor enough when they started out. Ah, them happy days in the old House of Dreams, as they used to call it! It grieves me to the heart they'll never return. Thank you, Mary, but I must be getting back to Ingleside. I have duties there. I'll have a cup of tea with you some other day when things have quieted down. And I'm real thankful to you for telling me the rights of the whole story. If you knew the gossip—"

"Sure and I can be guessing," said Mary. "But take my advice, Susan Baker, and larn to drive a car. Ye can niver tell whin the knack'll come in handy."

"At my age! That *would* be a sight. No," said Susan firmly, "I'll trust to my own two legs as long as they'll carry me, Mary Hamilton."

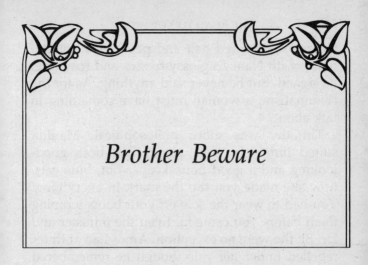

Brother Beware

There had been no change in the Randebush household in the Upper Glen for fifteen years ever since Nancy, beloved wife of Amos Randebush, had died. Amos and his brother Timothy and Matilda Merry just jogged along peacefully and contentedly.

At least Amos and Timothy were contented. If Matilda Merry, who belied her name if ever a woman did, was not contented, it was her own fault. She had a good place as housekeeper and a pleasant grievance of chronic rheumatism. People said she was a fortune to Dr. Gilbert Blythe. Amos paid her fair wages and never growled when the biscuits were soggy or the roast was over-done. Sometimes when he looked at her sitting at the head of his table and contrasted her skin-

ny mouse-coloured hair and pessimistic counte-
nance with Nancy's glossy tresses and rosy face,
he sighed. But he never said anything. As for the
rheumatism, a woman must have something to
talk about.

Timothy was more philosophical. Matilda
suited him very well. Nancy had been good-
looking and a good housekeeper but, blue cats,
how she made you toe the mark in everything!
You had to wear the sole off your boots scraping
them before you came in. Even the minister and
Dr. Blythe were no exception. Amos had at times
rebelled under her rule though he remembered
only her good qualities now. That was what
women did to you, even after they were dead.
Timothy thanked his stars that none of them
had ever succeeded in bamboozling him. No
thank you! He had always hated them all in
general, except Mrs. Dr. Blythe, whom he tolerated, but he hated the Winkworth woman in
particular. Dimples, by gad! Airs and graces,
by jiminy! Taffy-coloured hair and come-hither
eyes! Blue cats! Could anyone have supposed
that Amos could be such a fool? Wasn't one
lesson enough? Evidently not, when you had
a spineless creature like Amos, and a plotting,
wheedling, designing, desperate hussy like the
Winkworth woman to deal with! Hold your
horses! Amos might be quite helpless before
her fascinations, and Mrs. Blythe might be
helping things along—hadn't he heard she
had a passion for matchmaking? But Amos

had a brother to save him in spite of himself.

Miss Alma Winkworth was boarding with the Knapps at Glen St. Mary. It was reported through the Knapps that she worked in Hillier's Beauty Shoppe in Boston, that she had had an operation and needed a longer vacation than her usual two weeks before going back to work. Timothy hadn't a speck of faith in that operation. Very likely the doctor and Mrs. Blythe were in the plot. Alma Winkworth wouldn't look so blooming if she had had an operation. It was merely a play for sympathy. She had just come to Glen St. Mary to see if she couldn't catch a man, and, by golly, she was on the point of succeeding. Would succeed if he, Timothy, didn't put a spoke in her wheel.

They had seen her first in church, sitting in the Blythe pew in front of them—Maria Knapp never went to church—a smiling creature, looking, as far as hair and complexion went, like a remarkably good advertisement for a beauty shop.

Amos had never been the same man since. Next evening he went down to the Knapps on some trumped-up excuse and that was the creature's opportunity. Look what she had done to him already. For all it was harvest time, when men had to work and sleep, Amos mooned through the day and when night came, shaved and dressed, touched up his moustache and went to the Glen on some excuse about a meeting of the Fox Breeders' Association.

Another bad sign was that Amos had suddenly

become sensitive about his age. When, on his fifieth birthday, Timothy congratulated him on attaining the half-century mark, Amos peevishly remarked that he didn't feel a day over forty. The Winkworth woman had told the Blythes that *she* was forty, no doubt to encourage Amos, for would any single woman admit to being forty if she had no nefarious purpose in it?

It seemed to Timothy that nothing less than a miracle could prevent Amos from asking the Winkworth woman to marry him. He had not done it yet; Timothy was sure of that, from Amos' continual air of nervousness and uncertainty. But very soon he would screw his courage to the sticking point. He would have to do it before another ten days elapsed for then he had to leave for the National Exhibition in Toronto, in charge of a consignment of silver foxes the Fox Breeders' Association was sending there. He would be absent for two weeks and the Winkworth woman's vacation would be over before he returned. So Timothy felt quite sure Amos would propose to her before he went.

No, by gad, he wouldn't! A lifelong harmonious brotherhood was not going to be destroyed like this. Timothy had an inspiration from heaven. Joe's Island! There was your answer to prayer!

The details caused Timothy considerable anxiety. Time pressed and, rack his brain as he might, he could think of no way to lure the Winkworth woman to Joe's Island unbeknownst to anyone.

But Providence opened a way. Mrs. Knapp

came to the Upper Glen store and dropped in to have a visit with Matilda Merry. They sat on the back porch and rocked and gossiped until Timothy, lying on the kitchen sofa just inside the window, heard something that brought him to his feet in another flash of inspiration. Miss Winkworth, so Mrs. Knapp said, was going to Charlottetown to spend a day or two with a friend who lived there. She was going on the boat train. So was Mrs. Dr. Blythe who was going up to Avonlea for a visit.

So this, Timothy scornfully reflected, was why Amos had seemed so dull and depressed all day and talked of getting some liver pills from Dr. Blythe. Blue cats! He must have it bad if the prospect of being parted from his lady-love for a couple of days drove him to liver pills. Well, the hotter the fire the quicker it burned out. Amos would soon get over his infatuation and be thankful for his escape—yes, before Dr. Blythe's pills were half taken.

Timothy lost no time. He felt sure Amos was going to take her to the train but Amos' car was still visible down in the store yard. Timothy strode to the barn and got out his own car. His only fear was that Amos was going to call for Mrs. Blythe too.

"Now where is *he* going?" said Mrs. Knapp, as Timothy's car swung out of the yard.

"Must be to the harbour after fish," said Matilda. "He'd have to have shaved and dressed if he was going visiting, even if it was only to Ingleside after liver pills. Timothy's forty-five if he's a day but vain as a peacock."

"Well, he's a real good-looking man," said Mrs. Knapp. "Away ahead of Amos if you ask me. Amos is what you might call insignificant, as Mrs. Blythe would say."

"Do you think Amos and your boarder are going to make a match of it?" asked Matilda.

"I shouldn't wonder," said Mrs. Knapp. "He's certainly been very attentive. And Mrs. Dr. Blythe has done her best to bring it about. Nothing can cure *her* of matchmaking. And I think Miss Winkworth is pretty tired of struggling along by herself. But I can't be sure, she's one to keep her own counsel."

The Winkworth woman was sitting on the Knapp veranda when Timothy drove up. She was dressed for travelling in a natty suit and a smart little hat with a green bow and she had her packaway at her feet.

"Evening, Miss Winkworth," said Timothy briskly. "Sorry my brother couldn't come. He was detained by some fox business. So I've come to take you to the train."

"That is lovely of you, Mr. Randebush."

She certainly had a pleasant voice. And a very elegant figure. And a way of looking at you! All at once Timothy remembered that he hadn't shaved that day and that bits of chaff were sticking to his sweater.

"I guess we'd better hurry," he said grimly. "It's near train time."

The Winkworth woman stepped into the car unsuspiciously. Timothy glowed. This was far easier than he had expected. And thank goodness there had evidently been no arrangement with Mrs. Dr. Blythe.

But the crux would come when he turned off the Upper Glen road down the deep-rutted, grass-grown track that led to the bay. She would smell a rat there. She did.

"This isn't the road to the station, is it?" she said with a little note of wonder in her voice.

"No, it isn't," said Timothy, more grimly than ever. "We aren't going to the station."

"Mr. Randebush—"

The Winkworth woman found herself staring into a pair of very stern eyes.

"You are not going to be hurt, Miss. No harm of any kind is intended if you do just as you are told and keep quiet."

The Winkworth woman after one gasp, kept quiet. Probably she thought you had to humour madmen.

"Get out," said Timothy when they reached the end of the road. "Then go right down the wharf and get into the boat that's tied there."

There was nobody in sight. The Winkworth woman walked down the old wharf, Timothy following closely behind, feeling splendidly bold and buccaneery. Blue cats! This was the way to manage them! And yet Dr. Blythe was always saying that women were the equal of men!

When they were off and skimming merrily over

the harbour she said gently, with a disarming little tremor in her voice, "Where—where are you taking me, Mr. Randebush?"

No harm in telling her.

"I'm taking you to Joe's Island, Miss. It's four miles across the harbour. I'm going to leave you there for a few days and my reason is my own business, as Dr. Blythe would say. As I've said you won't be hurt and you'll be quite comfortable. Kenneth Ford's summer house is on the island and I'm caretaker for him. The Fords went to Europe this summer instead of coming to Glen St. Mary. There's plenty of canned stuff in the house and a good stove and I reckon you can cook."

She took it admirably—you had to hand it to her. Almost any woman he knew, except Mrs. Dr. Blythe, would have gone into hysterics. She did not even ask what his reason was. Likely she guessed, durn her. Sitting there as cool and composed as if being kidnapped was all in the day's work!

"Don't you think someone will raise a hue and cry when I'm found missing?" she asked, after an interval.

"Who's to miss you?" he said. "Amos will think you got afraid of being late and took another ride."

"Your brother wasn't taking me. I was going up with the Flaggs," said the Winkworth woman gently. "But when I don't come back day after tomorrow won't Mrs. Knapp wonder?"

"No. She'll think you've just been induced to

stay longer in town. And the doctor and his wife
are going to stay for two weeks in Avonlea.
Besides, what if people do start wondering?
They'll just think you've gone back to Boston
to get out of paying your board."

The Winkworth woman said nothing in reply
to this cruelty. She looked afar over the sunset
harbour. She *had* a way of tilting her head.
Little taffy-coloured curls escaped from under
the edges of her hat. Suddenly she smiled.

Timothy experienced a queer tickly sensation
in his spine.

"The wind is west tonight, isn't it?" she said
dreamily. "And oh, look, Mr. Randebush, there
is the evening star."

As if nobody had ever seen the evening star
before!

Of course she knew she was showing off that
pretty throat of hers when she lifted her face to
the sky!

This kidnapping of women was a durned dangerous business. He didn't like that sensation in
his spine.

Maybe she didn't think he really meant that
about leaving her on Joe's Island. She'd likely
be good and mad when she found he did. Well,
there was plenty of room to be mad in. Four
miles from anywhere. Nothing but fishing boats
ever went near Joe's Island when no one was
there, and they never landed. No light would
show through the solid shutters, and if anybody
saw smoke coming through the shutters they'd

think it was only he, Timothy, airing the house.

By golly, but it was a masterly trick, this!

"Stars are quite common in Glen St. Mary," he said shortly.

The Winkworth woman did not speak again. She sat and looked at that confounded star until they were close to the boat pier on Joe's Island.

"Now, Miss," said Timothy briskly, "here we are."

"Oh, Mr. Randebush, do you really mean that you are going to maroon me on this lonely place? Is there nothing I can say will make you change your mind? Think what Mrs. Dr. Blythe will think of your conduct."

"Miss," said Timothy sternly—all the more sternly because there was no doubt in the world that there *was* a fascination about her and he really did care a good deal about the Blythes' opinion— "Try molding granite if you want an easy job, but don't try to change a Randebush when he has once determined on a course of conduct."

"Mrs. Blythe told me you were all very stubborn," she said meekly, as she stepped out on the pier. A very beguiling fragrance seemed to exhale from her—another advertisement for the beauty shop, no doubt—though Mrs. Blythe did smell the same when she came into church.

The Kenneth Ford house was built on the high rocky point on the north of the little island. All the windows were shuttered with good strong wooden shutters. Doors and shutters were securely locked and Timothy had all the keys, or thought he had. He felt quite sure that even the Blythes did not have one. There was everything in the house one wanted for comfort: canned foods, coffee, tea, running water.

"You can be quite comfortable here, Miss. It's dark, of course, but there's plenty of lamps and coal oil. The bed in the north room upstairs is aired, I saw to that yesterday."

Timothy's face was red. He suddenly felt that it was a most indelicate thing to talk about beds to a lady.

Without another word he went out and locked the door. As he did so, he felt a twinge of compunction. It was too much like locking the door of a jail.

Don't get maudlin, Timothy Randebush, he told himself sternly. *Amos has to be saved and this is the only way. You know she can't be let run loose. She'd signal some fishing boat quicker than a wink. The boats sometimes run close to Joe's Island when the wind is east.*

Halfway across the bay he suddenly thought, "Blue cats! Were there any matches in the Ford house?" He had lighted a lamp when he went in but when she had to refill it, it would go out and what then?

To his wrath and amazement, Timothy found himself unable to sleep.

Well, you didn't kidnap a woman every night. No doubt it did something to your nervous system. If he could only stop wondering if she had any matches!

Blue cats! If she hadn't she couldn't light a fire to cook with! She'd starve to death. No, she wouldn't. The meat in the cans was already cooked. Even if it was cold, it would sustain life.

Turn over and go to sleep, Timothy Randebush. Timothy turned over but he did not go to sleep.

The worst of it was he could not take her matches in the morning. The wheat had to be got in and for him to start off on a cruise to Joe's Island, which would take the best part of the forenoon, would be to arouse Amos' suspicion or so thought Timothy's guilty conscience.

The day seemed endless. When the last load was in, Timothy shaved and dressed in a hurry and, not waiting for supper under the pretence of having to see a man at the Harbour Mouth on business, got out his car and started for the shore, stopping at one of the village stores to get matches.

The evening had turned cold and foggy and a raw wind was blowing up the harbour. Timothy was chilled to the bone when he landed on Joe's Island. But when he unlocked the kitchen door after a preliminary knock, for manners' sake, a most delightful sight greeted his eyes and a most delightful smell his nostrils.

A cheery fire was burning in the range and Alma Winkworth, in a trailing lacy blue dress, protected by a rose-coloured apron, was frying codfish cakes on it. The whole kitchen was filled with their appetizing aroma, blent with the odour of coffee. A plate of golden-brown muffins was atop of the warming oven.

Her cheeks were flushed from the heat of the stove, her rich hair curled in tendrils around her forehead and her eyes shone. Timothy actually thought this and then was horribly ashamed of such a thought.

Maudlin! That's what it was! Worse than Amos. Blue cats! There was something the matter with the pit of his stomach. It had been the spine before, now it was the pit of his stomach. It must be the smell of that supper. He hadn't had a mouthful to eat since twelve o'clock.

"Oh, Mr. Randebush, I'm so glad to see you," she was saying.

"It occurred to me that you mightn't have any matches and I thought I'd better bring you some," said Timothy gruffly.

"Oh, wasn't that clever of you!" she said gratefully.

Timothy didn't see where the cleverness came in but she contrived to make him feel like a wonder man.

"Won't you sit down awhile, Mr. Randebush?" she was saying.

"No thanks," Timothy was gruffer than ever. "I've got to get back and get my supper."

"Oh, Mr. Randebush, won't you have a bite with me? There's plenty for two—and it's so lonely eating alone. Besides, these cakes are made after Susan Baker's famous recipe. She imparted it to me as a special favour."

Timothy told himself that it was the smell of the coffee that was weakening him. The dishwater that Matilda Merry called coffee!

He found his hat was taken and he was gently pushed into a chair.

"Just sit there until I lift my codfish cakes. I know better than to try to talk to a hungry man."

Such codfish cakes—such muffins—such coffee! And such common sense! No bothering you with conversation. She just let you eat your fill in comfort.

To be sure, that queer sensation still persisted, even though his stomach was no longer empty. But what matter? Dr. Blythe always said the less attention you paid to your stomach the better. Not many doctors knew as much as Dr. Blythe.

"It's really very nice to have a man in the house," said Alma Winkworth after Timothy's second cup of coffee.

"I s'pose you find it rather lonesome," said Timothy gruffly, then reproached himself for his gruffness. It was necessary, of course, to save Amos from her clutches, but one didn't need to be a clown.

The Randebushes had always prided themselves on their good manners. But she wasn't going to get around him with her blarney and her lonesomeness. *He* had cut his eye teeth.

"A little," she said wistfully. "You might sit awhile and talk to me, Mr. Randebush."

"Can't do it, Miss. You must get your gossip from Mrs. Knapp and Mrs. Blythe."

"But Mrs. Blythe never gossips and Mrs. Knapp is a newcomer."

"Can't do it, Miss. Thank you for the supper. Susan Baker herself couldn't have beaten those cakes. But I must be getting along."

She was looking at him admiringly, with her hands clasped under her chin. It was years, he thought, since a woman had looked admiringly at him.

"I suppose you haven't an aspirin about you," she said wistfully again. "I'm afraid I've a head-ache coming on. I take one occasionally."

Timothy had no aspirin. He thought about it all the way home and most of the night. Suppose she was there alone, suffering. There was no help for it. He'd have to go again the next night and take her a supply of aspirin.

He took the aspirin. He also took a brown paper parcel containing two pork chops and two pounds of butter wrapped in a rhubarb leaf. Matilda Merry missed it but never knew what became of it.

He found Alma Winkworth sitting by a rock maple fire in the living room. She wore a cherry-red velvet dress with little red drops in her ears. Blue cats! What women could carry in packaways!

She ran to meet him with lovely dimpled hands outstretched.

"Oh, I've been waiting for you all the evening, Mr. Randebush, *hoping* you would come. I had such a dreadful night without the aspirin. And you've brought some!"

"I hope it's fresh. I had to get it at the store since Dr. Blythe wasn't home."

"I'm sure it will be all right. You are really so kind and thoughtful. You *must* sit down and talk to me for a little while."

Timothy, who had come to the conclusion that the feeling in the pit of his stomach was chronic and that he'd better consult Dr. Blythe about it, sat down slowly.

"Amos worked his first wife to death," Timothy found himself saying, without the least idea why he said it. Then he was overcome with remorse.

"No, he didn't. She worked herself to death. But he didn't prevent her."

Again, remorse. Blue cats! What sort of a man was he, slandering his brother like this?

"I don't suppose he could have prevented her. Some women are like that."

Alma Winkworth was laughing. Her laugh, like everything about her, was pleasant. "You *have* such a knack of putting things, Mr. Randebush."

The firelight sparkled and shimmered over her shining hair and beautiful dress. Timothy could see her thus quite clearly all the way home.

She had thanked him so appealingly for his visit and asked him if he couldn't come again. Well, he might—after a night or two. Of course it was mighty lonely for her there with not even a

dog to talk to. Suppose he took her a dog. No, that
would never do. A dog might attract attention by
barking. But a cat, now. The very thing. She had
mentioned that she was fond of cats; also that she
had heard a rat. He'd take her a cat. He'd better
take it the next evening. Rats sometimes did a
lot of damage.

By four o'clock the next day Timothy was
skimming across the harbour. In the bow was
a yowling squirming shapeless thing: Matilda
Merry's cat tied up in a potato bag.

Timothy suspected that Matilda would raise
Cain when she missed her pet, but after kidnapping women you grew callous about cats.

Alma insisted that Timothy have supper with
her and vowed she was delighted with the cat.
While they sat and talked after supper she held
the creature on her lap and caressed it.

Timothy had a spasm of horror when he realized that he was envying the cat.

The next day Amos suddenly announced that
he was starting for Toronto on Monday instead
of Wednesday. There was some fox business
to be attended to before the exhibition came
on. Timothy was relieved. Amos had not been
a very cheerful housemate of late. Worried
because Alma Winkworth was lingering so long
in Charlottetown, most likely. He didn't know
her address so he couldn't hunt her up.

Well, Amos would soon be gone so he could set
Alma free. The thought plunged him into gloom
instead of exultation. It took him some little time

to realize what had happened to him. He did not go to Joe's Island that night or the next night—would not have gone for a million dollars, he told himself.

But he had to go the third night for Amos was safely on his way to Toronto and there was no longer the slightest need for keeping Alma Winkworth mewed up. Besides, the Blythes were back and he mistrusted Mrs. Blythe. She was entirely too clever for a woman.

"I thought you were never coming back," said Alma with tender reproach. "I've missed you so."

With one look of those soft eyes Alma could say more things than most women could utter in a year. Their sorcery had undone Timothy and he knew it at last—and did not care.

I'm a wreck—shattered fore and aft, he thought dismally. He had really felt it since the moment she looked at the star. It was a kind of relief to admit it, though everyone would laugh at him, except Mrs. Blythe. Somehow he felt she would not laugh.

"Amos has gone to Toronto and I've come to let you out," he said desperately.

For a fleeting second it struck him that she didn't look overjoyed. Then she said slowly, "Would you mind telling me now why you brought me here in the first place?"

"To keep Amos from proposing to you," Timothy blurted out. She might as well know the worst of him.

"Your brother asked me to marry him the night before you kidnapped me," she was saying quietly. "I said no. I felt I didn't—couldn't—marry anybody unless I really loved him. I really couldn't, much as I'd like to have a home of my own."

She had said it. But it didn't make sense. Timothy stared blankly at her. She smiled mischievously at him.

"Of course it would have been nice to have been related to *you*, dear Mr. Randebush."

Timothy cleared his throat.

"Miss Winkworth—Alma—I never was one to beat around the bush. Mrs. Blythe would tell you that if she was here."

Mrs. Blythe had told Alma a good many things about Timothy, but she kept her own counsel.

"Will you marry *me*?" said Timothy. "I—I am very fond of stars. Mrs. Blythe could tell you that. I've got a good house on my own farm—if it's fixed up a bit and a veranda built on. I'd like to take care of you—"

Alma Winkworth smiled again—with a little relief in the smile. No more insolent and absurd customers for renewed beauty; no more lean vacations in cheap boarding-houses. *And* the fine-looking man she had admired so much the first time she had seen him in Glen St. Mary church. ("Why don't you set your cap for Timothy Randebush?" Mrs. Blythe had said once teasingly. "He's away ahead of Amos in every way.")

She came close to him. Timothy Randebush, tingling with the thrills of first love in all his forty-five years, found himself clasping her in his arms.

An hour—or a century—later, Timothy, carrying the cat and the packaway (Matilda Merry often wondered where the cat had been so long but then cats had their ways) turned down the hall to the side door.

"We'll go out this way, Miss Winkworth—Alma, dear. It'll be easier for you walking down to the beach than from the other doors."

He set down the packaway and the cat, selected a key and tried to open it. It would not turn. He tried the knob. The door opened easily.

"Blue cats! The door is unlocked!" he exclaimed.

"It has been unlocked ever since I came here," said Alma Winkworth demurely. "Mrs. Blythe and I were over here one day and I suppose we forgot to lock it. She has a key to it, you know."

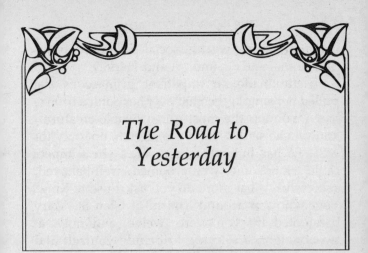

The Road to
Yesterday

Susette was not actually engaged to Harvey
Brooks, but she knew that when she came
back from her visit to Glenellyn she would be.
When Harvey had gone so far as to invite her to
Glenellyn to meet his mother and Aunt Clara and
his Great-aunt Ruth and several other relations, it
meant only one thing: that he had at last made up
his mind to marry her. It would not have occurred
to Harvey that there was any other mind to be
made up.

And, indeed, there wasn't. Susette had long
since decided to say "Yes" when he said "Will
you?" What else could a little-known sub-editor
of a small provincial paper really do when Harvey
Brooks condescended to her? To accept Harvey

meant accepting wealth, social position, a beautiful home, and . . . and . . . and Harvey.

Susette made an impatient grimace as she pulled her smart green hat over her golden bronze hair. "You are the most unreasonable creature I know," she said. "Harvey is a catch, not only for what he has but what he *is*. He's—he's impeccable. Handsome, well-groomed, well-behaved, successful. What more do you ask, Susette King? You, who ran around a farm at Glen St. Mary barefooted till you were twelve, and now, at twenty-eight, are trying to delude yourself and your world into the belief that you have a career? You ought simply to be dying of joy to think that Harvey Brooks—*the* Harvey Brooks who was always supposed to be too busy making money out of black foxes ever to find time to make love, but who would have been expected to choose a countess if he did—has taken it into his head to fall in love with you, to the horror of his clan."

Still, she liked Harvey very well. She loved what he could offer her, and she was going to marry him. There was no doubt in her mind about that as she ran down to Glenellyn that afternoon in her own little car. Nevertheless, she was a trifle nervous. It was a bit of an ordeal to be appraised by Harvey's family who thought so very highly of themselves. And the minute she saw Glenellyn she hated it.

Mrs. Brooks condescended and Aunt Clara kissed her. Susette had not expected that. It seemed to include her too quickly—and too inescapably—in the family. The rest of the house party, almost all of them relations of Harvey, shook hands dutifully and most pleasantly. On the whole, in spite of Aunt Clara's kiss, she felt that they did not quite approve of her.

Aunt Clara, who had a reputation for saying the most poisonous things in the sweetest way, asked her if she wasn't tired after her hard day in a stuffy office.

"Let me see—it's *The Enterprise* you work on? It's supposed to be Conservative, isn't it?"

"No—independent," said Susette, her green eyes shimmering wickedly.

Mrs. Brooks would have sighed, if she had ever done anything so human. She did not trust green-eyed women. Mrs. Gilbert Blythe had green eyes and she had never liked her.

"Harvey," Susette said at lunch next day, "I'm going to play truant this afternoon. I'm going to take my car and go off for a real spin on the road to yesterday. In other words, to see an old farm at Glen St. Mary where I used to spend my summers when I was a kid."

"I'll go with you," said Harvey.

"No." Susette shook her head. "I want to go alone. To keep a tryst with old memories. It would bore you."

Harvey frowned a bit. He did not understand this whim of Susette's and when he did not understand a thing he condemned it. But there was a mutinous tilt to Susette's beautiful chin that warned him it was of no use to protest.

She drew a long breath as she spun out of the Glenellyn gates. There was a delightful road ahead of her. Not a straight road. A straight road was an abomination to Susette who loved curves and dips.

She wondered what had become of all the half and third cousins who had had such fun at the farm with her. And the Blythes who were there half their time. She had lost track of them all—forgotten all of them except Letty, who had been her especial pal, and Jack Hall who was so straight and stiff and was nicknamed Ding-dong—and Dick. She could never forget Dick, the bully and braggart and tell-tale. She had hated him. Everybody had hated him. She remembered how he used to fight with Jem Blythe.

What a little pig he was! remembered Susette. *If he had been ugly, one could have forgiven him. But he was a good-looking kid. He had fine eyes—big grey, devilish eyes. I wonder what has become of him. He'll be married, of course. He'd have to have a wife to bully as soon as he could. Oh, I'd love to meet Dick again and slap his face—as Di Blythe once did.*

Big clouds had come up when Susette finally turned in at the well-remembered gate of the farm at Glen St. Mary. Her heart bounded to see the same wooden gate posts. The old house was there still, unchanged. The old lawn, the old garden, the gleam of the pond through the dark old spruces. Everything was trim and shipshape so it was evident that Roddy or somebody still lived there. But it was equally evident that the place was temporarily deserted. A thunderstorm was certainly coming up and if she couldn't get into the house she would have to scuttle back to Glenellyn.

She was on the point of turning sorrowfully away, when a young man came around the corner of the house and stopped to look at her.

"Why, Dick—Dick," she said.

She ran to him with outstretched hands. She was glad to see even Dick. Hateful as he had always been, he was still a part of the old life that had suddenly become so near and real again.

Dick took her hands and pulled her a little nearer. He looked earnestly into her green eyes and Susette felt a queer inexplicable thrill such as no look of Harvey's had ever given her.

"This must be Susette—Susette King," said Dick slowly. "Nobody else could have those eyes. They always made me think of Mrs. Dr. Blythe's."

"Yes, it's Susette. I'm staying at Glenellyn—the Brooks' summer place, you know."

"Yes, I know. Everybody knows Glenellyn." He seemed to have forgotten to let go of her hands.

"And when I found it was so near, I just had to come. I think I expected to find the old gang and perhaps some of the Blythes. But nobody seems to be at home. Who lives here now? Where did you drop from, Dick?"

Susette was rattling on because she didn't know just what had happened to her and she was afraid to find out. But she remembered that she had hated Dick—they had all hated Dick—and pulled away her hands.

"Roddy and his wife live here. I've been staying with them for a few days, getting ready for my flight to Peru. I'm a humble civil engineer, you see, and I'm leaving tomorrow. I very nearly left this morning. Thank any gods there be that I didn't."

Something darted into Susette's memory. This Dick had once kissed her against her will and she had slapped his face for it. She didn't know why her face should burn over the recollection. Or why it should all at once have ceased to be an enraging humiliation. When Jem Blythe had wanted to make her mad, he used to tease her about it.

"I ought to thank them too," she laughed, "because since you're staying here you can probably let me into the house if it starts to rain. I *do* want to see all round the place now that I'm here but I wouldn't have dared to stay for fear of a downpour."

"Your laugh hasn't changed, Susette," said Dick. "There was nothing like it in the clan— except perhaps Nan Blythe's. And your eyes— what colour are they really? I never could decide. Of course, it's hard to photograph grey-green starlight."

Whom you hated, thought Susette. *You didn't make such pretty speeches in the old days.* All at once—everything seemed to be happening all at once this amazing afternoon—it seemed to her vastly important that Dick should know she had always hated him. And hated him now. Always would hate him. "Do you remember how we fought? How I detested you? How we all detested you?"

"We certainly didn't hit it off when we were kids," admitted Dick. "But . . . be fair now, Susette, was I altogether to blame?"

"You were," cried Susette passionately, much more passionately than there seemed any need for. "You were always doing the meanest things. Do you remember how you pushed me into that bed of nettles and ruined my pink chiffon dress— and called attention to my freckles before everybody—and burned my doll at the stake—and filled poor Bruno's coat with burrs and . . . and . . ."

"Kissed you," said Dick with an impish grin. "But so did Jem Blythe once and you didn't seem to mind—much."

"And do you remember what a whack on the nose I gave you for it?" cried Susette with relish, ignoring the reference to Jem Blythe who had escaped with a very mild slap. "How you bled!"

"Of course I was a little beast in those days, but it is all so long ago. Just forget for this afternoon that you hate me—though I'd rather you'd hate me than think nothing about me, if it comes to that. Let's have a prowl around all the old spots. If you don't like me you needn't pretend to."

"I really ought to go back, you know," sighed

Suzette. "It's going to rain and Harvey will be peeved."

"Who is Harvey?"

"The man I'm going to marry," said Susette, wondering why she felt so keen to let Dick know that.

Dick took it in slowly. "Oh, of course—the big fox man. But you're not wearing any ring—I looked to see first thing."

"It . . . it isn't absolutely settled yet," stammered Susette. "But it will be tonight. He's going to propose tonight. That's really why I ran away today. I think . . ."

"Of course I've heard of the great man. Everybody has," said Dick slowly. "Well, he has a good start on me but a fast worker can do wonders in an afternoon, as Jem Blythe used to say."

"Don't talk nonsense," said Susette curtly. "Let's prowl. I want to see all I can before it does rain. I'm glad the farm hasn't changed much. Even the old whitewashed stones round the flower beds are the same. Do you remember how Susan Baker at Ingleside always insisted on white stones round their flower beds and how we used to laugh at her for it?"

"Susette, you are beyond any question the most exquisite creature I have ever seen," said Dick.

"Do you say that to every girl half an hour after you've met her? Remember I've long since crossed the old maid line."

"If I'd ever happened to think it I would—but I never happened to before. I decided recently that

I'd always say what I really thought the moment
I thought it. Rilla Blythe said she always did.
You've no idea what pep it gives to life. And
things go stale if you keep them unsaid."

"I daresay." Susette wondered what would
happen if she said everything she thought—just
when she thought it—to Harvey.

"Besides, it isn't half an hour since I met you—
it's years. We're second cousins, aren't we? And
old fr . . . enemies. So why shouldn't I say that
you're exquisite and beautiful and wholly charming, with hair like the sunset light on old firs and
eyes like that pond down there at dawn and a
skin like a tea-rose petal?"

"Do you remember the time when you pointed
out all my defects to the assembled gang?"
demanded Susette. "You said my hair was like
a stack of dried hay and that I had eyes like a
cat and a million freckles. Jem Blythe knocked
you down for it," she added, with a feeling of
gratitude to Jem Blythe she had never experienced
before.

"My aunt, there you go again," groaned Dick.
"Why can't you let the dead past bury its dead?"

Why indeed? Susette wondered herself. Why
did she feel that she *must* drag up these things?
Remember how hateful Dick had been? Must not
let herself forget it for a single moment. Because
he couldn't have changed, really. People didn't.
He had just learned to cover up his meanness
with a certain debonair charm made possible by
his indisputable good looks. Suddenly Susette felt

oddly panic-stricken. She must start for Glenellyn instantly before—well, before it rained.

"You can't," said Dick. "There's the first growl. You will be sensible and come into the house until the storm is over. Then we'll finish our prowl."

"It is five now," she protested. "If I don't start at once, I'll be late for dinner."

"I can get you a bite. Nan Blythe taught me how to cook."

"I don't believe it! Nan always hated you," cried Susette, stung out of her resolution.

Dick grinned. "Nan and I were a good deal better friends than you knew, though we did fight in public. Anyway, it's out of the question to think of starting to Glenellyn with a storm coming on. You were always a fearless little demon but that is a thing I'm simply not going to let you do. You know what our roads are like in a rain."

Susette yielded. She knew she couldn't negotiate that winding road in a rainstorm. It would be hard enough after it was over. Besides, she wanted to scare Harvey just once as a sort of dying protest. Moreover, she felt that she had not yet made Dick realize that she hated him as much as ever. And she was not going to leave the farm until that job was completed.

They went into the house. It was changed: new furniture; new curtains; new rugs; new paint. But the old rooms were unchanged. Susette ran all through them while Dick did something in the kitchen. When she came back to the living room—it had been the parlour in her childhood—

the rain was flooding against the windows and
the thunder was crashing overhead. Ordinarily
Susette revelled in thunderstorms. She wondered
if Harvey would be sorry. She didn't think Aunt
Clara would.

Dick came in carrying a tray whereon was a pot
of tea, a plate of toast and a jar of jam. He went to
the corner cupboard and took out dishes—Aunt
Marian's old fluted set with the rosebud on the
side and her little brown jug with its creamy
lining.

"You remember Di Blythe gave her this in place
of one she broke?"

What a memory he had for everything connected with those Blythe girls! But Susette put them
resolutely out of her mind.

"Oh," she sighed, "this toast is heavenly."

"I had a good teacher, don't forget," grinned
Dick. "Pull up to the table and let us break bread
together. Don't forget to compliment me on my
tea. I'm an expert at making tea."

"I suppose Nan Blythe taught you," Susette
could not help saying.

"She gave me some hints. But I had a natural
gift for it."

"Boastful as ever." But she sat down at the table
obediently. The tea *was* good. So was the toast. It
seemed hard to think of Dick making toast. As
for the jam, it had evidently been made from
Susan Baker's famous recipe. It had been known
all over the Glen St. Mary neighbourhood.

"A jug of tea, a crust of bread and *thou*!"

said Dick impudently. Susette refused—temporarily—to resent it. But why, oh why, should it be so delightful to sit in this half-dark room drinking tea and munching toast with detested Dick?

"I ought to telephone Glenellyn," she said weakly.

"You can't. This line never works in thunderstorms. If I were Harvey Brooks I'd be scouring the countryside for you. Susette, did any poor devil ever tell you that the way you looked over your shoulder at him drove him entirely mad? It even eclipses Rilla Blythe's famous smile."

"Do you remember," said Susette slowly, "how, when we were going to play Robinson Crusoe, you wouldn't let me be Man Friday because I was a girl?"

"And quite right I was! How could Crusoe have a distracting Man Friday like you? I showed my sense. I remember the Blythes agreed with me."

If he mentions the Blythes again, I'll throw that pitcher at his head, thought Susette.

Much later—it might have been hours—months—years—Susette awoke to the fact that although the thunder and lightning had ceased, the rain was still pouring down in a business-like way as if it meant to keep on for days. She looked at her watch, and exclaimed in dismay.

"Half past six! It will be dinner time in an hour at Glenellyn. I can never get there!"

"I should think you couldn't," said Dick. "Have some sense, Susette. The road from here will be absolutely impassable for that little car of yours.

You can't go back tonight. You've just got to stay here."

"Nonsense! I can't stay here. I must telephone. Harvey will come for me somehow . . ."

"Just try to phone . . ."

Susette tried. There was no reply. She stood for a few moments before the telephone, wondering why she didn't mind.

"I . . . I don't know what to do," she said miserably. "I know it would be madness to try to get back in this storm, but I have to be at the office tomorrow morning and . . . and . . ."

"And how about Harvey's proposal in the meantime?" grinned Dick. "Never mind, Susette. There are other proposals. I'm going to make one myself in the morning. I'll be awkward—I've never had any experience—but I'll get the thing said. I was on the brink of proposing to Rilla Blythe once, but of course she and Ken Ford . . ."

Susette sat down in fury because there didn't seem anything else to do. Dick lit the candles on the mantelpiece—informing her that Dr. And Mrs. Blythe had given them to Roddy and his wife for a wedding-present—and crossed one long leg over the other. He didn't pay Susette any more compliments or rag her about Harvey or drag in the Blythes by the skin of their teeth. He talked all the evening about aviation. Susette listened greedily. She almost forgot, until she found herself between the lavender-scented sheets of Mrs. Roddy's guest room in the upstairs southeast corner of the farmhouse, that she hated Dick.

Think, she told herself desperately, *how he used to bully the other boys; how he once twisted Jack's arm to make him apologize; how he told Aunt Marian it was Jack who took the pie; what he did to the kitten* . . . That memory was intolerable. Susette buried her face in the pillow and groaned. She was glad to recall what Jem Blythe had done to him for it. Still, the memory was intolerable. She hated him. She did hate him. She would get up ever so early in the morning and sneak away before she saw him again.

Suddenly Susette sat up in bed and shook her small white fist at the darkness. She had just remembered what had happened to her sensations when her fingers had happened to touch Dick's as he gave her the second cup of tea.

"I won't fall in love with him! I won't! I won't!"

She was aghast. When she put her danger into words, it terrified her. There was nothing for it but an early morning flitting back to safety and sanity and—and Harvey.

When Susette awoke she knew something she had not known when she went to sleep. She had only been afraid of knowing it. She got out of bed very softly and tiptoed to the window. The sun was not yet visible but the whole morning sky behind the eastern hill of spruces was rose-hued, with gossamer clouds of pale gold strewn over it. Little shivers were running over the silver-green pond. The distances were hung with pale blue mists. Susette knew she must drive instantly away through those lovely morning mists or she was a lost woman.

Swiftly and noiselessly she dressed. Swiftly and noiselessly she crept down the stairs, opened the front door and stepped out. She looked about her and caught her breath with delight. The sun was up now and a new lovely world, with its face washed, was blinking its innocent baby eyes at it. She had forgotten what the farm was like at dawn. And she hadn't seen all the dear spots she had loved. Wasn't there time at least for a sneak down to the pond? Dick wouldn't be up for an hour yet.

She would take a stolen run through this golden world. She would slip down to the pond on the old pathway with the wind as a gallant companion. The grasses would bathe her feet in green coolness and the water would sing to her—just once before she went back to Harvey.

When she was almost at the pond a suspicious fragrance met her nostrils. Before she realized the truth, she had broken through the trees and saw Dick squatted by a wood fire, broiling bacon, with a coffee pot beside him. A tablecloth was spread on the ground and—*what* was on it? Wild strawberries? Wild strawberries on a green leaf! How long was it since she had eaten wild strawberries of any kind, much less the kind that grew at the farm? She recalled as in a dream that Jem Blythe had always claimed to know a secret place where they grew bigger and sweeter than anywhere else.

Dick waved a fork with a piece of bacon on it at her. "Good girl! I was just going to call you. We've got to start soon to be in town in time. Besides, I didn't want you to miss such a chance to bathe your soul in dawn, as Nan Blythe used to say. Look what I have for you—I found Jem Blythe's old plot in the back pasture field. Such amazing luck! But then this farm has always been noted for its good luck. Besides—see—a bunch of the little red columbines you used to love. Pick out a soft spot on that rock and sit down."

Susette did as she was told. She felt a little dazed. Dick poured her coffee and fed her on bacon and wild strawberries. Neither of them said much. There were zones of beautiful colour on the pond, with little pools of pellucid shadow here and there. Great white cloud-mountains with amber valleys rose up in the sky over Glen St. Mary way. Presently, she supposed, Dick would be flying over them. The idea drove her to the banality of offering him a penny for his thoughts.

"I was wondering what would happen if I suddenly called you 'darling,' " he said solemnly.

"I should go away of course!" said Susette. "I'm going anyway. We can't sit here forever."

"Why not?" said Dick.

"That is a silly question and of course not meant to be answered," said Susette, getting up.

Dick got up too.

"I'm going to answer it. We can't sit here forever, heavenly as it would be, because I've got to sail the day after tomorrow. There isn't a great deal of time for us to fly to Montreal, get a special license and be married."

"You're quite mad," said Susette.

"Do you remember Walter Blythe's favourite quotation? 'And it's a poor family that can't afford one madman.' I never was much of a one for poetry, but didn't somebody once write something like this? I'm sure I've heard Walter quoting it:

> 'There is a pleasure sure in being mad
> That none but madmen know.' "

"I was never as intimate with the Blythes as you seem to have been," said Susette coldly.

"That was a pity. They were a delightful family."

"And I am going to the house to get my car and hurry back to Glenellyn," said Susette firmly.

"I know that's what you intend to do but it won't take long to change your mind."

Susette looked about her a bit helplessly. Then she happened to look at Dick. The next moment she was caught tightly in his arms and was being kissed—one long, wild, rapturous, breathless kiss.

"Don't you know that when you look at a man with eyes like that you are simply asking him to kiss you? You are mine, Susette. I've made you mine with that kiss. You can never belong to anyone else."

Susette stood very still. She knew this was one of the rare splendid moments of life. She knew she would never marry Harvey.

"We'll be on our way to Charlottetown in fifteen minutes," Dick was saying. "It'll take me that time to put away Mrs. Roddy's frying pan and lock your car into Roddy's barn. We can leave it there until we come back from Peru in three years' time."

Susette went back to her room for her watch which she had left under her pillow. She supposed she was bewitched—literally bewitched. Nothing else would account for it. She remembered that Dr. Gilbert Blythe had been rather laughed at because he had said there might be such a thing, at the time of the goings-on at the old Field place. Nothing else would account for it. If she could only forget about the kitten! But so many boys were cruel at first.

When she got back to the pond she could not see Dick anywhere at first. Then she saw him standing a little way off in the shadow of some spruces. His back was towards her and a red squirrel was perched on his shoulder. He was feeding it with something and the squirrel was chattering to him.

Susette was very still. She knew another thing now. And she would have run if Dick had not wheeled round at that moment. The squirrel made a wild leap to the trees and Dick came striding to her.

"Did you see that little chap? And do you

remember how Jem Blythe always loved squirrels? They've always been fond of me too . . . the folk of fur and feathers."

"*You are not Dick,*" said Susette, in a low tone, looking up at him.

Dick stopped.

"No," he said, "I'm not. I was wondering how I was going to tell you. But how did you find out?"

"When I saw the squirrel on your shoulder. Animals always hated Dick—he was so cruel to them. People don't change as much as that. No squirrel would ever have climbed on *his* shoulder. That was why the Blythes hated him so much. And may I ask who you really are?"

"Having promised to marry me you have a right to the information," he said gravely. "I am Jerry Thornton, a second cousin of Dick through Aunt Marian, but no earthly relation of yours. Jem Blythe and I were great pals. We lived in Charlottetown but I was here one summer when you weren't. I heard all about you from the others, especially Jem who had a youthful passion for you before he took up with Faith Meredith. And remember you called me Dick first. I was afraid, if undeceived, you wouldn't stay long enough to let me make you love me. I thought I'd a better chance as Dick—even though you had such a grudge against him. We always looked alike—our grandmothers were sisters—but, honest to goodness, we aren't alike under our skins. Besides, Dick is married, as are most of our old gang."

"He would be," said Susette.

Jerry looked down at her a bit anxiously. "A little thing like a mistake in the man isn't going to make any difference, is it, Susette?"

"I don't see why it should," answered Susette. "But tell me two things. First, how did you know that Dick once kissed me?"

"As if any boy wouldn't kiss you if he ever got the chance!" scoffed Jerry.

"And how did you know I loved wild columbines?"

"Everybody loves wild columbines," said Jerry.

A Commonplace
Woman

It had been raining all day, a cold, drizzling rain, but now the night had fallen and the rain had partially eased, though the wind still blew and sighed. The John Anderson family were sitting in the parlour—they still called it that—of the ugly house in the outskirts of Lowbridge, waiting for their Great-aunt Ursula, who was dying in the room overhead, to die and have done with it.

They never would have expressed it like that but each one in his or her secret soul thought it.

In speech and outward behavior they were all quite decorous but they were all seething with impatience and some resentment. Dr. Parsons supposed he ought to stay till the end because old Aunt Ursula was his grandfather's cousin and because Mrs. Anderson wanted him to stay.

And he could not as yet afford to offend people, even distant relatives. He was just starting to practise in Lowbridge and Dr. Parker had been *the* doctor in Lowbridge for a long time. Almost everyone had him except a few cranks who did not like him and insisted on having Dr. Blythe from Glen St. Mary. Even most of the Andersons had him. In Dr. Parsons' eyes they were both old men and ought to give the younger men a chance.

But at all events, he meant to be very obliging and do all he could to win his way. One had to, these days. It was all very well to talk about unselfishness but that was bunk. It was every man for himself.

If he could win Zoë Maylock apart from all considerations of love, it would help him quite a bit. The Maylocks were rather a run-down old family, but they had considerable influence in Lowbridge for all that. *They* never had Dr. Parker either. When any of them were sick they sent for Dr. Blythe. There was some feud between the Andersons and the Parkers. How those old feuds lasted!

Dr. Parker might laugh and pretend he didn't care, but the young doctor thought he knew better. Human nature was better understood nowadays than when poor old Dr. Parker went to college.

Anyhow, young Dr. Parsons meant to be as obliging as he could. Every little helped. It would be some time yet before his practice would justify his marrying, confound it. He even doubted if the John Andersons would pay his bill, and it seemed the old girl who took so long in dying had no money. They said Dr. Blythe—and even Dr. Parker sometimes, though he was more worldly minded—attended poor people for nothing. Well, *he* was not going to be such a fool. He had come to old Ursula because he wanted to ingratiate himself with the Andersons, some of whom were well enough off yet. And cut out Dr. Blythe if it were possible, though it was wonderful what a hold that man had on the countryside, even if he was getting along in years. People said he had never been the same since his son was killed in the Great War.

And now another war was going on and they said several of his grandsons were going—especially Gilbert Ford, who was in the Air Force. People were constantly dropping hints that they thought *he* ought to volunteer. Even Zoë at times seemed to have entirely too much admiration for this aforesaid Gilbert Ford. But it was all nonsense. There were plenty of ne'er-do-wells to go.

Meanwhile he would do what he could for a poor run-down family like the John Andersons. The progenitors of the said Andersons had, so he had been told, once been rich and powerful in the community. The biggest stone in the Lowbridge cemetery was that of a certain David Anderson. It was moss-grown and lichened now, but it must have been considered some stone in its day.

Well, thank goodness—young Dr. Parsons stole a sly look at his watch—old Ursula Anderson was dead, or as good as dead. He was sure the John Andersons in their secret souls would be very glad. And he did not blame them in the least. Trouble and expense was all she had meant to them for years, though she had earned her way as a dressmaker until late in life, he understood. The idea made him laugh secretly. It was more than funny to think of anyone wearing a dress made by Ursula Anderson, he thought. The wearer must have looked as if she had stepped out of one of those awful faded photographs or crayon enlargements he was so often called upon to admire.

Would that old woman overhead *never* die? He wished he had invented some excuse for going long ago. One could carry obligingness too far. And it was too late to go to Zoë now. Perhaps Walter Blythe—named after his uncle of course—had been spending the evening with her. Well, let the best man win! Dr. Parsons had little doubt who it would be. Zoë might be angry—or pretend to be—but a doctor could always think up a good excuse. And Gilbert Ford, of whom he was secretly more afraid than of Walter Blythe, had gone back to Toronto.

Zoë, with her wonderful eyes and lovely white hands and cooing voice! It seemed so absurd to think that Zoë and old Aunt Ursula belonged to the same sex. Well, they didn't—they couldn't—that was all there was about it. Ursula Anderson could never have been a young girl, with softly curving flesh and ripe red lips. If it had not been for Mrs. Anderson's fussiness he might just as well have spent the evening with Zoë instead of sitting here in this stuffy Anderson room, waiting for a tiresome old woman, who had never been of the slightest importance to anyone, to die, and wondering how on earth Mrs. Anderson managed to live with such a carpet in the house.

He fell to planning the house he and Zoë would have if—when—he won her. There was nothing in Lowbridge that suited him. He would have to build. A house something like Ingleside but more up-to-date, of course. Though it was strange how up-to-date Ingleside always seemed. Dr. Parsons had to admit that. Nor could he tell just why. Was it because it was generally overflowing with children? No, it was just the same when it was empty. Well, he and Zoë would have the very latest in everything, at all events. As for children—they would have to wait a while for them. Big families had gone out of fashion with many other things. *And*, thank heaven, such carpets!

Mrs. John Anderson was really very proud of her carpet which a Charlottetown uncle had given her from an out-of-date stock. But just now she was feeling very fretful and irritable. It was such an inconvenient time for Aunt Ursula to go and die, with Emmy's wedding to be planned and Phil's outfit for Queen's to be got ready. And all the expense of the funeral. Well, people would just have to wait for their bills. Dr. Parsons, now of course they had to have him because he was a distant relative. But she would much rather have had Dr. Blythe from Glen St. Mary, or even old Dr. Parker. What did old quarrels matter now? And why was Dr. Parsons hanging round when he could do no good? Of course she had asked him to out of politeness, but he must have known he wasn't wanted.

And Aunt Ursula was so maddeningly deliberate about dying. Well, she had been that about everything all her life. Likely that was why she had never got a husband. Men liked girls with some dash to them.

She might even live till morning. She had known a woman who lived for a week after the doctor had said she could last only a few hours. Doctors knew very little after all. She had told John they should have an older doctor. None of them might get a wink of sleep that night and John was half dead now. He had been up so many nights. You couldn't trust Maggie McLean. And of course she had to have some sleep.

To be sure, John was at present snoring on the sofa. It wasn't just the proper thing, she supposed. But she hadn't the heart to wake him. If that goof of a Dr. Parsons *only* had enough sense to go she might get a wink, too. As for Emmy and Phil, they had been looking forward so delightedly to Bess Rodney's dance tonight. And now they hadn't been able to go after all. No wonder they were disgruntled, poor darlings! And what earthly difference would it have made to anyone? Talk about gossip! It was the most powerful thing in the world and always would be.

Mrs. Anderson yawned and hoped Dr. Parsons would take the hint. But he showed no signs of doing so. An older doctor would have had more gumption.

She wondered drowsily if there was really anything between him and Zoë Maylock. If there was she pitied him. Everyone knew what Zoë's temper was. Dr. and Mrs. Blythe had done very well to stop Walter's going there. As for Gilbert Ford, everyone said he was engaged to a girl in Toronto and was just amusing himself with Zoë Maylock. Thank goodness, Phil was of a different type. *He* was not a flirt. And if he had a bit of the Anderson temper he knew how to control it. She supposed she ought to go up and see if Maggie McLean had fallen asleep. But she might wake poor John.

Emmy and Phil Anderson were very much disgruntled. It seemed positively absurd to them that they had to stay home from the dance because old Great-aunt Ursula was dying. She was eighty-five and for fifteen years she had been exactly the same—an ugly old woman who hardly ever talked, though she was given to mumbling when she was alone. She belonged to a dead and forgotten generation—the generation of those dreadful crayon enlargements on the walls which mother wouldn't have taken down, pictures of bearded gentlemen and high-collared women. *They* could never have been human either, Emmy reflected.

But at least they were dead and out of the way. How very stern and proper Grandfather Anderson looked, the embodiment of unbending rectitude, whose great pride had been that there had never been any scandal in the Anderson family. And yet hadn't she heard something about his brother, David Anderson? *He* had not been a model, according to Susan Baker. But it was all old stuff. Who cared now? They had been Aunt Ursula's brothers. How funny to think of Aunt Ursula having brothers! She couldn't imagine her feeling any family affection.

I'm sure she has never liked any of us, thought Emmy. *And we have been so good to her!*

Uncle Alec, who had come in from his farm at Glen St. Mary because it was the proper thing to do, was the only one who was not bored. He rather enjoyed occasions like these, though of course it would never have done to admit it. How many things it would never do to admit!

But you couldn't deny that there was something "dramatic" about deaths and funerals. To be sure, there was nothing very dramatic about poor old Aunt Ursula's death, any more than there had been about her life. Her sisters had been gay enough in their youth, if gossip spoke truly, but Ursula had been the quiet, retiring one.

Still, death was death: and the night, with its wailing winds and its vicious spits of rain, was quite in keeping with it. Uncle Alec always thought that a moonlit summer night, with flower fragrances, was very incongruous with death.

Though people died every day and night of the year, if it came to that.

John and Aggie were calm and dignified as became the occasion—at least John had been before he went to sleep. But the young folks couldn't quite hide that they were jittery with impatience. He didn't blame them. Of course it never occurred to them that *they* would die some time, too.

But Aunt Ursula wouldn't die till the tide went out. She had been brought up by the sea and when you had lived by the sea for eighty-five years you couldn't die till the tide went out, no matter how far away from it you were. He had heard Dr. Parker laughing at that "old superstition." Dr. Blythe had not laughed, but Uncle Alec knew he did not believe in it either.

"If he'd kept records he'd know," murmured Uncle Alec.

Ursula was quite a way from the sea now but that didn't matter a mite.

"Think of being an old maid for eighty-five years," said Emmy suddenly. She shuddered.

"Poisonous," agreed Phil.

"Children," said their mother reprovingly. "Remember she is dying."

"What difference does that make?" said Emmy impatiently.

"You must remember she wasn't always an old maid," said Uncle Alec. "They used to say twenty-five was the first corner. But Aunt Ursula has always been just a commonplace woman—a forgotten woman." He liked the phrase. People were always talking about "the forgotten man." Why not a forgotten woman? She was a creature even more to be pitied—and despised. For Uncle Alec despised old maids. And it was said Aunt Ursula had never even had a beau. Though he really did not know much about her. After all, she was only a poor old soul about whom nobody ever talked. Certainly she was not a subject for gossip. And she *was* a little long in dying. But of course the tide was late tonight. He almost envied John his nap. Poor John! He had made rather a mess of things. Most of the Andersons made money if they made nothing else. Old Great Uncle David now . . . he had been a rich man in his day. But his son had soon made ducks and drakes of his inheritance. It was generally the way.

"If I had to live a dull colourless life like Aunt Ursula," said Emmy, "I'd kill myself."

"Emmy!" said Uncle Alec in a shocked voice. "That is a wicked speech. We have to wait until our time comes."

"I don't care," said Emmy flippantly. "Eighty-five years and never a thing happen to you! Well, of course, you couldn't imagine anyone ever being in love with her—you simply couldn't."

"You can't imagine any old person being in love," said Uncle Alec. "Me, now. You know in your heart you think just the same of me. Yet I was quite a gay blade in my youth. You'll be old yourself some day, Emmy, and people will think the same of you. Perhaps Aunt Ursula did have some beaux."

"Not she." Emmy shrugged her shoulders. How dreadful never to have been loved! Never to have known love! "She just spent her life in other people's houses sewing till she got so queer and old-fashioned nobody would have her. I wonder they ever did. Fancy Aunt Ursula making dresses! I never saw her do any sewing except patching trousers. She did enough of that, poor old soul."

"Oh, I believe she wasn't a bad dressmaker in her day," said Uncle Alec. "Twenty years from now your fashions will seem just as funny."

"People won't have any fashions twenty years from now," grinned Phil. "They won't be wearing clothes at all."

"Phil!" said his mother in absent rebuke. She didn't believe in Alec's nonsense about the tide but certainly old Aunt Ursula . . . perhaps Maggie had fallen asleep. She supposed she ought to go up and see. But her bones ached enough now with rheumatism. As for the old maid talk, she didn't like it. *She* had been an old maid when John married her.

"Aunt Ursula was the best hand at a sponge cake I ever knew," said Uncle Alec.

"What an epitaph!" said Emmy.

Dr. Parsons laughed. But her mother rebuked her again because she thought it was her duty. Yet she had a pride in Emmy's way of saying things.

"She is dying," said Uncle Alec because he felt he ought to say it.

"And taking hours about it," grumbled Phil. "Oh, I know your theories about the tide, Uncle Alec, but I don't believe in them. Dr. Parsons, haven't you seen scores of people die when the tide was coming in?"

"I don't believe I've ever thought about it," evaded Dr. Parsons. "I suppose, Phil, you hold with Osler's theory that everyone should be chloroformed at sixty?"

"Well, it would rid the world of a lot of nuisances," yawned Phil.

"Phil, I won't have you talk so. I will be sixty in three more years," said his mother severely.

"Can't you take a joke, Mums?"

"Not with death in the house," said Mrs. Anderson, still more severely.

"What do *you* think of the Osler idea, doc?" said Phil.

"I don't think he really said just that," said Dr. Parsons. "What he did say was that a man's best work was over at sixty. Of course there are exceptions. You and I are still far enough from sixty not to have to worry about that," he added, remembering that John Anderson and this queer old Uncle Alec were both over sixty. One must not offend people. Sometimes they remembered the smallest things when they wanted a doctor.

Phil subsided. After all, there was nothing to do but wait. It couldn't last forever. Aunt Ursula would die and be buried—as cheaply as possible. And then let the undertaker whistle for his bill. Parsons, too, for that matter. Aunt Ursula would be taken out of the house for the first time in ten years and buried in the Anderson plot; there would just be room to squeeze her in. And there was room on one of the monuments to say when she had been born and when she had died.

God, what an existence! But that was all there was to say about her life. She probably had never enough pep in her to be rebellious at it. People of her generation accepted everything as the will of God, didn't they? They just vegetated. And why did *they* have to take her in when she was no longer able to earn her living? There were plenty of richer Anderson families. But they had never given a cent to her keep. Well, he, Phil was not going to be such a sap. When he got old there would be no useless relatives hanging round *his* neck. The poorhouse for them, if they hadn't enough to keep them. He felt sure Dr. Parsons would agree with him—though he didn't have any especial liking for the fellow.

"It's strange what a liking that old dog has for Miss Anderson," said the doctor abruptly, partly by way of making conversation. He didn't care much for Phil and was certainly not going to argue about Osler's theories with him.

Somehow, he couldn't say, "It is strange how that old dog loves her." Imagine even a dog loving Ursula Anderson! It was comical. Probably she had given him bones. "He will hardly leave the room for a minute. He just lies by her bed and stares at her."

"She always seemed glad to have him near her ever since he was a pup," said Uncle Alec. "I suppose she felt he was a sort of protection for her when she was alone. She was alone a good deal."

"Well, I'm sure we couldn't stay home *all* the time," said Mrs. Anderson peevishly. "She was quite well, and she said she didn't want company."

"I know, I know," said Uncle Alec soothingly. "You've all been very kind to Aunt Ursula, Aggie."

"I should hope so," said Mrs. Anderson in an aggrieved tone. "I know we took her in and gave her a home when others on whom she had more claim, one would suppose, never offered her even a week's lodging."

"She was a very fortunate woman to have such a good home to come to in her old age," said Dr. Parsons placatingly. "I suppose she won't leave much behind her." He was thinking about his bill.

"She won't leave anything," said Mrs. Anderson, still preserving her aggrieved tone. "She has never had a cent since she came to live with us. It surprised us, I will admit. She must have made a good deal of money in all those years she sewed. What did she do with it? That is the question the Andersons have always been asking. Certainly she never spent any of it on herself. I never remember seeing her in a decent rag even when I was a little girl, and she was no more than middle-aged . . . though, of course, like all young people," with a resentful glance at Emmy and Phil, "I thought anyone ten years older than myself was Methuselah."

"Perhaps she had a hoard of it somewhere," suggested Phil. "What a jolly thing it would be to come across a box or roll of it when we go through her things!"

Mrs. Anderson, who had gone through old Aunt Ursula's few things many times, frowned majestically. What a thing to say before Dr. Parsons! Of course he would tell Zoë Maylock and that was equivalent to telling all the countryside. She would give Phil a good talking-to when she got him alone. Though what good would that do now that it had been said?

"Maybe I shouldn't say it, but I've always thought she may have helped Brother Will out a bit," said Uncle Alec, with a deprecatory glance at the doctor. It was not just the thing, maybe, to hint that any Anderson was hard up, even before a distant relative. "With his big family, you know, he was chronically hard up."

"Then some of *his* family should have looked after Aunt Ursula when she got past work. Or at least have helped a bit," snapped Mrs. Anderson.

But she instantly composed herself. There was death in the house. And Dr. Parsons was there, too, which was about the same thing as Zoë Maylock

being there. It was all nonsense having a doctor
for old Aunt Ursula anyhow. No doctor could do
her any good.

But then how people would have talked!

Yes, Death was in the old house and a welcome guest to all, and to none more welcome
than to Ursula Anderson. She had longed for
him for many years and now she knew he was
near. Never was a bridegroom more welcome.
She knew no living soul would regret her but
that did not matter either.

The bare, dingy room, that had always been
thought good enough for old Aunt Ursula, was
full of shadows from the winking candle on the
little stand by the bed. Aunt Ursula would never
have anything but a candle. Lamps were dangerous and electric light something she could not or
would not understand. The John Andersons had
fixed up the room a little when they had to call
in a doctor, but it was very shabby still. A vase of
faded artificial flowers on the bureau cast strange
exotic shadows of enormous blossoms and sprays
on the stained, unpapered plaster above the bed.
Emmy had been thankful that at last something
had induced her mother to remove them from the
niche in the wall on the stairway. She had heard
Zoë make fun of people who cherished artificial
flowers.

Maggie McLean, who was supposed to be waiting on old Ursula, was asleep in her chair, just
as Aggie Anderson had known it was likely she

would be. Maggie owed a small debt to John Anderson or they would not have been able to get her. She knew that otherwise she would never be paid. How the Andersons had come down in the world! Maggie was old enough to remember them in the days of their prosperity. She even remembered the queer scandal at the time of old David Anderson's funeral. Few people had believed it. They said Clarissa Wilcox was quite out of her head and the Wilcoxes had always hated the Andersons and nobody but Susan Baker at Ingleside took any stock of it. And the Blythes had soon squelched *her*.

She might as well take a nap. Ursula Anderson was unconscious or nearly so and she couldn't do anything for her. But of course somebody must watch by the dying. In a way she felt sorry for old Ursula Anderson. She had had such a dull drab life of it.

The wind moaned eerily in the old spruce by the window—moaned and wailed and sometimes suddenly snarled and then died away to let the occasional spits of rain be heard. Occasionally the window rattled as if something that was rather impatient and overdue was trying to gain entrance.

Ursula Anderson lay motionless on the bed. You might have thought she was already dead had it not been for her large sunken grey eyes. They had been dull and bleared for many years, but they were bright and clear again, burning with a steady flame in her parched face.

A grey flannel nightgown was buttoned about her ugly, wattled throat. A coarse sweep of grey hair lay over the pillow. She had an amazing lot of hair for such an old woman. Her gaunt old body was quiet and flat under the faded patchwork quilt and thin blankets. Her knotted, discoloured hands lay over them motionless.

She knew she was dying and that everybody was in a hurry for her to die and that there was not a living creature that would regret her death. Except perhaps the old dog.

She knew she had become very ugly, but she had not been ugly in youth, though no one had ever thought her pretty. She had just been one of "those Anderson girls" with no beauty except her long, thick, sloe-black hair. But she had soft, large grey eyes and creamy skin and lovely hands. Yes, she had had lovely hands—he had often told her so; the most beautiful hands he had ever seen—and he had seen the hands of queens. Her sisters were counted pretty girls but they had fat, pudgy hands. She had never received a compliment about hers, except from him. It was faces and figures people looked at.

Her hands were very ugly now—they had grown warped and roughened by constant sewing and by age. Yet even now they were better shaped than Maggie McLean's. She had been rather small and thin in her youth and nobody had ever paid much attention to her amid her dashing, handsome sisters. She had never tried to attract attention and it was quite true she had never had a beau. It was equally true that she had never wanted one, though nobody would have believed such a statement. None of the youths of Lowbridge or Glen St. Mary or Mowbray Narrows had attracted her in the least. They did not think or talk as she did—or would have done if any of them had ever tried to talk to her.

She had spent her childhood and early youth under her mother's thumb and she was supposed to have no opinions of her own. Sometimes she thought they might have been surprised if they had known her thoughts—surprised and shocked.

Then there had come a change. The old grey eyes darkened and quivered and glowed as she thought of it. Her Aunt Nan had written and asked for "one of the girls" to spend a year with her after her only daughter had gone to India as a missionary. Aunt Nan lived in a little fishing village and summer resort many miles down the coast and was a widow. Ursula had never seen her. But she was chosen to go because none of her sisters would consent to bury herself alive in Half Moon Cove for a year.

But Ursula had been glad to go. She liked what she had heard about Half Moon Cove and she liked what her father had said about his sister Nan. Ursula gathered the impression that Aunt Nan was very different from all her other aunts— that she was still and quiet like herself.

"Didn't talk a man to death," she had heard her father say once.

There was not a great deal to do at Aunt Nan's and Ursula had spent much of her time down at the shore among the dunes. The summer colony was much further down and few of them ever strayed so far. It was there she had met him, painting. He was the guest of a wealthy family who were summering at the next Cove but who never came near Half Moon. There were no amusements there.

He was a young Englishman, an artist already on the way to the world-wide fame he afterwards achieved. It was said his older brother had a title, which was likely the reason he had been asked to be the guest of the Lincolns. They were certainly not artistic.

But to Ursula he was just Larry—and her lover. She loved his paintings but the brother with a title meant nothing to her.

"You are the most unworldly creature I've met in my life," Larry had told her once. "The things that mean so much to most people seem to mean absolutely nothing to you. I don't believe you belong to this world at all."

Never had she known, or even dreamed, of anyone so utterly charming. They had loved each other from their first meeting. Ursula knew it could never have been any other way. She did not doubt he had loved and been loved by many women before her, but she felt no jealousy of them. He was too wonderful to love any woman very long, especially an insignificant little thing like her. But, for the time being, he did love

her. She knew that beyond a doubt. For that
one enchanted summer he loved her and nothing
could ever take that from her. And nobody in the
world but herself knew it. She would never tell his
name even to Aunt Nan. Poor old Maggie McLean
pitied her. But Maggie McLean had never been
loved like that. Aggie Anderson pitied her but
Aggie did not even know the meaning of love.
She had married John to escape being an old
maid and she thought nobody knew it, while
everybody knew it and laughed about it.

But nobody knew her, Ursula's, secret. Of that
she was sure.

She knew he could never marry her. The idea
never entered her head—or, for that matter, his.
Yet all his life he remembered little Ursula—remembered her when beautiful and brilliant wom-
en caressed him. There was something about her
he never found in any other woman. Sometimes
he thought that was why he never married.

Of course he couldn't have married her. The
very idea was absurd. And yet . . . what great
artist had married his cook? On his deathbed
Sir Lawrence thought of Ursula and of no other
woman, not even the Princess What's-her-name,
who would have taken him, they said, if he had
ever asked her.

They had loved each other through lingering
days and soft emerald evenings and nights of
crystal splendour. She had not forgotten one of
them. He had said mad, sweet things to her—she
had not forgotten one of them either, those old

words of love spoken so many years ago. Fancy anyone saying such things to Maggie McLean, snoring in her chair!

Her hair was grey and coarse now. But she remembered the day he pulled the pins out of it and buried his face in its sleek flow.

Then she remembered the moonrises they had watched together on that far shore, where the bones of old vessels were bleaching. He revelled in the windy nights, but she had liked the calm nights better. She recalled the dim hills and the mysterious dunes—the fishing boats sailing in— and always his tender, passionate words. Maggie McLean would have felt insulted if anyone had spoken to her like that. Poor old Maggie, snoring away there, who had never lived. How Ursula pitied her!

She lifted her withered hands for a moment and then let them drop back on the quilt.

He must have painted her hands a hundred times. The hands of his pictures were famous. Nobody knew that but old despised Ursula Anderson. He had never tired of exclaiming over the wonder of them. "A kiss on the tip of every sweet finger," he would whisper. Only old Ursula knew that people had gazed on those hands in scores of European art galleries. She had a collection of engravings of his pictures in a ragged old box which she carried everywhere with her. Nobody knew why. But then Ursula had always been queer. The only time she had ever come near to quarrelling with Aggie Anderson

was one housecleaning time when Aggie had
wanted to burn the box. It was full of nothing
but faded old pictures, she said.

"What on earth can you see in them, Ursula?"
she said. "If you are so fond of pictures, there are
some old chromos and mottoes you can have . . ."

"Have they hands like those?" Ursula had
asked quietly.

Aggie Anderson shrugged her shoulders and
gave it up. After all, old people grew very childish. You had to indulge them. Hands, indeed.
And most of the women were very ugly in spite
of their titles.

Then the season had ended. The cool September
winds began to blow across the haunted dunes.
Larry had gone away, promising to write, but he
had never written. For a time life had wrung
Ursula in its merciless hands. She had to tell
Aunt Nan. There was no one else to whom she
dared go. She could never go home to her self-
righteous father and mother. Better to slip down
to the dunes some night and end it all. She was
very glad now she had not done so. It might have
hurt Larry if he had ever heard of it. She would
suffer anything rather than do that.

And Aunt Nan had been very good to her after
the first shock was over. She was pitying and did
not blame Ursula very much.

"I should have looked after you better," she
mourned. "But then of course I thought an
Anderson . . . and now that scoundrel has led
you astray."

Ursula hid her anger for Larry's sake. She knew Aunt Nan blamed an entirely different man. But a strange little flame came into her tired grey eyes.

"I wasn't led astray," she said. "I am not such a weakling. I knew what I was doing—and I'm not sorry—I'm not sorry."

Aunt Nan could not understand. But she stood by Ursula staunchly. She kept Ursula with her on one excuse or another, and had in an old woman she could trust for the birth, since the Anderson name must be saved at all costs. Ursula nearly died—even Aunt Nan thought it would be better if she had—but Ursula was very glad that she managed to live.

The baby was a little girl with Ursula's grey eyes and Larry's golden hair. The James Burnleys in Charlottetown were wealthy people who had long wanted to adopt a child.

Ursula thought she could not bear it, but for Larry's sake she consented. And she wanted his child to have a good home. She went back to Lowbridge, a little quieter and more insignificant than before. The Andersons, who had been hoping she would pick up some kind of a husband when she was away, did not welcome her very effusively. They tried to patch up a marriage with her and an old widower of Glen St. Mary but to Ursula all men seemed common or unbearable after Larry.

But she had her own keen sweetness in life which no one knew or suspected. So she did not mind any longer when the men ignored her. A distant cousin, in need of an assistant, offered to teach her dressmaking and, to everyone's surprise, Ursula developed an unsuspected talent for the art.

She went out sewing by the day and she often went to the Burnley home. Mrs. Burnley said there was nobody could fit a dress like Ursula Anderson. Ursula saw little Isabel often (Mrs. Burnley had named the baby after herself). She saw her grow up through dimpled childhood and adorable girlhood. At times she looked so like Larry that Ursula's heart gave a bound. She had little tricks of manners and voice like his. Ursula could never see anything of herself in her except her eyes. She was as beautiful and charming as Larry's daughter should be. The Burnleys adored her and showered everything on her. Ursula made most of her dresses. When she fitted them on, her fingers sometimes touched the girl's flesh with rapture. It was almost like touching Larry himself.

Isabel liked her.

"I believe that queer, quiet little dressmaker really loves me," she used to say. "She never says so, of course, but sometimes I've seen her looking at me in the queerest way—almost as if I belonged to her, you know."

"The poor thing has so little in life," said Mrs. Burnley. "Her own people never made anything of her. Always be as kind to her as you can, Isabel."

There was one thing that Ursula was hardly able to bear: to hear Isabel call Mrs. Burnley "mother." It seemed to tear her soul in pieces. At such times she hated Mrs. Burnley—and reproached herself bitterly for hating her when she was so good to Isabel. But she gave no sign. Mrs. Burnley never dreamed of it. She never thought of Ursula Anderson as feeling any particular emotion.

Finally Isabel married. The Burnleys were quite delighted over the match, much as they hated to lose Isabel. He was a handsome fellow, of good family and rich. Everybody thought Isabel was a lucky girl. Of course, there were some stories . . . but stories were always told about rich young men who enjoyed themselves. Mrs. Burnley said they had to sow their wild oats. Once married to Isabel, Geoffrey Boyd would settle down and make a good husband. She hadn't a doubt of it. Her own husband had been wild enough in his youth. And what a husband he had made!

Ursula made most of the trousseau, even to the dainty underthings. Yet she was not happy or easy. She did not like Geoffrey Boyd. Of course Isabel was wildly in love with him, and Ursula knew quite well that most young men were no saints—even Larry could not be called a model. But it was not that. It was something about Geoffrey Boyd himself. But Isabel was radiantly happy and Ursula tried to stifle her uneasiness and rejoice in that happiness.

She was allowed to help dress Isabel for her marriage, and Isabel was a little amused to see how old Miss Anderson's hands trembled. She was always "old Miss Anderson" to Isabel—always had been, although she was barely forty. Isabel was very fond of her and made up her mind that she would give her all the work possible. Ready-made dresses were coming in and home dressmaking was not so plentiful as it had been.

So Ursula was much in Isabel's home during the next four years. They were years of torture for her. She had to watch the change in Isabel's love, from passionate adoration to fear, horror and—worst of all—hatred.

Geoffrey Boyd was tired of his wife within a year and he never made any pretence of hiding it. He was blatantly unfaithful to her, as everybody knew—and he was hellishly cruel. Sometimes it seemed that his only pleasure was in inflicting pain on her. And he always laughed so horribly when saying and doing cruel things, though he always took good care that nobody except that little half-witted Anderson creature heard him. The Burnleys knew that the marriage had been a failure but they would not admit it. Such things in those years were best covered up. And riches made up for a great many things.

Ursula hated him so bitterly that it seemed to her that her hate walked beside her, a tangible thing. In spite of her insignificance he must have felt her hatred, for he never passed her without some bland, suave sneer.

She was always being "pumped" about the Boyd ménage but never a word could be got out of her. That was probably the reason Geoffrey Boyd allowed Isabel to have her in the house. He was not afraid of what she might tell. The Anderson gang were notorious gossips and although this Ursula creature was no more than half there, still, there were things she could say if she wanted to. And the Burnleys were still rich—or supposed to be. Geoffrey Boyd had his own reasons for keeping on good terms with them. He was always so nice to Isabel in their presence that they did not believe half the stories they heard.

The marriage was six years old when it became known that the Burnleys had lost most of their money. Then Isabel knew that her husband meant to divorce her on some trumped-up charge, naming as co-respondent a certain man about town.

Divorce in those days, in the Maritimes, was a naked tragedy. And everybody knew she was an adopted child. "Blood will tell," they would say significantly. Everybody would believe the charges against her—except old Ursula Anderson. Somehow, Isabel felt that *she* would never believe a word against her.

Geoffrey told Isabel that if she contested the suit he would take her son away from her. Ursula knew he meant to take the child anyway, just to torture Isabel, although he had no affection for the boy. He had never pretended to have. Little Patrick was a delicate child and Geoffrey Boyd had no use for sickly brats. Once he asked Isabel if Patrick inherited his constitution from her father or her mother. He knew that Isabel always had felt some secret shame that she was only an adopted child, and it delighted him to flick it on the raw. He had once told her, in their courtship days, that it made her dearer to him.

Suppose, thought Ursula, *I told him her father was the great artist, Sir Lawrence Ainsley.*

"Fancy the sly old thing," she could hear him saying. And the Burnleys would be furious. Aunt Nan was dead and she had no evidence whatever to prove that she had been a great artist's light-of-love. But she made up her mind that there would be no divorce for all that. Some way she would prevent it.

She was sewing in one of the upstairs rooms of the house the day Geoffrey Boyd came home drunk and whipped Patrick mercilessly in the library, while Isabel crouched on the floor outside the door and moaned in her helpless anguish. The last time Geoffrey had come home drunk he had hung his fox terrier up in the stable and whipped it to death. Would he kill Patrick, too?

When he came out and the sobbing boy ran to his mother, he said to her, "When I have Patrick all to myself—as I shall have sooner or later, my darling—he shall have a good dose of the whip every day. You have made a baby of him with your coddling. I shall make a man of him. Was your father a minister, do you think?"

Ursula had sewed quietly and steadily through it all. Not a stitch was misplaced. Even Isabel thought her very unfeeling. But when Geoffrey came reeling up the stairs, she was standing at the head, waiting for him. Isabel had taken Patrick to his room. There was nobody about. Her eyes were blazing and her gaunt little form in its plain black gown was quivering.

"Get out of my way, damn you," snarled Geoffrey. "You have always backed her up."

"I am her mother," said Ursula, "and her father was Sir Lawrence Ainsley."

Geoffrey laughed drunkenly. "Why not the King of England and be done with it?" he said. "*You* the mother of anybody!" He added something too foul to repeat.

Ursula put out both hands, hands, still beautiful in spite of everything—the hands Larry had kissed and painted—the hands that had been so much admired in his portrait of an Italian princess.

Ursula gave the unsteady Geoffrey a hard push. She did it quite deliberately, knowing what she meant to do, knowing the probable consequences. She did not care in the least if they hanged her for it. Nothing mattered except saving Isabel and Patrick.

Geoffrey Boyd went backwards down the long staircase and fell on the marble floor at its foot. Ursula looked down at him for a few moments, with a feeling of triumph such as she had never experienced since the day Larry had first told her he loved her.

Geoffrey Boyd was lying in a rather dreadful limp heap beneath her. Somehow, she felt quite sure his neck was broken. There was no noise or disturbance anywhere. After a few moments she went back to the sewing room quietly, began another piece of work and went calmly on with her sewing. Isabel was safe.

There was no trouble, as it happened. The maid found Geoffrey and screamed. The usual formalities were gone through. Ursula, examined, said she had heard nothing. Neither had anybody else, apparently. It was known Geoffrey Boyd had come home drunk—*that* was almost a daily occurrence, it appeared. Almost the only bit of scandal that came out at a very dull inquest. It was supposed he had missed his footing on the stairs and fallen. People said they had often wondered it hadn't happened long ago. Good riddance to bad rubbish. Only they rather regretted there would be no divorce trial after all. A good many spicy things might have come out of that. They guessed the Burnleys would be relieved. Though it would have served them right for adopting a child of whom they knew nothing—or pretended to know nothing. Though she *did* look amazingly like James Burnley's mother!

As for Ursula Anderson, nobody talked of her at all, except to say she would miss the Boyd sewing.

The worst of Isabel's troubles were over. But it was found she was left quite poor. Both the Burnleys died within a week of each other—oh, no—no question of suicide or anything dreadful like that. She took pneumonia and he had had some long-standing trouble—and they left nothing but debts. Well, that was so often the case with those high-flyers.

Isabel and Patrick lived in a tiny cottage in Charlottetown. Some comedown for Isabel Burnley, eh? Geoffrey Boyd had squandered his fortune almost to the last penny. But she was happier than she had been for years in spite of the lean times she and Patrick experienced.

Ursula sent Isabel some money every month. Isabel never knew where it came from but she thought that an old aunt of Geoffrey, who had always seemed to like her, must be sending it. She never saw old Ursula Anderson now—at least, not to notice her. But Ursula saw her very often.

When Ursula was fifty and Isabel thirty, Isabel married a rich man and went to live in the States. Ursula followed her career in the papers and made exquisite dresses for her children—Larry's grandchildren, whom he did not know existed. Isabel always wrote and thanked her sweetly. She was really rather attached to the poor old thing. She wanted to pay her, too, but Ursula would not take a cent.

Ursula did not get much sewing to do after Isabel went away. She had done so much for her that she had lost most of her clientele. But she managed to make a living till she was seventy and then her nephew, John Anderson, took her in—much, it was said, against the wishes of his family. Isabel was dead by that time, and so was Sir Lawrence. Ursula read of their deaths in the paper. It did not affect her very much. It was all so long ago and they seemed like strangers to her. They were not the Larry she had known or the Isabel she had loved.

She knew Isabel's second marriage had been a very happy one and that contented her. It was well to die before the shadows began to fall.

As for Sir Lawrence, his fame was international. One of the finest things he had done, so she had read somewhere, had been the mural decoration of a great memorial church. The beauty of the Virgin's hands in the murals was much commented on.

Yes, life has been worth living, thought old Ursula, as Maggie McLean snored resoundingly and the old dog stirred uneasily as if he felt some Great Presence nigh. *I am not sorry for anything. Not even for killing Geoff Boyd. One should repent at the last, according to all accounts, but I don't. It was just a natural thing to kill him—as one might kill a snake. How the wind blows! Larry always loved the wind . . . I wonder if he hears it in his grave. And I suppose those fools in the parlour down there are pitying me. Fools! Fools! Life has been good. I have had my hours. Have they ever had one? Nobody ever loved Aggie as Larry loved me—nobody ever loved her at all. And nobody loved poor John. Yes, they have despised me—the whole Anderson clan have always despised me. But I have lived, oh, I have lived, and they have never lived—at least none of my generation. I have been the one who has lived. I have sinned—so the world would say; I have been a murderess—so the world would say.* "But I have lived!"

She spoke the last words aloud with such force and emphasis that old Maggie McLean awakened and started up in alarm. She was just in time to see poor old Ursula Anderson die. Her eyes lived on for a moment or two after the rest of her died. They were triumphant and young. The old dog lifted his head and gave a melancholy howl.

Thank heaven I was awake, thought Maggie. *The Andersons would never have forgiven me if I had been asleep. Shut up, you old brute! You give me the creeps. Somehow, she looks different from what she did in life. Well, we all have to die sooner or later. But I don't think there'll be much mourning for poor Ursula. There never was anything in her! Strange, too. Most of the Andersons had lots of pep, whatever else they didn't have.*

Maggie went downstairs, arranging her features properly as she did so. "She has gone," she said solemnly. "Died as easy as a child going to sleep."

Everyone tried not to look relieved. Aggie roused John with a nudge. Dr. Parsons got up briskly and then tried not to look too brisk.

"Well, she had lived her life . . ." *Such a life!* he added mentally. "If you like I'll stop in at the undertaker's on my way back and ask him to come out. I suppose you'll want things done as—as simply as possible?"

He had just saved himself from saying "cheaply." What a blunder that would have been!

Enough to ruin his career. But would Blythe or Parker ever have thought of offering to send to the undertaker? Not they. It was the little things like that that counted. In ten years' time he would have most of their practice.

"Thank you," said Aggie gravely.

"That's mighty kind of you," said John. To his own surprise John was thinking he would miss Aunt Ursula. No one could put on a patch like she could. But then she had sewed all her life. She could do nothing else. Queer where all the money she made had gone to.

The doctor went out. The rain had ceased for good and the moon occasionally broke through the windy clouds. He had lost his evening with Zoë but there was tomorrow night . . . if some fool of a woman didn't up and have a baby. He thought of Zoë in her ripe beauty—and then he thought of old Ursula Anderson upstairs in her grey flannel night dress. She was dead.

But then, had she ever been alive?

"Didn't I say she couldn't die till the tide went out?" said Uncle Alec triumphantly. "You young folks don't know everything."

ABOUT THE AUTHOR

LUCY MAUD MONTGOMERY was born on November 30, 1874, in Clifton, Prince Edward Island, Canada. Although few women of that time received a higher education, Lucy Maud attended Prince of Wales College in Charlottetown, P.E.I., and then Dalhousie University in Halifax. At seventeen she went to Nova Scotia to work for a newspaper, the Halifax *Chronicle*, and wrote for its evening edition, the *Echo*. But Lucy Maud came back to rural Prince Edward Island to teach, and lived with her grandmother at Cavendish. It is this experience, along with the lives of her farmer and fisherfolk neighbors, that came alive when she wrote her Anne books, beginning with *Anne of Green Gables* in 1908. First published as a serial for a Sunday school paper, *Anne of Green Gables* quickly became a favorite of readers throughout the world, so much so that L. M. Montgomery published eight novels in all featuring Anne Shirley and her family. Lucy Maud Montgomery also wrote the popular *Emily of New Moon* in 1923 followed by two sequels, and *Pat of Silver Bush* in 1933 with its sequel. She and her husband, the Rev. Ewen Macdonald, eventually moved to Ontario. L. M. Montgomery died in Toronto in 1942, but it is her early years of lush green

Prince Edward Island that live on in the delightful adventures of the impetuous redhead, the stories Mark Twain called "the sweetest creation of child life yet written."

Anne of Green Gables has been translated into seventeen languages, made into a number of movies, and has had continuing success as a stage play.

The success of these productions inspired *The Road to Avonlea*—enchanting new tales based on characters created by L. M. Montgomery for a television series as well as the new paperback editions.